HABITUALLY GREAT

PRAISE FOR HABITUALLY GREAT

"As Governor I expect action and results and I have seen firsthand Mark's ability to bring out the best in groups or individuals. In _Habitually Great_ he reveals how anyone can identify and break down the barriers holding them back from achieving their goals. The man I call 'Coach' Weinstein has created a roadmap for success and satisfaction that is as inspiring as it is informative."

> – Bill Richardson, Governor of New Mexico

"This is the book you are looking for. Mark's ability to inform and inspire, to be practical and profound, all the time keeping everything in light perspective, reminds me why he has been my friend for over fifteen years. Mark doesn't just talk the talk: using the methods of this book he has achieved great success for himself and for those who have come to him for help. If Phil Connors had read _Habitually Great_ he would have gotten out of Punxsutawney a lot sooner!"

> – Danny Rubin, Screenwriter of "Groundhog Day"

"In _Habitually Great_, Mark Weinstein delivers Peak Life Habits that will change your life. This book is a great gift to leaders in all three sectors, public, private, and nonprofit, and to families everywhere at every stage of the journey. _Habitually Great_ is a remarkable guidebook for understanding ourselves, redefining our futures, changing our lives and living our dreams."

> – Frances Hesselbein, Chairman and Founding President, Leader to Leader Institute

"I love this book! Our greatest challenge in life is not 'knowing what to do' – our greatest challenge is doing it. _Habitually Great_ provides a step-by-step guide on how to do it and helps us make the connection between the values that we believe – and the behavior that we live. Change your habits – change your life! Mark shows you how."

> – Marshall Goldsmith, _New York Times_ best selling author of _What Got You Here Won't Get You There_, Harold Longman Award – Best Business Book of 2007

"'Coach Weinstein' 'gets it!' Lots to learn here."
– Phil Lader, Former US Ambassador to the Court of St. James's

"In our bestselling book, *Trump University Real Estate 101* (written with Donald Trump), we emphasize that knowledge alone does not produce success. You need Right Action. So, we strongly urge our readers to first "Review your habits. Make sure they are directing you towards the goals you want to achieve…Become your best." In *Habitually Great*, Mark Weinstein shows you how to do exactly that. Mark Weinstein has learned the how and why of habit formation—and most importantly—how you can break through the habit chains that limit you and replace those habits with the behavior that leads to the life outcomes you desire. If this sounds as good to you as it does to me, read (and put into action) *Habitually Great*."
– Gary W. Eldred, co-author, *Trump University Real Estate 101*

"Mark Weinstein's *Habitually Great* offers the guidance that we each need to actualize our potential. Habits define us and are hard to alter because they are so familiar. To change requires stepping back, gaining perspective, and finding the wisdom and will to move in a new direction. Mark Weinstein provides insight and practical exercises that aid us in assessing our detrimental habits and the encouragement and understanding that enable us to foster the habit of greatness with faith in ourselves and the goodness of life."
– Rabbi Elie Kaplan Spitz, Congregation B'nai Israel

"*Habitually Great* is a masterpiece. I've witnessed first-hand the positive effect that Mark Weinstein can have on individuals and organizations. Everyone has Limiting Habits that act as anchors in holding them back from greater success and happiness. This book provides a commonsense blueprint for recognizing your individual Limiting Habits, and replacing them with Peak Life Habits that lead to greater success."
– Sam Allred, Founder & Director, Upstream Academy

PRAISE FOR **PEAK LIFE HABITS**® PROGRAMS

"The *Peak Life Habits* program empowers me where I need it most: in the daily practice of becoming my best. I've overcome Limiting Habits, made enormous leaps in my career, improved communications with co-workers, brought more love home to my wife, and had numerous other breakthroughs that have led me to believe that I can actually achieve the life I've always wanted. I recommend the *Peak Life Habits* coaching program to anyone who wants to create a wave of breakthroughs in his or her life."

– Tucker Parsons, Creative Director,
Ignition Creative

"Since my *Peak Life Habits* coaching sessions, I've formed habits in my marriage that have transformed my relationship. I'm receiving flowers from my spouse weekly."

– Ramona King, Storyteller & Speaker,
Catch A Story Productions

"Over the past year, *Peak Life Habits* has facilitated a series of retreats that have fostered levels of trust, teamwork and accountability previously thought impossible by our team. Taking our partners down to ground truth brutal facts and then building us back up to a level where real discussions can take place over partner relations, organizational infrastructure, strategic planning and marketing has lead to genuine actions and results. It now seems remarkable that we operated for so long without *Peak Life Habits*' help. *Peak Life Habits* has gone from being an interim program facilitator to a permanent fixture at Aldus."

– Saul M Meyer, Partner,
Aldus Equity

"Mark's *Peak Life Habits* keynote to our event set the tone for a great day! The audience was plugged in, enlightened, and truly alive during Mark's presentation. Our attendees were talking about him for months afterward."

– Georgie Ortiz, President,
Association of Government Accountants

HABITUALLY GREAT

Course Certificate

a $2,599 value*

Mark F. Weinstein
and Peak Life Habits, Inc.

invite you and one friend or family member to attend the
Habitually Great Intensive Seminar,
as complimentary guests.

To register and for more information:
www.habituallygreatbook.com

REGISTER NOW! SEATING IS LIMITED

Use Reference # __**HG2009**__

*If you were not given a Reference #, use your book receipt #
or special promotion code.*

---

* This offer is open to all individual purchasers of *Habitually Great* by Mark F. Weinstein. (For corporate or organizational purchasers, please contact customprograms@habituallygreat.com.) Thank you for understanding this is a limited time offer; please go to www.habituallygreatbook.com and sign up for your free seminar. The value of this **FREE** admission for you and a companion is $2,599. Please use the reference number in the certificate above when you register at www.habituallygreatbook.com. Admission to the program is complimentary; participants are responsible for their travel and other costs. For planning purposes there will be a $150 no-show deposit at the time of registration that will only be charged if you do not attend. The offer is limited to the Habitually Great Intensive seminar only, and your registration in the seminar is subject to availability of space and/or changes to the program schedule/details. Seating is limited. REGISTER TODAY!

HABITUALLY
GREAT

Master Your Habits, Own Your Destiny

Mark F. Weinstein

Printed in the United States of America. Distributed by BookSurge, 7290B Investment Drive, N. Charleston, SC 29418

Visit www.amazon.com to order additional copies. For quantity orders and special sales orders, please contact the BookSurge Ordering Department at: 1-866-308-6235, option 6. Or, send an email to customerservice@booksurge.com with your order request.

PEAK LIFE HABITS®
Positively Inspiring Success!

Peak Life Habits®, Peak Work Habits®, and Habitually Great® are registered trademarks. Company and product names mentioned herein are the trademarks or registered trademarks of their respective owners.

Library of Congress Number: 2008910523

ISBN: 1-4392-0114-5
ISBN-13: 9781439201145

To my father, Harvey J. Weinstein, who taught me that the best way to achieve a goal in life is to draw a focused line of action to it and go for it (which is not as easy as it sounds). He understood the context of an individual choosing at all times their place and purpose, and he admired anyone who created their life with passion and integrity, whether they flipped burgers or ran a country.

Thank you, Dad, for being such a beautiful and wise human being. I was blessed to have you as my father.

CONTENTS

CONTENTS (CONT'D) . . .

ACKNOWLEDGEMENTS

This book is written upon the shoulders of all the Peak Life Habits and Habitually Great staff, coaching clients, keynote, retreat and workshop participants, who through laughter, rigor and remarkable discipline, ascend their lives. I intend and hope that this book exceeds their expectations. My heartfelt thanks extends to the countless teachers, mentors, coaches, family members and friends whose life paths have intersected with mine and from whom I have received so much wisdom and love. I dedicate this book to you all, with an infinity of gratitude.

Gracious and huge thanks to: Alexia Paul, who appeared right on schedule as the book's superb spit and polish editor; Bonnie Juul, who kindly assisted with countless details of my life and organized hundreds of workbook pages and case study compilations; Emily Crawford, who tirelessly spent four years transcribing, editing, sorting, and organizing thousands of pages of raw material from my work and research; Melinda Walker, an exceptionally wise, solution-focused therapist who spent numerous hours providing editing comments and suggestions; Gail Carey for her outstanding graphics work; Dr. J. Ann Dunn, for her wizardry in taking care of my health and well-being; Sarah Flatow, the playful soul who asked me to develop a program based on my understanding of human change; Bruce Malott, the insightful executive with a huge heart who, by engaging me to facilitate his breakthroughs and those of his company, helped put Peak Life Habits on the map during its infancy; Rabbi Elie Spitz for his eloquent wisdom, friendship, and Scripture interpretation; generous colleagues who provided astute input; Julie, Roy and my wonderful team at BookSurge; and the book's dedicated "beta" readers who volunteered countless hours and gave vital feedback.

A special thank you is in order here. This book project was stuck for several years, ping-ponging between my "Perfection Habit," "Almost Habit," "Procrastination Habit," and "There's No Time Habit." (Your humble author has his share of limiting habits, too!) In the fall of 2007 a miracle occurred: I met Dr. Wayne Dyer, fortuitously in Hawaii while I was at an accounting conference, of all things. Wayne was holding a workshop in the same hotel, and I attended one day of his program. During the day Wayne offered the opportunity for any of the attendees to accompany him on his regular afternoon swim in the ocean. For the three days that followed, I was the only one who accepted the invitation. On the final day, as we walked along the beautiful beach in Kaanapali after an invigorating swim, Wayne suddenly stopped. Although the book had only been mentioned once in passing during our time together, Wayne looked me straight in the eye as only Wayne can do (I felt as though he was peering inside my soul), and said in his deep authoritative tone: "Mark, you have to finish your book, you have to finish it now, no matter what hardship that causes; no matter what difficulties that creates financially or with your clients. You have to finish writing your book now!"

In that moment I felt strangely elated, and I thanked Wayne for the gift of his counsel. It was one of those artificial "highs" with a conundrum waiting in the wings. A few days later, back on the mainland, the inspiration subsided. I was left with my habits, those familiar trances of procrastination and busy-ness. I knew that I had been issued a call to action. Yet to finish the book would require my willingness to act in the larger context of my place and purpose in this life, rather than the comfort zone of where I was. Wayne was right. The difference between "almost" and "all the way" does require stretching oneself beyond what is familiar and comfortable. The book that is in your hands may have languished for yet another six years or more if it had not been for that moment. Thank you, Wayne, for calling me out to myself.

PREFACE

And God called to him from inside the bush, and He said "Moses, Moses." He answered, "I am here." And God said, "Do not come closer. Remove your shoes from your feet, for the place on which you stand is holy ground."

—Hebrew Scripture, Exodus 3:4, 3:5

The story of God's first words to Moses is the inspiration and trajectory for <u>Habitually Great</u>. Moses is a shepherd and he is up in the hills. His attentiveness to the circumstances of that moment identifies him as prepared to hear the call. First he hears his name: "Moses, Moses." The repetition is rare for the Scripture and it is meant to say: pay attention; this is a pivotal moment in the story.

Biblical scholars engage in seeing words as mirrors that you can hold up at different angles to find meaning. Wordplay is a way to find meaning. In Hebrew, the word for "shoes" shares the same root as the word for "locks," while the word for "feet" shares the same root as the word for "habits." My friend, Rabbi Elie Spitz, explains the wordplay in the Scripture above: "God is saying, 'Moses, remove the locks that are upon your habits for then you are standing on holy ground.'"

These are the very first words that God speaks to Moses, adding to the sense of importance and the foundation for what will unfold. This is the prologue to the call: be attentive and hear a message.

What call are you hearing in your life? What are you called forth to accomplish and achieve? What have you been saying to yourself about those changes in your life and the goals you desire?

The messages we hear today are often ones we say to ourselves, sometimes with power and commitment, other times with quiet desperation. These thoughts are about finding our place and purpose in life. They are about doing. They are about taking action. What messages, what intuitive thoughts or thunderous voices do you want to heed within your life?

For much of Western Civilization, Moses is identified as the prophet who models the possibility of change and hope. Now here's the conundrum: the biblical story is about accepting the call to action and doing what feels dangerous and seems unlikely to be a success. God instructs Moses to go back to Egypt and convince the Pharaoh to release his best asset, the Jewish slaves. This was going to be a long shot, to say the least! Yet despite the odds Moses felt compelled to act, because ultimately it was not just about feeling inspired by an encounter with God, rather it was the willingness to pursue, with a solid dose of perseverance, a good that felt necessary. That is why the story persists through generations: the call was not a simple thing, as it was not obvious on any level that Moses would succeed.

The calls to action that you hear will likely require you to release the locks from upon your habits. The challenges those calls present may look quite implausible at times. Heeding them may require deep courage, entrusting your heart to strongly stand in the face of the unknown. In the story, God commanded Moses to take action beyond the limits of his old habits. The metaphor is perhaps directed to all of us, to transform ourselves, to rid ourselves of habits that interfere with our greatness, to create new habits that will take us to the promised land of joyful success and happiness within the context of our place and purpose in this lifetime. Welcome to *Habitually Great*!

A note regarding spirituality:

Habitually Great is a non-religious, non-denominational, professional self-improvement book and program designed to help you take important steps toward the life you want to live. The human propensity for habitual behavior crosses all religious and cultural boundaries. With that in mind, it is my sincere hope that the strategies within these pages will speak to *all* readers, no matter where they anchor their faith.

CHAPTER 1

UNDERSTAND YOUR HABIT MECHANISM

"Whatever you put your attention on will grow stronger in your life. Whatever you take your attention away from will wither, disintegrate and disappear."

—Dr. Deepak Chopra

Jim is forty pounds overweight and has smoked since age 15. He plays golf, lifts weights, and has wanted to treat his body better for his entire adult life. His "Someday/One Day Habit" keeps him from making a fitness plan and staying disciplined about it. At age 40, he received a terrifying wake-up call: his overweight father died of a heart attack on the golf course. Two years later, Jim still has not heeded the call, and sees himself failing yet another plan to improve his health.[1]

* * *

Cathy's son is 11 years old and suffers from fetal alcohol syndrome. She frequently blames herself, believing that she "should have" known that even a little wine while pregnant would hurt the baby. Because of

---

[1] The examples presented in Habitually Great are of real people, actual issues, and bona fide changes. To protect individual confidentiality, personal details have been altered.

a strong "It's All My Fault Habit," she obsesses over the past and spends all her time online, researching prenatal nutrition and reviewing past mistakes. As a result, she is not focused on the future and has not researched how to get her son better schooling and care. To complicate matters, her son's learning disabilities are causing even more heartache in an already strained marriage.

* * *

Tyronne is the CEO of a large company, attends several leadership seminars a year, and works with an executive coach. Despite his attempts, his staff does not work well under him and inadvertently undercuts his performance. The company is suffering due to Tyronne's "Seeing What's Wrong Habit" and "Victim Habit." Rather than acknowledging his own responsibility in the matter, he blames his employees for "persecuting" him, and as a result has become stuck in a downward spiral of disempowerment that frustrates his employees and overloads him with negativity.

* * *

Maria is a single woman who runs a highly successful bridal shop. She is on what seems like a perpetual search: she has dated many men, a few who were serious about her and had good qualities, yet still she can't find her ideal mate – even though she says she would love to have a man with whom she can share her life. Her "Seeing What's Wrong Habit" and "Being Critical Habit" have crept far into her personal life. Even with the "good" men she has dated, she becomes a relentless watchdog uncovering annoying details. She then finds herself distracted by her sharp judgments and breaks off the relationship.

* * *

Do you yearn for a better life – a life that offers a glowing sense of achievement, more satisfying friendships, enhanced respect from your colleagues, richer relationships with your family and loved ones, and, yes, even a grander feeling of challenge and excitement? We all crave these lofty, yet quite human aspirations. However, as you know – as we all know – craving does not automatically lead to fulfillment.

So, why do you fall short? What blocks you from closing in on your ideal life? Your habits. It's as simple – and as difficult – as that. "Whoa," you may be thinking. "I've already read Covey (or at least I tried to read him) and I'm still not where I want to be."

Like you, millions of eager readers have tried to plow through Stephen Covey's _The Seven Habits of Highly Effective People_ and many other motivational and self-improvement titles. And yet they still do not experience the life-long boost to the level of achievement and joy they desire. Book after book, seminar after seminar, workshop after workshop, session after session, life goes on as before with only a modicum of lasting benefit to show for all of this effort. Why?

The reason is that none of those programs address the fundamentals of the habit mechanism and the underlying habits that run us. For example, Covey's philosophy has attracted book buyers from all over the globe. However, you are not going to be effective in Putting First Things First (Covey's Habit Number Three) if your "Procrastination Habit" keeps springing back into play. You will never master Seeking First To Understand (Covey's Habit Number Five) while your "Seeing What's Wrong Habit" runs you. You can't become a model of Being Proactive (Covey's Habit Number One) if your "Avoid Accountability Habit" thwarts that intention. Let's put first things first.

You really can climb off this treadmill of frustration, not only by recognizing the habits you want to infuse into your life, but more critically by exorcising the destructive habits that keep you stuck. Even with the best intentions, your destructive habits will squeeze out and vanquish your productive habits – the habits that help you progress to greatness – unless you first take charge of your habit mechanism.

Unlike any book or seminar that you have previously experienced, _Habitually Great_ helps you "fess up" and eliminate your life-diminishing attitudes, beliefs, and habits that steer you away from right action. Then, as you create that vacuum, you simultaneously fill it with productive, life-affirming habits – those habits that place you in the world of real accomplishment.

Habits are the elephants in the room of personal and professional improvement. They are burrowed into our brains so deeply that we fail to see their power and influence even though elephants are, indeed, huge. They leave their tracks across our lives day after day. We have habits about everything: how we brush our teeth, how we sit in chairs, how we think, how we manage our time, fitness and nutrition, relationships with partners, friends and colleagues, spirituality, integrity, and accountability. Some are good habits – or *Peak Life Habits*, as I'll refer to them in this book. We could not get through a day without good habits, which could be anything from an "I'm Worthy Habit" to a "Healthy Exercise Habit" to a "Compassion Habit." There are dozens of admirable patterns you act out in your life without ever having to think twice about them.

If somebody were to offer Jim, Cathy, Tyronne and Maria a magic wand for the price of the book you now hold in your hands, which they could wave at their lives and make significant changes, do you think they would buy it? For that matter, would you?

Congratulations. There is no need to dream of magic wands. Something even better is in your hands right now. With the help of this book, you are about to learn – as they have learned – how to take control of your situation, no matter how dire, frustrating, heartbreaking immobile, or even how good it may be already. Magic wands don't exist, yet we ourselves have the power to shift how we respond to anything and everything, the ability to identify and manage our habits, and in so doing, find and attract opportunities that increase our joy and contentment and our spiritual and material wealth.

For example, you can say to yourself, "Well, I'm making $100,000 a year and I really want to make $250,000 a year," and yet you keep bumping into a ceiling that holds your income at $100,000. Everybody confronts their own *Success Ceilings*, from professional athletes and top CEOs to middle managers. We can get stopped when a habit saboteur kicks in, the covert unconscious. And when we see a failure take shape, we scratch our heads and say, "What just happened there?" Habits are what happened. That's worth repeating:

HABITS HAPPEN!

Do we have good habits? You bet! Many of these are Peak Life Habits. Yet we all are also run by our *Limiting Habits* – sponsored by our doubts and fears, conscious or subconscious, which interfere with the positive effects of our Peak Life Habits. Limiting Habits are driven by unconscious, forceful beliefs that undercut our performance and our self-presentation at critical junctures in our lives. In the grip of these habits, we are left in the realm of "almost," again and again.

And do you know what? That is just how we human beings operate. The minute you put down this book, you walk out of the room, you get a message on your cell phone, you check your email, you go right back into life, and – BOOM – You snap right back to your habits – habits in the form of annoyance, criticism, self-loathing, distraction or distress. These are all your unconscious ways of being in the world, and chances are that they are not serving your highest dreams. Deep within you, there may be underlying doubts, assumptions and beliefs that do not support your heart's intentions. The likely result is a habit (or two, or ten) that jeopardizes your success. These habits may reflect some of your earliest life experiences. You could be 70 years old or 25 and – just when you are inches away from the winning the gold – still only achieve "almost" because of habits you unwittingly created when you were six. It is time to go beyond "almost."

Positively inspiring success happens in two stages. The first is in our immediate power: to recognize our embedded beliefs and our corresponding habits that keep us in the realm of "almost." This stage is important, because really our beliefs and habits have become so ingrained that they are now running us, instead of the other way around. That's right: our habits are in charge of us, and in many fundamental ways they are determining our lives, not vice versa. To help reverse this process, you hold in your hands an unparalleled self-improvement methodology, a whole new way of identifying, articulating, and cognitively shifting out of autopilot. You are about to name your elephants so clearly and so effectively that you will have the power to move them out of your subconscious mind and into conscious control.

This book was written to give you a remarkably simple language for understanding your unique self. You will be able to recognize patterns and say, "My 'Insecurity Habit' is being triggered," or, "My 'I'm Not Good Enough Habit' is being triggered." And by being conversant in your habits, you can also articulate for yourself what triggers them – and ultimately reroute them to Peak Life Habits that serve you better. That is the goal of this book: to give you the ability to preempt the habits that are giving you predictable futures in all areas of your life and achieve the life of your dreams. This book will guide you through that task, A-Z.

The result is an exceptional return on your investment of time and effort. You will go beyond former thresholds, stopping any covert or intentional sabotage as you take the wheel, press the accelerator to the floor and feel the exhilaration of intentional effectiveness. Shifting your habits, you will gain even greater mastery over your heart, mind, actions and schedule. (And, from this point forward, I will be capitalizing "Shift," as it is a central, vital concept to keep in mind. To Shift means to choose proactively to exchange your Limiting Habits for Peak Life Habits.) Along the way, you may choose to become a model of success and excellence in the way you speak to your colleagues and loved ones – because our habits of language can inspire the people with whom we communicate. Best of all, your dreams and passions will gain a never-before-imagined clarity. You will watch yourself achieve them one after another. You will removed the roadblocks that kept you stuck at "almost," and the gates to your ultimate life will be wide open in front of you.

Perhaps you have heard of the Law of Attraction, a simple phrase signifying that the outcomes we see in our lives are based on our beliefs and thoughts (conscious and otherwise). You might have even read a few books or attended a workshop or two. Yet come Monday morning, the only guarantee is that the habits that have been running you return in full force. No matter how brilliant the insight of these books and programs may be, without a pre-emptive habit intervention that you deploy to master your habits once and for all, you will revert back to your old ways of living. That is about to change, because when you master your habits, you tap into your personal capacity for greatness. You tap into the Law of Attraction in a focused, positive way. When you send upbeat, focused positivity into your universe from the core of your being – in thought, word, and deed – the universe reflects it back to you. Understanding your habits is the ticket to attracting the relationships, wealth and experiences you have always wanted.

The Law of Attraction is more than a mental gambit. It's a fact. The brain is fundamentally mechanical. If you imagine something powerfully, strongly and repeatedly, you are far more likely to manifest it. The brain helps facilitate it; the synapses fire away, initiating actions that generate the outcomes they are fixed upon. If you are playing tennis and, preparing to serve, you say to yourself, "I can't double-fault, it'll blow the match. I really, really, really can't double-fault." Guess what? Your brain is picturing and recalling what it feels like to double-fault, and as the ball falls through the air and meets your racket, your muscles are already obeying a command from your brain to double-fault.

Here is a bigger example. If, daily, you picture yourself living in the same house, working the same hours, making the same pay ten years from now, and if, daily, you act as if you will be living that same old life ten years from now – your habits will conspire with your environment to keep the status quo. If, daily, you picture yourself living in the house of your dreams, spending your days pursuing your favorite hobby alongside the partner of your dreams, and having more than enough money, and if, daily, you *feel* yourself stepping into this inspiringly successful life – your habits will collaborate with your environment to help you realize your wishes.

If you are not familiar with the Law of Attraction, here it is:

When you believe at the deepest level – the level where those huge "elephants" of your habits dwell – that you are powerful and capable of being or creating what you want in your life, you can walk straight toward success. Even if you stumble on that path (because we can't control every situation) you are likely to still end up with your face in a pot of gold, because your belief is stable. Put another way, when you feel positive, you create and act positively, and in turn, you reap abundant positive rewards, joys, and happiness.

And yes, this is still just "life on earth," as I am apt to say. There will always be those perfect moments of imperfection when events, circumstances, or the behavior of others challenge us. Miracles can happen when we rigorously focus our thoughts on the best outcome and support those thoughts with disciplined actions. To others, we seem to have attracted the miracle…though we know better!

The key to _Habitually Great_ is that it takes the Law of Attraction one step further, into an exciting new area of metaphysics that is called the _Law of Right Action_. The Law of Right Action says we attract our success by aligning our efforts with our intentions, i.e., by transforming our thoughts and feelings as well as focusing on and changing our actions. So the Habitually Great program is at heart an integrated one – its goal is to transform our thoughts, our feelings, and our actions all together. In short, we seek to transform our entire _selfhood_ so that we can become the best version of ourselves. After all, we attract true transformation, truly new outcomes, a truly greater life, only by addressing the big picture. And our selfhood is a direct expression of our habits.

THOUGHTS lead to FEELINGS and FEELINGS lead to THOUGHTS, so
THOUGHTS + FEELINGS → HABITS = SELFHOOD

A focused, clear, positive sense of self allows you to create the discipline of continuous Right Action, and *voila*, greatness! Without changing your habits, you cannot expect real, lasting, and different outcomes in your life. When you master your habits, you release yourself from vicious cycles and avoid getting stuck at "almost." That journey begins now.

From Negative to Positive: Habit Gaps and Habit Chains

What do you not want to regret in thirty years? Take some time and think about it. Survey your life this very day – the hassles and struggles that really get under your skin – and multiply by three hundred and sixty-five. Then multiply again by thirty. What don't you want to struggle with by a factor of 10,950? Do you want 10,950 days of debt? Or, like Cathy, 10,950 days of anguish over a perceived failure as a parent? Like Jim, 10,950 days of denial that steadily chips away at your lifespan? Maybe 10,950 days of hating your job? How about 10,950 days to reflect on failures in love?

Now, hold that thought. Feel it out. Can you feel its opposite – its antidote, the solution that washes all the fear, regret and tension out of your veins? I bet it is difficult; in fact, I would not be surprised if your brain is still ticking through images of 10,950 days of negative feelings. The brain is truly mechanical. Whenever you feed it images, it says, "Ok!" and dutifully processes them into your current reality of thoughts and feelings. So, what about 10,950 days of being happily in love? And 10,950 days of being so abundant that you could provide anything you wanted for yourself and anything anybody you love wanted? How would you feel if your heart is bursting its seams with joy for 10,950 days because, on every one of those days, you know you have total freedom to create the life you most desire? The brain is mechanical, and as you read these words, simply pause, take a deep breath, relax and picture images of a life that brings you great or greater joy, heartfelt smiles and happiness, consistently. In that visual, as you fill in the details of the people, the feelings, the accomplishments, the joys and fun, your brain is now saying, "Ok!" and perhaps filling you with tingly good thoughts and feelings. You change for the better. If you are challenged by feeling this now, be patient, and we will work through it in this book. It may be "natural" for you to get hooked on your negative character traits, those familiar doubting thoughts, beliefs and habits. No worries! Soon, you will begin to spend more time in the antidote, consistently creating great joy and great success. That's where we're headed.

So far in your life, you probably have not been able to find and keep this antidote. It exists on the other side of a gap, so to speak, forced out of your grasp again and again by "almost" moments. You can "almost," yet never quite, get over the gap once and for all and lead a life of steady ease, joy, and continuous ascension. In habit language, we call this obstacle the *Habit-Gap*. The Habit-Gap is the difference between what we have/are in life today and what we want to have/be either today or in the future.

Fig. 1.1

The Habit-Gap is caused by – surprise! – Habits. (From now on, I'll give a capital H to Habits so that we remember what a huge influential force they are in our lives.) Even if we know we can reach our goals, often we don't have the Habits to get there. This gap is responsible for regrets. When people speak of their regrets, they never talk about "pie in the sky" dreams that they regret not fulfilling. No. What people regret is not achieving the goals they knew were realistic. Something hooked them and held them back – their Limiting Habits.

LIMITING HABIT SPOTLIGHT:
THE "AVOID ACCOUNTABILITY HABIT"

The "Avoid Accountability Habit" has a few manifestations:

1) When you have a routine of success that's working, a feeling of pressure and burden creeps in. Then you hesitate and take a quick side step out. You avoid greater success (and perhaps sabotage the success you already have) because the accountability of continuing to be successful makes you uneasy; your friends, family, co-workers, even strangers are watching and you shrink to get out of the spotlight.

2) You invoke your "Avoid Accountability Habit" in the name of spontaneity, feeling that the perceived drudgery of accountability impedes your life and interferes with your ultimate success. "Too boring, too predictable, too oppressive, too regimented and too inflexible," you say.

3) Your "Avoid Accountability Habit" gives you a safe harbor for your "I'm Not Worthy Habit," "Procrastination Habit," and "Victim Habit." Under its cover you feel falsely safe and comfortable, blaming the world for your circumstances, yet going nowhere quickly.

The Solution: Take it on! Be accountable! Don't worry about it! If you are great at what you do, people may notice. So what? Be bold by being accountable and achieve <u>your</u> dreams, live <u>your</u> ultimate life. Be accountable for your health, prosperity, and happiness. Fulfill your vision about your place and purpose on earth. Go, go, go, go!

PATTERN INTERRUPT PEAK LIFE HABITS:

Accountability Habit, Create My Destiny (vs. Fate) Habit, Courage Habit, No More Excuses Habit, Playing Big Habit

SL 1.1

Starting today, begin to cross your Habit-Gap by aligning your whole self with your authentic desires, sidestepping and interrupting your Limiting Habits, and creating powerful Peak Life Habits along with disciplined actions to achieve what you want. Your relationship to Habits is about to do a U-turn; *you* are going to master *them* instead of the other way around.

At the moment, you are grappling in the dark with an unseen challenger. Let's begin by turning on the lights. At the heart of this book is a pair of straightforward tools that will change how you perceive your world and operate within it. The first is a *Habit Chain*. Our Habit mechanism is best pictured as a chain comprising a Belief, Action, Outcome and the resulting Habit, as well as the unspoken connections between all four components.

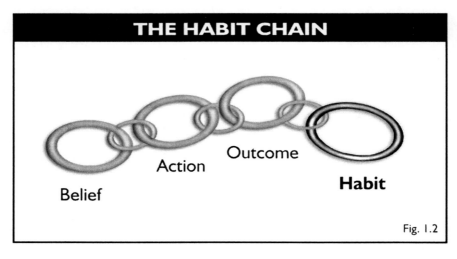

THE HABIT CHAIN

Action

Outcome

Belief

Habit

Fig. 1.2

You will see big links and little links in Figure 1.2. (If you are wondering what the little ones are and why they are there, hold that thought, because the explanation is coming shortly.) First, let's talk about the big links. You've heard of a whole being more than the sum of its parts? A Habit Chain is both a whole and the sum of its parts – it is a way of seeing that the whole Habit is in fact the sum of the parts of which it is composed. The Habits you experience every day are the final products of these complex Habit Chains.

Dozens of these chains operate your behavior and feelings, controlling them like puppet masters. Some of them work in your favor, for instance, allowing you not to take the receptionist's bad mood personally, and in so doing, to stay upbeat with your colleagues. Some Habit Chains work against you, say, when you let a curt tone of voice send you into a tailspin of second-guessing your worth as a human being so that you can't get any work done until you have a piece of cheesecake. Every single time a Habit guides your Actions, it starts with one of your Beliefs, and then moves toward an Action that produces an Outcome. And it doesn't stop there: Outcomes reinforce themselves. Truly, the Habit Chain is not a linear structure; it is a circular one, often a paralyzing vicious circle. Figure 1.3 illustrates this cycle.

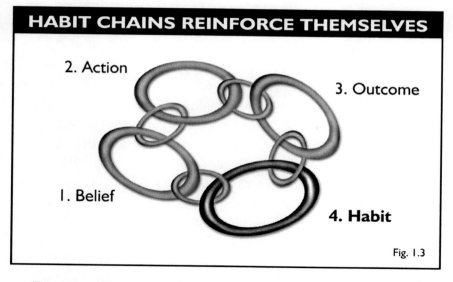

HABIT CHAINS REINFORCE THEMSELVES

2. Action

3. Outcome

1. Belief

4. Habit

Fig. 1.3

Tyronne, the executive we mentioned at the beginning of this chapter, is a good example of how a Habit can reinforce itself. When life doesn't go according to plan (and life, being life, often doesn't), Tyronne's "Seeing What's Wrong Habit" gets triggered. We have lots of Habits, and they often work together, feeding off of one another. In Tyronne's case, he sees what's wrong and then looks for someone to blame by falling back on his "Blame Habit." So, when he noticed a downward trend in the company's productivity, he spent a lot of money on a self-improvement workshop for his staff. He expected to see an immediate upward reversal in productivity, yet when they returned to work, what happened was nothing of the sort. Rather than recognizing that: 1) Shifting productivity Habits takes time, and 2) the root of the problem might be *him*, Tyronne chose to see only the evidence that, yes, his employees were a big problem. Because he believed that other people always screw up, he tried to remedy the problem by scheduling the workshop for them, and although the lack of immediate results was a predictable Outcome, his "Blame Habit" colored his interpretation of it. Therefore, he rested in the comfort of knowing he had been right all along, and became even quicker to blame them the next time around. Chalk up another victory for Tyronne's Habits.

To turn the game around, let's start by addressing the root of the Habit. If we follow a Habit Chain back to its first component, we come to a Belief about ourselves or about how the world works. The journey takes us underneath the surface, into our subconscious. If you imagine your Habit mechanism as being an iceberg, the 10% that sticks up from the water is the Habit. The other 90% is submerged in your subconscious, in your automatic Beliefs and expectations about the world and other people. Between the Habit and the Belief on which it is founded, at the "waterline" so to speak, is the *Belief-Link*, the point of connection between Beliefs and Actions. When we look at that link, we can see connections we may have never recognized before. The Belief-Link is our second tool. Placing the insights you gain from working with Belief-Links alongside the modeling power of Habit Chains, you will begin to see why your Beliefs and Actions keep yielding Outcomes that you don't want and haven't been able to change, the reason why your Limiting Habits may have stalled you at "almost." Let's pencil in a more complete drawing that reflects this process, so that our Habit Chain looks like Figure 1.4 on the following page.

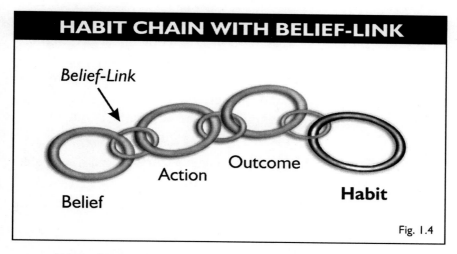

HABIT CHAIN WITH BELIEF-LINK

Belief-Link

Action

Outcome

Belief

Habit

Fig. 1.4

In Tyronne's case, his core Belief, i.e., the root of his Habit, is that other people cannot be trusted. His Belief-Link, therefore, is that he can't possibly trust them to do their jobs well. For the 20 years of his career, his Belief-Link carried that Belief into frequent Actions that garnered his employees' resentment of being micromanaged and blamed when things did not unfold according to plan. The key to Tyronne's breakthrough was ultimately an ability to recognize a feeling of agitation that preceded acts of blame and micromanagement, and then STOP, and say, "Ah-ha, I'm feeling that lack of trust again. Does it have anything to do with this situation?" The answer turned out to be a resounding *No* just about every time. The feeling came from another situation a long time ago, and whenever he felt this sudden urgency and angst as an adult, he learned to STOP and unhook his current reality from core Beliefs about trust.

Our Beliefs cause us to take Actions that do not result in the Outcome we want. Take a look for yourself. Is there an Action in your life that often backfires? For example, are you yelling at the dog for urinating in the house and thus making the problem worse because the dog is stressed out about being punished? Are you clamming up at the beginning of any disagreement with your partner and actually making the moment tenser? These are situations in which you want to achieve one Outcome, and consistently get another. Trying to fix somebody is another great example. Maybe your roommate comes home from the office every day totally drained and upset, and you suggest that she might feel better if she just stood up for herself more often at work. How's that effort working? Laugh and shake your head. It is a great example of how we can hold the Belief that we know how to fix a person's problem, and then take the Action of telling him or her what they "should" do, and getting the unintended Outcomes of feeling ineffective and probably upsetting you both.

Think of a time when you have taken an Action that has created a negative Outcome, and write that Action here: _____
_____.

Then ask yourself:

- How did I explain or justify that Action in my mind at the time?
- What Belief caused me take that Action?
- What is the origin of the Belief?

Identify an underlying Belief and the Belief-Link you attached to it. In our "clamming up" example, the guy may answer, "I clammed up in a disagreement with my girlfriend last night because in my family, when I was a kid, we argued a lot and whatever would make my parents mad never got any better, even if they screamed about it." He consistently and automatically bases his decision to clam up on this Belief, even though it actually perpetuates some deep dissonance from the past in an important, present-day relationship. Can you see the result? It is a clear "Avoid Conflict Habit."

What is important in these examples and this exercise is that together they provide a hands-on demonstration of how a Belief and the decision to act upon it are in fact separate, and that the link is forged by our own choice. That is a key concept, so let's write it in stone:

> **YOUR BELIEF AND YOUR DECISION TO ACT ON IT ARE SEPARATE.**
> **YOU CREATE A BELIEF-LINK BY YOUR OWN CHOICE!**

And therein lays freedom. Once you are able to recognize these connections, you will learn how to rewire them to generate the Habits and Outcomes that serve you better. The emphasis is practical, not theoretical. Beliefs often exist below our conscious awareness. Nonetheless, they guide all our Actions, with Beliefs and Belief-Links becoming Outcome predictors. No exceptions. In the coming chapters, you will learn how to get your pliers into that Belief-Link, pry it wide open, and pick and choose the links that will anchor you to a brilliant, powerful selfhood that won't fail you when your cell phone rings, when you go to your mother-in-law's for dinner, or when life tosses you one of its little adventures.

CHAPTER 2

IDENTIFY YOUR HABIT CHAINS

"For all our insight, obstinate habits do not disappear until replaced by other habits . . . No amount of confession and no amount of explaining can make the crooked plant grow straight; it must be trained upon the trellis by the gardener's art . . ."

—Carl Jung

This is your first peek at the Habit mechanism, the understanding of which will illuminate the path to freedom from the status quo. Remember, there is nothing wrong with how you have been in the past. If perfection was possible, we'd all be billionaires, star athletes, and Captains of the Starship Enterprise. We are human, and this is life on earth. That means we all have Limiting Habits. It also means we can lighten up and chuckle at the folly of our humanity. By exposing Limiting Habits with kind compassion, you will soon begin Shifting to a life of more fun, more play, more joy – in short, a life rich in Peak Life Habits. With the Habitually Great tools and training in your hands right now, you can look forward to the huge achievements and high spirits that come with transforming your Limiting Habits into powerful, energetically positive Peak Life Habits.

Here is the key: the first step toward disengaging the subtle and often subconscious Habit mechanisms is to reveal them, to bring them out into the light of day. We will label them in a new way, because there is power in naming. Naming gives your conscious mind the ability to recognize your Limiting Habit mechanisms, slice them, dice them, and Shift them from active duty to the scrap heap. At that point another Habit can take over – one that makes good on its promise to help you become who you truly want to be.

Master Habits

Pause from your reading and flip to Appendix B on pages 257-259, where you can peruse the Limiting Habits Chart. Notice any familiar ones? Are there ones that make you say, "Hmm… these are my old friends! Sure, I've been thinking/feeling/doing that for 30 years, I just never saw it that way before." Amid many Habits that may resonate with your experience, you may notice a few, even five or so, that have an especially strong timbre. Those are your *Master Habits*.

If Habits are the elephants in the room of change, Master Habits are the biggest bulls in the herd. They control our Habit mechanism more than any other. Master Habits are so powerful and comprehensive that they take over our thoughts, perspectives, and Actions; we are in many ways addicted to their control and to the context and color of our lives that results from them.

Master Habits are excellent diversions. They give us an excuse to avoid what we don't want to face: accountability for our own successes and failures. They create vicious cycles that keep us stuck in "almost." They perpetuate nagging dissatisfactions, those perpetual "good"s rather than "great"s that bar us from our ultimate lives. They keep us in familiar distress instead of allowing us to be fully satisfied with becoming everything we can be. Master Habits are the ones that remain fully intact despite all the other breakthrough and self-improvement workshops, books, and therapy. They come from our families of origin and from our early experiences. Master Habits keep us from sustaining goals and successes even if we are able to achieve or attain them momentarily.

Sally has the "I Have To Worry About Money Habit," which for her is a Master Habit. This Habit created quite a conundrum in her life. On the one hand it drove Sally to success, and she relentlessly climbed the corporate ladder, becoming the President of a leading international sporting goods company, earning over $1 million dollars per year. How perfect! Sally was making so much money that she really had to try to worry about money, and in fact she momentarily became free from worrying about money. Paradoxically, this created its own anxiety, as her insistent Master Habit kept looking for a home it no longer had. After all, Sally had worried about money her whole life, just as her parents had, and it was a Habit that truly ran her. Her career had given her freedom from the chain, so to speak. Or had it? A closer examination of what happened next reveals the power of a Master Habit.

It all felt so easy, too easy in fact. After just a few years at the top, Sally left her job, started her own retail store, invested most of her savings in the store, and re-created a life where she could and did worry about money. At the time Sally made this fundamental change, she thought she was getting herself out of the fast-paced high profile life. Upon closer examination as she unveiled her Master Habit, her jaw dropped. In the sinewy world of her covert unconscious a determined Habit lurked. Deeply ingrained, Habits were running her life, just as they are doing with many of us.

Triggers, Trances and Tire Marks

Habits don't exist in a vacuum. The 10% of a Habit that is above water has an impact on your world, and your world – including the people in it – can just as surely collide with your Habits.

Remember Maria from the beginning of Chapter 1? As she began to observe her Habits around dating and relationships, she noticed that the dazzle always wore off by the third date. It waned just as she was starting to get a good glimpse of the person on the other side of the dinner table – and, also important, just as he was starting to get a good glimpse of her. A parting of ways inevitably followed.

Here is the complex beauty of the Habit mechanism: Maria applied to herself the fierce standard against which she measured the world when in the grips of her "Being Critical Habit". Buried under that Habit in her unconscious were important Beliefs – Beliefs about her own worth, Beliefs that she would never measure up, Beliefs that she wasn't "good enough." These Beliefs linked to her "Being Critical Habit" as well as an "I'm Not Good Enough Habit," an "It's Never Enough Habit" and an "I Don't Deserve Habit."

When the new guy in Maria's life was just starting to appreciate and compliment everything that was wonderful about her, from her successful business to her assertiveness and strength – BOOM – she felt the dissonance between what he believed and her own negative Beliefs about herself. She slipped into her "Being Critical Habit" and all the shades of perception that resulted from it, and she could then justify pushing herself out of the relationship and away from the dissonant contradiction.

As Maria learned to identify that Belief-Link at the waterline, that connection between her Beliefs about herself and her habitual Action to push away from anyone who contradicted them, she was able to step back and see the iceberg for what it was and ultimately chart a new course around it.

We will always have moments when our reactions are beyond our control, and that's only human. We will begin to notice causal chains – a *Habit-Trigger* – and then the immediate feeling of distress, and we will default to a Limiting Habit. Tyronne learned that the iceberg in his path was his "Seeing What's Wrong Habit." Our culture stamps us with the ability to see what's wrong everywhere we look. Tyronne is a great example – he would turn on the news, review the company's earnings and his employees' performance reports and identify what was less than perfect. He was already harried and wanted life to go more smoothly. Whenever he felt that life threw him a curveball, for instance in the form of an annoying data point, the 90% of his "Seeing What's Wrong Habit" that was underwater started to rumble and activate his "Distress Habit," his "Blame Habit," his "Victim Habit," and all of a sudden he would be saying,

"Woe is me," and "It's your fault, so fix it." As he learned more about his Habit mechanism, he was amazed at how easily those curveballs had been throwing him off track throughout his life.

LIMITING HABIT SPOTLIGHT: THE "SEEING WHAT'S WRONG HABIT"

The "Seeing What's Wrong Habit" is a Habit embedded in American culture. It is a good example of a helpful perspective that has become overemphasized. This Habit permeates the way information is presented and shared throughout the media. It is so pervasive that our conversations are cast in its mold; we rush to judgment and spend a lot of time talking about what's wrong, criticizing an event or people or anything, rather than seeing what's right.

The "Seeing What's Wrong Habit" is synergistic with the "Being Critical Habit" and the "I'm Right Habit." This cluster is troublesome in our relationships, impedes us in our careers, and deteriorates our health with its negativity.

The roots of this Habit can often be found within our families of origin. Perhaps your mother or father was an expert at seeing what's wrong. And there you were at three, four or five years of age listening to somebody who is an authority on what's wrong. Given such a history, it would be hard for you not to grow up with that Habit; you would have been stamped with it.

The Law of Right Action is about moving in a positive direction towards what you want instead of being stuck with the perpetual movie in your head about what you don't like or want. Interestingly, you can use the "Seeing What's Wrong Habit" for contrast – to see what is right! Contrast is good. It helps you to focus on what you want and also what you don't want.

Are you in the grip of this Habit? Then ease up on the righteousness. The "Lightening Up Habit" is a good antidote here, one that you want to administer with keen intent!

PATTERN INTERRUPT PEAK LIFE HABITS:

Compassionate Habit, Lightening Up Habit,
Seek First To Understand Habit, Seeing What's Right Habit

SL 2.1

An event, circumstance, interaction with your family, or even something that happens in the news can act as a Habit-Trigger. Because it is a familiar and often loaded explosive charge from your past, it triggers you – BOOM – right into your "Life's Not Fair Habit," "I'm Not Good Enough Habit," or "I Don't Trust Anybody Habit," etc.

We can practice getting farther and farther away from a particular Habit-Trigger by recognizing the patterns that lead to it. When we are triggered, we default to a Habit. As long as that activated Belief-Link is buried in our subconscious, away from our ability to pry it open and examine it, we will follow our Habit Chain through to completion like a zombie. In other words, we are in a *Habit-Trance*. We don't even notice it because it is so familiar.

On the mantle above my fireplace I keep a vivid reminder of the power of a trigger: a small orange traffic cone scarred with angry, black rubber skid marks. In 1989, I was a syndicated automobile journalist with one of the nation's highest circulations – which helps explain my fondness for using driving metaphors in Habitually Great keynotes and workshops. Those were exhilarating days: Acura was introducing the NSX, a new mid-engine aluminum sports car designed to compete with Ferraris and Porsches, and had invited me to test drive the NSX at the Portland International Speedway. Of course, I accepted the invitation, and was flown first class to Oregon, where I joined an esteemed group of fellow journalists.

Acura had also brought in several competitors' models for us to drive for comparison and had hired a few race drivers to teach us the art of handling these exotic performance cars at high speeds. I was assigned to a successful driver named Parker Johnstone, who effortlessly piloted the NSX around the track, pointing out the perfect way to set up and execute the turns, while blasting through the straights at high velocity. Then I took the wheel and, after a few warm-up laps, got very comfortable with my speedway education. Both of us were wearing heavy helmets with no provisions for radio communication, so it's a wonder I could hear anything over the engine wailing at 8,000 RPMs and the tires squealing against the banked payment. We were having a good time yelling back and forth to each other from 12 inches apart, exchanging important tactical comments about the driving and the track. In the middle of a sweeping bend I was taking at 115 mph, all senses full on, pushing the car to the brink of adhesion, Parker yelled to me, "Mark, you're a great driver!" What do you think happened? I snapped out of the "zone."

I immediately thought, "No I'm not." In nanoseconds I instantly became nervous, felt like I was out of my league, and lost my confidence. Startled, without realizing what I was doing, I lifted my foot off the gas – which is exactly what you don't do in a mid-engine exotic sports car driving at the edge of adhesion through a sweeping curve at 115 miles per hour. The rear-end shot around like a boomerang and we went into a noisy, violent spin. Round and round we spun, veering directly onto the inside track grass, where the out-of-control NSX tore up yards of grass on its way to shredding and scarring countless orange cones that had been carefully placed to mark the proper line for taking the curve.

I wasn't hurt (except my pride, of course); though it wasn't the sort of event I could easily shrug off. The spinout caused me many moments of soul searching. It was really a terrifying experience. I had almost killed myself and Parker. Why? Until I understood how Belief-Links, Habit Chains and Habit-Triggers work, it haunted me for years, stuck in the back of my mind as one of those moments I knew was important yet did not understand why. Parker had made many comments to me prior to that one, as we shrieked around the track. What had that comment triggered? Of course, I wasn't exactly a regular at the racetrack, so whatever relevance the event was going to have to my everyday life involved a lot more than high-speed driving. As it turns out so often with Belief-Links, the Belief that was triggered that day at the track resonated far beyond my decisions behind the wheel of that car.

My NSX spinout was one of countless expressions of a basic, fundamental default Belief I had been operating with as long as I could remember. This happens to many of us. We are in the "zone," an expression used to describe the state of performing above and beyond our normal patterns or Beliefs. Then a comment or event occurs that snaps us back. In my case, Parker's comment snapped me back into my head, and to the iceberg below. At that time, I simply was not wired to accept Parker's compliment, as it contradicted my underlying Belief that I wasn't "great," either as a driver or in general. My parents hadn't instilled in me a "great" Belief, nor had it ever been planted in my subconscious through any other consistent experiences of "greatness." So as soon as I got triggered, I fell into a Habit-Trance of believing "I'm not great" that in turn prompted an unconscious Action of proceeding with caution – literally, taking my foot off the gas – which as any physics expert will know, led to a hellacious spinout.

And what Belief would such an Outcome naturally reinforce? Simply put, I didn't really know what I was doing, for which one can hardly imagine a more dramatic validation than my head-spinning, ear-splitting humiliation before my peers. Thank goodness for humility and a sense of humor! At dinner that night, my new race-car buddies roasted me for being a "great driver" and gave me that scarred orange cone, which today I look at often and smile because it reminds me of how much laughter we all shared that night – and the valuable lesson I learned.

Master Habits in Operation

A Master Habit is powerful because it colors your world for as long as you are in its trance. It can hold you in its power for seconds, days, months, or even years at a time. For example, if you have a "Guilt Habit" dominating you, you may feel perpetually responsible for everything at work, at home, and on the road; you feel guilty before you are even accused. You may suffer from thoughts of fault and liability for breakdowns that were completely out of your sphere of influence. In order to Shift a Master Habit from negative to positive, you must first understand how it does its work – because on your cognitive journey toward creating a more powerful life, there is power in recognizing, naming and transforming your Habits. There is power in mastering them, because if you are not the driver, they are.

Master Habits operate in one of three ways.

Master Habits in Operation #1: Alone

The first is a Master Habit operating as a lone wolf. My "I'm Not Great Habit" display on the racetrack is a perfect example. It ran rampant without help from any other Habit, and when it was triggered, my world was the purest color of that Habit for the split second it took me to lift my foot off the pedal.

Master Habits in Operation #2: Habit-Spirals

In the second way, a Master Habit recruits other Limiting Habits, creating a forceful compound effect on behavior: this is the Habit-Spiral, which occurs when there is one Master Habit that triggers a domino effect among a set of other Habits. The image of a spiral is helpful because it captures a sense of hierarchy and continuity. The Master Habit initiates the cascade of Action like an army general who orders his subordinate Habit into active duty, who then orders the next subordinate Habit into active duty, and so forth. In each Habit-Spiral, each subsequent, unique Habit is triggered by the previous Habit and set into motion (Figure 2.1).

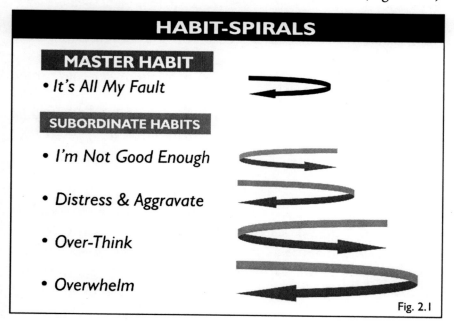

HABIT-SPIRALS

MASTER HABIT

• *It's All My Fault*

SUBORDINATE HABITS

• *I'm Not Good Enough*

• *Distress & Aggravate*

• *Over-Think*

• *Overwhelm*

Fig. 2.1

Cathy, the mother from the beginning of Chapter 1, had a set of Habits that operated in a Habit-Spiral. Sometimes her son had especially tough weeks – he acted up and punched the sitter, threw a tantrum in a store or shut down with his brothers. His behavior upset her terribly and triggered her "It's All My Fault Habit," which was a Master Habit that had its roots in the turmoil she felt when he was born with fetal alcohol syndrome. The resulting Habit-Trance sent her online at every spare moment to read about what she "should have" eaten and drunk while pregnant. However, the time she spent on the Internet upset her husband and, predictably, he criticized her for not spending more time away from the computer and with the family. The criticism triggered her "I'm Not Good Enough Habit" around her ability to be a good partner and mother.

In the grip of both of these Habits together, she would fall into her "Stress & Obsess Habit," getting stuck in the quicksand of discomfort and disagreement in her household. Subsequently, her "Over-Think Habit" got triggered as she started dissecting every exchange with her husband and looked for a way to communicate that would dissolve the tension and resolve any conflicts that arose from her son's initial acting-up. Finally, the "Over-Think Habit" led straight to her "Overwhelm Habit" because her mind was so busy working overtime that its capacity to function at peak level diminished. She would become tired, stressed, irritable, and so wound up from scrambling that she exhausted herself and further undermined her power to be a great mother, partner and human being. Luckily, Cathy saw the pattern and how she had unwittingly yielded her power to the Habit-Spiral shown in Figure 2.1. She resolved to break the pattern then and there.

Master Habits in Operation #3: Habit-Clusters

The third Master Habit sequence does not cascade like Cathy's Habit-Spiral. Rather, it is a cluster. A Habit-Cluster is just that – a group of Habits that are all triggering one another simultaneously and independently. In the case of the Habit-Cluster, there is no domino effect. Habit-Clusters work in one of two ways: the first has a

Master Habit that operates like a puppet master. In this model, once the primary Master Habit is triggered, it engages all its subordinate Habits at once, like the limbs of a marionette. You may recognize Figure 2.2 as Tyronne's Habit-Cluster.

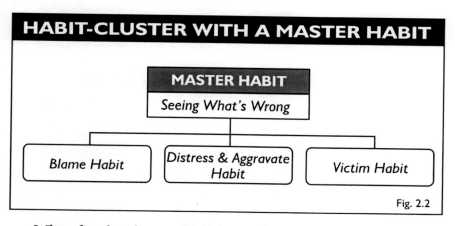

HABIT-CLUSTER WITH A MASTER HABIT

MASTER HABIT
Seeing What's Wrong

Blame Habit   *Distress & Aggravate Habit*   *Victim Habit*

Fig. 2.2

When faced with any of life's many deviations from his goal, Tyronne trained his laser-like focus (which has the potential to serve him well in his own work and is why he is capable of becoming a fine CEO) on what could be better. At this point, instead of focusing on making positive changes, his worldview became colored by everything he perceived as having gone wrong. He simultaneously and unconsciously started assigning blame for the deviations, stressed and obsessed over the urge to be better, and feeling like the victim of it all. He did not know how to turn off his "Seeing What's Wrong Habit."

Some Habit-Clusters do not require a single, specific Master Habit to be the ringleader. Instead, they are just a group of Limiting Habits that, once triggered, subsequently operate, activate, and reinforce one another, all at once or in any combination at any given time. We get stuck occasionally in the quicksand of this type of Habit-Cluster, and often don't even recognize the Habits at work – we just feel bogged down. Remember Jim at the beginning of this book? His repeated and failed attempts to quit smoking and get in shape have a root in the Habit-Cluster shown in Figure 2.3.

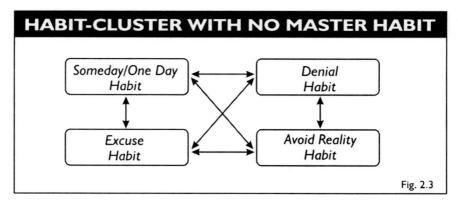

HABIT-CLUSTER WITH NO MASTER HABIT

Someday/One Day Habit

Denial Habit

Excuse Habit

Avoid Reality Habit

Fig. 2.3

Habit-Clusters without a Master Habit are just a bunch of inter-related Limiting Habits, equally triggered and equally committed to the game of controlling your behavior. Each Habit shares an emotional undercurrent, and they feed off of one another, perpetuating a negative state of mind. Jim allowed himself to duck accountability, avoid making specific and measurable fitness goals for himself, and fall short of making a change in his life. He held a Belief that what he did really didn't matter anyway, and whatever fate had in store for him was going to come true regardless of any Actions he took. That Belief sourced the strong Habit-Cluster that kept him off the path to better health even when confronted with his father's heart attack. His path to a better lifestyle began with a powerful acknowledgement of the root Belief and the Habits that resulted from it. Once dragged into the realm of the conscious mind, the Habit-Cluster could be explored, probed, and dismantled. That's slicing and dicing for you!

When we approach our Habit mechanisms methodically and with positive Peak Life Habits verbiage, we can examine ourselves as we never have before. This inquiry allows us to begin a journey out of "almost" toward self-mastery, and into the possibility of greatness. This is a fun game worth playing. So come on and play. Remember, you don't have to change anything, though you might want to Shift a few small things. It's your choice!

Now that you've gotten a taste of how all the pieces fit together, take some time to see which ones compose your own puzzle. Figure 2.4 contains the top 15 "Master" Limiting Habits to get you started – and there is an even more comprehensive list in Appendix B on pages 257-259 if you really want to dive in. Identify one Limiting Habit that resonates strongly – you'll find that it's probably one of your Master Habits.

TOP 15 "MASTER" LIMITING HABITS

- Avoid Accountability Habit
- Can't Say No Habit
- Distress Habit
- Excuses Habit
- Fear Of Failure Habit
- Fear Of Success Habit
- I Don't Trust Habit
- I'm Not Worthy Habit
- I'm Right Habit
- It's All About Me Habit
- Logic & Justify Habit
- Looking Good Habit
- Seeing What's Wrong Habit
- Victim Habit
- Waiting For The Shoe To Drop Habit

Remember, your Master Habits are Limiting Habits they just happen to be the ones in your Habit "control center" pulling the levers of the other Habits.

Fig. 2.4

MASTER HABITS

The following exercise will guide you through understanding how thoroughly Master Habits affect our Actions.

1. Identify one of your Master Habits:

_____

2. What do you believe triggers this Habit?

_____

_____

3. From the Limiting Habits Chart, choose a few Habits that this Master Habit calls forth, if any, and then list them:

_____

_____

_____

_____

4. Do you believe this is a Habit-Spiral or a Habit-Cluster?_____

Explain: _____

_____

_____

Once you have identified one of your Master Habits, its trigger, and its respective Habit-Spiral or Habit-Cluster, you are now in a place to begin interrupting and Shifting your Limiting Habits to Peak Life Habits. You have begun a journey away from "almost," across the Habit-Gap, toward a life of abundance – one that begins with a cognitive workout that defines your Beliefs, Actions and Habits in a powerful new way. As you assimilate this straightforward new paradigm for pulling what were once the shadowy subconscious workings of your Habit mechanism out into the light, stop and take a deep breath. Drop your fishing line into the muddy water, pull out those old tires, sodden work boots, weird pieces of junk, and say, "Wow, look at that!" Your curiosity and sense of wonder can make this a fun expedition. It's not every day that you get to peek at the real obstacles that have been snagging your forward progress.

Let's move into Chapter 3 and muse about how to gain control over your unique, complex Habit mechanism and launch yourself forward in any moment from covert negative to cognizant positive – and into your ultimate life!

CHAPTER 3

GET BEHIND YOUR BELIEFS

"Our deepest fear is not that we are inadequate. Our deepest fear is that we are powerful beyond measure. It is our light, not our darkness that most frightens us. We ask ourselves; Who am I to be brilliant, gorgeous, talented, fabulous? Actually, who are you not to be? You are a child of God. Your playing small does not serve the world. There is nothing enlightened about shrinking so that other people won't feel insecure around you. We are all meant to shine, as children do. We were born to make manifest the glory of God that is within us. It's not just in some of us; it's in everyone. And as we let our own light shine, we unconsciously give other people permission to do the same. As we are liberated from our own fear, our presence automatically liberates others."[2]

— Nelson Mandela, inauguration speech, 1994

How "dare" we not be great? Who are we not to be happy? Let's take on the challenge of filling our bodies with health, filling our

---

[2] Marianne Williamson, *A Return to Love: Reflections on the Principles of A Course in Miracles* (New York, NY: HarperCollins Publishers, 1992), 190-1.

lives with joy and passion, filling our pockets with that $500,000-a-year income (or more), sharing joyfully with our friends, fulfilling our place and purpose, providing for our families and pursuing the life of our dreams. In _Good to Great_, Jim Collins metaphorically and directly speaks of greatness. While his book is targeted to a business audience, it cogently speaks to individuals. What we do in our own lives parallels what happens at the company level – some companies get comfortably good enough, become complacent, and over time are eclipsed by competitors who are not satisfied with "good." The successful companies – and people – are the ones that push onward toward "great." That's why he says, "Good is the enemy of great." And that is what this excerpt from Nelson Mandela's speech is – beautifully written by Marianne Willamson – about, too. Really, when you look at successful people, they are the ones who leap the chasm of "good" to pursue a life of greatness. And greatness equates with abundance in joy, happiness, health and wealth.

Every one of us is truly a CEO. We are the CEOs of our own lives, always at the top of the pyramid of our personal world. And yes, though our circumstances may at times conspire to hold us back, each one of us has all the power in his or her life to play big. Yet we get comfortable in our own good-enough situations for months, years, even our whole lives. We may "almost" have a great career, "almost" have great relationships, "almost" have great health. Certainly there are times when "good" is good enough. Use your personal judgment to decide which parts of your life and experiences are good enough. Don't slip out of this conversation because you are attached to your comfort zone. Because if you picked up this book, chances are that you want more. I'm the same way. I've got that constant yearning, a positive and serious interest in going further and getting beyond "almost."

"Almost" is like "Someday;" it misses the mark, and whether it happens three or thirty or three hundred times in a the span of a life, one day we may wake up and see these "almost" moments and experience distress and disappointment along with the familiar comfort of sameness. When we do this, we are looking at a repeated tendency to stop short of our goals: in other words, we are looking at a Habit.

It is your own personal decision whether or not to go for "great." If you are not satisfied with what you are currently achieving in your life, take a look at the times you have decided to be satisfied with being merely "good." Confront the Habits that have kept you safely in the realm of "good" and off the track to "great." The challenge is to stop doing whatever keeps you off the path to your greatness, and start playing with the Habits and Actions that will take you there.

Our Limiting Habits are, in a manner of speaking, old friends. We are so accustomed to them that we anticipate and expect them. We rely on them to stick around and keep us occupied. They are the trouble-making cool kids whom we like to hang out with even though they aren't really the path to greatness. They keep us strangely comfortable, and we are often so used to their presence that they can cut in and take us for a turn around the dance floor, so to speak, without us really recognizing their influence on our Actions and Outcomes. We may even be heading metaphorically across the room toward the partner of our dreams, a glass of champagne in hand, ready to introduce ourselves and ask for the next dance, when our "Almost Habit" or our "I'm Not Good Enough Habit" or our "Playing Small Habit" pulls us in another direction. In spite of our best intentions, we may never make it across the room.

That is about to change. Let's explore the likely sources of the "Almost Habit," the pattern of getting tripped up and falling short just when you are at the threshold of playing big and getting the gold, getting the girl or the guy, or reaching an important milestone in your life's place and purpose. Let's focus on seeing the patterns or situations in your life in a new way (the Peak Life Habits way) so that you can tap your positive, creative power – and start running your Habits instead of letting your Habits run you.

Chapters 1 and 2 explored the Habit mechanism in a way that allowed you to look a few Limiting Habits straight in the eye and see if they are the ones snagging you. In this chapter, we will go to a different link in the Habit Chain: Beliefs. Here, you will have a chance to dive deep and recognize how your Beliefs feed your Habits. This is where we learn about how the psyche creates Habits, and from that knowledge, you can lay the foundation for mastery of your Habit mechanism.

Your challenge right now is to embrace the wonderful responsibility for your own greatness. It is a tough and powerful first step. It requires practice, action, discipline, and a sharp (and often very difficult) focus on greatness. At the same time, all you really have to do is tap into your courage and play big. If you are going to suffer this week, you choose the suffering. If you are going to have a great week, you create it that way. You have the power right now to send your Limiting Habits back to the chairs along the wall whenever they reach for you. Which dance will you choose?

Habit-Stamps

Babies come into this world with brains like sponges, ready to absorb any and all information about how to cope with life. Just like a little girl might learn to dance by standing on her father's feet, we humans grow up imitating the footsteps of others while we are young. Years later, long after we have forgotten the pattern those steps make on the floor, we continue the dance. We dance while our minds are busy with other things, and it is only with a conscious effort that we can look down at our feet and realize our movements continue to echo the lessons we learned decades ago. Have you ever driven several miles while your thoughts were wandering, and then all of a sudden snapped back to attention with no memory of turning the wheel? Your Habits were driving! Acquiring Habits is a big part of being human.

Gordon, the executive director of a nonprofit organization, is a good example of how Habits can move from person to person. His young daughter, Amy, was developing a "Disappointment Habit" because her dad spent so much time at work and often did not follow through on commitments he made to her. She was just seven, and like all children she was already developing Habits that would guide her behavior and color her worldview for the rest of her life. Gordon broke promises to her almost every day, and as a result she was beginning to learn that people always disappoint her and that the world is a disappointing place. She resisted that Belief to the best of her ability yet, left to perpetuate itself, the Belief would have deepened into a big Master Habit, a "Disappointment Habit." Like so many people, she might have ended up working with a coach or therapist twenty years down the line, searching for the root of her constant disappointment in herself, her career, and other people.

Fortunately, this story has a happy ending. Gordon noticed his daughter's distress, and in a Habitually Great coaching session, he and I had an eye-opening conversation about the pattern he was unwittingly perpetuating. He took a good look at the old dance steps his feet were taking, and at his daughter and himself, and he made a powerful decision to Shift his Limiting Habits and start keeping his promises. The goal was to model Peak Life Habits so that she might get free of the Limiting Habits he had begun to pass on to her from his own adolescence and adulthood, and ultimately to achieve a better Habit-Stamp.

A *Habit-Stamp* is the source of our oldest, most ingrained Habits. One of the ways that children learn about life is by what we represent to them through our personal examples without forcing it on them. If we model taking on the challenge of being great, of breaking through the Success Ceilings that restrain our success, then our children are more likely to break through their own ceilings at critical junctures in their lives. At Amy's young age, she was already acquiring Limiting Habits, and the instrumental piece in Gordon's Shift was realizing that he had to keep his word to his daughter so that she could be Habit-Stamped with the most basic and fundamental feeling of success. This dynamic holds true for all of us, and understanding it will help you approach your own Habit-Stamps with wisdom and compassion.

Habit-Stamps can come from anything. During the formative childhood years, and to a lesser though still powerful degree as we get older too, we are strongly influenced by events and experiences – with our families and friends, in romantic relationships, from our teachers, from strangers, television programs, music, movies, the Internet, the news and advertising media, school, and first jobs. We might have been born into the best, most loving, most easy-going family in the world, and one day at age five we are eating an ice cream cone and drop it on the pavement – and a moment later hear from Mom, "Oh well, too bad." BOOM, there's the early root of a "Disappointment Habit" later in life. Our young minds are talented at absorbing (and creating) these subliminal messages about worthiness, success, relationships – anything! From our early experiences with people and events, we develop Beliefs about many things.

The irony is that, although we employ a certain type of rudimentary logic in shaping those beliefs, we are still too young to use clear-headed, cognitive, critical thinking. (That capacity does not usually arrive until long after all these Beliefs have settled into our synapses, far below the surface of our awareness.) We lack the capacity to choose our Beliefs during those vulnerable early years, and so they become Habit-Stamps, stamped into our subconscious. By the time we are adults, we have accumulated a wide collection of them.

We have so many Habits that sometimes it may seem like we are running smack dab into a different one everywhere we turn. (Some are pretty comical too.) As we move forward in this chapter, each step taking us further into the origins of these Habits so that we can change them, I urge you to hang in there. If at any point you feel like you want to pause and take a deep breath to clear your head, do it! Grab a glass of water; roll your shoulders around a bit. The next milepost will always be just around the corner, and at the end of the chapter you will cross the tape into a series of chapters that use everything you learn in these pages.

The milepost in front of us now is understanding how our Beliefs create our Habit-Stamps. That is the root of our Habits, the first link in the chain. The next milepost is about getting to see where those Beliefs come from – our families, for instance – and understanding the force behind our knee-jerk loyalty to those Beliefs. The third milepost is about accepting that the resulting Habits we hold today may have been sabotaging our success. And the final milepost in this chapter is the delicious one about taking on our power, taking on our greatness, and taking action to become everything we want to do and be.

Now, let's go!

The Beliefs Beneath the Habit-Stamps

In the previous chapter, you learned about your Master Habits. They are the ones that really hit a chord, the two or three (or ten) that are always loaded in your mental CD changer and have colored your experience of life for years. Those Habits are almost certainly products of Beliefs rooted in your Habit-Stamps. We have Beliefs about work, failure, success, vulnerability, dependence, independence, worthiness, money, relationships, marriage, politics, religion, food, fitness, men, women, children, mothers-in-law – everything. Most are from our formative years, yet as adults they are firmly imprinted as Habit-Stamps that leave their mark on everything we do.

When Reese Witherspoon won her Oscar for Best Actress for *Walk The Line*, her speech was kind, humble, and heartwarming. She thanked her parents for always praising her and offering positive reinforcement for anything she did as a child, even simple things like making her bed. She explained how their parenting gave her the confidence to succeed, the foundation of a Belief that she could be great at whatever she did. This is a beautiful example of positive Habit-Stamping. She developed extraordinary yet simple Peak Life Habits like the "I Can Do It Habit."

Music lyrics are a good example of how we can absorb outside messages other than what we receive from our parents during childhood. Once outside messages make their way into our Beliefs, they may then shape our behavior and Outcomes – ones that may limit us rather than help us. Take for example some forlorn song on the radio, one that is all about unfulfilled love. You can probably think of one or two (or ten), right? If, every day for years, you turn on that radio or stereo and so many songs are about failed love, how will the music shape what you expect from your own relationships? Chances are, you are training your Habit mechanism to create consequences in alignment with those messages. Remember, your brain is mechanical and impressionable, and if it gets enough of the same image, it may form a Belief (say, that love leads to heartbreak) that links to a Habit that guides your Actions and produces an Outcome of unfulfilled, disappointing relationships, thus reinforcing your Belief. Next thing you know, you're a walking heartbreak song.

You are hardwired to act on your Beliefs as if they are absolute truths about life. You take Actions and create Habits that reinforce them. These Habits perpetuate what you believe, and the Outcomes in your life reinforce those Beliefs, and around and around it goes. You can have a Belief and a Habit-Stamp about anything. You may have Beliefs, for example, about how much money it is safe to make. You might say you want to make $500,000 this year, net in your pocket. And yet if you look at your Belief about making $500,000, you might not believe: (a) that it is possible; (b) that you are worthy of it; (c) that you are capable of being smart enough or outgoing enough to get it; (d) that there is enough time; or (e) fill in your reason here: _____. You will have all these Beliefs getting in the way of success, and without any conscious input from you, your Actions will flow out of those Beliefs. Let's restate that idea:

> **WHEN YOU ARE ON AUTOPILOT,**
> **YOUR ACTIONS WILL FLOW FROM YOUR BELIEFS,**
> **EVEN IF YOU DON'T REMEMBER THEM!**

You are guaranteed to have a certain Outcome (and income) – every time. Even though you think you are doing something different with each new business plan, job, or work schedule, the only guarantee is the repetition of an Outcome unless…read on!

The irony is that the originating Beliefs slip out of our conscious mind. We forget them and retain only the Habits, the 10 percent of the iceberg that sticks up from the water. We stop noticing that the music on the stereo is telling us that we're in for heartbreak and disaster, and we go about perpetuating an "I'm Alone Habit" and a "Waiting For The Shoe To Drop Habit." Amy won't make the link to Gordon letting her down between ages three and seven, even if she ends up with a "Disappointment Habit" at age 35. We may notice that we simply cannot get the breaks we want in business, yet won't realize that our Beliefs have been predicting our Actions all along. The good news is that, with a little effort and practice, we can wake up from our Habit-Trances and start taking Actions that lead to the Outcomes that we really want.

LIMITING HABIT SPOTLIGHT: THE "WAITING FOR THE SHOE TO DROP HABIT"

In this Habit's grip, we are always on the lookout for what will be the next thing to go wrong. We'll be waiting to get sick, waiting for the next car accident, wondering if we'll twist an ankle, fearing we'll lose our job, etc. We are so certain that something will go wrong that we cannot fully enjoy the feeling of life running smoothly.

If you are currently or have ever been within the spell of this negative Limiting Habit, you know its domination. In a puzzling twist, we steer toward what we most want to avoid, inviting it in, and actually make a sabotaging contribution to our lives. It quickly turns to struggle. We are not living powerfully, not taking the reins, and instead letting our fearful Beliefs pull us along.

PATTERN INTERRUPT PEAK LIFE HABITS:

The lightening Up Habit, Living Powerfully Habit, Living In Reality Habit, Creating A Powerful Future Habit

SL 3.1

Reese Witherspoon could look back and see how her Habit-Stamped Beliefs affected her positive life choices, i.e., her Peak Life Habits. To unlock the door to our own Peak Life Habits, we can begin by examining the Beliefs behind our own Limiting Habit-Stamps, the ones that have been holding us back. Here is a short case study of someone who had an "ah-ha" moment around her limited success in business and her family's Habit-Stamps. After this case study, you will have a chance to invite your own "ah-ha" moment to please step forward in your conscious mind.

Lisa was an executive at an advertising firm in San Francisco, and she saw herself repeatedly failing to close the biggest deals. At the last minute, prospective clients often backed out and hired other firms. She chose to confront this pattern when declining revenues finally compelled her to lay off three employees. She dug deep into two of her Master Habits, an "I'm Not Good Enough Habit" and "Fear Of Success Habit," that manifested as feelings of extreme anxiety and pessimism whenever she came to the threshold of pulling in a million-dollar client, and that kept her from really getting behind the deals to make them happen.

Lisa was the first person in her family to finish college. The usual pattern in the family was to follow your parents' footsteps, drop out of college, struggle, find your way into a marriage, have kids, and un-consciously pass your Habit-Stamps along to them. The first year Lisa made $100,000, she was unnerved. She felt she could only go so much further, could only allow herself a certain level of success before she bumped against the ceiling and fell back on Habits that undermined her success. She unconsciously didn't want to get light years ahead of her parents back in Spokane. Her father worked at the DMV and had struggled to pay for his kids' education. He always talked about money in a negative way – that it only came with great effort and could dis-appear in a heartbeat, and his Belief had been transferred to her and affected her success in the present day.

In short, with this Habit-Stamped Belief, Lisa's resulting anxiety at making a good salary as an entrepreneur made total sense! In a Habitually Great coaching session, she articulated that she was ready to Shift. She decided she would rather have a "Believe In Myself Habit" and a "Playing Big Habit" to help herself grow as an entrepreneur. Over the course of several months, she started using the tools you will find in this book to Shift away from her limiting Beliefs.

Change comes only after the Habit's soul has been laid truly bare. Once Lisa could bring the power of her Beliefs into her conscious-ness and see how those Beliefs had been running the show, some new options became available to her. Like Lisa, once we expose our Beliefs, we can then choose to make a change. We can start to work with our Habits. We can produce better Outcomes. We can take more appropriate, powerful, cognitive Actions. In short, we can form posi-tive Peak Life Habits.

Even if you can't locate the Belief that is the root of a Limiting Habit, do not worry. Sometimes those Beliefs are just so deep in the past that they are totally beyond our access. Our power comes when we trust that our old Beliefs, whatever they may have been, are no longer serving us, and then preempt or sidestep them. That is where the power is. You can choose when you are going to be disappointed and when you will work harder, when you are going to stress and worry and when you will persevere, when you are going to let human folly get to you and when you will laugh it off. You get to choose instead of letting those Limiting Habits lead you around the dance floor whenever you get triggered.

You may be thinking, "Yeah, but…" right about now. Your finger may be pointing outward at those who caused you grief and suffering or some type of malady despite their best (or perhaps because of their worst) intentions. The fact is that many of us had truly terrible experiences during our childhoods, at the hands and minds of others. Jack Canfield, author of the original _Chicken Soup for the Soul_, suggests that 85 percent of human beings grow up in varied degrees of dysfunctional family situations. Yet there is no going back. No matter how outraged you may be about the past, no matter how victimized you may feel, the only power you have is to take care of yourself from this point forward. Canfield calls this powerful decision: "So what, do it anyway." So what, it is in the past. So what! At the end of the day, you are still responsible for your own joy, happiness, and greatness.

We humans have a rather funny tendency to blame or attempt to change the people around us when things aren't going according to our hopes – it seems easier than transforming ourselves. Is there anyone you've tried to change lately? How's that working? These are my two favorite questions to ask in Habitually Great workshops. The sheepish laughs in the room erupt into a full chorus as we all at once see the futility of those attempts.

So let's hold in our minds a truth about life, one of the big ones: _we don't have the power to change people._ Parents, siblings, teachers – they are just who they are. Their stamps on our lives are inevitable, the good ones as well as the challenging ones, so no pointing fingers at Mom. No blaming your first grade teacher. No getting stuck in the "Victim Habit." The only true source of power comes when you turn your finger around and point it at your own chest, accept the Habits that manifest in your life today, and then make choices about how and who you want to be tomorrow, next week, and next month. This is the "U-Turning My Finger Habit." Whether you are 20 years old or 75 years old, you can make the powerful decision to be accountable and choose the Habits that allow *you* to lead the dance, to take the wheel, and to construct the success, happiness and joy that you really want.

In Chapter 2 you took some of your Habits out of the dark. Now, we are taking that exploration one step further. Here is a chance to look deeper into the influence of your Habit mechanism on your day-to-day Actions, and in so doing, step onto the path that leads from "good" and all the way to "great."

PEAK LIFE HABIT SPOTLIGHT:
The "U-Turn My Finger Habit"

Often we find ourselves pointing our fingers at people and events in our lives, blaming and shaming them for whatever is going wrong in our lives. The "U-Turn My Finger Habit" is about taking those outward-pointing digits and pointing them back at ourselves. If you don't like someone or something, take a look at how you have contributed to, and perhaps even directly caused, the circumstances, events, and behaviors that you don't like.

This important Peak Life Habit involves both accountability and humility. The trick is to U-turn your finger without being too hard on yourself, and without lowering your self-esteem. This Habit can actually raise your self-esteem because with it you naturally take on personal humility and accountability. Your life is likely to be more jubilant, powerful, and compassionate with your "U-Turn My Finger Habit." You can put in the positive changes you are going to make, stop finger pointing, focus on yourself and concentrate on your own great goals.

You've got a lot more power than you've been willing to believe to create the results and satisfactions you truly desire. Use it well, and get on with it!

The "U-Turn My Finger Habit" Interrupts:

Being Critical Habit, Knight In Rusty Armor Habit, Seeing What's Wrong Habit, Victim Habit, Excuses Habit, Blame Habit

SL 3.2

Many of us have strong Beliefs about failure, success, vulnerability, money, relationships and family. Those Beliefs may get their strength from old Habit-Stamps and, years later, fuel Outcomes that might stop us short of achieving our true intentions. We look back, scratch our head, and wonder, "How come I keep coming up short? I can see the finish line, yet never cross it." It's because our Actions are grounded in Beliefs that were stamped into us when we were most impressionable, and now we choose them again and again without reexamining their source.

It does not matter if you can or cannot remember the exact Belief behind some of your Limiting Habits. What *is* important is that you are interrupting the power of your Beliefs. (And you thought your free will was in charge!) Link by link, you are freeing yourself from the bondage of no choice, the bondage of living at the whim of your Habits.

BELIEFS BENEATH THE HABIT-STAMPS

As you practice your "Detachment Habit," see what wisdom the following short exercise can help you uncover about your Beliefs. It is an example of the powerful questions you can ask yourself as you go about exploring your own Beliefs about life. Have some fun playing with this, and see if you can unveil how some of these Belief categories have a significant effect on the Habits and the Outcomes you see in your life right now. Below are the questions you can ask yourself. You can choose to examine your Beliefs about anything at all. Some heavy-hitter categories are:

•	Money	•	Relationships
•	Success	•	Sexuality
•	Authority	•	Fitness
•	Failure	•	Spirituality
•	Vulnerability	•	Men
•	Family	•	Women
•	Trust	•	Myself

There is no limit to the number of things you can have a Belief about!

My Belief(s) about _____ are: _____

_____

_____

At what age did the Belief(s) form? _____

By what event(s)? _____

_____

_____

What are the Habits and Outcomes of the Belief(s)? _____

_____

_____

What positive Habit-Stamped Belief(s) would I rather have? _____

_____

_____

If you feel these questions are huge – you're right! Remember, this is a chance for you to learn about yourself. Dive deep and fill up a whole page, or skim through the questions in your mind. We will use the example of Lisa to walk us through the exercise, and then you can spend as much time as you want examining one or more of your own Beliefs. Ready?

Here's how Lisa approached this exercise.

My Belief(s) about money: You only get money with great effort, and it's easy to lose. It's humanly impossible to work hard enough to be rich. I'm not good enough to be rich. As a woman it is much more difficult to become rich...

At what age did the Belief(s) form? About 13 or so

By what event(s)? Dad would always complain when he got home from work about how hard he worked and how impossible it was to get ahead and become wealthy in spite of his efforts. Mom would parrot it the next day if she talked to family on the phone – "Oh, he's working so hard to pay for this or that... etc." Once, when he had gotten ahead and saved a bunch of money, he lost it in an investment he made with his friends. And Mom never considered herself a breadwinner, so I had no female role model at home.

What are the Habits and Outcomes of the Belief(s)? I feel lazy when I work 70 hour weeks. Money never seems to be enough. I don't do a good job closing big deals because the more money on the table, the more inferior my company looks next to the competition. So...the Habits are: I'm Not Good Enough Habit, Fear of Success Habit, and the Safe In My Misery Habit.

What positive Habit-Stamped Belief(s) would I rather have? I am smart and resourceful. I know how to do this right. I believe in myself and I am taking the right actions to create great results, starting now. I am good at getting advice from the most successful people I know. This company is so good, people are eager to pay us for the use of our products and services.

Now take a look back at the questions in the exercise. Do any interesting patterns or Beliefs reveal themselves? How were you parented? Do some of your Beliefs trace back to the childhood years when you were most impressionable? If so, you may also be recognizing some Habits and Habit-Stamps that parallel those of the adults closest to you. Did you ever wake up one day and think, "Oh my god, I'm just like Dad!" (Or Mom!) Have you noticed that your ability to have awesome (or not-so-awesome) success in your career, relationships, parenting, or fitness might have some hooks back to your family's patterns? This is the juicy stuff. So many of our Beliefs come from what we see and experience as kids, and those Beliefs have a predictable and ongoing impact on our lives as adults, thanks to our Limiting Habits. When we understand where we stumble, we can learn to sidestep the Limiting Habits that have been fettering us in our efforts to realize our full potential for greatness.

Here we are at the next milepost: seeing where our Beliefs come from – especially those we get from our families – and understanding the force of our knee-jerk loyalty to those Beliefs. Onward, you're doing great!

Staying Loyal to the Family

Children often mimic their family's Habits, and consequently their successes and failures. As babies, we do not come into the world wired to go forth and create our own path out of thin air. A natural pull exists toward being loyal to our family's Habits, because imitating them teaches us how to live and love and be in the world. The resulting Habit-Stamps affect our patterns of emotional expression, success, and even physical fitness later in life. We call this tendency the "Loyal To The Family Habit," and sometimes it is the Habit that keeps us at "almost."

To clarify: you aren't born thinking, "Oh, wow, life on earth; this is going to be one heck of a struggle." What happens is that when you are a kid, you are around the energy of your caregivers. It might be the energy of very loving, relaxed people whose lives came very easily and in a healthy way, and they pass that onto you. Or there you are at age two or six, listening, observing or experiencing some-body who is an absolute expert at seeing what's wrong with the en-tire universe. The Habits get stamped into you and set a baseline for what you expect from the world. After that, it is only human to fight to maintain the baseline – to stay "loyal to the family" even if their Habits do not serve us well in our lives. That loyalty can be either a conscious choice or a subconscious pull; either way, the old adage seems to hold true: misery loves company.

A few years ago, I witnessed a great example of this Habit. Shortly after a client, David, and his wife divorced, he and I went for a walk around the baseball field near his house. As we strolled the perime-ter, shoes wet from the dew in the grass, David said to me, "All the women I've ever loved seem crazy. They harass me, yell at me, and alternately push me away and pull me in. Whenever things are going great, whammo! What am I doing wrong?" He pointed out that the one time he had a great girlfriend – one who was so predictably giving and nice – he ended the relationship because she didn't seem to have enough "fire" or, he admitted, he felt used to a little more zaniness, a little more uncertainty about whether the woman he loved would em-brace him or yank him around.

This was an old "Safe In My Misery Habit," and the resulting situ-ations echoed back to his earliest relationship with the first woman in his life. He grew up in a household with an erratic mother, and the Habit-Stamped Belief was that you never knew if the woman you loved was going to embrace you or hate you. As David told me the story, it was clear that there was a Habit-Spiral operating in his rela-tionships. It started with an "Insecurity Habit" as the Master Habit, which came from his mother's unpredictable affection or lack thereof. The spiral would then cascade into a "Waiting For The Shoe To Drop Habit," which triggered a "Drama Habit" because conflict was in some ways easier to bear than waiting for the next rejection. (The women he chose, of course, had a "Drama Habit," too, and they triggered each other. He and I had a good chuckle at the predictable clashes that re-sulted!) Finally, the resulting emotional chaos of the "Drama Habit" would feel familiar and comfortable, and in turn it would trigger a

"Safe In My Misery Habit" that had kept him in the relationship with his ex-wife for so long.

Figure 3.1 illustrates this Habit-Spiral.

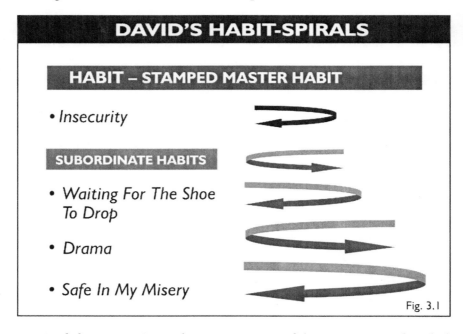

DAVID'S HABIT-SPIRALS

HABIT – STAMPED MASTER HABIT

- *Insecurity*

SUBORDINATE HABITS

- *Waiting For The Shoe To Drop*

- *Drama*

- *Safe In My Misery*

Fig. 3.1

And there is more to the picture. Part of the reason David ended up in the same type of relationships over and over again was that he had a "Loyal To The Family Habit." He was hardwired to be loyal to his family's Beliefs and ways of being. The pieces fit together: his mother may not have been a classic mother hen, yet she was still Mom, and the stamp made by her relationship with him was something David carried well into adulthood. He was utterly bonded to his Habit-Stamped Belief about how a relationship with a woman was supposed to look and feel, which was basically (and this is in his subconscious, the iceberg under the water), "My important relationships with women are supposed to be topsy-turvy. I expect that; it is how those relationships are supposed to be." Subconsciously, he was drawn to women who validated this Belief, and broke up with the ones who did not. So when the relationship was easy, available, and consistent, those qualities didn't resonate with him. It wasn't because he was crazy or a masochist; it was just that his association with love and bonding in a relationship was so tied up with riding an emotional rollercoaster. So a relationship of ease and consistency was unfamiliar to him, and he would sabotage one if it came his way.

David's "Loyal To The Family Habit" is pictured in Figure 3.2.

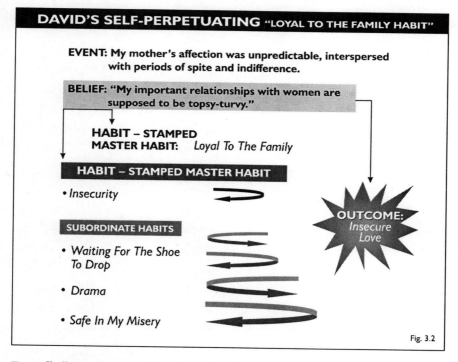

DAVID'S SELF-PERPETUATING "LOYAL TO THE FAMILY HABIT"

EVENT: My mother's affection was unpredictable, interspersed with periods of spite and indifference.

BELIEF: "My important relationships with women are supposed to be topsy-turvy."

HABIT – STAMPED
MASTER HABIT: *Loyal To The Family*

HABIT – STAMPED MASTER HABIT

• *Insecurity*

SUBORDINATE HABITS

• *Waiting For The Shoe To Drop*

• *Drama*

• *Safe In My Misery*

OUTCOME: *Insecure Love*

Fig. 3.2

David's "Loyal to the Family Habit" took the Action of choosing the same type of woman over and over again. On one hand, his Habit mechanism let him feel the love that felt most familiar to him, which was predictable in its unpredictability. This familiarity was a benefit, and a deeply satisfying benefit at that. On the other hand, he prevented himself from ameliorating the pain and unhappiness of unstable adult relationships. This "almost" situation caused him much distress.

Many people find their Habits pulling them in two or more different directions, impeding their progress toward greatness. In spite of our best intentions, we may often end up looking back and wondering, "What just happened there? Why did I fail again?"

And by the way, congratulations – another milepost down! Two more to go, and you will have the foundational understanding that will support you as you take back the power, embrace control over yourself, and start to implement the techniques that will allow you to start attracting positively inspiring success.

Self-Sabotage: "Thanks, But No Thanks…"

Sabotage is a strong word, and an apt one. When we are undermining our own efforts to succeed, we do so through our old, covert Habits. As long as we have been safe in "good," we sabotage greatness because greatness is scary. Our Habit-Stamps may have taught us to feel we don't deserve success, are not worthy of it, or that success puts us too far outside the "safe zone" of our family of origin.

The Beliefs behind our Habit-Stamps are entrenched and buried out of sight in the most vulnerable corner of our psyche. Marshall Goldsmith, one of the brilliant founders of the executive and life coaching movement, labels this mental warehouse the "covert unconscious." It is the source of those out-of-sight and powerful Habit-Stamped Beliefs that act up when we are about to change our lives in a big way – they do us the "favor" of putting us in a Habit-Trance, keeping us cozy, comfortable, and safe in the world of "almost."

The "Loyal To The Family Habit" is a heavy hitter in the sabotage league – the MVP of our Limiting Habits. It is rooted in Beliefs that were stamped into us as kids, and it is on the same team as many of our other Master Habits. Its influence is often far reaching.

What David – and Lisa, too – have in common is that their "Loyal To The Family Habit" perpetuates and is reinforced by a big group of Limiting Habits that collectively we call "*Self-Sabotage Habits,*" which I also refer to as "*Covert Unconscious Habits.*" We often fall back on these Habits to keep us in comfortable "good" rather than unfamiliar (and sometimes challenging) "great." Our "Self-Sabotage Habits" can undercut our ability to take consistent, disciplined, positive Action. What trips us up are the Beliefs we were born into, stamped with, and we manifest covertly. These Habits pull the strings from offstage, in the unconscious mind, to give us a dose of Action that keeps us from moving upward to "great." Figure 3.3 contains examples of some "Self-Sabotage Habits."

TOP 15 "SELF-SABOTAGE" LIMITING HABITS

- Avoid Commitment Habit
- Avoid Vulnerability Habit
- Drama Habit
- Distraction/Interruption Habit
- Fear Of Success Habit
- Good Person Habit
- Impatient Habit
- Insecurity Habit
- I'm Not Great Habit
- Loyal To The Family Habit
- Over-Think Habit
- Overwhelm Habit
- Perfectionist Habit
- Playing It Safe Habit
- Procrastination Habit

Fig. 3.3

These "Self-Sabotage Habits" can give us a litany of headaches and heartaches. It's not like we are out there in the world saying to ourselves, "Oh, I'm going to shoot myself in the foot now." "Self-Sabotage Habits" are almost always covert. Gordon's daughter, Amy, is surely not going to suffer intentionally in relationships twenty years from now because of an overpowering Belief that her lover is letting her down. Lisa gets excited every time she imagines landing a huge new client. David genuinely believes in the possibility of a stable, loving relationship. Our "Covert Unconscious Habits" are old and automatic, and they send us into a Habit-Trance and prevent us from stepping outside our family's patterns and taking on the accountability of major league success.

As you read this book and sift around in your own thoughts, feelings, and Actions for evidence of "Self-Sabotage Habits" like the "Confrontation With Success Habit" and the others in Figure 3.3, consider the following three common manifestations/types of self-sabotage. Recognize the role these Beliefs played in protecting you through the years, and then start to guide yourself in a direction that allows you to release these so-called "protection" methods. With each type of self-sabotage, we will also look at a brief example of how it unfolds in everyday life. It is often hard to see on your own, so that is why there are a few extra glimpses into the lives of men and women who are on the same path to greatness!

Self-Sabotage Pattern #1: Feeling Unworthy

The first obstacle that confronts you when you come face-to-face with a chance at ongoing success may be a feeling of unworthiness in the moment of greatness. BOOM—a "Covert Unconscious Habit" such as the "I'm Not Good Enough Habit" kicks into high gear to undermine your success pattern and, in so doing, reinforces a root Belief that you don't deserve awesome success. Right when you are about to take the gold, the love, the life of your dreams—when something great is about to happen—a feeling of unworthiness or pessimism pops up. Like when I'm in the driver's seat next to Parker Johnstone going 115 mph and he's telling me that I'm a great driver when BOOM, the thought, "No I'm not!" gets triggered subconsciously and I spin out. There it is: a "Self-Sabotage Habit."

This dissonance between actual success and our Beliefs about success activates a "Self-Sabotage Habit" that reinforces our Habit-Gap. All of a sudden we are in a situation as adults where we are on the verge of a huge life success, and then we put ourselves in a spin-out. Here's another example:

Ruth suffered a sexual assault in her teens, which she kept secret for many years. Even after several years of therapy in her thirties, she was experiencing a consistent pattern of unfulfilling relationships. Though she wanted to fall in love, feel safe, and play big in affection and trust, she acknowledged that her pattern was to keep herself at a distance and push away whenever she felt a bond forming. Behind the Action of "pushing away" was a Belief that the people she loved would betray or abandon her when she most required their help. The realization led her to recognize a strong "I Don't Trust Anybody Habit" in herself around love and commitment.

Ruth enacted a pattern of self-sabotage. Whenever she found a good guy, someone who cared about her and was genuinely sensitive to her past trauma, she would be thinking in one part of her brain, "Wow, I love this person and he seems really committed to supporting me," while her unconscious Belief was saying, "Wait a second! I can't trust people to be there for me if things get really hard." In that moment of dissonance, the deep Belief always won out. She found her mind filling with more doubts, feeling more longing to be alone, and struggling with the ideas of love and commitment. Her resulting Actions would slowly push her boyfriend away, and soon she would self-sabotage her commitment to making the relationship work.

If you have an "I Don't Trust Habit" you may test and challenge people until they ultimately have no choice other than to let you down. Yet there is a way out: awareness and understanding of the pattern, followed by an active decision to change and some rigorous, careful interruptions to this pattern. In Ruth's case, perhaps continued therapy would help. We will learn all about parachuting out of these Limiting Habits after we complete our walk-through of the remaining two Self-Sabotage Patterns.

Self-Sabotage Pattern #2: Preemptive Sabotage

The second common possibility is that we covertly, preemptively sabotage ourselves. Here the "Self-Sabotage Habit" works in tandem with a "Waiting For The Shoe To Drop Habit." We say something to ourselves like, "I'm just going to do whatever I want to do because this other stuff isn't really going to work out anyway." We facilitate our own breakdowns and then encounter the pain of having turned away from our desires, of having disallowed the structures of success to fall into place, of having found excuses to stop at "almost." Here's an example.

Carlos moved to a new city and made new friends who got him into rock climbing. He started taking better care of his body so he could go on the same trips and do the same workouts, yet he couldn't quit smoking. He found himself finding excuses to avoid more and more climbing dates, and he started to lose the physical strength he had recently taken so much pride in building.

He saw that his Actions resonated with his early experiences of moving from school to school because of his father's job – every time he would adjust to a new routine, his father would be transferred and the routine got disrupted. The resulting Habit-Stamped Belief was that any successful pattern was destined to be broken, and so he wound up taking Actions that reinforced his Belief and fed a cluster of Habits like the "Waiting For The Shoe To Drop Habit," the "Why Bother Habit," and the "Backsliding Habit" that preemptively sabotaged his commitment to a peak fitness pattern.

Carlos saw the same Outcome over and over again. In childhood, his father's frequent relocations caused him so much suffering – he said goodbye to numerous homes, friends, teachers and after-school sports teams. Many times he started at a new school halfway through the year and couldn't join a new team, couldn't adjust to the curriculum, and couldn't find his groove in a new peer group. His grades would plummet, and he would be lonely and bored. The moves also created tension in his parents' marriage and brought arguments and a strained family atmosphere into the home. He absolutely dreaded the news of another move because he was totally helpless to control the fallout. As he got older, his Belief that success patterns couldn't last led to a "Waiting For The Shoe To Drop Habit," which had served him by giving him some control over his failures: rather than living in conscious (or unconscious) fear of disruption, he created the failure himself. His smoking was a good excuse to backslide on his commitment to physical fitness and disengage from another group of friends. Although these "almost" moments hurt him, they hurt far less than having the rug pulled out from beneath him unexpectedly.

What happened? Carlos ultimately made powerful changes to his life and his health, beginning with a determined and rigorous letting go of the old Belief, and with it the Limiting Habits that kept him at "almost." Of course there was so much more. As you read the upcoming chapters about the Habitually Great methodology you will understand how.

Self-Sabotage Pattern #3: Logic & Justify

It works like this: once you have reached a threshold of success—say, for instance, you have been running three times a week and are about to lay down the cash for your first 10K race—you may again find yourself in the territory of self-sabotage. The last thing that can "save" you from achieving your goal, the final gasp of limiting energy that can "help" you avoid totally taking on the confrontation and the commitment to having the life that you want and the goals that you are committed to achieving, the last obstacle when all else has failed to stop you is your brain.

The voice of sabotage whispers in your ear, "Oh, that's right; you can't do this." You may come up with any number of good reasons: "I might get injured," or "I might get busy, and then my money will have been wasted." Other common ones are: "I've got to keep working; I don't have the time; they won't let me; the time isn't right; I don't want to seem pushy," and on and on!

We tend to save logic for last because it is our ace in the hole. The fact of the matter is that logic, like the "Over-Think Habit," is a "Covert Unconscious Habit" that is designed to boomerang us back to our comfort zone. Again and again, it helps us justify sliding right back into that safe, comfortable place—and too often directly back into the world of "almost." Let's take a look at Sabrina's story:

Sabrina built a successful salon business with several locations. She was the mother of a ten-year-old son. Although she was financially secure and had saved several hundred thousand dollars, she skimped and saved on everything from groceries to family vacations, and she often felt deeply upset about money.

She had grown up watching her mother's anguish over her father's uncontrollable spending and was Habit-Stamped with a Belief that if you didn't strategize and save as much as you could, your money was unsafe. Her resulting Habit was an "It's Never Enough Habit." Instead of enjoying her success, she was consistently anxious, and her young son had developed his own anxieties about his ability to please his mother.

Sabrina manifested self-sabotage in her financial life by pouring her focus into a poverty mentality. She planned, skimped, and strategized so well, yet at the end of the day, she denied herself the ease and sense of victory that came with accomplishing her savings goals. Her logic kept telling her, "It's not enough, Sabrina; you had better figure out how to spend even less and save even more, just to be safe." She saw the whole world through a lens of dollars and cents, and that filter created enormous distress even as it let her rest safely in the knowledge that she was not repeating her father's reckless spending mistakes.

Her relationship with her son began to transform for the better as she experimented with taking different Actions, spending a little more once in a while, and confronting her Belief with the fact that the world didn't have to fall apart every time she opened her wallet. We'll take another look at her Pattern Interrupt method in the next chapter, along with some others.

And that brings us to our final milepost of Chapter 3!

Your Head: Dangerous and Powerful

In this chapter we've talked about how the undertow of our Beliefs can interrupt success in our careers, relationships, and health. In a nutshell, when those Beliefs get triggered, our Limiting Habits grab the wheel and drive us straight into familiar and unproductive thought patterns. We start worrying, stressing, and ruminating our way into the world of self-sabotage. Those thought patterns really make our heads some dangerous places to be. That's worth repeating:

> **YOUR HEAD IS A DANGEROUS PLACE TO BE!**

As we saw with Sabrina, logic and justification are great examples of how self-sabotage patterns are totally tied into our dangerous heads. You may pick out a goal and then immediately see what is wrong with it. You may say something like, "No, it wouldn't be right for me to have that." Thanks to our brains, we can troubleshoot our dreams and rationalize why they are out of reach. We can tell ourselves some great stories about what is wrong with what we want and, at the end of the day, ensure that we play small and sabotage our greatness.

Remember, we are absolutely run by our Habits. Maybe we get triggered by a demanding partner, child, parent, the guy who cuts us off in traffic, a migraine, an argument with the boss, or even weighing in on the scale. Maybe we get triggered by getting too close to love in a relationship, or by having too many really great times with someone we love when our Beliefs subconsciously insist that "this can't possibly be real!" Our steady, pervasive Beliefs about ourselves and how much success we are "allowed" to achieve can orchestrate our Actions in a predictable, limiting pattern over time. However they get triggered, when our Limiting Habits step up to the plate, three things are certain: (1) we are not in control anymore, (2) our Limiting Habits have us completely in their power, and (3) we are stuck. There is an alternative and it is up to us. We can get our power back. We can become great. This is where we break the tape at the finish line and cross into a new way of taking on our selfhood.

One of the purposes in this book is to offer you a way to preempt your Limiting Habits and stay out of that dangerous, self-sabotaging head. You can harness the power of what psychologists call the front-brain, the executive function that is the essence of Habit-Wisdom. In short, it is where your power of choice lives. You can choose to get wise about your Limiting Habits, look out for and act upon Habit-Triggers, break your Habit-Trances and choose Actions that eliminate old Habit Chains. It is the place from which you can see and interrupt your Limiting Habits and choose new, Peak Life Habits to practice instead. You can choose to transform the energy of struggle and self-sabotage into Peak Life Habits and, in so doing, make your head a powerful rather than a detrimental place to be. That is the heart of the next chapter.

One of the perks of greatness is that you get many more choices. You can choose to detach from all the worry, suffering, impatience, struggle, and instead let your foibles and flaws be cause for some wise laughter. This whole book is about lightening up, although I am not minimizing the difficulty of change. We don't know when things are going to happen: when people are going to live and die, when a kid is going to break an arm, when we are going to do something that makes other people laugh at us—even little things, like spinning out an expensive, state-of-the-art racecar in front of somebody you admire. There is real pain, heartache, and suffering, and some of life may be really unfair. The point is to come into your power, master it, and create the best life possible—to have fun and play big, to live with passion and to be the one who holds the accountability for your own happiness.

What you can do now in your own life is close the chapter of incomplete success. You can Shift. You can break through the barriers, you can break through the Habit-Stamps, you can break through the mold that has been passed down from generation to generation and been proven ineffective time and again. The tools you were given by your family may only allow you to live life one way. The great news is that you have the power right this moment to say, "Thanks, but no thanks." In Chapter 4, we talk about how to preempt our Limiting Habits and make a new reality—one in which, as we say in Habitually Great workshops: "Shift Happens!"

CHAPTER 4

INTERRUPT YOUR
DESTRUCTIVE PATTERNS

*"We are what we repeatedly do. Excellence, then, is
not an act, but a habit."*

—Aristotle

Ultimately, much of what we do in the course of a day is motivated by either a Peak Life Habit or a Limiting Habit. For instance, how do we allocate time for our loved ones, our fitness, our jobs, etc? What are we eating and drinking? How do we communicate? When do we let ourselves dream big? What actions are we taking (or not taking) to fulfill those dreams? Among the thousands of people who have gone through Habitually Great coaching and Habitually Great workshops – parents, athletes, students, all levels of employees, entrepreneurs, all of whom are the CEOs of their own lives – is they all have one thing in common: they are creatures of Habit. Our decisions and behaviors follow a pattern over time. So here is a hypothesis for you: if our Habits determine our successes and failures, and we desire different results, then the surest way to achieve our dreams is to Shift our Habits. Let's say that again:

IF OUR HABITS DETERMINE OUR SUCCESSES AND FAILURES, AND WE DESIRE DIFFERENT RESULTS, THEN THE SUREST WAY TO ACHIEVE OUR DREAMS IS TO SHIFT OUR HABITS

So far, we have examined the important nuts and bolts of the Habit mechanism. Take a moment and check in with yourself. How has this process been so far? Inspiring, motivating, fun? Perhaps thought provoking and challenging, too? If our grand strategy is to fully understand the many layers and workings of our Habit mechanism, we must then use our knowledge to detach from and interrupt our Limiting Habits – especially those rooted, automatic, Habit-Stamped Master Habits that tend to hog the driver's seat when we want to be on the road to success. Like Ruth, Carlos, and Sabrina in the previous chapter, we can make a conscious decision to Shift to Habits of greatness, stand by that decision, and cause the Shift to manifest.

In Chapters 1 and 2, we focused on the Habit link in the Habit Chain. In Chapter 3, we moved to a different link, Belief. Now, we are going to take a look at two interrelated links: Belief-Link and Action. Let's first play with the idea that our deepest Beliefs don't have to govern our Actions so completely that by taking new Actions we can pave the road for new, positive Outcomes.

There is no magic involved in Shifting your Habits. As you read this book, you will simply begin to see that there is an alternative, and once you make that leap you can consciously practice the alternative by working directly with the Belief-Link in the Habit Chain using the techniques in this chapter. As you read on, take a look at the Shift Chart in Appendix C on pages 261-271. This tool illustrates exactly how each Limiting Habit has the potential to Shift to a Peak Life Habit. Three, six, or twelve months from now, you can turn around, survey the road behind you, and realize, "Wow, I've come a really long way" (though it might not have been apparent in the moment). Thanks to the interrelation and overlap of the Habits, which you have probably noticed in many of our examples, tackling and interrupting one Habit can Shift a whole Habit-Spiral or

Habit-Cluster, so that over time you will see significant changes in your Habit Chains and life situations.

You have by now pulled your Limiting Habits out of the shadowy subconscious mind into conscious recognition, named them, discovered what triggers them, and explored their origins. In short, you have been slicing and dicing them. Now it is time to break their control and re-train your mind so that new, positive Peak Life Habits can sift back down into your unconscious and move you onto the path of Right Action toward greatness. The crucial next leg of your journey is to take over the wheel and turn off the autopilot. Have you been looking around for the switch? Here's the switch: a *Pattern Interrupt*. A Pattern Interrupt is your intervention tool for discerning, interrupting, preempting, and Shifting your Belief-Links in order to choose new Actions. The end result will be new Peak Life Habits that gradually allow you to reach your highest potential.

Pattern Interrupts

A Pattern Interrupt is straightforward and profound. It is a method to dig down to the core of your Habit mechanism, where your Beliefs reside, and make a Shift. Even if you keep your Beliefs (and they can be awfully hard to change sometimes), it is within your power to rewrite the script of any Belief and replace almost any Belief-Link by actualizing a Pattern Interrupt. You have the bolt-cutters for your Habit Chains and the power to link yourself to different Actions.

Remember David (with the "Loyal To The Family Habit") from Chapter 3? He began to Shift his Habit-Spiral by choosing to interrupt his "Waiting For The Shoe To Drop Habit." It's the one that would guide him toward topsy-turvy women in the first place. The inevitable argument would begin, or the expectation would go unmet, which then fed into the "Drama Habit" and eventually the familiar and comfortable "Safe In My Misery Habit" (Figure 3.2). As you have likely seen by now, that's just how the Habit mechanism works. Yet David was powerfully committed to Shifting the pattern of his relationships so that he could experience the joy of a stable, loving partnership. His next step was to implement the Pattern Interrupt technique.

As David and I strolled around the baseball field that day, we walked through a fun visualization. I asked him to imagine that he had grown up with the blessing of a mother who was kind, stable, and predictably loving. He envisioned a mother whose love and affection were always constant. If he were disciplined by her, it was for a good reason, and the discipline was offered firmly and with genuine care for his well-being. "Now," I said, extending the visualization exercise, "imagine that having had those maternal Habit-Stamps, you are back at the beginning when you first met your ex-wife. Picture going on a date with her. How many times would you go out with her?" He said, "None!" She would have appeared unstable and erratic from the start, and he would have moved right on to find a better match for himself. And with that realization, he saw how his Belief about relationships with women could Shift. In that moment, he glimpsed the power to change.

By gently re-scripting his Belief about relationships with women, he began to clear a path into a new kind of relationship. He Shifted his Belief from, "My important relationships with women are supposed to be challenging," to, "I'm committed to having a stable, trusting, loving partnership." He reminded himself of this radically new and positive Belief continually and let it nurture new, more positive expectations from his romantic relationships. Over time, the energy that once went into his old ruminations and struggles went instead into nourishing a joyful "Seeing What's Right Habit" and an easy-going "I'm Worthy Habit."

As we see with David, a Pattern Interrupt is composed of two parts. The first is to detach and notice that a Limiting Master Habit (or a cluster or downward spiral of Limiting Habits) is in control. If you notice that you are often being triggered, reacting, getting angry, and being right, then (even though it may seem paradoxical) jump right in and detach! This first step is about selecting your "Detachment Habit." Right Action isn't about being right; it is about being wise and appropriate to the Outcome that you truly want, to your place and purpose. It helps you U-turn your finger so you can be in charge again and make different, powerful choices. The second step is to select a Peak Life Habit that you want instead. Again, you may want to flip to Appendix

C on pages 261-271 and peruse the Shifting Habits Chart to see how each Limiting Habit has one or more Peak Life Habit counterparts.

Just like learning a new exercise at the gym, interrupting your Habits takes practice. They're automatic, they're safe, and they've worked well enough in the past—at least to get you to "good." At first, you may not want to exercise those new muscles all the time because, like exercise, it feels difficult. Your old ways, like your weak muscles, sometimes have a strong, elastic pull on you. You will stretch toward a new way of being, yet your subconscious draws you back. Like David, we are loyal to our families, loyal to our Beliefs—in short, we are creatures of Habit. It's just how the Habit mechanism works. Without a Pattern Interrupt, your Habit mechanism is guaranteed to win every time. If you are in the game for "great," it is time to head for the gym and build your new Pattern Interrupt muscles. As you work your Pattern Interrupt muscles more often, they grow stronger, and each choice to interrupt a Limiting Habit becomes easier. Soon you may be able to rapidly preempt the Habit Chain created by your self-sabotaging, Habit-Stamped Beliefs—the ones that have kept you at "almost" (Figure 4.1).

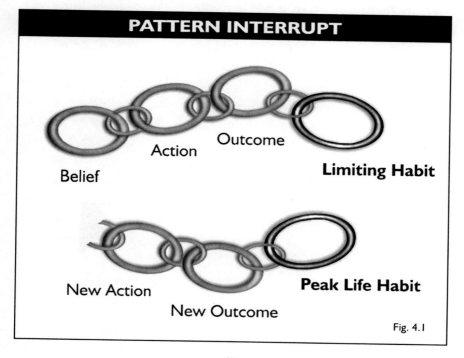

PATTERN INTERRUPT

Belief
Action
Outcome
Limiting Habit

New Action
New Outcome
Peak Life Habit

Fig. 4.1

By breaking and Shifting the Belief-Link in the Habit Chain, you will be able to take new Actions, which provide for new Outcomes. Carlos manifested a Shift in his life (see Chapter 3) that is a good example of the preemptive power of Pattern Interrupts. As he created a structure for the Actions that linked great Outcomes and Habits like the "Living Powerfully Habit," he started to push his old Habit Chain out of the game. He drafted his doctor to support him in keeping his commitment to a smoke-free life, scheduled free time back into his days so he could spend it with friends, and laid out money for a gym membership. With his self-sabotaging Actions no longer in play, the old, familiar, limiting Outcomes had less of a chance for a repeat victory over Carlos's greatness in friendship and fitness.

It is no small undertaking to set yourself onto a new groove, and it is okay if your transition from the old groove to the new isn't without a few bumps. Nobody is giving you a grade or watching for the "perfect" transition, so don't sweat it. For example, like a lot of people, Carlos also had a couple of saboteurs who wanted to wreak havoc on his newfound clarity: the "I Don't Wanna Habit" and the "Why Bother Habit." Carlos had to challenge those Habits more than once, and early on he gave into them now and then. When he did, at first he would be elated at the freedom to eat, smoke, drink, and not work out – and yet that feeling quickly subsided into a hefty dose of guilt and remorse. Over time Carlos spiraled into a "Hard On Myself Habit" about not working out, which fed his depression about falling off the wagon and, in the downward spiral we've seen before, undercut his motivation. During your Shift, detachment and discipline are so important. The key for Carlos was to be disciplined, even when he didn't feel like it. My advice to Carlos was simple and rigorous: stick with the accountabilities of the program he created, and if he fell off the wagon, get right back on without anger or regret. Just get back in the saddle for a longer and longer time, every time. No judging yourself!

As you can see, at first Pattern Interrupts take a good bit of focus and consciousness (though perhaps no more than to read and think about what you are learning in this book), because you are really inventing a new way of living and being in the world. You are lining up your synapses in a new way. Instead of your Habits driving you, you are taking conscious control of the wheel and choosing different turns. The more you do it, the deeper you carve the new groove.

There are four very effective types of Pattern Interrupts that you can use to block the grip of a Limiting Habit. Each of them will pry open your old Belief-Links and let you forge more powerful Actions, no matter what your old Belief is. These Pattern Interrupts are like bolt-cutters in the Habit Chain. First, let's take a quick glance at where we have been, and then spend some time with these simple yet powerful new tools.

Pattern Interrupt Preparatory Steps: Awareness & Understanding

Chapters 1 and 2 were about awareness, focused on training you to recognize a Limiting Habit, to have an awareness of the saboteur in your midst. After all, awareness is the essential step in making change happen. There is an old adage that states, "A problem recognized is a problem half—solved." And yet, it turns out that a problem recognized is not solved, half-solved, or resolved in any way, shape or form. Most of us know about our "problems." And what have we done with that awareness? Maybe not much.

Chapter 3 was about understanding why you may not have acted to solve those problems. That is the second preparatory step before you can really take on Shifting your Habits. We learned about Habit-Stamps, those troublesome saboteurs that more often than not have nothing to do with our truth. Our understanding now extends to the roots of our Habits—that is, to our Beliefs—and further, to the foundational experiences and events that created those Habit-Stamps.

Chapter 4 is a new, positive, and proactive place, a place to move ahead and break through your Limiting Habits using the Peak Life Habits cognitive paradigm. We will learn about the Pattern Interrupt techniques in four parts, one to address each link of the Habit Chain. You can approach the Shift by focusing on your underlying Belief, the Actions you take, the Outcome you desire, or the new Peak Life Habit you want to cultivate—and once you obtain a foothold, you can focus on all four. At each link, you have a solid option for shaking off the grip of your Limiting Habits (Figure 4.2). I'll discuss each in turn in the upcoming sections.

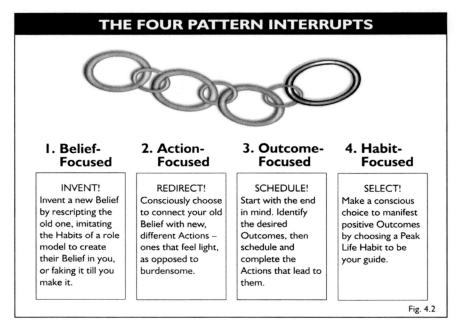

THE FOUR PATTERN INTERRUPTS

1. Belief-Focused	2. Action-Focused	3. Outcome-Focused	4. Habit-Focused
INVENT! Invent a new Belief by rescripting the old one, imitating the Habits of a role model to create their Belief in you, or faking it till you make it.	REDIRECT! Consciously choose to connect your old Belief with new, different Actions – ones that feel light, as opposed to burdensome.	SCHEDULE! Start with the end in mind. Identify the desired Outcomes, then schedule and complete the Actions that lead to them.	SELECT! Make a conscious choice to manifest positive Outcomes by choosing a Peak Life Habit to be your guide.

Fig. 4.2

"Uh-oh, not so fast," you say. "This sounds too easy." And you're right! Shifting is not simple, and part of your work happens in tandem with truly coming to grips with three other emotions I identify as one Limiting Habit: the "Fear, Doubt, & Worry Habit." It can stop you in your tracks. It is one of the most debilitating and falsified Limiting Habits that exist. As you read the next section, set an intention to check in periodically with the negative stories and images that you have manifested in your mind from your "Fear, Doubt, & Worry Habit." Especially if you feel skepticism in your openness to these new ideas – often, that bit of struggle signals a Limiting Habit. Maybe its root is a fear of change or a cynicism about the possibility of a Shift? Or perhaps you feel that big, passionate successes are for other people? Or you worry about whether your friends and family will still like you if you are different?

No matter what, the "Fear, Doubt, and Worry Habit" can be pretty huge. You are invited to park that one at the door – because, hey, you can always pick it up later if you decide you want it back. For now, take the "Playing Big Habit" for a test drive. It is your accountability to keep yourself wise, happy, healthy, safe and playing big. Now, let's go:

1. Belief-Focused Pattern Interrupt: Invent!

Remember how our Habit mechanism has us trained to act as if our Beliefs are the absolute truths about life? Well, guess what – we can have a little fun with our training by inventing some new Beliefs for ourselves. We're not erasing the old ones just yet. (Oh, if only it were so easy!) We do get to try on new ones to see how our outlook changes and what new Actions become available to us. Think of it as trying on new clothes: you can leave your old, worn out duds on the dressing room bench, pick out the sharpest or most flattering outfit from the rack, walk around in it and see how your confidence Shifts. The crux of this Pattern Interrupt is that the sky's the limit.

There are three styles of "Invent!" These subtly different approaches to trying on new Beliefs can get you started on the exciting road of visualizing and attracting new Actions and Outcomes in your life.

1a. Re-script the Old Belief

The first style is to invent a new Belief by re-scripting the old Belief. Basically, you insert or create a new Belief that supports the Outcome or Habit you seek. Let's say you have an "Avoid Authority Habit" and a "Defensive Habit," and you want to stop butting heads with authority figures. You've seen how those Limiting Habits keep you stuck in a pattern. It doesn't matter whether it's the traffic cop, your mom, or your boss. You have identified that your actual Belief is "I know what's best and I don't want anyone telling me what to do," or perhaps it's "authority figures are always trying to cut me down, make me feel small, and make me look like a fool." Are you ready to say, "Enough's enough!" and script a new Belief, regardless of where your original Belief came from? It may go something like this: "I have and always will have the ultimate power over myself. Nobody can take that away from me, and the authority figures in my life only want what is best for me, so I am going to become better at trusting them, listening to them, and communicating well with them about what is important to me, and why. I am going to become a great team player, and build powerful, trusting relationships with integrity and purpose." What a great, positive Belief! With continued emphasis on that new script, it will absolutely support you as you interrupt that Limiting Habit in any moment of struggle. Rather than getting triggered and defensive, you can play with staying grounded and clear to handle the reality of the situation, whatever it may be, and Shift toward productive, positive Habits like the "Accountability Habit" and the "Humility Habit."

Your accountability is to be proactive, play big with this and reinforce the new Belief continuously. At every opportunity, in every scene or sequence in your life, play with visualizing your new intention, your new Belief, your new Outcome. Remember to keep these thoughts big and make your positive intention so huge that every time your Limiting Habit hooks you, you can dwarf it with your new Belief. Make sure you identify the Actions that are consistent with your big, new, invented Belief and bring about the Outcomes the new Belief supports. Practice this with discipline and persistence.

1b. Choose a Model

The second style is to create a new Belief by imitating someone else's Habits. One of self-improvement guru Tony Robbins' favorite modalities for change is to model the behaviors and actions of someone whom you admire, the way they are and the results they create. The key is to identify what Habits they are using to generate their success. Once you identify those Habits, then you articulate a conscious intention to adopt those Habits for yourself and take the Actions that your role model takes. To use our clothes metaphor, pick out somebody whose style of dress you love, research and identify the type and style of clothes they are wearing, and purchase ones to wear yourself. Again, this requires discipline and follow through, two keys to greatness. We are not talking about doing this for an hour, a day, or a month. Go all the way, and over time your whole Habit Chain Shifts toward the model of success that you are emulating, including your Belief. Interestingly, we often select our clothing based on what others are wearing and the current perception of what fashions are considered "in" for the image we want to present. When you are modeling yourself after someone else, remember to dig deep, always looking at the whole package of selfhood.

A good example is a person's work ethic. In our professional lives, it is quite natural to identify a mentor or role model – somebody who creates fantastic Outcomes expertly and quickly, works with interesting people on interesting problems, is highly respected in the field and attracts a steady stream of new opportunities – while in contrast you may see yourself perpetually stuck in a "Procrastination Habit" or "Fear Of Failure Habit." How do you put yourself forward in the world and start having similar successes? It does not matter if that person works directly with you, on the other side of the street, or on the other side of the planet; how they approach their work and other people is a gold mine of information. With your growing Habit Wisdom, identify what kinds of Actions they take, what Outcomes they create and, most importantly, what Beliefs are at the head of those positive Habit Chains. The results are great Peak Life Habits like the "Discipline Habit" or the "Power Scheduling Habit," which will be explored later in the book.

In short, if you choose a model to guide your Pattern Interrupts, identify the components of their positive Habit Chains and replicate those in your own mind and life. Consciously and continually choose the components of those Habit Chains. As you begin to manifest the desired results, keep up your discipline with this key Pattern Interrupt and take pride in watching yourself align with your model over time.

1c. Act As If, or Fake It Until You Make It

Have you ever heard of "acting as if?" In our third approach, you can "fake it until you make it" with a new Belief by pretending it is true so that, eventually, it will become true.

Our Beliefs are powerful, and our righteous attachment to them is not to be underestimated – it is a magnetic pull. Those Beliefs often appear immovable, and for good reason. After all, we have believed them for a long time and have always believed we are right. So if you want to take on this very effective Shift, the first step is to forcefully acknowledge the reality of your Beliefs and the truths they hold for you. Then, with that acknowledgment, challenge and impose on yourself a different Belief: fake it. This is truly "acting as if." The "Acting As If Habit" cultivates the internal state that allows successful Outcomes to happen. You want to be a millionaire? Declare yourself rich, learn rich, act rich, create rich, and *become* rich. You want to attract the best partner ever? Study relationships, read and learn about relationships, and choose to *think* like somebody who allows love and commitment into their life. Believe it, act it, make it real, and *keep* it real.

If you are getting stuck in expectations of how people will behave or how life will treat you, have some fun with this Pattern Interrupt. Ruth's Belief, for example, was that people could not be trusted to help her when their help was most needed, and the trauma associated with this Habit-Stamp made it tough for her to imagine what Actions were available to her in spite of the Belief. She could, however, imagine which Actions linked to an entirely different Belief, such as: "I draw good people into my life, and they will always do their best to help me when I ask. In fact, their love helps me every day." She faked it with positive Actions like taking healthy risks in honesty and vulnerability – and threw a curveball at her old Belief whenever her Actions were rewarded with great Outcomes, such as feeling a growing bond of trust in a relationship in the months that followed.

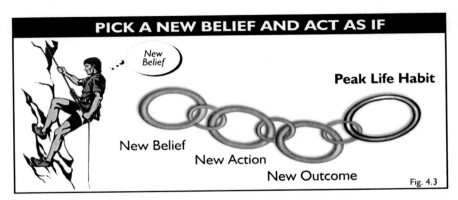

PICK A NEW BELIEF AND ACT AS IF

New Belief

Peak Life Habit

New Belief

New Action

New Outcome

Fig. 4.3

Our expectation is not that our old Beliefs immediately vanish. In that case, we would definitely be setting ourselves up for disappointment. No, we simply want to put ourselves in a new pattern of Action and witness the surprising Outcomes they produce. Over time, with our "Discipline Habit" and "Persistence Habit" as our guideposts, our old Beliefs will begin to fade. Figure 4.3 shows how it works.

The fun of this Pattern Interrupt is that you can also visualize some of the changes this new Outcome will bring and start to draw them into your life. The best approach is to suspend concern over whether or not you believe your new Beliefs; you are just going to identify the Actions that support the Beliefs, and then take those Actions. Focus on the Actions that your invented Belief will produce, and the Outcomes will spring to life.

* * *

All three styles of the "Invent!" Pattern Interrupt are effective offsets to Limiting Habits such as the "Disappointment Habit," "I'm Not Good Enough Habit," "Unsafe World Habit" and "Waiting For The Shoe To Drop Habit." Whenever you want to side step your ingrained, limiting expectations of life, you truly can invent any other Belief you want and try it on for size, especially in the areas of your life where you want to see new success.

2. Action-Focused Pattern Interrupt: Redirect!

First, let's clarify: every single Pattern Interrupt in this chapter is about being in Action, because Action paves the road for change. This particular Pattern Interrupt focuses specifically on the Action link of the Habit Chain. In other words, we are looking at what Actions we have taken in the past, saying "no thanks" in a moment of struggle, and carefully choosing new Actions as replacements. It is an in-the-moment, rapid intervention to shake off the grip of a Limiting Habit.

Several years ago, I backed my brand-new Camaro SS convertible into a cement post at a gas station. OUCH! I could have really beat myself up over a minor mistake, and believe me, those feelings of a "Hard On Myself Habit" – "I'm stupid. I'm an idiot! How could

I do this?" – all came flooding in. It was a moment ripe for a Pattern Interrupt because it was a moment full of struggle, so I caught myself and said, "Wait a minute. What is the solution to this?" The car had less than 1,000 miles on it, and I drove it right over to the Chevrolet dealer where I had bought it, and I said, "Okay guys, here's what I've done. How do we fix it?" They said, "It's going to cost you about a thousand dollars, Mr. Weinstein." I said, "Great, let's make an appointment." And that was that – a new Action. Did I have the money allocated for that? No. And yet by just taking an appropriate Action, I knew that I would manage my budget and pay for the repair. It was a good moment in the journey of my own Shift, and it supported a nice "Lightening Up Habit."

The point is, instead of spiraling into those moments of self-sabotage and negative rumination, you can instead lighten up and say, "Okay, that's pretty funny, how the heck did I do that?" and pull a Pattern Interrupt into the game to take your power back. I could have suffered over my backing into that cement post. I know myself. I am an avid auto enthusiast, drive on many racetracks, love high performance cars, and I'm a guy who takes pride in his cars (if you're a guy, you know the type; if you're a girl, you know the type too!). So you can imagine the extent to which I could have suffered about that incident for quite some time. Instead, after a few good minutes dwelling in my "Hard On Myself Habit," I said, "Oops. Pattern Interrupt. What can I do to resolve this and move forward?" And the story has a happy ending: the shop fixed it perfectly; I couldn't even tell the damage had ever occurred.

The fun part of this technique is to find a challenging situation, resolve it, and move toward the future with an exultant heart. Maybe that means having an authentic, honest conversation with a friend who has upset you rather than getting stuck in your "Victim Habit" or "Anger Habit." Maybe it means sorting through the clutter in your home office rather than feeling suffocated by a "Chaos Habit." The goal is to pick an Action, even a simple one that takes just 15 minutes, focus on it and follow through. And when the same old Belief raises its voice in that moment of struggle to tell you that you can't succeed, you detach for a split-second and begin, step by step, to take a new course. It does not matter whether you change the originating Belief one iota. You just make the choice to connect that old Belief with new, different Actions – ones that don't steer you naturally toward the same old Limiting Habit – and enjoy the success of creating new Outcomes. The new Peak Life Habits and Beliefs will form gradually and naturally over time.

This second type of Pattern Interrupt is shown in Figure 4.4.

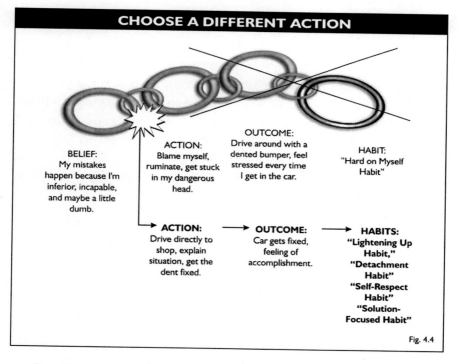

CHOOSE A DIFFERENT ACTION

BELIEF:
My mistakes happen because I'm inferior, incapable, and maybe a little dumb.

ACTION:
Blame myself, ruminate, get stuck in my dangerous head.

OUTCOME:
Drive around with a dented bumper, feel stressed every time I get in the car.

HABIT:
"Hard on Myself Habit"

ACTION:
Drive directly to shop, explain situation, get the dent fixed.

OUTCOME:
Car gets fixed, feeling of accomplishment.

HABITS:
"Lightening Up Habit,"
"Detachment Habit"
"Self-Respect Habit"
"Solution-Focused Habit"

Fig. 4.4

In my car example, I said to myself, "Hold on a second. The wheels in my brain are spinning like crazy again. I'm angry, frustrated, insulting myself, and it doesn't feel good. I want to get out of my Dangerous Head." And while I was making the appointment, the guy at the desk told me a story about the time he pulled his car into his garage and forgot about two carbon fiber road bikes attached to his roof rack. Both of the frames were totaled—and he was actually laughing about it. We all make mistakes, because we are human.

Therefore, we can give ourselves a break, lighten up and put our energy into a positive Action.

Our new Actions produce surprising, great, and unpredictable Outcomes that challenge our old Beliefs and gradually re-script them over time. We feel burdened less often, and when we do, the burden is lighter. What a beautiful success! Now let's take a look at a Pattern Interrupt to use when we know exactly what Outcome we would like to manifest.

3. Outcome-Focused Pattern Interrupt: Schedule!

This third Pattern Interrupt is really about starting with the end in mind. Peak Life Habits are about knowing the result you want and using your Habit mechanism to generate the change in yourself necessary to make it happen. By seeing your Beliefs as simple components of Habit Chains, you can choose to side step your limiting, default Beliefs and recognize them for what they are: obstacles and limiting thoughts that are not real truths. Rather than spending years searching for their roots and causes, you identify the Outcomes you desire, then schedule and complete the Actions that lead to them. Easy? Yes! Do-able? Absolutely!

Lisa, who we met in Chapter 3, is a great example of how this Pattern Interrupt can jump-start a success pattern. She held a Belief that she could not overshoot her family's working-class lifestyle by too much. Yet she saw that her greatness in business would serve her family as well as herself. She wanted to take the fast track to a specific and measurable Outcome: land a pair of million-dollar clients in three months and another one by the end of the fiscal year, and then make a gift to her parents' retirement fund. She scheduled the Actions of signing her company up for a trade show, reconnecting with people in her address book, and doggedly following up on leads and speaking opportunities. (Clearly, she had also hired a Habitually Great coach to strengthen her pitch and follow through skills!) This type of Pattern Interrupt is shown in Figure 4.5.

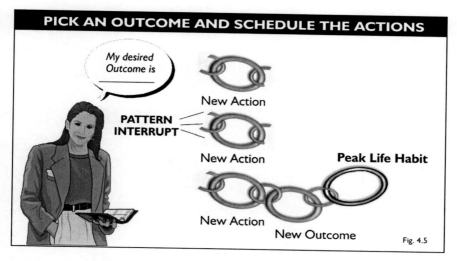

Fig. 4.5

Lisa took the Actions that made sense for her desired Outcome and landed all three million-dollar clients in only six weeks. All along, those opportunities had been waiting like fruit on the branches – she only had to look up, get a ladder, and do some harvesting. She kept herself so engaged with her desired Outcome that anytime her Limiting Habits (in her Dangerous Head) told her that her company was too small to handle big clients, that she didn't have the power to taste the sweetest successes, she could recognize and interrupt those disempowering Beliefs right away. The reason? They contrasted so sharply with the intention and schedule she had set for herself. She looked at her list, picked the next Action, and got moving again.

So get into your Powerful Head and schedule Actions that lead step by step to your happiness and greatness. Then all you have to do is fulfill those Actions.

4. Habit-Focused Pattern Interrupt: Select!

TOP 15 PEAK LIFE HABITS

PEAK LIFE HABITS

- Accountability Habit
- Always Learning Habit
- Being Appropriate Habit
- Compassion Habit
- Detachment Habit
- Discipline Habit
- Gratitude Habit
- Great Listener Habit
- Ground Truth Reality Habit
- Humility Habit
- Lightening Up Habit
- Patience Habit
- Power (vs. Force) Habit
- Success Structures Habit
- U-Turning My Finger Habit

Fig. 4.6

The fourth and final Pattern Interrupt is to choose a Peak Life Habit and walk, talk, live, and breathe it. If you identify a Peak Life Habit as your guiding star, you are choosing to manifest the positive Outcomes of that Habit through your thoughts, feelings, and Actions, whatever that means in your life and dreams. You adopt and consciously enact everything that your chosen Peak Life Habit means for you.

Here is an example. If you have a "Fear, Doubt, And Worry Habit," you know how you feel when you are inside of it: maybe a little (or a lot) cynical, anxious, or just full of pessimistic "yuck." And you declare that you want to catapult beyond it – so far beyond it that soon it will be just a speck on the horizon. Next, you read through the Peak Life Habit List above (or the comprehensive list located in Appendix A on pages 253–255) and identify an alternative that strikes a chord. Maybe it's the "Always Learning Habit" that makes you sit up and say, "Yes! That's exactly how I want to be!" And then, starting today, you nudge aside your fears, doubts, and worries and make more room for your courage. You look for healthy risks (maybe it's in emotional honesty, or in whatever goals you are willing to set for yourself), and then you get out there and find those healthy risks and pursue them. At every opportunity, you look up at your guiding star and ask yourself, "What Action will take me one step closer?"

If you were in a situation like Lisa's, where she doggedly pursued the biggest clients for the first time in her life, you would schedule time in your day to follow up on leads. You would trust a coach to help you. You would create courage by thinking about and actualizing the supporting thoughts, Actions and Outcomes that accompany the "Always Learning Habit." You would let courage and lightness take root in your brain. Even if they only stay rooted for a few seconds at a time, as Carlos experienced when he Shifted his Habits, you wouldn't expend the energy being hard on yourself. Just get right back into the saddle! And over time, you will find yourself going there automatically. No longer are you in a one-way alley headed into the "Fear, Doubt, & Worry Habit."

Other great Habits for this type of Pattern Interrupt are the "Discipline Habit," "Patience Habit," "Lightening Up Habit" and "Right Action Habit."

This Pattern Interrupt is about the power of choice, and ultimately it is the heart of this book. At the end of the day, your ability to catapult to habitual greatness can be found in that instant when you release your fear of the unknown and merge onto a new highway. There's the old maxim again: "A problem recognized is a problem half-solved." Not always the case, right? Well, let's give it a better twist: "A problem half-solved is a problem I am choosing to solve right now." Now that's Right Action! Chapter 5 will take you even deeper into power of Pattern Interrupts with strategies to help you make the most of these tools for success.

CHAPTER 5

NOW, SHIFT YOUR HABITS

"Man does not simply exist, but always decides what his existence will be, what he will become in the next moment."

—Viktor Frankl

Let's do a little exercise. First, make a fist and hold it out in front of you so that you are looking at your knuckles. Got it? Now, extend your index finger. Does that feel familiar? Ok, good. Now, turn your whole hand around 180 degrees so that your palm is facing up and bend at the wrist so that your finger makes a U-turn in the air. Congratulations! Like all great CEOs—and remember, whether you're a teacher, a teenager, a parent, or a partner, we are all the CEOs of our lives— you have just located the center of all power in your life. Right there, where your finger is pointing right now: at yourself! You have also just performed the first step of every Pattern Interrupt you will ever do.

The four Pattern Interrupts discussed in Chapter 4 are 100 percent guaranteed to get rid of all blame, procrastination, and struggle in your life—as long as you hold yourself accountable for applying them. You hold all the cards to your future. Practice them and you are taking on the most basic form of responsibility for whatever situation you face. You are asking yourself what Actions you can take to Shift in any situation. When there is a problem, when there is a struggle, you detach for a second and ask yourself two questions: "What's really going on here? And what can I do about it?" Each Pattern Interrupt gives you a unique way to ask and answer those two questions, pick an Action and follow through. That is the biggest, greatest, most powerful choice you can ever make in your life, and it all starts with your index finger.

Just a reminder: any time you feel negative, when you are being reactive, triggered, fearful, manipulative or controlling, that is when a Limiting Habit is vying for control. You are being taken over and, without a Pattern Interrupt, you are a goner. Positive, powerful, successful Outcomes are not predictable. The beauty of our work here is that you can get your power back in an instant. Simply hold out your fist, point your finger, make that U-turn, and then pick one or more Pattern Interrupts and give them a go. In fact, the four types we have talked about are interrelated, and they completely support each other. Figure 5.1 is a quick-reference summary of the four (well, really six!) Pattern Interrupts:

TYPES OF PATTERN INTERRUPTS		Fig. 5.1
PATTERN INTERRUPT	**HOW TO USE**	**EXAMPLE**
1a. Invent! *Rescript the old Belief.*	Create a new Belief that supports the Outcome or Habit you seek.	Interrupt an "Avoid Authority Habit" by re-scripting the Belief that authority figures want to make you feel inferior. So the next time you feel that struggle, you can detach and commit to the Belief that you have ultimate power over yourself, and nobody can take it away from you.
1b. Invent! *Choose a model and imitate.*	Identify someone whom you really admire – either the way they are or the results they create – then adopt the Habits and resulting Actions that they employ. You naturally also create their Belief.	Imagine your favorite athlete. What Actions does he or she take to get from good to great? Chances are, a good dose of discipline and a "Yes, I can!" Belief. You may not be training for the NBA, yet even so, choosing the Right Action can apply to any walk of life.

TYPES OF PATTERN INTERRUPTS (cont'd)		Fig. 5.1
PATTERN INTERRUPT	**HOW TO USE**	**EXAMPLE**
1c. Invent! *Fake it until you make it.*	Acknowledge the reality of your Beliefs and the truths they hold for you. Then, with that acknowledgment, challenge yourself to adopt a different accountability, to "fake it," thus creating new Beliefs.	**Ruth invented the Belief, "I draw good people into my life, and they will always do their best to help me when I ask," and from that mindset she could identify the Actions that linked to it, like taking good risks in honesty and vulnerability.**
2. Redirect!	Consciously choose to connect your old Belief with new, different Actions – ones that feel light as opposed to burdensome.	**I could have really beat myself up over backing my Camaro SS into a pole, thanks to the feelings of a "Hard on Myself Habit" like I'm stupid, I'm an idiot. Yet instead of ruminating, I drove directly to the shop and made an appointment to fix it. This Action produced an immediate feeling of personal effectiveness – as well as an understandable dose of good humility!**
3. Schedule!	Preempt Limiting Habits by identifying the desired Outcomes, then scheduling and completing the Actions that lead to them.	**Lisa created an Action plan for landing new, big clients that kept her on track when her "I'm Not Good Enough Habit" tried to pull her toward hesitation and inaction.**
4. Select!	Make a cognitive choice to manifest positive Outcomes by selecting a relevant Peak Life Habit to be your guide.	**For example, if you choose the "Success Structures Habit," then identify and implement Action structures that support your goals and success. The key is to go beyond empty motions and lip service, instead calling yourself forth to have a breakthrough in discipline, focus and follow through!**

Have fun with this technique in a way that works for *your* life, *your* dreams and *your* commitments to greatness. Pattern Interrupts let you step out of your Habit-Trance, take a breath, get your power of choice back and make your head a powerful place to be. Even if your deep-down Beliefs are locked in place for now, that's okay. It is difficult to counter those Beliefs. The whole idea behind Pattern Interrupts is that it does not matter if our original, underlying Beliefs linger, because we still have the freedom to take new Actions.

Your Beliefs may be giving you some "Yeah, but…" thoughts right about now. If so, the resistance is natural. Your Habit mechanism is hardwired to create allegiance between yourself and your Beliefs, and your first knee-jerk reaction will always be to hang onto those Beliefs and let them keep their status as "unshakeable" truths about life. Old Beliefs and Habits want to stay hidden and continue to pull your strings – so if you find you can't let them go immediately, that's okay. The real, empowering message is that every human being is born with the freedom to test-drive any and every kind of new Action, no matter the underlying Belief, and then observe (and enjoy) the new Outcomes. Meanwhile, Shift happens under the surface, and as you take new Actions, your Beliefs may evolve or dissipate over time. Pattern Interrupts are positive, playful Actions to jump-start this process.

Each positive Action we take is one of accessing our greatness in the moment – even simple Actions like laughing and shaking your head at a moment of knee-jerk worry, or kicking your feet up, lighting a candle or a fire, and using your Powerful Head to meditate on gratitude and happiness instead of going down the road of over-thinking and getting stressed out after a challenging day at work. We make ourselves great one moment at a time, and moment-to-moment greatness takes discipline.

The Secret: Discipline and Persistence

Anthony Robbins likes to say that human beings have two motivations, pain or pleasure, and that those two things are what drive people to change. With Peak Life Habits there is a third way to make Shift happen. When you don't have enough pain, and you don't have the promise of pleasure, the only thing that can get you to greatness is discipline and persistence. Treat them as two sides of the same coin, because discipline without persistence may give you a really great week of Pattern Interrupts followed by a backslide into "good" for the rest of the month. Persistence without discipline means that you might play with Pattern Interrupts like a hobby – once in a while, when you have time, because "someday" you'll get your Shift, and "one day" you will arrive at greatness. Together, discipline and persistence empower you to take the steady, measurable, bite-sized Actions that will move you from "good" to "great" in a predictable way.

PEAK LIFE HABIT SPOTLIGHT:
The "Discipline Habit"

The "Discipline Habit" is somewhat of a paradox because once discipline is a Habit, there is actually nothing to be disciplined about. Self-discipline is an absolute key to greatness, and we see it in almost all highly effective, successful people. They keep a strong degree of personal accountability, they allow the results to show up in their lives, and then they keep being disciplined.

What carries us through the day is a certain measure of discipline, and we each have our own individual measure that we will want to sustain and increase. We want to develop our discipline muscles so that our mind's eye stays focused on our intentions with each disciplined choice we make.

If you're struggling with your "Discipline Habit," you are almost certain to also have the "Doing It My Way Habit." You'll find yourself slipping in the area of discipline and defending your rights to do things your way. You may have a fear of discipline. Being good enough is okay with you. If this is the case, you will want to ramp up your "Discipline Habit" by being persistent and creating everyday systems for accountability that facilitate Right Action.

The "Discipline Habit" Interrupts:

Fear Of Commitment Habit, Looking Good Habit, Reward Habit, Self-Sabotage Habit, Struggle Habit

SL 5.1

The value of discipline and persistence is time-tested and true. Napoleon Hill wrote _Think and Grow Rich_ in 1937, and in identifying what causes greatness and wealth, he wrote a whole chapter on persistence. Despite the truth of this concept, however, many of us have learned to see discipline and persistence as a burden – something hard and austere, maybe something that is synonymous with deprivation. Rolled up with that idea, perhaps, is a feeling of "why bother?" Why bother sticking to disciplined, persistent Pattern Interrupts if they take us off of the familiar, known road of "almost?" At the end of a long day, we can fall back on our Limiting Habits, such as the "Reward Habit" that justifies eating the pint of ice cream. We can fall back on our "Victim Habit" to avoid the accountability of U-turning our fingers when our old Self-Sabotage Habits create crisis and distress in our lives. Being merely good is pretty easy; falling back on a default behavior takes less effort than traveling a road to greatness for the first time.

So, really, is the "Discipline Habit" about freedom and joy or is it about burden? How do you define it and inspire change? Try on this idea: a life without discipline is a life without the taste of great success, great joy and great achievement. Here is an interesting reflection from successful author and counselor Earnie Larson:

> "Wait a minute. Isn't joy a matter of doing what we want? Isn't freedom the state of never "having to" do what we don't want to do? And isn't discipline – which we learned from our parents – the burden of having to do what we don't want to do?
>
> Actually, joy is the freedom to do what needs to be done. And gaining that freedom takes discipline. Why? Without discipline, we usually end up doing what is familiar to us. And our experience clearly tells us that old thinking and old behaviors bring us anything but joy."[3]

To illustrate my point about how discipline works, the typical Olympic athlete will train about four hours a day for at least 310

---

[3] Larsen, Earnie, _Days of Healing, Days of Joy_ (Hazelden Publishing and Educational Services, 1987)

days per year for six years before even getting to the Olympic games. Extreme? Yes! Absolutely! Yet these athletes are so utterly determined, so focused on their goals that they don't quit at a mere 250 days a year or give up after five years. Our "extreme" regimen may simply be the discipline of committing to 55 minutes at the gym rather than 45 minutes (or a happy 15 minutes of exercise instead of none), or taking an extra-deep breath of Pattern Interrupt detachment with a loving, compassionate Shift toward being a great listener to our partner even when we are triggered, or asking a question rather than assuming we know the answer.

The athletes that are training day in and day out know that slacking off won't kill their chances of making the Olympic team. Yet there is something else at work that makes a disciplined and persistent Action preferable to falling back on an "easier" way of being. There is a window into something beyond the task at hand, a commitment to a goal and a promise to oneself. Whether your goal is happiness, competitive victory, fitness, better communication, abundance, or improving an aspect of the world, that seemingly crazy regimen of Olympic hopefuls represents the power of a commitment and the effectiveness of the techniques we apply to interrupt our Limiting Habits and Shift toward the fulfillment of our greatness, place and purpose. The individual task itself does not matter as much as the willingness to take the step, again and again and again. Now, are you willing to take your step? What will it be?

Seeing It Through: Faith Vs. Optimism

In short, your discipline and persistence prepare you for your success. The point of discipline is not that you love it. It does not require pleasure. What it does require is trust that if you stay in Action and follow through step-by-step, no matter what Limiting Habit goblin jumps out from under the iceberg, you will achieve freedom and discover the joys that await you in the life of your dreams.

Still, how do we know if those dreams will come true? Simple answer: we don't. Nobody's a Nostradamus here. This is the point where you may start hearing the voices of your "Fear, Doubt, &

Worry Habit" and your "Why Bother Habit," because without a guarantee that your methodical discipline and persistence will pay off, even while knowing that these are qualities which lead to success, we meet a paradox. How do we maintain faith in working toward an Outcome without any certainty that our efforts will get us there?

Jim Collins talks about the *Stockdale Paradox* in his classic book, <u>Good to Great</u>. Admiral Jim Stockdale was the highest-ranking military officer to be imprisoned in Vietnam, and he survived over eight years of torture when many POWs died after a few months. He credited his survival to what I call a "Keep The Faith Habit" (and I'm not necessarily talking religious faith). His disciplined emphasis on that Habit let him trust that someday he would be free again, though he did not know when that day would come. The prisoners of war who survived were the ones who thought, "I'm going to get out of here. I don't know when so I'm going to keep moving along, keep myself in shape, keep my mind sharp, and it may be five years, ten years—who knows?—and still one day I know I will be free."

According to what Admiral Stockdale recounted, the ones who didn't make it had a different Habit – and this is may surprise you. They had an "Optimist Habit." They thought, "I'll be out of here by Christmas," or "I'll be out by Easter." And Christmas came and went, and then Easter came and went, and Thanksgiving, and Christmas came and went again. Each time they set up those optimistic goals, they did so with a measure of fantasy. In the midst of their optimism was torture and fatigue, yet ironically their spirit and will were crushed by the devastation of their optimism as well as the physical hardship. They set their dreams up with too much optimism, and therefore they were heartbroken and ultimately destroyed by the reality.

All right you "eternal optimists" out there! Perhaps you are more faith-based than you realize. The other side of this paradox – faith in a goal despite a lack of certainty about how it will happen – applies to anyone. When we approach our Shift with an acceptance of the Stockdale Paradox, we tap into the power of faith, the power of our capacity for vision. We don't ignore reality. We powerfully acknowledge that we don't have control over anything beyond ourselves, and in so doing set ourselves up to take the appropriate Actions (connected to the "Being Appropriate Habit," the "Keep the Faith Habit," and the "Right Action Momentum Habit") that get us fit and ready for that day when the door finally opens. That is the heart of discipline and persistence, and it is how success becomes predictable. *Shift happens!*

While Olympic athletes and Admiral Stockdale are great role models for discipline and persistence, there are many more. For example, look at the people you admire most in your own life. Just like you, they may feel uncomfortable some days, and they may want to throw in the towel after a poor result or life blow, yet they still make a choice to stick with their Action plan. That is because their Discipline and Persistence gives them stamina, inspiration, and faith in themselves, and in the place, purpose and goals they aspire to. They believe, and then believe some more. They keep doing things over and over again with mental intention until they are metaphorically (or actually) standing on the pedestal wearing a gold medal on their chests in front of millions of people. They have paved the way for their miracle to happen. Ah, the power of Right Action! That power is within all of us, right now. Habits take time to make, take time to change and Shift. So use your "Patience Habit" and play for whatever gold medal is important to you.

Rico Washington was a baseball player. In high school he had become a star pitcher with a 92-mph fastball. That's not blindingly fast, and yet it is the speed of a competent major league pitch. After high school he played minor league baseball for over 11 years. By that time, his hairline was receding and he had lost his mother, who along with his high school coach were his biggest fans. Rico was just another prospect, of which there were thousands, hoping to get to the major leagues. He was no longer a pitcher, having become an infielder in the minors. He had plenty of reasons for quitting the game. Yet he never considered it. "You're getting to play the game you love. When you compare it to people that work a 9-to-5 job and hate it, you're pretty lucky to be mak-

ing a living in the minors."[4] Rico always believed that one day he would play in the major leagues. That day happened on April 1, 2008.

Are you willing to break through the ceiling of your success? You must break that "Loyal To The Family Habit" or that "Almost Habit" or any of your "Self-Sabotage Habits" and say, "Now it's up to me. It's my turn to really create and invent my greatness!" You will have a chance at the end of this chapter to articulate the things you are positively inspired and passionate about. (Or at least moderately interested in…it's a good start!) Basically, you will be orienting yourself upward as you climb toward your own version of your ultimate life. While you may not have the exact coordinates to plug into the GPS, you can certainly identify which direction to focus your spotlight. Your discipline and persistence will move you in the right direction, and as your new Peak Life Habits take root, they will open the road before you.

Shift Happens

Here's a phrase to write on your bathroom mirror: "Shift Happens!" (Now that ought to put a smile on your face!) It really is beautiful. One day you are suffering, and a few months or years later you're living an awesome life, or you notice you are responding to life's imperfections differently, or you are in great shape, and you say, "Whoa! How did that happen?" What happened was a Habit Shift to Peak Life Habits, practiced with discipline and persistence. Your commitment to habitual greatness paid off in spite of pulls to the contrary. As you repeat your Pattern Interrupts with discipline and persistence, they become easier and more automatic. You will find yourself in a new place of being Action-oriented. That's the greatness of the "Pattern Interrupt Habit!"

The next step in Shifting your Habits is the process of letting your new Peak Life Habits trickle down into your subconscious and become as automatic as your old Limiting Habits once were. From there, they will start manifesting new Outcomes. Whether you have believed in the process or not until now, this final phase

---

[4] New York Times, 4/13/2008, Sports Sunday, p.3

is your proof. You have been setting yourself up for success by tak-ing the right Actions, and with time they start to pay off. Shift is a language you learn to speak with greater fluency the more you prac-tice it. Like Carlos and Lisa's examples, moment-to-moment Actions build momentum toward small successes and large victories, some so subtle and deep that they may manifest themselves simply as an overall feeling of being more satisfied than ever before with the way you live your life. You can look back over time and see it. As in ath-letic training, the Shift just happens. You are stretching, you're going to the gym, you're working out, and all of a sudden you hit the ball better, sharper, and farther. You dance perfectly within the tempo of your greatness. That's a tipping point.

You are not just putting band-aids on your life – you are going in deep to profoundly Shift the way you are in the world. You are debunking the myths inside your head, the "absolute truths" that are your old Habit-Stamped Beliefs, and you are giving them a reality check so that over time subtle changes start to manifest themselves. We never know where or how Shift will happen, at least not exactly, yet the Shift is predictable. You can put faith in the fact that once you pull your Habits into your conscious mind, focus on what you want in your life, and then put your attention on Pattern Interrupts, your unconscious mind will come along for the ride. (That's the Stock-dale Paradox for you!) Then your Habits, the Habit-Clusters and the Habit-Spirals will all Shift.

Great things will start happening seemingly by chance. This is where the Law of Attraction meets the Habit mechanism. Through disciplined, persistent Pattern Interrupts guiding new Peak Life Habits into the unconscious mind, we set ourselves up for success. Happy, successful folks focus on who they want to become and take many Actions to guarantee that attainment. They are coincidentally in Action when the right time hits, just like they were in Action in the days, months, and years before that "right time." From the out-side, their Outcomes – getting the gold, the girl, the guy, making an important contribution, creating the life of their dreams – may look like miracles, yet it is simply what they've already promised themselves through Action. What you focus on, what Outcomes you identify and pursue, what new Peak Life Habits and Beliefs you create with disciplined and persistent Pattern Interrupts create the miracles in your life.

Envisioning Positively Inspiring Success

Remember, the brain is mechanical. When you articulate what gives you passion (perhaps starting with the things that simply give you pleasure) and then get in Action toward those things, you draw the positive Outcomes of that passion into your life. Those Outcomes can be anything – more time outdoors, more great moments with a partner, new travel experiences, more great success and respect in your field, fun with the kids, a new degree, a fitness program, etc. You put vivid pictures into your brain of that Outcome. You then choose the new Beliefs, Habits, and Actions that will take you right to the open doorway of that success, allow you to walk through it and live in the light of who you've become. As you read these words, allow your passion and desire for accomplishing what you are picturing grow.

Passion can propel you and be a part of your success – though interestingly, there is no passion requirement for Peak Life Habits. Greatness requires discipline and persistence, not passion. We've all had those moments, sometimes even days or weeks when we feel the blahs, the lack of motivation and passion. An important way to generate passion is to stay in Action. Have you ever had those moments where you just didn't care, and yet you put yourself into Action and worked your way through your malaise and into a big smile of satisfaction? Sometimes passion is a destination rather than the driver.

The upcoming exercise on page 96 will help you start to clarify where you want your Shift to take you. It will lend your mechanical brain images to work with that give you passion and/or pleasure and start you on the road of taking Actions that will draw even more greatness into your life. The trick is to imagine your Outcome using vivid pictures of what you want to manifest and make them so clear that you can *feel* what's great about getting the gold, the girl, the guy, the life of your dreams. For instance, if you love spending time outdoors, what about it is most appealing? Is it the feeling of nature or freedom? Is it the sound or smell of the water or the trees? Do you feel a sense of joy as you're looking out over the expanse of water and sand dunes, or at an endless line of mountains in winter? Are you passionate about financial security? About the image of you standing in the bathroom mirror looking fit and healthy? About how good it will feel to wake up on a Sunday morning, peacefully, blissfully in love? Passion is full of positive energy. It is the bliss you feel when you are overflowing with feelings of good humor, success, competence and sharp focus.

Be as detailed as possible in your Passion List on the following page. Start with something that you love to do and then expand on it. Add color and use all five of your senses: sight, sound, touch, taste, and smell. For instance, if you love to travel, write down what the specific destination you have in mind and how you would like to get there. Use the space provided to list some Actions that you could take, beginning right now, that will lead you one step closer to living your life with more passion.

Once you have identified what you are passionate about and the Actions you can take to bring more of that passion into your life, conclude the exercise by identifying some new, more distant areas in which you may want to become passionate at some point in your future.

MY PASSION LIST

My personal definition of passion is: _____
_____
_____
_____

Using all of your senses – sight, sound, touch, taste and smell – make a list of some things you are or have been passionate about at points in your life. What do you love? Where do you love to be? What hobby do you have or want to have? What lights you up about your job or education? What touches you? Who are you passionate about? What topics are you passionate about? What in nature excites you? What causes are you passionate about? What excites you in life? This is a helpful exercise that you will build on during the book. Capture those points of passion along with any past or present feelings of passion with words right here, right now:

Point of Passion: _____

Good Feelings About It: _____

Point of Passion: _____

Good Feelings About It: _____

Point of Passion: _____

Good Feelings About It: _____

Point of Passion: _____

Good Feelings About It: _____

Point of Passion: _____

Good Feelings About It: _____

The Actions I can take in my life today to enjoy more passion, happiness and fun are:

- _____
- _____
- _____
- _____
- _____
- _____

New areas that I may become passionate about in the future are:

- _____
- _____
- _____
- _____
- _____

With practice, all of your big dreams can become your daily reality. This exercise is great preparation, a place to become aware of your desires in all their vivid possibilities. The next steps are to trust your discipline, to Shift the Limiting Habits that have held you back from your passion, and to let your new Peak Life Habits become integrated into the fabric of your life. To add even more skill and intention to your Shift, Chapters 6 and 7 will introduce you to some fundamental, positive changes you can make to how you talk about the great feelings and images you just identified.

Your potential for joyfulness is up to you, because one of the most important things we do in this book together is to delineate a path of freedom from the subconscious Limiting Habits that you didn't choose, that came into your life through your family of origin and your early life experiences. Retraining your Habits gives you free will, the power of choice. You can decide who you are, what your life is about, how you are going to live, and how you are going to manifest your place and purpose on Earth; your dreams come true. You decide, you choose – and then Shift happens.

CHAPTER 6

LISTEN TO WHAT YOU ARE REALLY SAYING

"Never underestimate the power of words, you make your world with words . . . If you do not like the world you have, you can begin building a new world by changing your words of command and decree."

—Catherine Ponder

With the words we speak, we open doorways of happiness, wealth and achievement. Or we close the doors and die unfulfilled, haunted by regrets. Words are that powerful. You use words all the time, and even though you sometimes may not think about which ones you choose, their impact is deep and pervasive. In fact, what you say out loud (your external voice/external dialogue) and what you think (your internal voice/internal dialogue) are perhaps the greatest habitual determinants of the results in your life.

Not only do your Habit Chains create Outcomes, your words make sure that your Beliefs come true; they provide the resilience and durability for the chain. This is an important concept, what I call *Vocal Invocation*. When you summon something into existence through the words of your internal or external voice, you are at the same time sending direct messages to your Habit mechanism, invoking both cognitive and subconscious Habits that will either support your dreams or undermine them, depending on the words. The implications are huge. Vocal Invocation means that many circumstances of your life – your relationships, your fitness, your career, your finances, your everything – are initiated by your words, vocally invoked! How you speak about something is how it *is*. Your Actions and Habits are the results, the mirrors that reflect back to you the thoughts and Beliefs you express with words.

In the Chapter 5, we turned a corner in our work with the Habit mechanism, taking Right Action toward our dreams by interrupting our Limiting Habits and replacing them with Peak Life Habits, then pursuing those dreams with discipline and persistence. In this chapter, we will further unlock our Habit Chains, starting with awareness and understanding of the language we have been using. *Limiting Language* can inject our best intentions with a dose of negativity that impedes our pace of progress, limits our leadership effectiveness, and depletes our health, strength and ultimate success. Then we will discover how to Shift to more powerful *Positive Results Language*, honing our greatness with the tools of thought and speech.

You have the power to invoke success by declaring intentions, articulating goals, specifying the benchmarks, and then keeping your words aligned with the Outcomes you've committed to. This is truly brain power, as this is about the images the brain receives through your thoughts and words. By tuning in to your internal voice you can get a clue as to when a Limiting Habit is vying for control, then interrupt the related Belief and redirect your internal voice to new words and Actions to circumvent your Limiting Habits. Monitor the words in your head because what they are saying is your first clue. Are they ruminating about what's wrong and what's not working? If so, STOP and perform a Pattern Interrupt. Your first goal in this chapter will be to gain awareness and understanding of your internal voice.

Greatness in any area of life is an individual choice, your choice. Sometimes good really is good enough. Not too often, though, because that is when your internal voice tends to ruminate about the "what if"s and wait for the proverbial other shoe to drop. However, when you choose to master an important area in your life, you are ready to stop letting your Limiting Habits speak for you. By Shifting your "Limiting Language Habits," you can learn to speak with a directed, powerful voice, remaking your world and inspiring the very success you desire. In the score of your life, it is time to Shift your voice to a different key and unlock your Limiting Habit chains.

Monkey Say, Monkey Do: Is Your Internal Voice Acting Up?

As you got out of bed this morning, were there any voices in your head? Chances are there were some "should do"s, "need to do"s, "have to do"s and "don't want to do"s, streaming through your synapses, as well as some finger pointing dialogues. By the time you were fully vertical, you might have felt exhausted all over again. When we default to *Limiting Language*, our internal voice phrases our intentions, thoughts, and feelings with words that send our power away. We can feel the effects of language in our bodies, wearing us out. Those words have consequences for our success, self-esteem, health and well-being.

A lot of the energy behind your daily language is not necessarily positive. For example, if an "I'm Right Habit" has you fighting it out with somebody, you may feel good in your brain when you win the argument – yet how does your body feel? Perhaps drained, weak, tired of the fight? The same goes for the "should"s, and "need-to-do"s that come with an "Overwhelm Habit." What does that do to your energy? Do you feel ready to move mountains? Probably not.

Right this second your internal voice is whispering the words of this sentence inside your head. It is also the part of your mind that has been comparing the examples in this book to what you have seen and felt in your own life, exploring what Habits you might want to Shift, and thinking about what intentions you want to set for yourself. And it's also wondering what's for dinner. Your internal voice is incessantly talking, talking, talking. Many of us have even experimented with different meditation techniques to control this chatter, or "monkey mind" as it is aptly called in Buddhist meditation. Getting a handle on this creature is indeed a challenge, and perhaps you have acutely felt the truth of the statement, "Your head can be a dangerous place to be!"

Your internal voice is giving you nonstop feedback without solicitation, providing an unending stream of observations during your every waking moment. The noise often keeps going whether or not you make any effort to sustain it or stop it. Listen to some of what the chatter is saying; you may start to hear pessimism, negativity, and other obstructive Beliefs that are directly related to your Belief-Links. Remember our earlier tennis example on page 7? If you have a "Fear Of Failure Habit" and your internal voice says, "I absolutely can't double-fault on this one!" or "I'm afraid of double-faulting," or "Don't double-fault!" what you are actually doing is a Vocal Invocation, giving your brain a sharp image of a double-fault. And, oops, the ball hits the net or goes long. Because the image the brain created was one of double-faulting, your synapses could only fire in a manner that created the result you envisioned.

Successful people in all areas of life focus their language on what they want to happen. Olympic athletes do countless hours of mental training, sharpening the positive words of their internal voices and the correlating images of success they picture. Here is another example:

Lakshmi, a nonprofit executive, is a great illustration of an internal voice run amok. She was in trouble at work only a month after receiving both a raise and a promotion as part of a truly slam-dunk job evaluation. In fact, within a week of hearing her manager's enthusiastic assessment of her performance, she had begun to under-perform in many of the areas that had been singled out for praise. An old familiar

Limiting Habit popped up of forgetting things like meeting times, keys, cash; you name it, she forgot it. With her Habitually Great coach, she took a look at what was going on and saw that the good review had triggered the voice of her old Habit-Stamped Beliefs – Beliefs that told her that she wasn't as good as they thought she was. The Beliefs came from her childhood experiences with her mother, who was excessively demanding and constantly undermined Lakshmi's self-esteem. Those oppressive experiences led her to be quite scattered whenever the spotlight was on her.

Like a monkey on her shoulder, her internal voice delivered its predictable lines as soon as the review came in: "What are they talking about? This isn't me! I don't want them getting used to this being me. I cannot be held accountable to this standard." When she had been performing so well, her internal voice had sat mute in its observations of what she was doing. She was in the moment, "in the zone." Yet when the evaluation suddenly made her conscious of what she was doing, the voice of her default Belief-Link was triggered and snapped her into her "Fear Of Success Habit," "I'm Not Good Enough Habit," and "Scatter Habit."

Like Lakshmi, a deeply entrenched doubt about your ability to succeed will hinder you from success by giving your mechanical brain images of failure. Let's say that again in more general terms.

> ## YOUR INTERNAL VOICE STRONGLY INFLUENCES YOUR SUCCESS AND FAILURE

The incessant chatter of that internal voice in your head is part of what keeps your Habit-Stamped Beliefs alive, because the words can color any new experience the same shade as those old Beliefs. The dialogue is predictable in what it will broadcast, and it will overwhelm any new data or perspective that tries to jump to the front of the line (Figure 6.1).

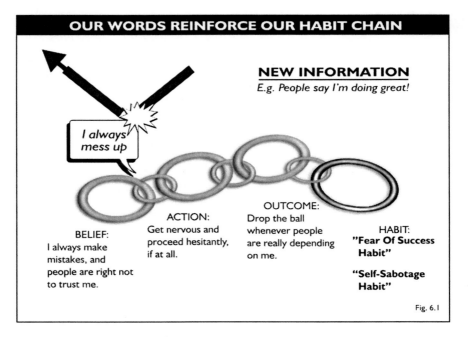

Fig. 6.1

Here are some short statements, each of which carries negative energy:

- "I'll try not to forget."
- "You're putting our marriage on the rocks."
- "Rich people get all the breaks."
- "I'm exhausted."
- "I can't lose weight."
- "I always mess up."

These statements and others like them can make a strong contribution to our "almost" moments. Just feel how disabling they are. The phrases in these examples are protecting all kinds of Limiting Habits: an "Overwhelm Habit," a "Victim Habit," and an "I Can't Habit," among others. I will come back to these phrases later in the chapter and, step-by-step, show you how to go from limiting internal chatter to empowering internal dialogue. Our goal is to use language carefully and consciously so that we can start invoking success and positive feelings every day.

WHAT IS YOUR INTERNAL VOICE SAYING?

Here is a fun exercise to help you get into the moment and start waking up to the Language Habits that distract you. It will also bring you into the heart of this chapter with a nice, relaxed focus. Turn your attention to your internal voice. What are you mumbling about inside your head? What are you thinking about besides reading this book? What are the top-of-mind issues, concerns, or excitements in different areas of your life? Tap into your "Lightening Up Habit," and don't be too hard on yourself. Pause and jot some notes below. What Limiting Habits are speaking through your internal voice? What is the conversation underneath the conversation?

ON MY CAREER

My Internal Voice Is Saying: _____

_____

Limiting Habits:_____

ON MY RELATIONSHIPS

My Internal Voice Is Saying: _____

_____

Limiting Habits:_____

ON MY FAMILY

My Internal Voice Is Saying: _____

_____

Limiting Habits:_____

ON MY PHYSICAL FITNESS

My Internal Voice Is Saying: _____

_____

Limiting Habits:_____

ON MY FINANCES

My Internal Voice Is Saying: _____

_____

Limiting Habits: _____

ON MY EDUCATION

My Internal Voice Is Saying: _____

_____

Limiting Habits: _____

ON MY EMOTIONAL HEALTH

My Internal Voice Is Saying: _____

_____

Limiting Habits: _____

ON MY SPIRITUALITY

My Internal Voice Is Saying: _____

_____

Limiting Habits: _____

ON MY INTEGRITY

My Internal Voice Is Saying: _____

_____

Limiting Habits: _____

ON DOING WHAT I LOVE

My Internal Voice Is Saying: _____

_____

Limiting Habits: _____

ON CREATING MY ULTIMATE LIFE

My Internal Voice Is Saying: _____

_____

Limiting Habits:_____

Great! I know that sounds funny to say, so let me explain: the 'great' part is that you have taken the first giant step toward noticing the extent to which your language Habits (the good, bad and ugly) are running on auto-pilot in your head without you so much as noticing their impact and tenacity. What people say to themselves is often disabling. Remember your Habit-Gap, the chasm between the reality of your life and the life you want? Language plays a key role in causing that gap. This exercise is designed to help you see with more clarity what you have been speaking into existence and how you can instantly make a verbal Shift. By hearing and writing down these internal, under-the-radar conversations, you can choose to turn down the volume in your head, leaving you more present to each moment in your life and able to consciously re-script your internal voice. I often use this exercise when starting a Habitually Great workshop.

"IT" HAPPENS

There is an "it" virus going around – can you hear it? "It" has all the power and we have none. "It" is amazing:

"It" shifted my whole mood.
"It" threw me for a loop.
"It" makes me paranoid.
"It" really irritates me.
"It" makes me crazy.
"It" is too difficult.
"It" ruined my day.
"It" is too hard.

Yet "it" can never be difficult. "It" doesn't have a life of its own. "It" can't ruin our day. We ruin our day or choose that the day is ruined; not "It."
Reality check: "I'm choosing to ruin my day because of how I've decided to feel about this." Vocal invocation starts with "I." The "I" is what gives us access to change. "I" choose to feel powerful and successful no matter what!

Fig. 6.2

What phrases do you use to give your power away and keep yourself in a holding pattern? We will come back to some of these vocal distractions in a bit to deal with them productively. Now you might be having some *new* internal thoughts and worries such as, "Oh no, have I been inviting failure?" Or maybe, "Do I really think this way all the time?" Good questions. Let's look together at our Language Habits in more depth. As we've discovered, cognitive awareness and understanding are the first steps in unhooking our Habit mechanism from an old pattern of "almost." If your Limiting Habits are causing you distress, either by keeping you at "almost" or by creating disharmony in your life, ignoring the context and content of your Language Habits while you attempt to Shift is like driving a car with the parking brake on.

Most of us have a variety of "Limiting Language Habits" and fall back on one or two more often than others. As you listed your internal voice musings in the previous section, you might have seen that some old stand-bys showed up in your thoughts more than once. For example, do you have a ton of stuff you "should" do? Are you going to "try" to stop smoking and get healthier this year? Are there phone calls you really "need" to make? Or do you just feel that "something" keeps happening and "it" is out of your control? All of these are indicators that you are sacrificing your power to a Limiting Habit, or several. The moment is ripe for your "U-Turn My Finger Habit" and a "Pattern Interrupt Habit."

Let's jump in! Depending on what Limiting Habits you are dealing with, your words may gravitate toward one of eight different Limiting Language subdivisions. We will define each of them, and in the section that follows you will learn how to migrate them to Positive Results Language and transform their impact.

Limiting Language Subdivisions

1. Burden Language

Picture this: You wake up in the morning and that litany in your mind begins: "Oh gosh – I should have done this, I've got to do this,

I need to do that." Whoa, you're tired when you get out of bed just from those initial thoughts! That doesn't make a lot of sense. And yet those are the Habits—more specifically, the Language Habits—that run you.

Welcome to Burden Language, the language that stresses us out with the pressure of all that we tell ourselves there is to do. It thrives in phrases like "I have to," "I need to," "I should," "I must," etc., and you can probably feel its negative energy, pressure, tension, and struggle in your muscles. This is exacerbated by the fact that there is no commitment to complete anything that you say that you "need," "should," or "must" do. It all hangs in the air as "not being done."

You are highly unlikely to achieve things that you feel you "need" to do. Burden Language supports a fantasy that someday you will follow through. You are not quite admitting that you don't want (and are therefore unlikely) to make the phone calls, get the car fixed, lose 30 pounds, spend more time reading, or take an important action with your businesses or co-workers that would really make a difference if you would actually do it. Nor are you saying *when* or *how* you will complete these things. The word "need" can be a powerful declarative force leading to immediate action when used to describe primal human necessities such as food, shelter, medical emergencies, etc. However, when it is used to describe less primary concerns, tasks, and issues, the word becomes a stress energy/force that does nothing to generate a resolution. Instead it perpetuates negative, unresolved pressure. It is a paradox that sometimes the more pressure we put on ourselves, the less effective we are.

Virtually every person whose story is told in this book speaks with a burdened tongue. We all do, not because we intend to, rather because that is the language of our culture. How often have you said to your staff, your partner, or your kids that they "need" to do something? Does that generate the action you want? Not often, and not without constant haranguing and likely distress.

Remember, the brain is mechanical in its perceptions and reflects most accurately the energy of the words and images it receives. More to the point, it creates your reality from the images and feelings you feed it. Therefore, if your internal voice speaks of pressure, burden, and negativity, you will likely perpetuate those feelings rather than resolve them. Using phrases such as "need to" or "should do" doesn't create images of follow through. Burden Language often supports and is reinforced by an "Overwhelm Habit," "Distress Habit," and a "Procrastination Habit."

Substitute and change those phrases! If there is an Outcome that you want, go easy on the burden. Here is an example: if you weigh 200 pounds and you "want" to weigh 150, picture yourself at 150 not because you "need" to, rather because you "want" to. Do this often, many times during a day, using what I call a bit of mental "imagineering." How do you look at 150 pounds? What do you wear? Who are you with? What is your wardrobe like? Picturing, thinking and speaking internally are stimulants for Action. This is the Law of Attraction in Action! No burden required.

2. Judgment Language

One of the miracles of life is this: there are several billion people on the planet, and each one of us has an "I'm Right Habit" to some degree. We are all running around with our fingers pointed outward, blaming and shaming one another. Yet somehow we live together and occasionally create great societies. The miracle is that we get along at all! For the most part, when we get off track and into the mud of these Habits, we eventually find our way back onto the pavement. You have likely had times when you've been stuck in your "Being Critical Habit," stalled and going nowhere. For some of us this righteousness can last a lifetime, causing limitations in many areas of our own lives. Do you want to be right or do you want to be happy? (As a side note, keep in mind that righteousness and integrity are two different contexts. We are talking here about your righteousness and judging and the surrendering of your power when you are mired in those.)

When you say to someone with your external voice, "You should have known XYZ" or "You're doing that thing again," you are using Judgment Language. You are pointing your finger outward and making somebody else wrong. You end up behaving in a self-righteous way, focusing on problems and likely making them worse. That is because Judgment Language implies that it is someone else's responsibility to "fix" the distress you are feeling. Be honest, how often does that distress actually get fixed when you don't tackle it within yourself first?

When you criticize someone else, often the person most impacted is you. That negativity takes its toll, right in your body. Take the phrase I mentioned earlier: "You're putting our marriage on the rocks." Even though it is the person speaking who is feeling the distress and pain, we place blame outside of ourselves. Negative energy creeps into our cells because underneath the blame is an outward-pointing finger. With this kind of language, we end up tense and uncomfortable throughout the day because behind the scenes, in our authentic minds and bodies, we probably don't like who we are being. Consequently, we generate even more disharmony in the world around us.

Remember Maria, on her perpetual search for her mate? Her Judgment Language Habit has both her inside and outside voices yammering. No man stands a chance.

Tyronne spends so much time judging his employees that he completely misses the opportunity for happiness, teamwork and success beyond the limitations his language engenders.

Figure 6.3 on the following page illustrates a familiar and covert way we often use Judgment Language.

SHIFTING YOUR "BUT" TO "AND"

"It was a great job, but...," "I'd like to go with you tonight, but...," "This looks really good, but...," "I'd be happy to work with you on that, but..."

Do you use the word "but" every day, and perhaps many times during the day? Become aware of how impactful a simple word like "but" can be.

For the person you are speaking with, "but" negates whatever you said before it, thereby eroding trust for you by your listener. If you tell someone they did a really nice job, and then add "but," then you have erased the compliment and in fact inserted a discreetly placed critique instead. "But" is a show stopper and trust breaker because it reveals your underlying reality of judgment and domination. For example: "You did a great job, but..." is not a compliment at all, rather it is a disempowering phrase that says: "You did not do a great job and here's why."

The nuances of language are very important. The people you are speaking with know this, they feel the negation yet they'll never tell you. They know the perpetration that just landed on them with your "but." You just dropped a notch in their eyes, and their trust for your compliments was thrown out the window. You have eroded their trust because you are using covert Judgment Language as well as Force/Control Language.

The Solution: Shift to the word "and" which is inclusive and validates both sides of the statement, before and after the "and," building trust and teamwork.

For example: "That's a great idea and ...," "I'd be happy to work with you and ...," "You've got the potential, and ...," "This looks really good, and..."

Fig. 6.3

Judgment Language walks hand-in-hand with Limiting Habits like the "Seeing What's Wrong Habit" and the "Being Critical Habit." These righteousness Habits do not often lead us to become personally accountable for Right Action, because too much effort is spent focused on what we don't want rather than on what we do want. This is why often we hear of "fallen" religious or political leaders who spend their careers espousing righteousness while criticizing the behavior of others, yet are then themselves exposed of being guilty of violating many fundamentals they presumed to uphold. It makes sense when you look more closely: their minds were so focused on what they did not like that they actually adopted some of the behaviors they claimed to abhor. There's that mechanical brain again. Focus on solutions, be proactive, manage your own integrity, and lighten up!

3. Force/Controlling Language

Have you ever tried to change someone? How has that been working for you (and for those you've been "trying" to change)? Not so good? Force/Controlling Language bullies, belittles, overcorrects and micromanages. You may say, "Because I'm your big sister," or "The customer is always right, and I'm the customer," or simply "Because I'm your boss, and I said so." Like Burden Language, Force/Controlling Language functions in a world of negative energy and pressure.

There are circumstances where you must use effective, succinct and powerfully compelling language. And that is different from this discussion. Commanding your child not to cross the street in front of a car is different than imposing unimportant rules on people or situations because you feel like it. Force/Controlling Language is about domination and power. There is no sense of teamwork or trust with this type of language, and in fact just the opposite occurs.

Sabrina, with her unyielding mistrust of spending money, was forceful in her approach to controlling every nickel. In the process her son was being Habit-Stamped by her insecurities and therefore developing his own control patterns in order to feel safe, which may take years of therapy to undo. Force and control tend to be rooted in insecurity.

Tyronne was a forcefully expressive, uncollaborative executive, and he constantly ordered his employees to do things because he was right, he was smarter, and he had the title.

If this is a "Limiting Language Habit" of yours, take a quick inquiry into its origins by examining the following questions. Do you feel insecure underneath the façade of this Habit? Do you have an "I Don't Trust Anybody Habit?" Which of your Habit-Stamps caused you to adopt this Limiting Language paradigm? How did you come to be this way? Was it to control your environment and feel safe? What are the fears/habits that perpetuate it? Do you really get the results you want? Do you constantly feel that you can't trust people to do what you want unless you really let them know how you feel and forcefully impose on them what they "have to do?"

Some Limiting Habits that reinforce and are supported by Force/ Controlling Language are the "Domination & Control Habit," the "I'm Right Habit," and the "I Have The Title Habit." This is pretty pervasive stuff. Force/Controlling Language causes significant turnover issues, productivity lapses, and invariably results in breakdowns in corporate settings. At home it often generates resentment and purposeful, covert sabotage by children and mates. With this language Habit you may also be inadvertently planting the seeds of burden and fatigue in others' minds, creating fear in your relationships instead of compassion, and undermining trust. Force stops you short of reaching your full potential because you sacrifice your accountability to yourself by pointing outward and paradoxically making other people responsible for your happiness, success and failure. Be bold enough to recognize when you fall into this language pattern, then be strong enough to rise above it. You will learn how to interrupt this pattern in the pages ahead.

4. Victim/Blame Language

Victim Language gives away all your power. These are especially hard Habits to break. When you identified your Habit Stamps back in Chapter 3, did one or two childhood experiences jump out? Those experiences and their impact are very real; I've been there myself. Yet how long have you been playing those hard-luck victim songs? Once you Shift to victim mode in your language, regardless of whether it is in regard to others, to circumstances, to bad luck, or to your own failings, you lose the ability to be in the driver's seat. The marionette reigns with the Victim Habit pulling the strings.

When we use Victim Language, we say things like, "It's your fault that I...," or "I have to," or "It's always like this and I don't have a choice," or "It's not fair," or "I'm not good enough," or "That (or it) always happens to me," or "I never learned to create stable relationships because my parents had a terrible relationship," or "My parents neglected me as a child." Whew. The "Blame Habit" has prominence here, both at work and at home. Are you blaming others: your customers, your boss, your spouse, kids or your staff for why things are wrong in your world and with your life? Blaming is a path taken to avoid the rigor of personal accountability; in the fine print is disempowerment. With Victim Language, you declare yourself powerless to change, yet nothing could be further from the truth. In those moments you may even blame yourself for your weakness and doom.

You always have a choice. Even deciding *not* to choose is making a choice. When you forfeit your personal responsibility as adults for the actions you choose, you stop yourself from moving forward and instead stay stuck in your circumstances, perpetuating your suffering. Sometimes we all find it easy to slip into this tendency, because this is just life on Earth (as you've heard me say), and accidents happen. Occasionally a bone breaks, fenders get banged, and people we love get sick (some even die). From now on, no excuses. Are you using your Victim Language to keep you from being responsible for being promoted, getting your workouts in, eating right, or making tough choices that will attract more love, happiness and success into your life?

Ruth was the victim of a sexual assault. What had evolved from that event was her internal voice repeatedly warning her to be careful in relationships, even a decade later, because of her fear of being betrayed and abandoned. She walked and breathed Victim Language. Hers is a special case, and in tandem with good therapy as well as Habitually Great coaching, she was able to make a cognitive Shift.

Jim, in spite of his knowledge that he was on the same path to heart disease as his Dad, felt powerless to change. He was run by a "Why Bother Habit" supporting his "Loyal To The Family Habit."

Maria was an incessant finger-pointer, always blaming the guys she "rejected" for breaking her heart by disappointing her, not seeing how she set them up to fail in her eyes.

We have all witnessed firsthand the experiences, situations and hardships in life that are blatantly unfair. I offer no insight to the reasons behind the challenges we face in our lives. Studies of people who experience true hardship show the extraordinary resilience and recovery we are all capable of. Our power lies not in changing the past, rather in *writing the story of your future*, starting right now. You have control over yourself, and can make the Habitually Great choice to enhance your power, accountability, integrity, and personal effectiveness in every situation.

You can Shift your Victim Language as you Shift the accompanying "Victim Habit," "Excuses Habit," or "Defensive Habit" to the "Accountability Habit," "Right Action Habit," and the "Empowered Language Habit."

5. Regret Language

Regret language is closely related to Victim Language—and just as disempowering. Have you ever whined or remorsefully ruminated about what you could have done that you didn't do? The promotion you could have gotten, the trip you could have taken, the great deal you didn't consummate, the financial opportunity you let slip away? People state regrets in the context of something that they believe they could have done or achieved or had in their life. You say, "I should have," "I wish I had," "I could have," "I wanted to but didn't." Regret Language is about suffering and represents yet another evocative way of burdening your psyche and well-being. The reason I say this is because when you are feeling regretful, you are usually deploying your "Hard On Myself Habit," as if suffering and beating yourself up has anything to do with taking Right Action. Regret exists in the world of inaction—it is about experiencing the challenges of the past without taking the lessons and moving forward powerfully and with wisdom. Instead, you dwell on the past and do endless instant replays in your head (dangerous!). When you use Regret Language at the same time, you suffer even more.

Yet failure is actually a pathway to success if we take appropriate Right Action inspired by the lessons in the event. Do you know anyone who learned to ride a bicycle without one fall? How many courses did you take in high school, college and graduate school on being a great leader, creating and maintaining great relationships, or how to create success in all areas of your life? Just like me, none. While we study and learn many subjects, these are the fundamentals—and yet there is no roadmap provided for them. Welcome to the trial and error of life. Being Habitually Great can Shift that to a masterful life.

With Regret Language, we may look back with heartache when reflecting on our "almost" moments, yet usually we don't commit to surmounting the obstacles next time around. For example, you might look back and say, "I regret that I spoiled that relationship," or "I regret I never finished my degree," or "If only I'd saved more money," or "If I'd have just taken my job more seriously at the time." Can you see the doom and gloom getting ready for a repeat here? When you use Regret Language you are keeping yourself mentally stuck. You reinforce old Beliefs that produce the same regret-causing Outcomes. Ouch.

Poor Cathy, she was so steeped in Regret Language that she had paralyzed herself in suffering. She had no idea that words were so influential. She really blended Blame, Victim, and Regret Language into one "Woe Is Me Habit" spiral. As we saw, that impacted her marriage, self-esteem, and her ability to help her 11-year old (who was being Habit-Stamped by his mom, an unintended consequence of her negative musings). Yet there are countless examples of children and adults miraculously building strong and inspired lives in spite of whatever hand they have been dealt. Cathy was stuck in her pattern.

Let's take back some of that power! The key to escaping from the doom and gloom of Regret Language is to contrast what you "could have" or "should have" achieved against what you are now going to do to be successful next time. What did you learn? What can you do differently? What lessons can you apply for the future? For example: "I regret that I spoiled that relationship. I caused a lot of unnecessary suffering and really suffered a lot of heartache too. I am committed to developing great relationship skills and finding a first-class partner. Here are the Actions I am going to take: I am going to hire a relationship coach or therapist and meet with them ten times; plus I am going to find and attend a two-day workshop on relationships; I am going to the bookstore and will buy and read three books on how to be great in relationships. I am going to learn from this failure how to make my relationships happy and fulfilling successes!"

That is a Habitually Great way to Shift a regret. Some of the Limiting Habits in the background of Regret Language are the "Safe In My Misery Habit," "Regret Habit," and the "Woe Is Me Habit." Invoke Peak Life Habits that circumvent these Limiting Habits with patience, diligence and determination.

6. Scatter Language

Do you repeatedly give yourself verbal reminders about something, yet still forget to do it? People with the Scatter Habit tend to be forgetful in spite of all kinds of efforts to remember. With Scatter Language we tend to say things like, "I don't want to forget to do XYZ" or "I don't want to lose this." Paradoxically, this language is giving our brains the wrong image of losing what we don't want to lose or forgetting what we want to remember. Do you recall our double-faulting tennis player? Here again, we are inadvertently encouraging our brains and subsequent Actions to misfire. Since the brain is mechanical, it has a tendency to obey the words we are using, turning those words into pictures and then fulfilling those pictures without a care in the world. With Scatter Language the brain gets such a clear image of what you don't want that it conveniently edits out the potent word "don't." Your mind focuses on the image of forgetting, because you have just pictured the "forgetting" and not the "remembering."

If you have a tendency to lose the car keys, the cell phone, phone numbers or to-do lists, and you tell yourself only, "Don't lose this again," or "I always forget things," guess what? The result is that you keep scattering your focus to the winds, making yourself a victim to brain function and missing the chance to make yourself accountable for a workable system of storing and retrieving the car keys whenever you are ready to leave the house. This may sound a little humorous, perhaps like the absentminded professor, always forgetting, losing, and confusing things which creates ongoing distress, annoyance, and delay that you are better off without.

Lakshmi's "Scatter Habit" is already known to her friends. However, it is exacerbated whenever her success attracts the proverbial spotlight. In her case the pressure to perform activates her sense of being overwhelmed and triggers her tendency to use Scatter Language which then reinforces her forgetfulness. This was a surprisingly easy fix: Lakshmi discovered that her language was just as much of the perpetrator as she was. A structural change to the words she used created remarkable memory Shifts, along with adopting some key success structures. This was particularly effective because she had identified the Habit-Stamps that had caused this subterfuge in the first place.

There are some language Shifts that you can practice with immediate effect to remember better and forget less. The Right Action solution to the dilemma of Scatter Language starts with a simple Action. If you have a tendency to be forgetful, practice this with a good bit of discipline and vigor. Be patient, trust and learn to remember what you want to remember! It all starts with the phrase "remember to." Use the words "I will remember to," and simultaneously provide a clear picture in your mind of what you want to remember.

There are some resilient Limiting Habits that fortify the Scatter Habit. They include "The Spacey Habit," "I'm Too Busy Habit," "Excuses Habit," "Avoid Accountability Habit," and the "I'm Disorganized Habit." Do any of these sound familiar? These Habits reinforce – and are reinforced by – Scatter Language. Imagine a world where you remember and follow through with all the calls you commit to, the letters and emails, the lunches, the appointments, the car keys. By imagining such a world, you have the choice to create it. Welcome to the "I Am Organized Habit" and the "I Remember Habit."

7. Self-Deprecating Language

We may use Self-Deprecating Language as a way to joke around others, break the ice, create a false sense of humility, or to chide ourselves when we push a door that says "pull" or walk face first into the glass in front of strangers. Often it consists of making a joke in front of friends, strangers, staff members, or customers that highlights our shortcomings and infers things like, "I'm so stupid" or "I always get it wrong" or "I'm such a klutz." Even your humble author catches himself doing this every once in a while, to polite laughs or, if someone is around who knows and loves me, an immediate, "Don't say that!"

Self-Deprecating Language is common, yet let's stop and look at this a bit closer. How appropriate would it be to speak to someone else the way we speak to ourselves? It is Judgment Language that we turn inward. The larger issue is that looming mechanical brain again. If you tell your brain that you are always getting it wrong…you know the rest.

Jim is a hard worker in a prestigious law firm. The partners want him to become one of them, yet one Habit sticks in their craw: his "Self-Deprecating Language Habit." He often makes what he feels are humorous and tension-breaking comments during client meetings that are directed at his weaknesses or flaws. "If only I could remember," "I'm so foolish that…," "Who's the fat guy that did this?" "Who was the idiot that did that?" At home he is a gifted musician who fears that his success will make his friends and family see him as somehow superior to them. He makes jokes that diminish his accomplishments such as, "Yeah, I always screw up when it counts!"

In the world of the Habit mechanism, this Limiting Language ties directly into the perception of being not good enough, such as with a "Hard On Myself Habit" or an "I'm Not Good Enough Habit." Whether you are using Self-Deprecating language lightly or being utterly earnest in your self-flagellation, you are cutting yourself down, diminishing your self-esteem and playing small in front of others.

The best Peak Life Habit to insert here is the "Being Appropriate Habit." You want people to respect you, appreciate and like you because they trust you on many levels. Self-Deprecating Language interferes with all of that. You may be wondering, "Isn't this all a good dose of humility?" Yes, humility is a welcomed Peak Life Habit; however humility is quite different than self-deprecation. Being a humble soul—and not self-deprecation—is what Jim Collins identified as one of the key tenets of being a great leader. Being humble is about not boasting, about acknowledging others, about creating great teamwork with discipline, accountability and exceptional communication. Having a sense of humor is a good thing, particularly when it lightens you up and uplifts those around you. The key is to have a sense of humor that doesn't take you or anyone else down.

We want to set ourselves up for success, starting by giving our brains a healthy, positive focus. Go light on the self-deprecation; go heavy on the compassion, humility, and positive reinforcement to yourself and others.

8. Excuses Language

Here is the "Catch-22" language Habit that more than anything else can interfere with great success. Are you in the mood for your workout, for your studying, for your meeting? Do you put things off until you feel that it's the "right time?" Have you heard yourself hedge, fudge, and outright avoid the very things that are the Right Actions in your life? Are you ready to tackle this elephant?

When you use Excuses Language, you are encouraging yourself to make vague, agreeable statements with your internal and external voices, saying things like "I'll play it by ear and decide later," or "I'll try," or "That's on my list." You might notice yourself carefully ducking under the accountability expressway, with words selected for the purpose of playing it safe, leaving out any chance for great success.

Gordon, like many people, had decided that life was "all about him," and with his "Wiggle Room Habit" and "Excuses Habit" had taken it to the point where he consistently changed his plans and commitments and constantly gave excuses for those changes. He lived in the world of "trying." Gordon's daughter, like all of his family and staff, suffered. The secret that Gordon did not know was that barely anyone trusted what he said, and trust is the foundation of everything important.

Jim had many excuses for not working out, a whole repertoire of good reasons that would help kill him if he kept using them instead of addressing his health.

"NICE TRY" SHIFTS TO "NICELY DONE"

"Trying" is a significant Excuses Language culprit. The word is full of failure. Think about this for a moment. "Nice try" is what we say to our kids, peers, staffs and partners when they fail at something. Have you ever been complimented on a success or achievement with "nice try!" No, that wasn't a "try." Yet we hide under the cover of "try," even before we begin something.

> "I'm trying to lose weight."
> "I'll try to be on time."
> "I tried to be a good ."
> "I'll try to explain this."
> "I'll try to be better."
> "Nice try."
> "Good try."
> "At least you tried."
> "I should have tried."
> "I'll try better next time."
> "If only I had tried harder."
> "I could have tried a lot harder."

What does "I'll try" mean? That whatever you are doing is not likely to be successful and you are already soft-pedaling your commitment. When you are growing up and you're on a sports team, what do you say to your teammate when they didn't quite make it? "Nice try." Listen for it. If somebody says, "I'll try," what does that mean? It really means that they're not likely to succeed.

The Solution: It's time to take "try" out of your vocabulary. Catch yourself saying, "I'll try," and Shift it to something positive, even tentative, such as: "I'm going to give my absolute best." Trying doesn't cause success. How about a new and permanent Shift: catch yourself saying, "I'll try," and Shift to a positive, committed expression: I will; I intend to; I expect to; I am going to; I will do my best to; I am committed to!

Fig. 6.4

As Figure 6.4 illustrates, greatness doesn't come from "trying," it comes from the determination to succeed. Yes, we have real life moments where we miss the mark and fall short of our intended goal, occasionally even in areas to which we are fully committed. Greatness is achieved by being 100 percent in the game called your life …play big! You then learn from your failures. The key is to play the game without straddling or hesitating.

Excuses Language circumvents being disciplined and persistent. Some Limiting Habits that support and are supported by Excuses Language include the "Avoid Accountability Habit," the "Wait And See Habit," and the "Fear Of Failure Habit." You'll see in the charts ahead a few more nuances of Excuses Language that you may be using unwittingly and invoking your personal "almost." Getting beyond "almost" is your mandate.

* * *

Now let's Shift our inquiry toward inspiring a much more positive internal and external dialogue, taking a giant step toward greatness. Awareness and understanding of our Language Habits has value that actually extends beyond language alone; remember, as we are looking at what we say we are also looking at what we do – what Habits are associated with our internal and external dialogue – and therefore the degree of success we allow ourselves to have on our journey toward our ultimate life. Figure 6.5 is a helpful summary of the "Limiting Language Habits" you just read about, and you will also see a more complete list of some common Limiting Habits that both stem from and reinforce our words. Notice where your thoughts may be supporting your Habit-Stamps and Limiting Habits.

SUMMARY OF LIMITING LANGUAGE — Fig.6.5

LIMITING LANGUAGE	PHRASES WE USE	LIMITING HABITS IN THE MIX
Burden Language is language that stresses us out and has no commitment. These words give our brain images of lack, not doing, pressure and fatigue.	• I should, I ought, I'd better • I must, I have to, I've got to • I should have • I'm too • I'll try • I need to	**Can't Say No Habit** **Fear Of Success Habit** **Hard On Myself Habit** **It's Never Enough Habit** **Overwhelm Habit** **Paralysis Habit** **Perfectionist Habit** **Procrastination Habit**
Judgment Language is often about making somebody else wrong – and is used as an escape from dealing with ourselves and how we're being. When we're criticizing someone or something else, regrettably, the person that is often most affected by the criticism is us, as the negativity impacts our well-being.	• What were you thinking? • What were they thinking? • It's you, not me • You're incompetent • Why did you/they do this? • This is your fault • That was dumb • They are stupid; they • If I were you • You screwed this up • You always do this • I'm stupid; I'm not worthy of • You should have known or done	**Avoid Vulnerability Habit** **Being Critical Habit** **Distress Habit** **Entitlement Habit** **Expect You To Know Habit** **I Always Have An Enemy Habit** **Logic & Justify Habit** **Seeing What's Wrong Habit**
Force/Control Language places the burden outside of ourselves, on other people, by (compelling) them. We may bully, overcorrect, or micromanage.	• Do this because I'm the boss (parent, etc.) • Do this because I have the title • Do this because I'm right • Do this because I'm bigger • Do this because I said so • Just do it this way • Do this because my rules are all that count	**Domination & Control Habit** **Forceful Habit** **Being Critical Habit** **Seeing What's Wrong Habit** **I Have The Title Habit** **Doing It My Way Habit** **Righteousness Habit** **I Don't Trust Habit**
Victim/Blame Language avoids accountability for changing our life, for being powerful, for being responsible for better success. We point our fingers at situations and at the world and blame it for our circumstances.	• I was abused; I was ___ • It's your fault • You/this ruined my day, life, ___ • Why did you/they do this? • This is because I'm not worthy • Because I'm fat, blonde, bald, ___ • That always happens to me • It's not fair • I have rotten luck • It/that/they/you make me feel • I had the wrong parents, job, ___	**Acting Small Habit** **Avoid Accountability Habit** **Defensive Habit** **Fear Of Failure Habit** **Feeling Incapable Habit** **I Always Have An Enemy Habit** **I'm Not Good Enough Habit** **It's All About Me Habit** **Life's Not Fair Habit** **Safe In My Misery Habit** **Victim Habit**

SUMMARY OF LIMITING LANGUAGE (cont'd)   Fig. 6.5

LIMITING LANGUAGE	PHRASES WE USE	LIMITING HABITS IN THE MIX
Regret Language is about suffering because we are picturing or assuming failures. Limiting Habits get in the way of success, as does ruminating about what could have been.	• I should have • I wish I had • If only I had • I could have done that • I regret ___ and I'll never ___	**Almost Habit** **Avoid Accountability Habit** **Hard On Myself Habit** **Hold Myself Back Habit** **Regret Habit** **Safe In My Misery Habit** **Sob Sister Habit** **Woe Is Me Habit**
Scatter Language is about inadvertently telling our brain to misfire by using words like "forget," "confused," "lose," etc. This language reinforces Limiting Habits instead of helping to change them.	• I'm forgetful, I always forget • I'm spacey • I always lose things • I get confused • I've got a million things floating around • Don't forget; Don't lose ___ • My memory is no good • I can't keep track of ___	**Avoid Accountability Habit** **Chaos Habit** **Fear Of Success Habit** **I'm Disorganized Habit** **Overwhelm Habit** **Spacey Habit**
Self-Deprecating Language is Judgment Language that we turn inward. Whether we're using it lightly or being utterly earnest in our self-flagellation, we undermine ourselves.	• I've got a pea for a brain • I'm too old, short, etc. • I'm not attractive; I'm ugly • I'm such a klutz; I'm such a loser • I always get it wrong • I'm incompetent; I'm dumb • I'm not smart enough • I'm stupid; I'm an idiot	**Hard On Myself Habit** **I'm Not Good Enough Habit** **I'm Not Worthy Habit** **Insecurity Habit** **Overwhelm Habit** **Woe Is Me Habit**
Excuses Language is the "Catch-22" of them all. More than any of the above, this Language Habit can interfere with the possibility of your great happiness and success. When you speak with these words you are truly stuck in that place where good is the enemy of great.	• I'll play it by ear • I'll decide later • If I could find a way, and I can't • There's no time • I don't know, if I can • I don't have to because • I don't want to, I don't feel like it • If I had more hours in the day • That's on my list • It slipped away • I'll think about it • I'll try, I'll work on that • It depends; If this happens – then • Maybe, maybe not	**Afraid To Be Wrong Habit** **Appeaser Habit** **Avoid Accountability Habit** **Can't Say No Habit** **Disorganized Habit** **I Can't Habit** **I Don't Wanna Habit** **I'm Too Busy Habit** **Over-Committed Habit** **Unable To Be Specific Habit**

It is amazing how pervasive these Language Habits are, which we can see just by performing this simple exploration. Limiting Language keeps us from taking the wheel in our lives and, ironically, we avoid changing the one thing we have the power to change: ourselves. However, as we Shift our Limiting Habits with discipline and persistence, we will also begin to Shift our Language Habits. In Chapter 7 we will learn how they can be interrupted and Shifted just like any other Habits to produce immediate feelings of ease and relief. We will also be making ourselves more accountable in the world outside our heads by Shifting how we speak in our *external dialogue* – the words we use when speaking with other people.

CHAPTER 7

INSPIRE YOUR LIFE WITH SELF TALK

"The greatest discovery of my generation is that human beings, by changing the inner attitudes of their minds, can transform the outer aspects of their lives."

—William James

If we look at the sports psychology behind today's leading athletes, the simplicity of excellence is revealed. They remain disciplined even when their internal dialogue is ruminating about strife and negativity. If they feel that they "always forget" or "need to do" or "should have done" something, they stop themselves and add the missing link to the conversation; they Shift (as we will be doing in just a minute) to words of Action: "I will remember to ___," "I'm going to score the goal/win the race," "I will talk to my coach tonight and put new focus and structure into my training." And then they put the Actions into play.

This is all about *Intention*. If you don't first ask yourself what you would like to do or make or achieve or build, then you won't do or make or achieve or build anything. It's just that simple. What are you intending to create in your life? What are you intending to achieve? What is your place and purpose? These are the questions to answer. So your first Action is to create a deliberate, clear thought about what you want. Moment after moment – in those of struggle as well as those when success is within your reach – you can engage in very powerful, important, encouraging conversations inside and outside your mind that let you reach the peaks in your life.

Here is the good news: you don't have to burn yourself out or hold yourself back. You no longer "have to" do things or "try to" Shift your Habits – because you can Shift your Language Habits, feel great and start manifesting your desires carefully and methodically. Positive Results Language eases off the brake and gets you into high gear by adding clarity, intention and resolution to the images in your mechanical brain. Here is a real life example of how our Language Habits can Shift the environment inside and outside our heads.

Hector worked in medicine and was experiencing some pretty high stress. He began working with a Habitually Great coach because he had recently been fired from his job at a clinic and just started a new one. In his session, he kept saying he was "trying to get his head together." As a doctor, he was already worn out from long hours at his new job, and knew he was wearing himself down further with his internal voice. First, notice the Vocal Invocation of his Excuses Language and Victim Language. His invocation called forth a "trying to" rather than a "committed to" or a "going to" and created a feeling of being stuck in his stress that in turn stressed him out even more.

Understandably, he was off balance and feeling the effects of his "Hard On Myself Habit" after being fired. The key to his Vocal Inspiration Shift was to commit himself to making a good transition to his new job. By saying instead, "I am committed to getting my head together and moving forward," he could U-turn his finger, powerfully decide to Shift the Habits that had stopped him at "almost" and start creating a better future at work.

When we want to accomplish something, the language we use is crucial. Like Hector, as soon as you notice how your "Limiting Language

Habits" have kept the parking brake on, worn you out and held you at "almost," you get to experience a truly invigorating "ah ha!" moment.

As we move ahead, here is an important word of wisdom on Shifting Language Habits: *play*. Instead of saying, "I'm going to *try*," you can say, "I'm going to *play* with this." Instead of "I'm *working* on this Shift," you can say, "Here's what I'm *playing* with." When you use the word "play," you give your brain a suggestion of fun. You choose to lighten up and enjoy yourself as you commit to making the Shifts. Now, let's play with interrupting our Language Habits and move on to the positive, committed, inspired language of Right Action!

Shifting Limiting Language, Step #1: Awareness

Until now you have been desensitized to the words you routinely use, so put your *awareness* driving gloves on. The first step in Shifting Language Habits is to listen in on your internal and external voices and pinpoint the Limiting Language. You are now on the alert; you've taken the wheel; the cruise control is off. 24 hours a day, from this point forward, monitor your words and phrases as well as those of others. This is actually a "no-brainer" because as you embrace the details of this chapter within your consciousness, the Shift of new information will cognitively assist your subconscious to be on alert too.

Maria never realized how engaged she was with her critical voices. Her jaw literally dropped when she began to listen to herself. She realized that the criticizing tape she was playing had no on/off switch yet had run on without her control. Now she could take charge of her Limiting Language Habits and her Limiting Habits, using her newfound awareness to give potential mates a chance instead of instantly judging them.

Shifting Limiting Language, Step #2: Understanding

With awareness comes *understanding*. You hear your words and now you understand the fatigue, disempowerment and distress that they may be creating in your body and mind. These are all signs that you have given your power away. The words you are using are betraying your good intentions for yourself and others. With your understanding of this impact, you can begin to make more powerful and conscious choices about your language as well as the Beliefs and Actions underlying it. Become fully conscious of the sabotaging contribution your "Limiting Language Habits" are making in your life. It's your life and your choice; perhaps today is the perfect day to begin to be on the lookout for subtle ways that you have allowed your Limiting Language to barricade your progress. Your ear will grow sharper for "Limiting Language Habits" and the Habit Chains they support. Awareness and understanding work together as your guides, leading instantaneously to step #3.

Tyronne's heart was momentarily heavy. It had taken several sessions for him to fully understand how his habituated thoughts and language had created a gap between himself and joy, camaraderie, and greater success while being the source of much distress to people who were invaluable to him. This understanding came about as he began to think back on specific interactions he had with colleagues. Like the time his marketing manager, Mark, was late with a press release. Instead of privately speaking to Mark about it in his office, Tyronne chose to berate him at their weekly staff meeting. Mark's humiliation and anger drove a permanent wedge between the two colleagues, shattering the chance for further collaboration.

Shifting Limiting Language, Step #3: STOP

The third step is identical to the next step of any standard Pattern Interrupt: STOP. Like successful athletes and CEOs, decide to end the conversation inside your mind so you can move forward. In other words, hit the brakes! In that moment take a quick pause, see the wall you are spinning toward, then take your eyes off it and focus instead on where you want to go. In auto racing we are trained to never stare at the curve we are driving through or the wall we are driving by, because if you stare at the wall you are apt to drive right into it. It makes sense once you understand the way your mind converts thoughts/words into images and images into reality. The only thing you have power over is yourself – and therefore, you have the power to shut off the tape when your negative Limiting Language tries to fill your mind.

Gordon agreed to make perhaps the biggest change he had ever made in his life: he STOPPED. With rigorous determination, he interrupted his excuses and halted all of his justifications for missing meetings, being late and breaking agreements. Now he is persistently on time to see his daughter's dance recitals and games, and he can't imagine how he could ever have willingly missed so much.

Shifting Limiting Language, Step #4: Choose Inspired Words

Once you have stopped the Limiting Language conversation in your head, you can begin an inspired conversation with yourself, accented with a bit of mojo. This is equivalent to our "Redirect!" and "Re-script!" Pattern Interrupts. You are choosing a new Action—in this case, the Right Action of speaking inside your head. At first, you don't even have to believe the new words you're using; you can use your "Acting As If Habit" to allow the new "Positive Results Language Habit" to take root.

You can immediately begin practicing this step of intentionally selecting another way of speaking. Start right now and keep at it today, tomorrow, the next day and the next and so on. Start with the "I" and say whatever inspires you. Speak powerfully with your mind and your heart and declare your passion, your ambition, your gratitude, your desire, invoking the pictures that you are committed to realizing in your life. Be bold, brave and inspired. Notice any Limiting Habits that attempt to curtail your voices and repel them! Repeat and hone your inspired declarations over and over and over. Then channel that inspiration and put yourself into Action. "I am taking my power and ..." or "I am totally going to achieve...and here's what it is and how I'm going to do it."

This is your "U-Turn My Finger Habit" in action. Engage in a powerful conversation with yourself that asks, "How can I improve? How can I be better? What is the lesson here for me? What can I do differently next time? What can I do now?"

Take a deep breath, pause, and reflect with your internal voice on those questions in the above paragraph. Words in our minds often speak with pictures, so notice that as you answer them you may naturally be creating images in your head and perhaps even a few motion pictures. Often we think so fast that we do not recognize there is a movie always running in our heads with action, words, everything. Slow it down and you will "get the picture." As the answers to those questions come into focus, you have taken the first step toward achieving the Outcomes they represent. In just a few short minutes or days, you are likely to be regularly preempting the old phrases and words that interfered with your aspirations. Enjoy being in command as the Shifts start happening.

Sabrina began practicing speaking positively to herself about her success and the abundance she had created. She chose new Peak Life Habits: the "Believe in Myself Habit," "Open Heart Habit" and "Ground Truth Reality Habit." She loosened the purse strings and treated herself and her son. This was not natural for her, so there was a bit of "acting as if" and trepidation in her voice as she began to Shift her perspective. In reality she was very wealthy, with stable investments. Even so, as she let go of her angst, her business pushed through its Success Ceiling to new heights.

Shifting Limiting Language, Step #5: Straddling The Fence, Positive Tentative Language

Here we take an interesting turn. As you apply the lessons of this chapter, you will notice that you are using language in an enhanced way. You are speaking and hearing words differently and you are seeing, both literally and figuratively, their impact. You will be more cognizant of the power your voice has always had.

Now let's discuss a persuasive and evocative phraseology that provides the right messaging to our brains. There are two types of positive action language: *Positive Tentative Language* and *Positive Results Language*. In this section we cover the richly nuanced Positive Tentative Language.

Positive Tentative Language is a first step toward Shifting to your goal of Positive Results Language. It allows you to modify your language toward the positive rather than the negative and provides a first glimmer of the accountability and power (without delivering the specificity and commitment) of Positive Results Language. Instead of saying, "I'm trying to finish writing this short story," make a minor Shift to: "I want to finish writing this short story tomorrow." You are not yet saying, "I am going to write three hours tonight so that I will finish this story by tomorrow at 5:00PM." Positive Tentative Language helps you make a disciplined and realistic Shift in the right direction without triggering your "Fear of Success Habit," your "Fear, Doubt, And Worry Habit," your "Doom Loop Habit" or your "Why Bother Habit."

Here's an example of Shifting to Positive Tentative Language: perhaps someone requests that you meet with them at 5:30 p.m. You say "I'll try to be there." In this simple example the "I'll try" can be Shifted to "I'll do my best to be there by 5:30." You see that it is still tentative because what you didn't say is "I'll be there by 5:30." The Shift is that "I'll try" does not suggest much of anything and certainly not that you will do your best. By making this Shift you have committed to doing your best, which in turn activates your "Integrity Habit" and your "Accountability Habit."

How about Shifting the phrase, "I need to do that" to, "I'm going *to play* with that" or "I want to do that." The word "want" and the word "play" come together well when we use them in place of the word "need." You can initiate different results by speaking with clear vigor. "Need" is not likely to get us to greatness, so we want to launch ourselves into forward movement with words like "desire" and "intend."

Here is a caveat: if you have a Limiting Habit like an "Incomplete Habit" (starting and not finishing many things) or a "Looking Good Habit" or a "Can't Say No Habit," you are at risk for the pitfalls of the Positive Tentative Language Habit. You likely use this Language Habit routinely as your framework for interacting with the world. In these cases, Positive Tentative Language keeps you out of commitment continuing to procrastinate and avoiding accountability.

Here is a second caveat: when you *hear* somebody say to you, "I'll try…" the message is clear. If a friend says "I'll try to make it to the movies with you tonight," or if a co-worker says, "I'll try to get that to you tomorrow," perhaps make different arrangements. If people are saying to you "I'll try to do that" or "I'll work on that," from this point forward for the rest of your life, just nod to yourself and ask, "What does that mean exactly?" Set your expectations up to align with the predictable Outcomes (or lack thereof) of those statements. No righteousness or blaming allowed.

Ruth's "I Don't Trust Anybody Habit" was a strong obstacle blocking her ability to measure people and situations. When she realized the deep impact her words and voices had in reinforcing this Limiting Habit, she was determined to Shift. She began choosing her language much more carefully and loosening the grip of "I Don't Trust Anybody Habit." Without giving herself a timeline, she initiated the practice of using words such as "I am learning to trust…" while at the same time going through accountable communication training so that she could stop inadvertently setting others up to fail her. She is learning that it's all in the words.

Shifting Limiting Language, Step #6: Choose Positive Results Language

As you play with these phrases, take a look back at the list of concerns and distractions you noted in the exercise "**WHAT IS YOUR INTERNAL VOICE SAYING?**" on pages 105-107 in Chapter 6. Look for any Limiting Language and choose how you can Shift it into Positive Results Language, the language of Right Action. The final two steps, *specificity* and *measurability*, join together to form the powerful Positive Results Language, taking you beyond Positive Tentative Language and toward your ultimate accountability. There is no "I'll try" or even "I'll do my best;" there is only "I will." Phrases like, "I will have the report to you by 5:30 p.m." and "I will remember to call my mother on her birthday this Thursday" Shift you toward achieving the positive Outcomes you desire.

Cathy's marriage was on the rocks, having been burdened for so many years by her "It's All My Fault Habit" regarding her son's fetal alcohol syndrome. Slowly, steadily, she began her climb out of the abyss, deploying her "Believe In Myself Habit," "Compassionate Habit" and her "Solution-Focused Habit." With those Habits, she created accountabilities with her words and Actions, giving herself timelines for getting into shape, reclaiming her femininity and initiating positive, proactive family events and dates with her husband. He was very grateful and took the male lead too, restoring a healthy balance to their home.

Shifting To Positive Results Language

The following Figures 7.1-7.8 are your handy guides for migrating Limiting Language into accountable, specific and measurable language that supports Right Action. If you don't see the perfect phrase in these tables, create your own words, the ones that call you forth with specificity, accountability and measurability.

You will see the word "No" in the charts, which may seem just a bit curious. If you have the "Can't Say No Habit," "Pleaser Habit," or "Avoid Disappointment Habit," it is time to break the "Yes" pattern. Perhaps saying "No" with conviction (and kindness too) is a great positive language breakthrough for you. Imagine living in a world where you are respected and appreciated for your "Yes" and "No" answers rather than taking on tasks and responsibilities that you won't be able to complete!

Each language category has familiar Limiting Language phrases along the left hand column, Positive Results Language in the right hand column, and in the middle, Positive Tentative Language phrases that initiate the "U-Turn My Finger Habit" while still giving us some wiggle room before we take the final, powerful leap to committed language. Remember, have fun and keep PLAYING!

SHIFTING BURDEN LANGUAGE

Fig. 7.1

BURDEN LANGUAGE Shifts to→	POSITIVE TENTATIVE LANGUAGE Shifts to→	POSITIVE RESULTS LANGUAGE!
I should, I ought to, I'd better I must, I have to, I've got to	I want to, I am going to, I'd like to Reality check: I don't think so!	I'll be completing that on (or by) I'm setting up the following plan
I'll try, I'm too ___ I need to, If only I	What I am going to play with doing is I want to, I am going to, I'd like to	No, sorry, I won't be able to ___ Can you get that to me by 1PM?

SHIFTING JUDGMENT LANGUAGE

Fig. 7.2

JUDGMENT LANGUAGE Shifts to→	POSITIVE TENTATIVE LANGUAGE Shifts to→	POSITIVE RESULTS LANGUAGE!
What were you/they thinking? Why did you/they do this? If I was you	What can I do to help? Here's how I contributed to this situation	Let's create a specific solution What I've learned is ___
This is your fault, That was dumb I'm stupid, I'm not worthy of ___	Let's figure out the best way to do this What can I do to make this better?	Next time, let's agree to do ___ I (we) will do this next time

SHIFTING FORCE/CONTROL LANGUAGE

Fig. 7.3

FORCE/CONTROL LANGUAGE Shifts to→	POSITIVE TENTATIVE LANGUAGE Shifts to→	POSITIVE RESULTS LANGUAGE!
Do it because I'm the ___ Do it because I have the title	I believe...this is best...because... These are my thoughts, what are yours?	Let's do it this way together Let's create a clear agreement
Do it because I'm right, I said so Do it because I'm bigger, smarter, etc.	What do you think the solution is? What do you think?	Let's create specifics together What specifically do you suggest?

SHIFTING VICTIM LANGUAGE

Fig. 7.4

VICTIM/BLAME LANGUAGE Shifts to→	POSITIVE TENTATIVE LANGUAGE Shifts to→	POSITIVE RESULTS LANGUAGE!
I was abused; I was ___ It's your fault; You/this ruined my life	I am responsible for my life I am done making excuses	I am going to make a clear plan I am taking the following actions
I'm not good enough That always happens to me	I am working on changing how I feel I am good enough to learn and master	I am great! I am going to do ___

SHIFTING REGRET LANGUAGE

Fig. 7.5

REGRET LANGUAGE Shifts to→	POSITIVE TENTATIVE LANGUAGE Shifts to→	POSITIVE RESULTS LANGUAGE!
I wish I had, I should have If only I had, I could have, I regret ___	I am going to learn from that! I am going to turn that into a victory!	I've learned my lesson, I'm ___ Here's my plan of action now

SHIFTING SELF-DEPRECATING LANGUAGE

Fig. 7.7

SELF-DEPRECATING LANGUAGE Shifts to→	POSITIVE TENTATIVE LANGUAGE Shifts to→	POSITIVE RESULTS LANGUAGE!
I've got a pea for a brain, I'm too old, short, fat, slow, etc.	I am throwing away my excuses! I'm going to play with improving	No more self-deprecating Here's my plan to improve
I'm such a klutz, I'm such a loser I always get it wrong	Now that was interesting I can do that better	Here are the changes I'll make Starting right now ___

SHIFTING SCATTER LANGUAGE

Fig. 7.6

SCATTER LANGUAGE Shifts to→	POSITIVE TENTATIVE LANGUAGE Shifts to→	POSITIVE RESULTS LANGUAGE!
I'm forgetful, I get confused I'm spacey, I always lose things	I want to be responsible and remember I am committed to remembering	I've enrolled in a memory class I have hired a coach to help me
Don't forget ___, Don't lose ___ My memory is no good	I am want to remember I am going to keep track of my stuff	I will remember ___ I will sign up today for a training

SHIFTING EXCUSES LANGUAGE

Fig. 7.8

EXCUSES LANGUAGE Shifts to→	POSITIVE TENTATIVE LANGUAGE Shifts to→	POSITIVE RESULTS LANGUAGE!
I'll play it by ear, I'll decide later It depends, If this happens, then ___	I will do this the best way possible I am going to play with finding solutions	I'll decide by Friday at noon No, sorry, I won't be doing that
If I had more hours in the day It slipped away	I'll decide within the week Well that was an oops!	My decision right now is ___ Here's what I learned from this

Using Positive Results Language

Have you ever known someone who was an "overnight success?" How many years, months and days were they focused on what they were doing before they achieved recognition? Success does happen (though overnight was likely a misnomer), and it results from steady and consistent forward movement that you are responsible for creating. Luck absolutely occurs—being in the right place at the right time, meeting the right people, getting the right breaks, good health—and it requires staying in Action, with your mind clearly focused on your desired outcomes. Discipline will open doors. The evidence of this is all around you. Just look at the people you most admire. Their persistence, even when there were few who supported their efforts, led to their accomplishments. The Vocal Invocation they used along the way was likely an example Positive Results Language.

Vocal Invocation is where all success stories begin. For you to manifest exactly what you want, start by thinking and speaking consistently about it. We begin with the words to ourselves and follow with the rigor of Right Action, then we Shift into Peak Life Habits with discipline and persistence. By transforming the conversations we have inside and outside our heads, we open the door for positively inspiring success.

Let's put our finger on what makes the inflection of the Positive Results Language (in the far right-hand column of Figures 7.1–7.8) so powerful. We can then learn how to transform any language into the language of Right Action. The antidote to the eight negative-energy Language Habits is language with three vital properties: *Accountability, Specificity, and Measurability*. Here it is again:

> **POSITIVE RESULTS LANGUAGE IS ACCOUNTABLE, SPECIFIC, AND MEASURABLE**

Together, these three properties make up the no-fail litmus test of your Language Habits. You will soon be effectively preempting the aid and comfort your Limiting Language has been giving to your Limiting Habits, and you will embolden a powerful, unique new voice that can make joyful greatness available to you in every moment and area of your life.

Positive Results Language Litmus Test #1: Accountability

Your accountability is litmus test #1. It puts the sphere of influence in your competent hands for managing, monitoring, and Shifting your Language Habits. Instill these Language Habits in yourself because of your commitment to your own greatness. Remember, you are the CEO of your life. We are all too eager to blame someone else, the world, or "it" when things don't go our way. Yet in the end, the only person we can control is ourselves. That is what accountability is about.

Become alert to feelings deep within yourself. Notice that when you are blaming another person or situation or ducking under your accountability, there is a dissonant feeling and a weakening in your own body. There is a disempowered sensation that arises when we assign blame to circumstances, someone else, fate, birth order, etc. You may notice a nagging dissatisfaction, a lack of ease when you are off track. Be accountable for your strength, power and health. We have empowered a nonentity, "it," to run roughshod right over us! Only "I" has that power in the context of Right Action. Shift back and be responsible for all circumstances. I can choose to have him, her, them, the situation, or "it" ruin my day. I can also choose to take a deep breath, STOP, INTERRUPT, SHIFT, and move on with my voice focused on resolution, starting with "I."

Your personal accountability starts with "I." Whenever we say "I," we create the option of U-turning our finger. When we stop blaming and make ourselves accountable, we set ourselves up for happiness and success. Here are some quick examples from earlier in the chapter, with a few modifications.

- "You're putting our marriage on the rocks" becomes "I want to figure out how to make our marriage better," or "I want to (am going to, am committed to…)."

- "They have put up roadblocks to my success" becomes "I intend to meet with everyone and have a straight conversation about how to move forward."

- "Rich people get all the breaks" becomes "I am going to play with appreciating and having more money."

- "It is simply exhausting" becomes "I am going to get more rest."

- "It's impossible to lose weight" becomes "I am committed to finding a fitness program that works."

- "Who dropped the ball?" becomes "What can I do to help?"

You may think that your "I" statements don't always have a results inflection. An "I" statement is often merely an observation of being overwhelmed or distressed. It's one thing to say, "I feel overwhelmed by planning my financial future" and quite another to state: "I will have the plan completed, printed out, and implemented by January

31st." Select which feels better: "I am upset" or "I am committed to improving my mood!"

Your accountability is at the heart of your Positive Results Language in two ways: one, you have the power to inspire yourself to dream really big, and two, you remove yourself from whatever disempowering "Limiting Language Habit" has you in its clutches, putting yourself back into the game of delicious, joyful success. Through your words you can free up the energy to discover and take Right Action, and that is where the power is. Just in case your internal voice is starting to squeak again, Chapters 8 and 9 will address the questions that may be percolating, such as "How am I going to do everything that I want to do or commit to do?"

Positive Results Language Litmus Test #2: Specificity

Be specific in your communication. Lead by example. Catch yourself saying, "I'll try," and Shift it to something accountable and measurable. If someone says, "Let me see what I can do for you," and you are wanting a specific timeline, your response to them could be, "That's awesome – when do you think you can get that done by?" Now we have put specifics into the conversation. That little language Shift changes everything in communication. The more we do this the easier it will become. Even when communicating by email, we can be specific by writing something like, "I really appreciate you doing this! Please send back a quick note today and let me know when you will finish this by, and thanks again." People don't take offense at that. If they do, then you know there are some Limiting Habits in the midst. Most people appreciate accountable, specific communication; it makes their lives easier because they know what you want and expect. Be mindful and intentional that your communication is kind and clear.

How specific are the statements below, and what do they mean?

- I'll work on that.
- Let me give it a go.
- I'll keep you posted.

- I'll think about dinner plans.
- Let me see what I can do for you.
- I want to get in touch with Dad.
- I'd feel more relaxed if I made more money.
- I want to take a vacation.
- I want to lose some weight.

How about these?

- I'll put five hours into that today, and send you an update.
- I'll send you a progress report tonight.
- Let's meet today and make a schedule for all stages of the project.
- I'll call you before 3 p.m. with some suggestions for dinner tonight.
- I'll get this to you tomorrow morning before noon.
- I'll call Dad today.
- I'm committed to making $100,000 a year in interest income.
- I will plan a vacation to Cozumel and schedule a call to a travel agent tomorrow.
- I am going to join Weight Watchers today and lose those 15 (or more) pounds.

As you might have noticed, the beauty of making a specific commitment is that the accountability we accept also begs the question, "How?" When we ask how to summit the peak, how to attract greatness and joy, we spur our brains to figure it out, setting a baseline, selecting actions, and identifying *how* to measure our progress.

* * *

LIMITING HABIT SPOTLIGHT: THE "SOMEDAY/ONE DAY HABIT"

The "Someday/One Day Habit" is about the future instead of today. It slows us down because when we put things off until someday or one day, it keeps us out of action and prevents us from achieving our goals and dreams. There is no structure for the objects of our "Some Day/One Day Habit," and our conversations about them are equally tentative.

I ask people, "What are the eighth and ninth days of the week?" The answer is that the eighth day is Someday and the ninth day is One Day. The challenge of this Habit is that we generally die first before Someday or One Day ever comes. The only day that exists is today!

PATTERN INTERRUPT PEAK LIFE HABITS:

Accountability Habit, Success Habit, Right Action Habit, The Right Time is Right Now Habit

SL 7.1

Positive Results Language Litmus Test #3: Measurability

There is one last step before we are on our way to mastering Positive Results Language. We have made our language accountable, and we have made it specific. Now is the time to step away from the "Someday/One Day Habit," "Optimist Habit," or any other Limiting Habit that has kept you from bringing your desired Outcome into the world (or effectively removing it from the world, if you are reducing the size of a flabby carbs belly). Positive Results Language is *measurable*. If you don't know what your baseline for success is, how will you know that you are achieving what you set out to accomplish? Get out the yardstick and measure everything you can possibly measure. Be even more specific: create checkpoints, milestones and specific results. Ask questions like:

- How and when am I going to achieve this?
- What milestones or timelines am I creating?
- How will I know the goal is complete?

- How am I going to know that the plan is working?
- How will I know if it is not working?
- What Actions am I going to take?

Using these types of questions, we can modify the statements from the last section one more time, down to the micrometer.

- I'll put five hours into that by 4 p.m. and send you an update by 4:30 p.m.
- I'll fax you a progress report that you'll have by 8 p.m. or earlier.
- How does 9 a.m. look for you to meet and plan all stages of the project?
- "I'm picking up the phone to call Dad right now."
- "I have a meeting with my broker on Monday to talk about financial goals, and based on that I will implement a plan for investing \$_____ by December that will increase my interest/dividend income to \$_____ a year."
- "I will look into the cost of travel and lodging to Cozumel after dinner tonight and put my name on the vacation calendar at work first thing in the morning."
- "I will lose 15 pounds by Labor Day. I'm joining Weight Watchers tonight and will be following their protocols, plus cutting out all sodas and sweets; and I will get on the stationary bike for 30 minutes, five days per week."

* * *

Maybe you would like to be earning a million dollars or more, or have your daughter's Ivy League education in the bank by the time she graduates high school, or find yourself in a partnership with a vibrant, loving, compassionate person. Here is a reminder: your goals will probably not arrive in your life all at once by tomorrow morning – you are still living in the real world, the world of discipline and persistence, keeping the faith and taking Right Action. As you saw in Chapter 5 when we talked about the *Stockdale Paradox*, dreams are realized with patience and discipline. We invite them into our lives step-by-step, word-by-word, Action by Action. At each stage of every great journey is a benchmark and that benchmark is delineated with language. So how will you articulate your next step?

Shifting To Vocal Inspiration!

Now is the time to practice Shifting your favorite "Limiting Language Habits." Paint a picture with your words that leads to the roadmap of your life. Then keep on painting those pictures more and more vividly. By Shifting your words, you invite action, happiness and vivid pictures of the passions you collaged in your head at the end of Chapter 5. In the upcoming exercise, jot down a few of those Limiting Language phrases that your internal voice has habituated. (You may notice that there are certain people in your life with whom you often use these expressions.) Also, list when and where you use these phrases, as this exercise can give you some insight as to why you use them in certain circumstances, assist you in the process of interrupting your Limiting Language, and help you begin to Shift to positive language that supports the Peak Life Habits you want. Then identify some Positive Tentative Language phrases you could have used instead. Finally, write down a Positive Results Language phrase that authentically Shifts the entire conversation and moves you toward the Actions and Outcomes you want. (For more exercises and structured practice on this, look at the companion Habitually Great workbooks available at www.habituallygreat.com.) Get your pen/pencil ready, and have fun as you amuse yourself by noting these Language Habits that you have unwittingly expounded for years. Now is the time to Shift them. Play Big!

CHANGING THE GUARD:
MY LIMITING LANGUAGE PHRASES

1. A Limiting Language phrase I've used recently is: _____

_____

- Where was I?_____
- Who was I with?_____
- Possible Limiting Habit involved: _____
- Positive Tentative Language phrase to substitute: _____
- Positive Results Language phrase to substitute: _____
- Peak Life Habit(s) I want to support with my words: _____

_____

2. A Limiting Language phrase I've used recently is: _____

_____

- Where was I? _____
- Who was I with? _____
- Possible Limiting Habit involved: _____
- Positive Tentative Language phrase to substitute: _____
- Positive Results Language phrase to substitute: _____
- Peak Life Habit(s) I want to support with my words: _____

_____

Now that you are claiming your power over your Language Habits, you will begin to see that you have the power to pull that repetitive, chattering monkey out of your head and focus your attention on the mileposts that lead beyond "almost" to your ultimate life. You will discover what remarkable energy becomes available when you begin to pay close attention to the words you've been choosing subconsciously up until now. Whether you have spoken those words inside your head or externally to others, whatever you say you create.

You can walk toward success or failure simply through your words. The power of choice and intention is life changing and exhilarating. You've got all the power!

You're doing great – onward to Chapter 8 where we are going to climb the peaks of Right Action.

CHAPTER 8

INFUSE YOUR LIFE WITH RIGHT ACTION

"Lots of people know what to do, but few people actually do what they know. Knowing is not enough! You must take action."

—Anthony Robbins

The Nike slogan, "Just Do It" speaks to the success that is within all of our grasps. There is only one problem with taking Nike's advice: the Limiting Habits that stand in our way. When your Limiting Habits threaten your focus, you must do whatever it takes: sidestep them, interrupt them, or create a substitute Habit. Greatness is a commitment and a Habit. Shifting Limiting Habits happens when you understand what you are up against, and then declare where you want to go instead, followed by taking positive, preemptive Actions with the discipline and persistence to get you there.

In this chapter you are going to learn how to take a detour from the familiar road of "almost." You are going to preempt the autopilot and put your hard-earned Habit Mastery to work. In the coming pages we are going to cover Right Action success structures and Right Action Habits that take you across the great divide of the Habit-Gap. When you close this book, you will be saying, "I am committed to _____" *and* have the tools and the structures in place to manifest great Outcomes.

Right Action is positive, disciplined, persistent Action undertaken with clarity, focus, specificity and measurability. Right Action is the antidote to the undertow of Limiting Habits. It reinforces and strengthens our commitment to our desired Outcomes. Right Action is being respectful and appreciative of others and of ourselves. Figure 8.1 shows you several important Right Action Habits (that are a subset of Peak Life Habits) you can adopt as your allies.

TOP 15 RIGHT ACTION HABITS

GREATNESS IN ACTION

- Completion Habit
- Discipline Habit
- Focus & Clarity Habit
- Ground Truth Reality Habit
- Modeling Well Habit
- Pattern Interrupt Habit
- Persistence Habit
- Positive Results Language Habit
- Power Scheduling Habit
- Preemptive Habit
- Proactive Habit
- Right Action Momentum Habit
- Saying No Authentically Habit
- Saying Yes Powerfully Habit
- Teamwork Habit

Right Action Habits are Peak Life Habits that help you catapult the Habit-Gap and achieve your ultimate life!

Fig. 8.1

Habits of Right Action act as Pattern Interrupts. When these Habits are in play, despite any of your Limiting Habits that may be lingering around, you are getting things accomplished and feeling satisfied. (Remember: Right Action also includes relaxation and taking care of your well-being!) Right Action Habits provide the framework for success to walk through your door. They also gather momentum over time and align with circumstances and events around you. The miracles that we perceive – the lucky breaks and "overnight" successes – happen because you are in Right Action. The next time you are in the "right place at the right time" you may recognize that your Right Actions, sourced by Peak Life Habits and Vocal Invocation, were the important contributors to bringing you there.

Now is the time to put the pedal to the metal in your ultimate life and enjoy an exquisite ride. Keep in mind, however, that the first few minutes may not be that sweet; you've got to blast some Limiting Habit sludge out of your system. By this point, your Habit Mastery is likely to have become a more straightforward proposition. What are you determined to change? What are you exhausted about, mad as heck about and not going to allow in your life anymore? What torments you about your past, about your Habits today, about life? Open your eyes to all those nails in your tires and choose Right Action success structures and Right Action Habits to manifest the Shifts and Outcomes you desire.

Inspiration Comes From Discipline

Have you ever wondered why 99% of your New Year's resolutions wither on the vine? Have you made the same resolution(s) two years in a row? New Year's resolutions are borne from inspiration, not discipline. Their aim is virtuous: to change, break or create a Habit. The pathway to their success runs straight into the walls of your Limiting Habits in spite of your inspired "in the moment" commitment and clarity of intent.

Are you inspired? What if you're not? (If you have the "Perfectionist Habit," you just might wait for the perfect type of inspiration before starting anything.) For the rest of you, how often have you been waiting for inspiration to knock you into Right Action? Often

I'm introduced as a motivational speaker, and the folks in the room excitedly clap as I head for the podium. They're getting ready for a nice dose of inspiration. At least they think they are. The first thing I ask them is, "Hey, how long is a good motivational pep talk going to last with you once you leave this room?" The answers are always predictable: "an hour...a few days...maybe a week." That's not what I'm committed to. If I'm spending my time with you to provide you with the possibility of more joy and success, those timeframes are not sufficient for you to make the Shifts you desire. The insights of motivational talks can give you great feelings. But here's the problem: insights disappear; Habits don't. That's worth repeating:

> ## INSIGHTS DISAPPEAR, HABITS DON'T!

Here's why: insights lead to inspiration which does not lead to sustained Right Action. And here's the good news: the "Discipline Habit" and "Persistence Habit" lead to sustained Right Action. Better yet, *discipline leads to inspiration*. That's right. You know that when you have truly applied yourself, whether in school, sports, at work or in another venue, success has soon followed. Think back to a time or a success that has felt really good (before your "I'm Not Good Enough Habit," "Confrontation With Success Habit" or other saboteurs jumped in). You were inspired! That inspiration happened *afterward*. Your discipline led to your inspiration, and that is the beauty of the equation. In my motivational talks, we roll up our sleeves and get to the real work, the conversations under the conversation, i.e., Habits.

Here's a compelling life example:

John was a divorced father of an estranged teenage daughter and the part owner of a family business mired in debt and ownership disputes with his father. He also weighed 330 pounds. He was so heavy that he avoided industry conferences due to his embarrassment about his weight. His "Victim Habit" ran the show. He felt powerless and unhappy. Here's what he changed: in twelve months, John lost over 80 pounds, reconciled with his daughter at this important time in her life and bought out his father. All of those took time, discipline and persistence. He had to push past the self-sabotage moments when all he wanted to do was throw in the towel. That was perhaps the hardest part for him. Coaching was critical in those moments for John. He created an accountable structure to keep him from folding up the tent and giving up.

Discipline and persistence is the way through the maze. In the second year of John's Shift, he focused on his company, building quality and accountability systems with a focus on teamwork, and he received a large multi-year contract from one of the top retailers in the industry. He also purchased a new home, adopted a healthy lifestyle and patterned himself for sustaining greatness. Today John fully enjoys the happiness that he generated, which inspires him greatly. Notice that the inspiration came <u>after</u> *the discipline. John appreciates his successes, takes nothing for granted and focuses on continuing improvement. There are always peaks to climb. His next peaks are joining the dating scene, expanding his social life and hobbies, and losing another 50 pounds. He uses Habitually Great coaching as a key part of his accountability and as a structure for establishing and exceeding his goals. Coaching is one of many types of accountability structures you can create for yourself in your quests. This book was written so that you would have access to every tool that I used with John.*

As we discussed in Chapter 5, Olympic athletes train with inner visualization techniques. They know that their body will manifest what their internal voice says and their mind pictures. They are not afraid of the spotlight; they embrace it. At the same time, their *discipline* defines who they are and where they are going, not the spotlight. Discipline is their motivator. Great athletes, just like all successful humans, accept that people are watching them. Regardless of the scrutiny, the accountability that they generate is to themselves first and foremost. Even those who bask in their fans' adulation detach from the crowd and go inside to ground themselves in their Right Action Habits, particularly the "Focus & Clarity Habit." With their internal dialogue they pump themselves up about success and accomplishment. You'll see them yell aloud in buoyant and defiant tones, leveraging the positive power of their voice.

It is the same for you as the CEO of your life. Embrace the fact that if you are great at what you do, others will notice, watch and comment. On those days when your game stumbles, you will want a tough skin. Critics and naysayers will appear. Yet if you are willing to master the path of Right Action, people will hold you accountable to be great. Your accountability is to maintain your focus and clarity as well as your Habits of determination, stamina, patience and discipline. Those Habits are your allies. Don't worry or even think about being watched, because the only spotlight that counts is you managing your own.

Managing your spotlight, just like for great athletes, involves creating structures of discipline and sticking to them no matter how you are feeling. There is nothing revolutionary about scheduling, staying in Action and following through. The catapult of Habitual Greatness is in your Habit Mastery, the process of interrupting what has stopped you in the past and instead getting all the way to the checkered flag of joyful completion and success. That's the breakthrough – keeping on and not stopping, no matter what. That is why great athletes and teams *are* great: because they practice, over and over and over. They practice with purpose and intention. They preemptively work on circumventing anything that could get in the way, like Limiting Habits. Then they practice some more. Those practices and drills are all scheduled; there's nothing random about their days. It is the same with great CEOs, great parents, and virtually all people who challenge themselves in their roles to truly be the best they can be: they continue to learn and grow, constantly training and retraining themselves. With discipline comes success. You decide what your trophy case will display and what is important for you to master and feel joyful about. Right Action is the remedy, the preemptive cure for disappointment and the formula for a grand and fulfilled life. It's not about buying lottery tickets; it's about taking sustained Right Action, applying the success structures of this chapter along with the magic of Peak Life Habits and Positive Results Language.

There is a saboteur, a Limiting Habit that I have often seen challenge sustained greatness: the "Every Other Monther Habit." I've seen this with sales persons who consistently over perform and then under perform, in relationships when things are getting too good, and in many situations when the spotlight of success creates a bit of paralysis in companies and individuals.

LIMITING HABIT SPOTLIGHT: THE "EVERY OTHER MONTHER HABIT"

There are people you observe and admire who are habitually successful. They say, "Thank you," to the spotlights of visibility that naturally accompanies their success. The adulation and acknowledgement inspires them to continue with their greatness. They may have the powerful Habits that generate this level of consistent accomplishment such as the *Believe In Myself Habit* and *Greatness Habit.*

For others, in the midst of the success spotlight all of a sudden the "Avoid Accountability Habit" pops up like a jack-in-the-box. We get queasy and uncomfortable with being noticed. We'll under-perform until the spotlight is off of us, and then we'll perform well again. And it happens just as soon as people don't have the expectation of us, so we have that freedom to be great again because no one is watching. Then the cycle continues because we are recognized, and then we panic, under perform, etc. You have likely seen this Habit with promising athletes, spouses, children, and maybe even yourself.

Welcome to the "Every Other Monther Habit." The root of this Habit is about being accountable for success. We all like to succeed, yet paradoxically many of us don't want to be held accountable for maintaining that success. We actually sabotage our performance so that the expectation is diminished. Often this sabotage is at the subconscious level based on the stranglehold of Limiting Habits such as the "Fear Of Success Habit," "I'm Not Good Enough Habit," and "Avoid Accountability Habit." Other Limiting Habits join the chorus too.

The "Every Other Monther Habit" directly correlates to Nelson Mandela's speech that: "Your playing small does not serve the world. There is nothing enlightened about shrinking…" Yet shrink we do. Instead, we have to develop that muscle and diminish those Limiting Habits, calling forth powerful Pattern Interrupts and substituting Peak Life Habits, learning that the light is nothing to be afraid of and is something to be consistently humble and proud of. Become Habitually Great at playing in the light!

PATTERN INTERRUPT PEAK LIFE HABITS:

Believe In Myself Habit, Playing Big Habit, Detachment Habit, Greatness Habit, I'm Worthy Habit

SL 8.1

There is no magic spell for greatness. What we have is something far more reliable – our discipline and persistence, our ever-growing Habit Mastery, and the real-world tools in this chapter that will keep you in Right Action. The key to the Law of Right Action lies in melding your power as the master of your Habits with productivity structures that facilitate your greatness. Are you ready to roll up your sleeves and pave the road for success? If you said yes – or even just "maybe" – then let's go!

The "Right Action Momentum Habit"

The "Right Action Momentum Habit" goes hand in hand with your "Discipline Habit" and leads to enduring happiness and success. Imagine that you took on the accountability or desire to start something from nothing (for example envision having to do 15 minutes on the stationary bike if you are seriously overweight and have not exercised even a minute for many years). Sound daunting? In fact, most great achievements begin with just an idea that has no muscle mass to support it. With the initial push and continuing discipline of the "Right Action Momentum Habit," your intention eventually gains mass and momentum, growing, developing and ascending.

The key is to engage your "Discipline Habit," schedule your Actions and keep pushing forward, inch by inch, step by step. It may involve a lot of sweat equity, as if you're trying to push a boulder that just refuses to budge, yet you keep pushing. So there may be some hardship, a bit of struggle, sweat, rigor, and then step by step, day by day, with a setback here and there and as you keep it all going, finally a tipping point is reached. Interestingly, perhaps that tipping point goes unnoticed because you are focused on staying with the rhythm, building momentum and recovering any missteps. As the weeks go by, all of a sudden you'll find yourself riding 45 minutes at a clip, easy as pie.

The "Right Action Momentum Habit" is a positive, intentional, step-by-step momentum builder that leads to the magic of inertia. Like a kid on a swing furiously pumping his legs hoping to soar, your dream may not pick up much momentum at first. Luckily, your "Discipline Habit" keeps you from giving up – and lo and behold, steadily the effort lessens and you are swinging with the treetops, feeling the exhilaration of success. That is how the "Right Action Momentum Habit" works with exercise, weight loss, career ascension, wealth, place, purpose and happiness.

Through your continuous, determined, and patient application of the Habitually Great cognitive methodology, even if you stumble at times, even if the rubber-band exerts its backward pull, your "Right Action Momentum Habit" will help you recover your ground and power forward. It will keep you ascending, sustaining and building your inspired path of greatness. Your victories and smiles of contentment are driven by your "Right Action Momentum Habit" as you stay in steady, determined Action.

PEAK LIFE HABIT SPOTLIGHT:
The "Right Action Momentum Habit"

The "Right Action Momentum Habit" is about traversing step by step toward your greatness, like a glider that soars over extraordinary terrain and lands in the field of change with grace and integration. It is about simplifying and taking small bites while not allowing ourselves to be overwhelmed by the large and important goals we have targeted. With this Peak Life Habit we place our "Self-Sabotage Habit" to the sideline while we act as our own mother ship, pulling ourselves to the tipping point of bright blue skies where our momentum is established and we are self-propelling with inspired confidence, soaring on our own.

It is exactly the opposite of the "Doom Loop Habit," which is all about optimistically expecting miracles to happen overnight and being disappointed and stressed when our immediate, frantic efforts don't pay off.

When we are exercising our "Right Action Momentum Habit" we are staying in Action, interrupting and side-stepping Limiting Habits, keeping our forward motion and achieving our goals. This is one of the most important Peak Life Habits. It will enable you to remain steadfastly in Right Action, ascending the important areas of your life, powerful and focused in your own right.

The "Right Action Momentum Habit" Interrupts:

Avoid Accountability Habit, Confrontation With Success Habit, Doom Loop Habit, Waiting For The Shoe To Drop Habit, Paralysis Habit

SL 8.2

A simple example of the "Right Action Momentum Habit" involved the following breakthrough:

Chloe is a Director at a large accounting firm and spent her days reading tax returns, reading tax research, reading emails, meeting with clients, etc. When she got home at night, she also had roles as wife, mother, homework assistant and Girl Scout Troup leader. She loved to read non-fiction yet had not read a book in a few years, feeling that there simply wasn't enough spare time. (She had developed a Victim Habit in her relationship with time.) She had a desire to be learning about all sorts of other subjects, feeding her starved curiosity. How could she develop a success structure around reading with so many roles to which she allocated time?

With her Habitually Great coach, she analyzed her time and roles, and she decided to implement something simple: a "Right Action Momentum Habit." She scheduled 15 minutes each night for reading. It did not sound like much at first, and she was interested to see if it would have any impact. To accomplish her goal, there was a Limiting Habit that had to be changed: her "Perfectionist Habit" from which, over the years, she'd come to believe that she must have at least an hour or more to immerse herself in a good book, and she liked to finish any chapter she started in the same sitting. Well, 15 minutes a night was not going to take her from chapter to chapter. It was time to change.

So she started, just 15 minutes a night, and found it fulfilling—and liberating, too, not to have to read a whole chapter. It was even more fun to discover just how much she was reading each week and how much she was enjoying it. The steady commitment to her reading list kept the material fresh and easier to retain from night to night. Within the first three weeks, with her steady "Right Action Momentum Habit," she had finished a book that she had wanted to read for three years.

Reading is a simple example and, for Chloe, an important one. With a little introspection, you might find that there are other clear-cut challenges—even if they may seem like minor ones—that you face and can turn into goals. Start today by taking small steps in developing an achievable success structure. Then, no matter what, follow through, maintain your commitment and momentum, achieve the fulfillment, resolution or completion of that issue or goal. This is how Right Action works; welcome to greatness. Use all the tools of this book. I am not over-simplifying the path to success. There is no single tipping point, no celebrity TV host or Fortune 100 CEO that saves your day, no point when somebody pulls a lever and turns on all the lights in the house and thousands of your favorite people stand to applaud. Instead, the companies and people that succeed are the ones that focus steadily, without fanfare, toward clearly articulated, specific, measurable goals.

Implementing and maintaining Right Action success structures is a big part of your "Right Action Momentum Habit." When you install those success structures in your life and then invest the steady push to get them going, you put yourself in power. As the wheel of success begins to turn, be on guard for Limiting Habits that "try" to get in the way, and use all your tools of Pattern Interrupting. The initial investment of effort—articulating your goals using Positive Results Language, designing and installing the Right Action success structures and following them with discipline and persistence—are the fuel for your "Right Action Momentum Habit." Your steadily increasing momentum will catapult you across the Habit-Gap. That might happen overnight, a month from now, a year from now, or ten years from now—just stick with it, and success will happen.

Time Is Just Time

All right, fess up. Let's tackle the issue of time with good old-fashioned honesty between us. How often have you justified something not happening and/or felt distressed about an intention or goal that was not completed or even started due to time constraints? The Right Action path to Habitual Greatness leads straight to the clock. Time often comes up in our conversations with statements like: "There is not enough time. I have no time. I need more hours in the day. I'd like to buy some time. What happened to the time? I wish I had more time." What are some of your familiar internal and external comments or phrases about time?

Our words about time are often a covert displacement of what we are not dealing with. We play the time card instead of looking directly at our Limiting Habits to see what really puts up the road-block. When your time conversation comes up, ask yourself, "What is the conversation displacing?" Is it a covert excuse for your "Confrontation With Success Habit?" Is it a cover-up for an "I'm Not Good Enough Habit?" There are certainly many demands today on our time, and that gives us many more excuses to hide behind the conversation about time. Down the road you'll be calling forth your "Regret Habit" and ruminating about how you could have "made the time."

Here's an alternative – deal with it! Identify what you are not dealing with when you put your "overwhelmed with not enough time" conversation into the forefront of your thoughts. Time is just time. Say it again, louder: TIME IS JUST TIME. It is "time" to alter your relationship to and prioritize your time in a manner that supports your joys and goals. In the pages immediately ahead are Right Action structures and Peak Life Habits that will assist you.

The good news is that time is not in exceedingly short supply. Actually, it is one of the great equalizers. There are 24 hours in a day, 60 minutes in an hour, 60 seconds in a minute, for everyone, no matter how privileged or disenfranchised. There is not more and not less, and there never will be. We get to allocate that time to our roles and priorities. Acknowledging this truth allows us to be authentic about what we can and cannot accomplish. You can alter your relationship to time by prioritizing what is important and being responsible about how you allocate your time. Immediately and for the long term, institute the practice of the "Saying No Authentically Habit" combined with the "Saying Yes Powerfully Habit." Both will go a long way toward taking control of how your time is allocated. I guarantee a Shift will Happen!

Your Roles In Life

Let's deepen our analysis of time in your life by looking at the key roles you play, the areas of your life in which you invest your time on a regular basis. For starters, you may have a role as a boyfriend/ girlfriend, partner/spouse, parent, son or daughter, extended family member, caregiver, pet owner, cook, shopper, carpooler, commuter, as well as the many roles you may have in your career and industry, plus your other interests in fitness, as a sports fan or team member, musician, hobbyist, member of your house of worship, community, boards, etc. Note there is also your individual role of "rest recharger." That role is one of the most important; at least 25% or more of your time is allocated to sleep and you must manage that role well so that you have enough vitality for your commitments. In our busy lives, regardless of age or status, the list of our roles has become quite extensive, perhaps too much so.

Most of us have five or more basic areas/roles that are best served by scheduling appropriate time for them. We have work, relationships, fitness, family, spiritual/religious practices, and hobbies. Notice that as you look at any single category, you are likely to see that you have multiple roles within each category. When you add all of your other roles, there is a lot of organizing and scheduling to do. Roles are areas of commitment and accountability, and most of us underestimate what we are accountable for and what others expect from us, as well as what we expect from ourselves. When the rubber meets the road, we often find we are behind and overwhelmed by the myriad of demands of our roles.

You may be thinking there are roles and areas in your life you want to invest more time into, leading you to wonder, "*Where is that time going to come from?*" If you don't schedule many of these areas, the greatness that you desire may never occur. Your relationships may only be so good; you may only get to enjoy your hobbies just so much. Perhaps you want to write a book and don't ever schedule or follow through on the time to do it. A quick look at your roles might explain why the time hasn't been allocated. Add a dollop of Limiting Habits into the mix and that book isn't likely to reach the printing press. Sound familiar? It does to your humble author too.

GOALS FOR YOUR ROLES

Grab a notepad or piece of paper and jot down a few of your roles, then sketch them individually through this exercise so that you have done it with four or five different roles. This simple exercise guides you through identifying specific goals for your roles:

Role: _____

Average time spent weekly: _____

Overall Theme/Intention For This Role: _____

_____

Determine some specific goals you would like to achieve with this role. Select an immediate goal, short-term goal (within six months), and also a long-term goal.

Immediate goal: _____

Short-term goal: _____

Long-term goal: _____

Remember: the abundance of a life well lived and savored includes committing to and scheduling for the roles and hobbies that are important. You will enjoy the satisfaction of knowing that you are investing your time in what *you* decide matters.

Buckets of Time

The upcoming "Buckets of Time" analysis gives you the nitty-gritty understanding of how you spend our time – and consume much of it without realizing the allocation or cost. You can see how much time you are parked, with the time meter ticking in each Bucket. Through this simple analytical tool, you can clarify what changes you want to make and how you will make those changes by investing your time in a manner consistent with the Right Actions and accountabilities of your goals and dreams. By doing this, you will be able to see how your time is allocated within any particular role. You may also want to pause and illuminate many different roles you have in your life that you may not even have realized existed, yet are time consumers too.

As you replicate the "roles" exercise for several of your stations in life, this reality check may confirm that you have been attempting magic tricks with time that have never been achieved. Let's save magic for the magicians and put some grounded reality in. As you move through the chapter it will become clear to you where to make changes in your schedule and in all your roles. (An in-depth analysis tool is included in the *Habitually Great Workbooks* available at *www. habituallygreat.com.*) To get started with an easy and persuasive application of this approach, apply the same role that you selected in the "Goals for Your Roles" section to the Buckets of Time exercise. You may recognize that the goals you select for that role are not currently supported by your Buckets of Time allocation. That contradiction must be corrected!

The key is to use this exercise as a tool, analyzing your roles and goals one at a time. Discern three goals as well as the allowance of time necessary to fulfill those three goals and the specific activities required. We allocate our time in so many areas that it is helpful to see where exactly it is consumed. With this full breadth of information, it's time to look at Limiting Habits like the "Do It Myself Habit," "I Don't Trust Habit," and of course the "Can't Say No Habit." What are you going to delegate/hand off and ask someone else to do? How are you going to achieve a balanced, awesome life with all the stuff there is to do already? The answer starts with a good hearty "Buckets of Time" investigation:

BUCKETS OF TIME WORKSHEET[5]

Role: _____

Average time spent weekly in this role: _____

Immediate goals within this role: _____

Short-term goals: _____

Long-term goals: _____

Specific Role Activity	Current Number of Hours Weekly	Ideal Number of Hours Weekly	Realistic Number of Hours Weekly	Time of Day/Day of Week
TOTALS				

Changes To Be Made: _____

_____

_____

Effect on Immediate goal: _____

_____

_____

[5] If you'd like a few copies of this exercise so that you can fill them in with your different Roles go to www.habituallygreatbook.com. Habitually Great workbooks that have more details and other productivity paradigms and tips are available at www.habituallygreat.com.

Effect on Short-term goal: _____

_____

Effect on Long-term goal: _____

_____

Note: If you are noticing your "Resignation Habit" or "Skepticism Habit," STOP! Step out of your box, identify what Limiting Habits are stopping you from taking Right Action and rework the box until you have your breakthrough. Do not allow your internal voice to talk you out of this. That is a clue that there is a conversation under the conversation, i.e. a Limiting Habit. Shift to being Habitually Great!

Interruptions and Distractions

As we are humming through life and work, it is inevitable that we get pulled aside by interruptions from email, the phone, co-workers, significant others, friends, family, customers, vendors, babysitters, another person's schedule, kids, and life's unforeseeable events. Despite our best intentions, sometimes it seems that these always prevent us from getting ahead. It's the Monday morning that greets us after the inspiring weekend workshop or self-help book. The difference is that by the end of this chapter, with your new understanding of what gets in the way, how and why, you can Shift even those disheartening moments.

Accountability, Right Action and discipline are the powerful tools in your Habitually Great toolbox ready to create results...right now. You and I both know that interruptions and distractions are real, and they happen. They may even occupy more of your time on a daily basis than you've been acknowledging. What are your interruptions during the course of a day, week or month? Pull out a pad or copy of the Buckets of Time Exercise and let's take a look and fill this Bucket (called "My Distractions"):

- Be as specific as possible. How much time do I spend on email? On the Internet? How much time do I allocate to breaks and meals? How much time do I spend on phone calls that are work-related? Personal phone calls? How much time do I spend daydreaming? How often do I get interrupted or distracted? How much time do those take (on average)?

- Which of your Limiting Habits step into the dance in moments of procrastination, escape, sabotage, avoidance, distraction, interruption and interference? There's your real culprit.

Even the greatest CEOs and Olympians among us are challenged in those moments where they have prepared to take Action, scheduled the Actions and are "in Action." Often, that's when distractions, interruptions and excuses make an appearance. These will be both aggravating and tempting. Your "Excuses Habit" may pop up along with your "Procrastination Habit," "Distraction/Interruption Habit" and "Struggle Habit." Then your "Perfectionist Habit" could circulate back again and say, "Wait a minute, is this the right way to do it? I'd better stop." Then your "Logic & Justify Habit" reasons with you, using your internal voice to talk you out of Action for a myriad of reasons. Whew! Welcome to the conundrum of Limiting Habits. This is what you are up against every day, and from now on you must win and overcome those deadbeats. Unfortunately, getting into Action doesn't necessarily circumvent all of them. On some or most days there may be twenty other things that we could be doing besides what we are doing. You know the feeling: sometimes it is simply an "Overwhelm Habit" triggering you into a circuit overload shutdown as your brain keeps telling you that you have more to do than you can possibly get done. The key to great success is discipline, actually doing what you committed to do while refusing to indulge those old distractions and interruptions. For the most part they aren't forwarding your life or your true happiness. Real contentment is much more satisfying than an in-the-moment distraction.

Here's a classic twist to the distraction scenario to be on the lookout for. Remember your "Self-Sabotage Habits" from Chapter 3? Another time they like to take the wheel is during those periods when things are going well and you're on the verge of achieving a goal you have set. The Beliefs in the background may be: "I'm not worthy of this success," "This success can't be real," "I can't keep this up," "This isn't who I really am," etc.

Sunil is a CEO who was overwhelmed running a $250 million dollar company when he sought my help. Sunil, like many, was both successful __and__ unhappy. He had been waiting to be inspired to make changes . . . instead, frustration had clouded his sunny skies. As we discerned together, he did not like being accountable to a schedule; he was used to winging it, a Habit from his early entrepreneurial days. Now he had a list of tasks that was a mile long. There were many things that he had said he would do that he hadn't done. His hours and days were becoming more and more stressful because of this.

Sunil also had a strong "Distraction/Interruption Habit," and it was common for Sunil to drop whatever he was doing whenever someone requested his time. A good example was a morning when he was picking up his dry cleaning on his way to work and coincidentally ran into a client. His client expressed an interest in a business chat. Even though Sunil had a fully scheduled day and was already running late, he accommodated his client and agreed to have coffee with him right then at a nearby restaurant. That simple accommodation threw his entire schedule off and exacerbated the stress he was feeling.

A much better alternative would have been to say to his client, "I'd love to talk with you, and my schedule is full for today. I'll have my assistant call you tomorrow to schedule a time for us to get together later in the week. I'm looking forward to it." Why was he so easily derailed?

The first step was to identify and address the Limiting Habits that were getting in his way. It turns out our CEO had a serious confrontation with accountability ("Avoid Accountability Habit" and "Avoid Authority Habit"). He resisted his schedule. He was also controlled by his "Good Person Habit" and his "Can't Say No Habit."

Leaders impact many people. As the leader of his company he saw that his employees often modeled his Habits. His behavior was emulated by the employees throughout his firm. The more organized he could become, the more organized the people around him would become. The better he could become at keeping his word, the better the people around him would become at keeping their word.

A proactive approach to handling distractions and interruptions is applying the Bucket of Time exercise to identify exactly how much time in a day you want to *allocate* for interruptions. Most of us are not budgeting enough time for these, and so we tap daily into our "Frustration Habit" instead of our "Power Scheduling Habit." Scheduling well requires applying the principles of your "Ground Truth Reality Habit," authentically seeing and dealing with the reality of your life. If you are interrupted on average two hours per day, schedule for those interruptions and stop complaining about them! Interrupt your "Victim Habit" about interruptions and start looking at how to change their pattern so that you control how and when they occur.

Peter owned a landscape contracting business that was very successful. He prided himself on his great installers and his one-on-one interaction with his customers. Here's the paradox: Peter used to react angrily every time his phone rang, occasionally even throwing the phone and cursing at it. He was frustrated with the interruptions of that phone during his work day. However, the callers were his customers. The irony is if his phone didn't ring randomly and sporadically, he wouldn't be able to pay for his house, cars, food, clothes, healthcare, fishing trips or his children's education. Those were paying customers old and new calling.

We reworked his perspective, changed his voicemail message so that he communicated clearly about when he would return those calls and redirected many of them to his assistant. Here's the most interesting part: we clarified that the calls weren't interruptions at all, rather they were actually part of his job description. Even though he had told clients to call the office, he'd also given them his cell phone number. He hadn't looked at it that way because his "Victim Habit" had insisted on being front and center with his internal and external voices saying that the calls were frustrating intrusions. That Limiting Habit had been stamped into his subconscious a long, long time ago.

Applying the Bucket of Time exercise to your distractions and interruptions allows you to *recognize* and *manage* them. Being aware of the interruptions and distractions that are inevitable in your daily life will help alleviate resentment, feeling overwhelmed, and even depression. This will go a long way toward creating a schedule that accommodates them and Shifts those moments so that you manage them instead of them managing you. Here are some Distraction/Interruption Tips:

1.   *Do Not Disturb:* Change your "Open Door Habit" at work (and at home, too) by interrupting your "Distraction/Interruption Habit" and perhaps your "Need To Be Needed Habit." At the office create or order a sign that allows you to close your door with the sign choices being: Knock or Do Not Disturb.

2.   *Solitary Work Blocks:* Create scheduled solitary work blocks to catch up, focus and catapult. This means having a breakthrough in your "Saying No Habit," closing the door, turning off the phone, shutting down the email and digging into your important priorities. A time span of between two to four hours works best, and thirty minutes is a great start too!

3.   *Answering The Phone:* At work or at home, when you answer your phone, create an immediate time boundary expectation: "I'm glad you called and I've got five minutes right now, will that be enough time or do we want to schedule for a longer call?" or "I know this is an important topic to cover, let's schedule a good time to talk about this." or perhaps "I really want to talk about this (or "to you"); I'm really busy right now, so let's pick a good time to talk this afternoon; let me check my schedule."

4.   *Authentic & Compassionate:* Express your feelings with compassion if you feel that you are not being recognized or heard: "Listen, I'm there for you and I understand the importance of this to you. It's just that right now I've got to stay on task. Let's find the perfect time to discuss this together, how does later today or tomorrow look for your schedule?" Be firm and powerful in your words (surprise yourself) by using your "Authentic Habit" with your "Compassion Habit."

5.   *Keep Your Word:* Be accountable to the time commitments you make so that others develop trust and respect for what you say. Use your "Keeping My Word Habit" while establishing parameters that work. People will learn from you and model the "Integrity Habit" you are demonstrating!

6.   *Say "No":* Do a Pattern Interrupt on your "Good Person Habit" and "Can't Say No Habit," substituting your "Accountability Habit," "Discipline Habit" and "Saying No Authentically

Habit." Actually when you apply #s 2 and 3, others will find your heartfelt "Compassion Habit" more open and generous, because your "Resentment Habit" and "Victim Habit" have been preempted by your "Authentic Habit." You will actually be happier and that will rub off on those around you.

7. *Transform Big Goals to Bite Sized:* When a big goal or a multitude of To-Do's triggers your "Overwhelm Habit" and you launch into a pattern of distraction/interruption, simplify immediately. Take a big goal and make it into something small and manageable. Keep shrinking it until there's something you can actually do. Narrow and transcend large goals by cutting them into small pieces and just focus on completing a small piece.

8. *Checking Email:* Start your day without looking at email first. Instead look at your schedule and dig in. Spend at least 30–60 minutes each day getting organized and launching into the important Actions scheduled for the day. Then schedule an email check. Additionally, effective immediately, turn your email alarms off and immediately stop randomly checking email. Schedule 15-minute blocks of time for checking and responding to email, based on a ground truth analysis of what is most efficient for your priorities while being appropriately responsive. Set clear guidelines for people so that they know they can count on you to respond to email every three hours, daily, etc.

9. *Text Messaging:* Repeat step 8 for text messaging. Our stress levels are getting higher and we don't realize it. If you have created expectations that you can be available for text messaging randomly throughout the day, change that now. This is another insidious form of interruption and distraction. Set clear guidelines for people who text you so they know when you will be responding to text messages. Remember, solitary work blocks (step 2) are best done without text or email interruptions!

Understanding how and where you spend your time sets you on a Right Action path, making it easier to employ Peak Life Habits. The other side of the time 'coin' is creating a schedule that optimizes your life. Come along to Chapter 9, where you will create a personalized Habitually Great Power Schedule of your very own!

CHAPTER 9

SCHEDULE FOR GREATNESS

"Overcome your inertia. Since to be inert is to be without action, agree to become a being of movement: Plan to exercise, make that call you've been avoiding, or write that letter . . . Experience the apprehension and do it anyway! It's the doing that brings you to a new level of inspiration."

—Dr. Wayne W. Dyer

I remember a time many years ago when I did not keep a schedule. Yet I was always scheduled; I just didn't have it written down or on a PDA. I was proud of the fact that I kept everything in my head and could always remember my schedule for the upcoming days and weeks. That was a lot of mental real estate occupied with scheduling. I didn't realize that the head gymnastics I was doing with my schedule were taking away from my capacity to be fully present in the moment. Today, after many years as a student of productivity and time management, I can see how much more in-the-moment freedom and brain power I have at the table, so to speak. My schedule is all accounted for on my PDA. I actually don't know what I'm doing tomorrow and never worry about it, because it is all written, organized and planned! When you blend Habit Mastery, Peak Life

Habits and Pattern Interrupts with this Shift of being a focused and diligent scheduler, you will bring all of your desires into reality with ease and brilliance. You will become comfortable starting *and* finishing anything you commit to.

If you have already achieved mastery with creating your schedule, you know that the structure of a schedule gives you the accountability, perseverance and the continuity to keep on going. Mastering a new level of attention to scheduling is often the missing link to great results and productively staying organized and in Action, no matter how much there is to do. Habitually Great power scheduling blends Right Action Habits and success structures.

If you prefer not to keep a formal schedule, be aware of pitfalls you may not have anticipated. We sometimes get the mistaken feeling that not having a schedule provides us with the ability to be free, flexible and spontaneous when, in reality that "freedom" is an empty void that doesn't get us anywhere. Without a schedule we have no accountability to actually do or accomplish anything.

At every Habitually Great keynote, workshop or seminar there are always war stories from the planner. I'm amazed by the methods of madness involving schedules. As I have mentioned before (I'm still astounded by this!), our education system neglects to teach us about a few key areas of life. How many of us have had training in Leadership, Relationships, Financial Management, Fitness/Nutrition and Time Management? I don't see any hands raised.

Whether you are the crackerjack of scheduling or less proficient with your calendar than you want to be, here are two real life stories from the planner that will make you smile.

Karen came to me after years of being at the mercy of a Belief-Link that was crippling her output in the name of spontaneity. She told herself that structuring her schedule would be too limiting, so she kept it all in her head. She knew exactly what day and time every appointment was, and she planned her days and weeks with her internal Memory Planner. She shunned watches—and always knew what time it was, too. She could remember phone numbers, dates—everything— and rarely missed a beat.

And therein lay the problem: her practice of keeping track of time and schedules in her Memory Planner left her mind so full that there was little room left for creative juices to flow. All the effort she was putting into avoiding the perceived limitations of a schedule was in fact completely limiting her productivity. Her devotion to her old story about her spontaneous schedule actually left her with few accomplishments and little freedom.

Today she is amazed at what she accomplishes. She uses a PDA, has a perfect To-Do system and has established structures and Right Action Habits that have her producing remarkable results every day. She reports that she has found a lot more spontaneity by keeping a specific schedule and tracking everything in an orderly manner. The freedom she has with this system is remarkable. If it is not on her schedule, she doesn't do it. Often she adds things that come up during the day to her schedule, inserted only if there is extra time. If she makes a mistake or is unable to complete a task, no suffering Limiting Habits are triggered; she just re-schedules.

Karen's breakthrough is in the discovery that with a rigorous "Power Scheduling Habit" her head is clear to focus in the moment because her schedule manages her life. With that freedom, she noticed a remarkable expansion in her ability to be fully present, and that provides for real spontaneity. Plus, she now has more free time than ever to do many more things that she loves because she schedules the time for them!

Take a look at your Belief-Links concerning scheduling and spontaneity. If it is independence you want, you can create it by actually depending on one straightforward system and freeing up the rest of your mind. If you are concerned and are equating a structured scheduling paradigm with lost spontaneity, then create a Habit of scheduling a few hours into each day where you have nothing scheduled except spontaneity. You will likely be more spontaneous than ever, because you have allocated the time to be so.

Jeff is a father, husband, heart patient and the General Manager for a large company. In the midst of a Habitually Great seminar with his key executives and managers, he revealed that he kept one schedule on his office computer, a second schedule on his refrigerator, another in his car and another for his personal life that he carried around with him. His fear and resistance to having one central schedule stemmed from the turmoil that had ensued a few years ago when he lost the one schedule he was keeping at the time. This event stimulated a Belief-Link that left him blanketed by a fear of losing everything if he kept a single planning system.

Remember the Habit Chain? This event changed his Belief, and what took over was a fear that it could happen again (internal voice chatter), so he created new Actions and a new Habit by having several schedules scattered about. In spite of his commitment to bxze great in all of his roles, his Habit-Gap was setting him up to under perform and disappoint everyone. He tried to cross-coordinate the various schedules every day even though it became increasingly impossible to do so. As a case in point, he told us about a single afternoon a few weeks earlier on which he had made it to a late-afternoon doctor's appointment noted on his personal schedule yet missed both his sons' soccer games (written months ago on the refrigerator calendar) and a brief sit-down with a job applicant (which one of his managers had set up with a secretary to whom he had mentioned neither the medical appointment nor the game).

His productivity was suffering because his (now subconscious) fear of losing his schedule was controlling him more than any considerations of how he could most effectively manage. Without the tools to recognize or change his Belief-Link, he was trapped in a Limiting Habit Chain that was easily replaced.

Yes, even top executives have Limiting Habits that are instilled by events, and then they manage either themselves or their businesses (or both) poorly. You can likely remember some of these moments in your own life and/or career. Manage your Beliefs so that they don't manage you!

The structure of a Habitually Great Power Schedule gives you a home for the desires and goals in your mind and heart, translating them into accountable action steps and milestones. Be gentle yet disciplined with yourself as you ramp up your scheduling and following through Habits. Well-designed schedules and your accountability to the Actions declared within them carry you forth across the Habit-Gap to where you want to be.

BENEFITS OF HABITUALLY GREAT POWER SCHEDULING

- *Organizing All Areas:* Work, Fitness, Relationships, Family, Goals
- *Fulfilling:* Your roles and your desires, dreams and goals
- *Transcending:* Large tasks by cutting them into small pieces
- *Keeping:* Your word – fulfill your commitments
- *Being Responsible:* For your "On Time Habit"
- *Practicing:* Reverse Timeline Scheduling
- *Notating:* Desired Outcomes & To-Do's
- *Rescheduling:* Strengthen your integrity
- *Completing:* Everything you touch
- *Automating:* Everything you can
- *Saying:* No and meaning no

Fig. 9.1

Habitually Great Power Scheduling begins by putting everything that is important to you in your schedule, including workouts, To-Do's, Honey-Do's, etc. By keeping track of your life in one universal place, nothing falls through the cracks. The particular type of schedule that works best is up to you. Most of us already have PDAs or Franklin Planners. Both types, paper and electronic, work well as long as you just pick one. The single most important change you can make in your life is to schedule it effectively, keep to your word and keep your schedule. As you implement or enhance your universal schedule, here are some worthwhile considerations.

Empower Your Schedule

Some us often have such a strong "Avoid Authority Habit" that we tend to avoid our schedule because it is telling us what to do. We don't like being told what to do, and yet somehow this inanimate object becomes an authority figure. Get over this one! As we take on being masters in time management, scheduling and staying in Right Action, we may once in a while sabotage our schedule with this old Habit. In those moments, pause, take a deep breath and do a Pattern Interrupt. Smile, remember your old Interruption and Self-Sabotage Habits, and then get right back into power by saying, "I love my schedule. I created it to assist me with my happiness; it is just part of me, not a separate entity!"

Notate Desired Outcomes

Begin the practice of writing the Outcomes you desire into scheduled items. This is a favorite practice of many people once they start it. You will feel a stronger sense of accomplishment and intention. For example, instead of writing: "5:00 strategy meeting with Diane," perhaps write "Upbeat meeting with Diane where we argue/cajole and create a great strategy to align on." Writing your desired Outcomes is good practice for your "Believe in Myself Habit" and your "Determined to Succeed Habit." Remember, the brain is mechanical. You have the direct power to create what you imagine!

Interruptions/Distractions Floater

As you take over and curtail the interruptions and distractions in your day, here is an excellent tool for dealing with the ones that remain. Take a notepad and, for a day or two, note all of your interruptions and distractions while also jotting down the approximate time that is consumed. For example:

Stopped to watch the news this morning- 10 minutes

Unplanned errand- 35 minutes

Stopped work and read a magazine article at my desk- 15 minutes

John came into my office to talk about personal problems- 20 minutes

Phone calls from Mom, spouse and two friends while at work- 25 minutes

That's an hour and forty-five minutes, right there! When you start to see how much time you are expending for the "unplanned," you may be surprised. Identify how much time on average in a given day you are interrupted or otherwise distracted. Scheduling well requires applying the principles of your "Ground Truth Reality Habit." If this calculates to one or two hours per day, schedule the time for those interruptions. This is what I call the "floater." Generally we don't know exactly what time those moments will occur; we just know that they will during the course of the day. So make sure that if the predictable amount of time for the daily *unexpected* is usually 1.5 hours, then be sure that you have blocked off a total of 90 minutes per day in your calendar.

You must schedule for this "floater" of time or else these distractions/interruptions consume time that you've already prioritized for other Actions. If you don't account for these, you may notice that you are perpetually driven by your "Overwhelm Habit" and "Distress Habit." Here's how you schedule this floater: take any block or blocks of time you choose and mark them as your "Interruptions Floater." For example, you may choose to rope off 1:00 p.m. to 2:30 p.m., three 30-minute segments, or any variety of time blocks that sums to the hour and a half.

Creating a floater of real time provides for daily interruptions. Perhaps interruptions are even part of your job description. Remember Peter, who was always cursing the phone every time it rang? I was always amused, because the calls were from his customers; if the phone stopped ringing, he wouldn't have a job! His new approach was to schedule a two hour floater every day to accommodate the reality that those calls would occur and were an integral part of his job.

Here is the secret to the "floater:" you allocate bona fide, specific times in the day for it, and it shuffles. You have two choices for how it moves:

One, simply proceed with your day, shuffling your schedule, knowing you have time for everything, and accommodate the interruption when it occurs. That's why we call it a floater; interruptions happen randomly during the day, not always "on schedule." As long as you've allocated real time for their occurrence, you simply use a portion of that time in the moment to the interruption/distraction. Your schedule accommodates the time, and the flexible parts of your schedule shift such that a report you scheduled to complete from 2 p.m. to 3 p.m. may have its actual start and stop time adjusted, yet no time was taken away from it. Meanwhile, the hard and fast scheduled meetings, conference calls, doctor's appointments, soccer games, etc. stay right on their timeline.

Two, funnel your interruptions/distractions into the exact time of the floater you have created. For example, if you have set aside 2:30 – 3:30 for unforeseen interruptions, and a client calls unexpectedly (and it's not a crisis), a staff member walks in for a chat, or your best friend calls at 10:00 for what is predictably a five or 15 minute conversation, what do you do? How about explaining your new system and making a compassionate request to schedule with them for a specific time that is within your scheduled floater for that day. Again, you won't feel stressed since you've already set aside the necessary amount of time, and they will appreciate that you are allocating real time to them. Both of these methods work well, and the result is that you feel complete at the end of a given day because you have created a schedule based on reality!

Rescheduling

Have you noticed that sometimes you get aggravated if you mess up your schedule – when you didn't do what you said you were going to do, when you forgot to do something, when something got in the way or when you were interrupted in the middle of something important? Starting right now, put negativity aside. What Limiting Habits are you invoking with these thoughts that are just making you wrong? Perhaps your "Hard On Myself Habit" or your "Perfectionist Habit?" How about a simple humble acknowledgement such as, "Oops, I missed that," or "I didn't finish that?" No self-judgment, just the facts.

Instead of suffering over it, reschedule it. Reschedule the meeting or workout, reschedule the piano practice and that hour to write. This is important because by taking positive, proactive steps, you get further into the "Success Habit" and "Feeling Good Habit." As soon as you stop suffering, trust me, it's going to be a lot easier to reschedule whenever a situation arises.

Scheduling Play Time

It is vital that downtime gets plugged into your schedule. Block out time to do what you want – social activities, recreational activities, hobbies, etc. This also means scheduling blocks of time without filling in what the time is for – that is *in-the-moment* time. You'll decide what to do in those moments. Remember also to block out time for vacation, perhaps weeks, months or even a year or two in advance. Invoke your "Lightening Up Habit!"

An Exercise To Discover Extra Time

What would life be like if you took one day and charted how you spent its entirety, start to finish, head on the pillow to head on the pillow? You would learn a lot about where that "lost time" is hiding. Take just one day with a yellow pad in hand, tracking and writing down how you spend all your time. Use five-minute increments so that you capture plenty of the little stuff that adds up quickly. How long did it take you to drive to work? What did you do while you were at work? What did you do with the family? Add up all those extra phone calls, distractions, interruptions, commuting/travel, chores and tasks (bathroom breaks, shower time too). Almost all of us will ultimately find at least an hour or more of utterly wasted time. Imagine if we could reclaim an hour or more every day. We could use that extra time to fulfill some of our goals. Or we could make the choice of doing absolutely nothing for an hour.

The Simplest & Most Effective Task/To-Do System

No more sticky notes framed in a random circling pattern on your computer screen or littering your desk, three or four To-Do legal pads in varying places, scribbles on paper napkins and torn paper tablecloths. From this point forward, discipline yourself to use just one location for all of your To-Do's, one place to keep all of your daily notes and jottings. In that single location, notate the things that come up during the day that you want to, have to, or must do. Choose a To-Do receptacle that is convenient to carry, such as a small notepad or your PDA's task list that can always be on your person throughout the day. (I prefer a small spiral pad that fits easily in a jacket, back pack, or pocket.) The caveat is this: from that single source, initiate a regular end of day review to move all undone items from your To-Do list directly into your schedule, giving each Task/To-Do a scheduled, specific, measurable date and time for completion. No more Task Lists a mile long and wide. (After all, anything parked on a list is something that is not being done and has no structure for getting done.)

This may seem a bit radical to you if you think a Task/To-Do list is always to be kept separately from your schedule. That productivity structure leads to missed deadlines and forgotten commitments. In a Habitually Great Power Schedule, all Tasks/To-Do's are placed into your schedule with specific, measurable dates and timelines for fulfillment. By doing this, you Shift individual Task/To-Do's into scheduled Actions and completions. (Yes, even for returning and making phone calls, paying bills, follow-up meetings, appointments, research—everything!) This will help you complete important and required To-Do's as well as the simpler ones.

In addition to this simple, five-minute daily practice, on a weekly basis (pick a regular time for this, such as Sunday night, Monday morning, Friday before leaving work, etc.), perform a look-back, reviewing your daily schedules for the week just finished. Examine and make sure all scheduled To-Do's in each day from the prior week were either completed, eliminated or rescheduled. This Right Action step will combat any "Procrastination Habit" or "Sabotage Habit" that may be lurking in the wings.

Melding your To-Do list within your schedule creates a synergy that is a Right Action tool for success. If you can't pick a time, you are not going to do it. "Never Doings" will easily identify themselves by their repeated need for rescheduling. On the 3rd reschedule of anything, check in with your "Ground Truth Reality Habit," have a breakthrough and toss the item out. Monitor your "Can't Say No Habit," interrupt your "Overwhelm Habit," and enjoy the satisfaction of your "Completion Habit." If you have an assistant, you can enhance this structure with a weekly 15-minute meeting together to input all of your tasks (don't leave any unsaid or parked in your head —download them all), and fine tune your schedule accordingly.

Are you worried about getting all of this perfectly right? Is that going to stop you from playing with this or picking a small step to implement? If so, that would be a quick and dirty sabotage undermining you. Let's move perfection off the table:

LIMITING HABIT SPOTLIGHT: THE "PERFECTIONIST HABIT"

If you have one or both sides of the "Perfectionist Habit," you spend a lot of time analyzing and organizing and procrastinating until you are certain that everything is aligned for your success. Perfectionists fall into two categories. One type will start many things yet finish very few. This is because once started, they will only finish something if they can do it exactly right. So this type also has the "Incomplete Habit." A flip side of the "Perfectionist Habit" is the version where they won't even start on a project, goal, or anything if they think they can't do it right. Often this might appear to be the "Procrastination Habit;" look a little closer and see that perfection is at the top of the spiral or cluster.

In Peak Life Habits and Habitually Great programs, we've seen this Habit cause many challenges, including:
1) Inability to settle on a mate, regardless of intention/goal.
2) Consistent dissatisfaction with career, co-workers and others.
3) Either obsessive with fitness/diet or unable to find the right health regimen.

Either side of this Habit can be paralyzing. If you are a Perfectionist, you know that you often get stuck in the throes of this Limiting Habit. The "Perfectionist Habit" relies on the "Logic & Justify Habit" for rationalization of why something cannot be done. Yes, a bit of perfectionism in life is a good thing. Remember, a Limiting Habit is caused by a pattern run amok! In this case most Perfectionists will tell you that the Habit runs them and leads to being in a perpetual state of dissatisfaction, both with their lives and with others.

PATTERN INTERRUPT PEAK LIFE HABITS:

Courage Habit, Detachment Habit, I can Do It Habit, The Right Time Is Right Now Habit, Pattern Interrupt Habit

SL 9.1

Reverse Timeline Scheduling

Reverse Timeline Scheduling (RTS) is a chance to articulate all the steps or milestones you want to achieve along the way to an Outcome you are passionate about. It is the rapid transit system of fulfilled Outcomes by deconstructing your schedule from the end to the beginning. Each step is clarified, invoked and scheduled for Action. A good place to start is to begin with one of those passions you identified in your Passion List on pages 96-97. The magic is in working backwards. The path revealed will lay out the Actions that lead straight to your goal. Reverse Timeline Scheduling is a nifty and straightforward mechanism that also aligns perfectly with accountability, specificity and measurability. This is how you take your life's successes from random to deliberate. Complex long—term and straightforward short—cycle objectives are sliced and diced into easy bite sizes, scheduled and fulfilled. *Voila*, you will arrive at the intersection where your destiny meets Right Action.

Select a role (old or new), select an objective that's worthy to you, schedule time to do some "imagineering" with the Reverse Timeline template, and map out your path of Right Action. Along with the timeline, place the path's coordinates in your schedule, fill up the tank and hit the gas. If there are some Actions you are unsure of, schedule for research time, preparation and follow through. If your "Perfectionist Habit" jumps into the fray, give it a hall pass. Be bold; take Action—even if you are uncertain, the Right Actions will reveal themselves as long as you're moving!

REVERSE TIMELINE SCHEDULING (RTS)

1. Pick an outcome or objective that you want to accomplish:

_____

2. Pick the exact date, month & year to accomplish that by:_____

3. On a separate pad or worksheet, do a little *imagineering* and write down in reverse order, starting with the final Action/Activity that completed your accomplishment.

4. Working backwards from that future date, use the template below or create your own with enough Action dates to list all of the important Actions, dates and milestones along the path backwards from your objective to the final date, which, remember, is for the first Action and is listed as today (placing all of the Actions identified into your schedule would be a good "Today" Action).

5. This method gives you the clearest perspective of the different Action steps and milestones to be met along the way to fulfilling the outcome listed above. Include key Actions and timelines for them, such as research, phone calls, personal/family/career Shifts, applications, conversations, results, classes, tournaments, trainings, steps along the way, etc.

6. Once you have completed the template, place all the Action/milestones in your schedule and fulfill on the Actions.

7. As you follow through on your vigorous plan, be flexible and willing to revise your plan as new information and unforeseen catapult opportunities or obstacles show up.

The key is to work backwards from your desired result/outcome, schedule the Actions in your planner, fulfill the Actions no matter how you feel or what excuses you have, and also to monitor and dismantle any interruptions, distractions, covert sabotage, and anything that your Limiting Habits and events of life place in your path along the way to success. Reschedule any missed Actions and fulfill!

Step by step, the momentum will build and you will achieve your Outcome. Apply both your "Discipline Habit" and "Patience Habit" to this RTS system!

REVERSE TIMELINE SCHEDULE: Outcome Achieved By:_____

Date:_____ Action/Milestone:_____

_____

Date:_____ Action/Milestone:_____

_____

Date:_____ Action/Milestone:_____

_____

Date:_____ Action/Milestone:_____

_____

Date:_____ Action/Milestone:_____

_____

Date:_____ Action/Milestone:_____

_____

Place the Actions and Milestones you identify into your schedule; achieve your Outcome!

* * *

An important aspect of Right Action lies within the combined discipline of being a focused and diligent scheduler along with keeping your word and following through on the Actions you place within your schedule. Therefore, creating a realistic schedule is central to achieving your objectives. This next section gives you the opportunity to upgrade some of your scheduling fundamentals.

CREATING A HABITUALLY GREAT POWER SCHEDULE

- Do you currently keep a schedule?

  _____

- Where do you keep your schedule/what do you use (a planner, PDA, wall calendar, legal or note pad, computer software, Internet-based system, your head, etc.)?

  _____

- Have you been scheduling solely work-related items and appointments, or do you also schedule the other areas and roles of your life, too?

  _____

- What scheduling enhancements and Shifts do you want to put into practice?

  _____

  _____

- What are the Actions you can take to implement those enhancements and Shifts? List the Actions below and then place them in your schedule for completion, being specific and measurable about what the Actions are, when you will do them and how much time you will allocate for them. Filter out hiccups, glitches and any Limiting Habits like the "Procrastination Habit" that get in the way. The right time is right now!

  _____

  _____

- Spread the love. Embed discreet reminders in your schedule to practice your "Acknowledgment Habit." Simple touch points – spoken words of thanks, written notes, gifts, etc., eliminate feelings of anonymity, build trust, and warm the hearts of those around you, yours too.

* * *

Many Habitually Great seminar participants have asked for a scheduling example, and on the next page is an illustrative model of a day in a Habitually Great power schedule – a day-in-the-life of your humble author, in fact. This is an example that may or may not be relevant to you. Your schedule will reflect your life's own cadence. Whether you are young or older, an executive, entrepreneur, working single person with no kids or pets, a home-based Mom or Dad or a primary caregiver, you have plenty to do. Your passions, desires and goals will inform your schedule, making it a daily, living document that is unique to you. For more sample schedules from a variety of walks of life, please visit: www.habituallygreatbook.com.

SAMPLE SCHEDULE

November 12

Notes/Added Action Items

6:30a – 8:15a	Wake-up/Picture the day and set positive intentions! 10-minute cardio warm-up. Organize/help around the house, shower/shave/toilet. Make and drink smoothie. Pack tennis bag and drive to work. (Drink water)
8:15a – 9:00a	Organize files/desk for today. Check and respond to email/vm messages. Reading time (20 mins).
9:00a – 9:35a	Great phone session with client. (Drink water)
9:35a – 10:00a	Meet with Julie, review Q1 program schedule, finalize travel arrangement decisions and workshop locations.
10:00a – 10:30a	Full staff meeting: review workshop handouts, timeline and logistics for today's program.
10:30a – 11:30a	Great phone session with client. (Drink water)
11:30a – 12:15p	Floater for interruptions, schedule changes, errands, calls, etc.
12:15a – 1:00p	Eat a healthy protein/veggie meal at desk, check email/vm.
1:00p – 1:20p	Drive to conference center, relax, get ready for workshop. (No phone calls)
1:20p – 1:45p	Check in with staff, final tweaks on room setup.
1:45p – 3:45p	Deliver fun and focused 2-hour workshop module (this is module 3 or 5), facilitate a good teamwork and accountability shift!
3:45p – 4:15p	Informal time with participants, quick debrief to thank staff.
4:15p – 4:45p	Return to office (15 mins), check email/vm (15 mins). Enjoy fruit snack. (Drink water)
4:45p – 5:15p	30-minute floater.
5:15p – 5:45p	15-min stand-up staff meeting. Finalize tomorrow's schedule/print.
5:45p – 7:15p	Drive to the courts, have a great tennis practice!
7:15p –	Head for home – fun dinner and movie night!

Fig. 9.2

The Habitually Great "Power Scheduling Habit" is a deliberate action structure that leads to inspiration. Yet each day and every life are different. Schedule the level of detail that is right for you and fulfills on what you want to accomplish. Ease up on saboteurs like distress or perfection Habits that engage your thoughts with confusion or aggravation about how to do this right. Monitor for any other Limiting Habits that may arise when you start to schedule this way, because as you step into this structure of Right Action and move steadily towards what you want, old Habits about worthiness and success may be triggered. Beat them down! In the words of William Shakespeare, "Action is eloquence."

If you have a story in your head about the "need" for spontaneity, get over it. Schedule time blocks for spontaneity if that's your thing, and don't let a false belief about having to be footloose and carefree inhibit your success any longer. There is nothing random about greatness; it is intentional and achieved with the support of discipline, follow-through, and scheduling for its occurrence! That being said, schedule time for daily relaxation and vacation time; that way you'll more likely make sure those happen.

A Deeper Look At Spontaneity

At first, Julie strongly resisted being more scheduled. She felt that she would lose her carefully guarded sense of freedom, that great feeling of spontaneity that was so innate to her soul. Julie loved to be spontaneous, whenever and wherever she could be. Yet she was dissatisfied with her life and the gap between where she was and what she wanted to accomplish. At the same time, she was a successful corporate trainer, interestingly, helping others understand how to get things done in teams, build trust and be accountable. Julie's inner conflict is a familiar one. She thought she'd be depressed and feel claustrophobic, boxed in by too much scheduling. Together we explored her Beliefs about freedom and spontaneity, along with how those Beliefs interfered with her being able to take Actions that would fulfill on her dreams and goals. In coaching, Julie took on the practice of creating Habitually Great Power Schedules. She discovered that she liked feeling satisfied and accomplished by moving forward on goals she'd always wanted to focus on.

She also allocated several time blocks in her week with nothing to do, spontaneous time.

No matter how busy we are, personal time is important. I love having blocks of time with nothing scheduled. Then I decide what to do (or not do) in those minutes and hours, whether it is for three hours on a Saturday, an entire weekend, a couple of hours in my midday—midweek schedule, or a long plane ride. If you have a story in your head about the "need" for spontaneity, cut loose from that noose! Allocate time blocks for spontaneity and don't let a false belief about having to be footloose and carefree inhibit your success any longer. There is nothing random about greatness; it is intentional and achieved with the support of discipline, follow—through, and scheduling for its occurrence!

Stop Doing!

A fundamental key to creating a realistic schedule is to generate a Stop Doing list. In many respects technology has increased the pace of our lives—not our happiness. People were happier 40 years ago, and time is one reason why. They had more flexibility with their time and fewer roles competing for it. With the ramp-up of high—speed communication, there are very few moments we have to ourselves. It was not that long ago that a car or train ride was Blackberry and cell phone free, not due to a ban, rather because people simply weren't carrying them. Mail took at least a few days, and fax machines were nonexistent. Even children today are bombarded with the demands of a world that is always busy with communication; kids can't take their bikes out for a spin without a helmet *and* a phone.

With this communication invasion has come a rapid expansion of To-Do's. The requests on our time are endless. Our To-Do list is getting longer as we struggle to do more and more and still never catch up. To master Right Action you must take that deep breath and start saying "No." Your happiness, success, and health are at stake. You know those roles, tasks, and other To-Do's that no longer fit with your plan for greatness. To cross the chasm of the Habit-Gap, you must take the Right Action and Stop Doing them!

Here is the key question: once you know the Right Action, do you have the discipline to take the Right Action? The key is to defeat all your Limiting Habits that have been stopping you from stopping! Are you ready to stop doing a few or several of those things that give you little joy, really aren't that important, can be done by someone else, or are being done because of Limiting Habits like the "Good Person Habit," "Drama Habit," "Domination & Control Habit," "Do It Myself Habit," "Looking Good Habit" or "Obsess Habit?"

It is time to create a Stop Doing List using your "Ground Truth Reality Habit" and then follow through with stopping what you say you are going to stop. This is a nice extension of the work we have done together on the "Saying No Authentically Habit." Which distractions and interruptions are you going to disallow? What activities and Actions are you going to courageously Stop Doing? Clear the pipes by taking Right Action and Stop Doing everything that has you missing your goals, feeling resentful and burning out. This is going to be fun, because you are going to feel refreshed and vibrant. Here is a further suggestion: maintain a Stop Doing list at all times and keep adding outdated Actions and obligations that don't align with your Habitually Great life and cart all the items off to the junkyard. What are you going to Stop Doing? (Remember, the Right Time is Right Now!)

STOP DOING LIST
List Here What You Are Going To <u>Stop</u> Doing

1. I am going to Stop Doing: _____

The Action I've added to my schedule to make sure
I follow through is: _____

_____

I will Stop Doing this: A. Immediately_____ or B: As of this
date: _____

I will contact the following person(s) to inform them of this: _____

2. I am going to Stop Doing: _____

The Action I've added to my schedule to make sure I follow through
is: _____

I will Stop Doing this: A. Immediately_____ or B: As of this date:
_____

I will contact the following person(s) to inform them of this:

_____

3. I am going to Stop Doing: _____

The Action I've added to my schedule to make sure I follow through is:

_____

I will Stop Doing this: A. Immediately_____ or B: As of this date:

_____

I will contact the following person(s) to inform them of this:

_____

LIMITING HABIT SPOTLIGHT:
THE "CAN'T SAY NO HABIT"

We field requests all day and every day from a multitude of sources. In the midst of those we find ourselves saying "Yes" to so many things that there isn't a prayer that we will achieve and accomplish what we've said "Yes" to. And once the overwhelm sets in, we are stuck feeling like the hamster on the wheel, round and round and round we go with no way off.

The "Can't Say No Habit" is one of the first Habits in the cluster when we are experiencing the challenge of a life and a schedule that is too busy, overwhelming, exhausting, etc. Most of us have a slice of this Limiting Habit, and it has a remarkable impact in disrupting our plans to accomplish what we say we want.

Become an expert at saying "No" so that you can say "Yes" powerfully. With the proper language skills, we can become experts at saying "No" while still leaving everybody happy, including ourselves. A simple practice to start now is to say "No" to spontaneous requests for your time and compassionately schedule an appropriate meeting time instead.

Being powerful in saying "No" is as important as being powerful in saying "Yes." Saying "No" authentically is a positive committed expression spoken with clarity and truth, for example: "I'd like to help, and No, I'm sorry, I won't be able to do that." Everyone is better off when they communicate "No" with kind, straightforward honesty. After all, how many times has your Pleaser Habit had you say "Yes" to things you either did not want to do or did not follow through with?

Is your "Can't Say No Habit" burning fires in your schedule? Are you side-tracked by all kinds of interruptions? Take a deep breath and say these words: "I am really buried right now, let's schedule a good time to meet." (That is a kind way of saying "Not right now.")

We respect people who say no. Their integrity draws a clear line, and we trust their "No" and their "Yes." This makes it very easy to communicate and work together. Adapt that style for yourself too, and you will earn greater appreciation and respect from everyone in your life. Oh, and you will be much happier.

PATTERN INTERRUPT PEAK LIFE HABITS:

Saying No Authentically Habit, Putting Myself First Habit, Ground Truth Habit, Power Scheduling Habit, Stop Doing Habit

SL 9.2

You may now want to go back, add to your Stop Doing list, and remember to contact whoever will be impacted by your decision. Schedule those communications. By the way, as you schedule them, practice writing some of those intended Outcomes too. You will enjoy seeing what happens during the actual moments. Follow through and hold yourself accountable for creating some great breathing space in your life and schedule.

Start Doing!

The pathway to Right Action is now illuminated. It is time for the "Saying Yes Powerfully Habit." Where there is something you want to accomplish, your roadmap is clearly marked for how you're going to do it, the way you're structuring it, how you're scheduling it and going to stay in Action to its fulfillment. Greatness happens with discipline and perseverance nose to the grindstone, patiently smiling, knowing that your inspiration will arrive and desired outcomes will become a part of the integration of permanent success.

You may want to leverage your new productivity and success structure Habits by resolving old commitments and resolving some of your old incomplete To-Do's. Areas that are incomplete in our lives take up important bandwidth in our heads, too. A simple practice is to list up to 10 areas of your life where you have made lingering and unresolved commitments—unfinished business, so to speak. Pick the easiest five and schedule the Actions that will tie up the loose ends and complete them. A few authentic "No's" can go a long way in clearing out the congestion. You will feel clearer, stronger and more focused on your future once you resolve the issues and incomplete commitments that have been weighing on your mind today. What Limiting Habits have kept those in circulation? It is your accountability to preempt those and clear the space for your ultimate life!

Now is the right time to throw your hat in the ring and get started. What are you going to Start Doing? (Remember, the Right Time is Right Now!)

START DOING LIST
List Here What You Are Going To <u>Start</u> Doing

1. I am going to Start: _____

The Action I've added to my schedule to make sure I follow through is: _____

_____

I will Start this: A. Immediately_____or B: As of this date: _____
I will contact the following person(s) to inform them of this: _____

_____

2. I am going to Start: _____

The Action I've added to my schedule to make sure I follow through is:

_____

_____

I will Start this: A. Immediately_____or B: As of this date: _____
I will contact the following person(s) to inform them of this: _____

_____

3. I am going to Start: _____

The Action I've added to my schedule to make sure I follow through is: _____

_____

I will Start this: A. Immediately_____or B: As of this date: _____
I will contact the following person(s) to inform them of this: _____

_____

As you become a greater master of time management, scheduling and staying in Right Action, once in a while your "Self-Sabotage Habits" are predictably going to step in the roadway. In those moments, smile knowingly at your old Limiting Habits and then get right back to taking the power, staying in Action. Shift to the "Focus & Clarity Habit" and you will be so organized that you will no longer even have to worry about being organized.

CHAPTER 10

CLOSE YOUR ESCAPE HATCHES

"I've missed more than 9,000 shots in my career. I've lost almost 300 games. 26 times, I've been trusted to take the game winning shot and missed. I've failed over and over again in my life. And that is why I succeed."

—Michael Jordan

In this chapter, we will examine some of the common loopholes that can distract and interrupt the road to success. Where do you waffle and wiggle? Where do you self- sabotage, lose your motivation, bump your head up against a figurative wall? Here, you will find some Right Action tools that can get you back on track when your Limiting Habits take the wheel.

Let's start by examining the Seven Escape Hatches in Figure 10.1 on the following page.

LOCK DOWN THE SEVEN ESCAPE HATCHES

You Believe In "Change A Habit" Timelines

Doom Loops & Optimism Get In Your Way

The Rubber Band Effect Pulls You Back

You Close Your Eyes To The Obvious

You Take Too Much Wiggle Room

Success Ceilings Stop You Cold

Fear of Failure Grips You

Fig. 10.1

How Long Does It Take To Create or Change A Habit?

Since this entire book is about Habits, let's examine this important and oft-debated question. We are a password obsessed society. More than likely you have changed a password at one time or another, replacing an old familiar one with a new one. How many times did you mistakenly enter the old password after you had changed it? Habits become so automated that their shadows remain for a long time during any Shift, making it easy for distractions and loopholes to interrupt our progress. Any time we have a familiar routine, changing it will cause a period of adjustment as we establish new neurological pathways. The answers I have heard with regards to the length of time required to change a Habit range from one second to twelve weeks to one year or more. Repetitive practice is deemed important, with some saying that 10 minutes every day for seven days will do the trick while others offer that 21-days of consistent, repeated practice is the only way to establish a new Habit. Which is the accurate measurement?

Let's be clear about this together: there is no "right" answer. I have never stated a timeline, nor do I believe there is one rule that applies here. Because there is a variable in the equation of establishing any new pattern, practice or Habit: your Habits!

How long it will take you to create a Peak Life Habit or permanently (more or less) interrupt a Limiting Habit depends on several

196

Habit variables in your Habit Cluster: motivation, accountability, distractions, sabotage and excuses. Plus, the time allotted will also depend on your cognitive commitment and follow through in practicing overall Habit Wisdom. Finally, there is the factor of the actual neurological imprint of the old Habit. These imprints are pretty sticky. There have been neurological highways built that lead you post haste to these old nemeses. They can be deeply entrenched. (The Habitually Great workbooks discuss Entrenched Habits in greater detail.) Here is where we apply the three P's: Be patient, persistent and persevere! (Using your "Keeping The Faith Habit" and not your "Optimist Habit.")

The bottom line: there is no accurate answer that applies universally to the timing of changing Habits. So keep the faith! Your accountability is to persevere no matter what gets in the way, no matter how large the effort or length of time. And once you have made the Shift, stick with it.

Doom Loops & Optimism

Often, in a wave of optimism or in quick fix mode, people and organizations rush into Action intending, with the wave of a magic wand, to create a desired result. Welcome to the "Doom Loop Habit." Sound familiar? While Right Action gets you to your ultimate life, the "Doom Loop Habit" keeps people and organizations stuck in a perpetual vicious circle of highs and lows.

Perhaps you have noticed that you repeatedly become inspired by solutions to a long-standing issue or problem and that, despite your confidence, the solutions always fail. Do you work with an executive who is always on the hunt for the next great initiative while at the same time failing to notice that skepticism is rampant? We have all seen examples where people, companies, even whole countries are distressed enough to cause immediate change, yet they fall just a bit short of going all the way. It is the pain of a sudden financial, health, personal, corporate or family crisis that overwhelms them with stress and pressure, causing a jump into Action. Often that Action is short term.

Let's say you are six feet tall and over the holidays your weight ballooned from 215 to 230 pounds. At 215 you were unhappy about it, yet still stuck in "trying" to lose weight, while at 230 you are a bit freaked. At 230 pounds you hit your pain threshold, your distress kicked in – and you became motivated. You headed back to 215 with rigor. As you hit 215 you intended to keep losing weight, however your motivation began to slack and old Habits reemerged. After all, you started well, and the compliments are coming in; people have noticed. The distress has diminished. Even though you know 185 would be a lot better for a 6-footer, your Limiting Habits have returned to power and stopped you along the path toward your goal.

Doom Loops are "flavor of the day" schemes that are unrealistic, usually require a rapid, fast-paced ramp up, and ultimately fail in their promises. If you have an "Optimist Habit" you may inadvertently participate in Doom Loops. You have likely never looked at optimism this way. Part of this is semantics, so don't worry if you've been considering yourself an optimist. Optimism can lead to disappointment because it is not sourced in anything concrete, such as being in Action. Optimism often has no context in reality, just a happy go lucky feeling that ends with a shade of the "Disappointment Habit." An optimist does not confront the brutal facts. This is where _Habitually Great_ varies from the simplicity of the Law of Attraction – it is not enough to simply hope. Seeing reality allows you to be preemptive. Ignoring reality is a set-up for failure. Optimism without hardcore, determined, sustained follow-through is simply a prevailing Doom Loop in the offing.

Here's your caveat: there is nothing wrong with being optimistic; that is perfectly okay. At the same time, you must be aware of its pitfalls and blend it with the "Ground Truth Reality Habit" for real success and follow-through. The best way to Shift is to source your optimism in hope and faith and then remember that hope and faith work together with Habits of Discipline, Persistence and sustained Action. Shift happens because you make it so!

PEAK LIFE HABIT SPOTLIGHT:
The "Ground Truth Reality Habit"

The Habitually Great program is a ground truth reality check about what your Habits (and you) have been up to. Are you really aligned with regards to your goals and desires? Are you really happy? What is in the way? When you peel back your public image, what are the real truths about your station in life? This is the contrast between the Limiting "Official Truth Habit" and the Peak Life **"Ground Truth Reality Habit."**

The "Official Truth Habit" is the façade that you often may live in. Are you putting a positive spin on things to avoid confronting the brutal facts? Are you an optimist with a "Fantasy Habit," pretending that your life is different than it is, avoiding making changes because a Limiting Habit about worthiness, effort or fear is holding you back?

At work are you courageous enough to manage people with accountability or do you choose artificial harmony over productive conflict? Have you been more concerned about popularity than accountability? Your "Official Truth Habit" has kept you paralyzed long enough. It is time to be accountable for seeing the ground truth and taking Action that aligns with your reality.

Additionally, when you apply your **"Ground Truth Reality Habit"** to your Language Habits, you may also see what you have been "trying" or "needing" to do for a long time. If you have been "trying" to do something for three years, the ground truth may be that you are never going to do it.

Look reality straight in the eye, stop dancing around it, and stop making compromises with your integrity. Root out the Limiting Habits that get in the way of your **"Ground Truth Reality Habit."** What are they? Be accountable for being brave, bold and authentic, for seeing the truth in the status of your well being, place and purpose, career and relationships, and be responsible for creating what you truly want, starting right now. Follow the prescription for Right Action with unwavering resolve. Bring some supporting Peak Life Habits along for your **"Ground Truth Reality Habit,"** including the **"Proactive Habit," "Courage Habit,"** and **"Playing Big Habit."**

The "Ground Truth Reality Habit" Interrupts:

Artificial Harmony Habit, Fantasy Habit, Optimist Habit,
Why Bother Habit, Looking Good Habit, Procrastination Habit

SL 10.1

Stepping Out of the Rubber-Band Effect

This may be your first book on greatness or you may buy a lot of motivational, and self-improvement books, sampling one after another. Yet many of us are not able to find the one that truly effects change. Do you have a "Rubber-Band Habit?" Do your inspired breakthroughs and transformations stretch you anywhere from a few hours to a couple of weeks before you snap back to your old ways? As you attain Habit Wisdom, it is your accountability to close the hatch on this pattern, now and for good.

The "Rubber-Band Habit" manifests itself in two ways. One, when we Shift into new Peak Life Habits, we may experience something akin to a gravitational pull, yanking us backwards. Those feelings may manifest themselves through a powerful discomfort with our new successes, Peak Life Habits or goals, because they are very different from the struggle and the suffering that we are used to. Familiarity is a comfortable place to be. In such moments we may actually snap back to our old Limiting Habits and failures because those feelings and patterns are what we are used to. Two, when you put this book down, within a minute or an hour you are likely to have a conversation with someone, get a message or text on your cell phone, check your email, feel pressure about something, and even though you were stretched and inspired while reading these words – BOOM – Without realizing it or making a conscious decision to do so, you have snapped right back into the jaws of a Limiting Habit, triggered by a word, an event, a feeling, you name it.

Any event, circumstance, interaction with our mates, or even something that happens in the news can act as a Habit-Trigger. Because it is a familiar sensitivity trigger (some people call these our "sore toes") from our past, energetically, viscerally or circumstantially, it triggers us right into the old emotions of distress and aggravation along with a "Life's Not Fair Habit," "I'm Not Good Enough Habit" or "I Don't Trust Anybody Habit." When we are triggered, we default to a Limiting Habit and follow our Habit Chain through to completion like a loyal puppy. In other words, we are in a *Habit-Trance*. We don't even notice it because it is so familiar.

STOP! You have Habit Wisdom now and you can STOP skidding off the track. Use your Habit Wisdom to apply a strong and successful Pattern Interrupt whenever you feel the contraction of the rubber-band yanking you back to old Limiting Habits, anxiety or frustration. Your accountability is to keep being the driver and chooser of your Habits in each and every moment. Master these Peak Life Habits: "Being Appropriate Habit," "Detachment Habit" and "Resolving Past Issues Habit." Be accountable and ready to sidestep any hint of the rubber-band snap. Cognitively snip the rubber-band within the guidance system and positive power of your Habitual Greatness.

Preemptive Visioning & The "Proactive Habit"

The Law of Right Action is based on you being preemptive, having forethought *and* foresight into what is predictable and acting accordingly to achieve your goals. That means sometimes you will look down the path you are taking, see where it's headed, and change course. Paradoxically, this will help you stay *on* course. While change is a constant in life, there is much that is predictable, and hence changeable, by you. Most of the areas in your life have just one driver: you. Working through this book, you are now keenly aware of your Habit mechanism. You are also well versed in predictable Outcomes in your life, career, health, and relationships, based on the Habits at play – both your Habits and the Habits of others whose lives intersect with yours. As Einstein wisely said, "Insanity is doing the same thing over and over again and expecting a different result." This rings particularly true once you have acquired Habit Wisdom.

Pause for a moment and select one of your goals to look at with your mind's eye, to discuss with your internal voice. Think about the obstacles that are in between you and that goal. How often in the past would have you waited for those predilections to turn up and then relied on an imprudent knee-jerk from your "Reactive Habit?" Even the Right Actions you commit to may have challenges all of their own, not to mention issues of money, time, other people's demands of you and other roles that require your attention. Are there physical or geographic obstacles in the way of this goal? What other obstacles can be at play here? Which of these could become a stopper? Perfect. You are practicing the "Preemptive Habit." With the answers to those questions, you can make early adjustments to your navigation and action plan.

Now bring in the "Proactive Habit" as your partner. Identify the Actions that will proactively preempt the obstacle(s) you have identified. Make sure those Actions are also in your Reverse Timeline Schedule and of course in your schedule itself. Follow through and preempt the predictable future and instead create your awesome destiny. Fate we lie down for; destiny we create.

One of the first steps in Preemptive Visioning is to start consciously changing your internal dialogue. You may notice where your internal thoughts are perpetuating your Habit-Stamps and Limiting Habits.

Randy wanted to be a better husband. Using his "Ground Truth Reality Habit" he knew he had failed on several levels, including having had an affair. Cindy, his wife, was wary of their future, yet was more comfortable in the relationship than out, and with two small children she also wanted to learn how to be a better mate. Part of Randy's coaching homework was to purchase a book called Love Busters. *Therein lay the rub. A little preemptive visioning is all it took for Randy to ascertain that Cindy would likely have a negative reaction when she saw the title of the book Randy was reading. What was predictable was that this would result in a magnification of her "I Don't Trust Anybody Habit" and create anxiety, which was exactly opposite of what Randy wanted. With coaching, Randy had come to recognize that he was accountable for building an ark of trust, affection and predictability for Cindy.*

Randy decided to be proactive, and he told Cindy: "My coach thought this was a really good book on relationships. It's what he recommends to his married clients so that they can create stronger love and understanding between them." They scheduled time to read the book together, in small bites, during evenings and on Sundays. They committed to finishing and they did within a three-week timeframe. They also preemptively committed to working with an excellent marriage counselor at least twice a month for six months. With some good counseling help, they were able to forge a reinvented relationship based on ground truth, listening and love. Randy preempted his "Self-Sabotage Habit" and learned to be a great and caring husband.

Be preemptive and proactive at work, at home, everywhere. Pre-emptively schedule for the predictable interruptions and behaviors in your work environment and stop playing the role of victim in the face of them. Choose from an "I" place: "I am compassionate and live my life with full integrity." "I stay focused playing in the Action Zone of my life." "I choose not to be distracted." "I schedule time for interruptions. "I keep to my schedule well and reschedule when conflicts arise." "I have great fun following through and succeeding with the dreams and intentions I have for my life." "I am the master of my Habits!"

That's why we call it Preemptive Visioning. The "Preemptive Habit" takes us out of being stuck, when in fact most of the future in many areas of our lives is totally predictable. The Habit-Patterns of individuals, organizations, groups, cliques, teams, etc., are largely established, and yet we have lived until now always being blindsided by those patterns as though "we didn't see it coming." With this Habit we will more readily see the shadowy Habit mechanisms of our own that are ready to be sprung by a hair trigger, and we can put the safety lock on.

You can apply the "Preemptive Habit" and "Proactive Habit" to your schedule. Allocate a two-minute preemptive analysis at the beginning of each day. Look at your plans for the day, sharp shoot for what is likely to veer off course and what Shifts you can make to prevent that before a gasket blows. Make the adjustments, call and Shift a meeting, cancel something, move something, stay rooted with your "Ground Truth Reality Habit" and command your day well. Are you ready for a calmer life that is at the same time more exhilarating, satisfying, and joyous? Then preempt your Limiting Habit inclination for distress and focus on how to make things in your schedule work really well and in sync! Take a deep breath and visualize. Life on earth will always give you speed bumps and curves in the road; the key to handling them is how well tuned your human machine is.

Squash the Wiggle!

An influential Peak Life Habit and Pattern Interrupt is the "Squash The Wiggle Habit." For example, Doug, proud father of two West Point students, has a Limiting Habit called the "Wiggle Room

Habit." This Habit shows up in a few of Doug's important life areas. One is a weight issue that is pervasive in the world today and causes significant health-related issues. His goal is to drop his weight from 230 to 175. He managed to get all the way to 188 and then wiggled all the way back to 210. This Limiting Habit has several other Habits in its cluster, including the "Good Is The Enemy Of Great Habit," "Avoid Accountability Habit," and "Confrontation With Success Habit." The bottom line is that the discipline, rigor and commitment which got him to "almost" became expendable once he was "almost" at his goal. He eased off the gas pedal, somehow tricking his minds into believing that he would coast the rest of the way to victory. Yet he hadn't crossed the finish line.

You've probably had a moment just like Doug. You know what has happened; wiggles reverse your success. We have all experienced this with New Year's resolutions and other determined intentions that we have sabotaged. What have you wiggled on?

LIMITING HABIT SPOTLIGHT:
THE "WIGGLE ROOM HABIT"

Remember a time when you picked a goal, got your act together and did everything right for a while. Yet there was a switch, and somehow you didn't quite attain your objective. Your "Wiggle Room Habit" is the likely demon.

Often people make the mistake of throwing out their accountability structures because they think they have the discipline thing figured out and know just what to do. Even champions have such moments. Tiger Woods is a good example of this. There was a point in his career when he decided he no longer required a coach, so he tossed out his coach for over a year and stopped winning tournaments. This is where good becomes the enemy of great. We begin to feel too good about our progress, become a bit pompous and feel as though we've got it all under control. We say, "Okay, I can manage this by myself." That is the mystical juncture where the covert demons of our internal voices tell us we can throw out the structures and disciplines that supported the Actions that got us to that point. No, we can't! Don't fall for this facade. It will derail you off your path of meeting your goal.

Don't give yourself wiggle room. You want to live in a world of success and greatness. The world of discipline and the results you will achieve, because of that discipline, will give you greater satisfaction than any wiggle.

The key is to interrupt the wiggle! Notice it, STOP it! Put the cupcake down (whatever the cupcake is, for example, an inappropriate communication because you've been so good at being appropriate, skipping a workout or five, being slightly dishonest because you've been so good at honesty, cutting yourself any slack that is out of integrity, distracting yourself with email, other's problems or worries, etc.).

PATTERN INTERRUPT PEAK LIFE HABITS:

Accountability Habit, Right Time Is Right Now Habit, Completion Habit, Teamwork Habit, Pattern Interrupt Habit

SL 10.2

Another instance of the "Wiggle Room Habit" is in a business setting where the bar is set by the competition, and those rivals haven't set the bar very high. Doug's company worked in such an environment:

Doug's commercial development company gave him a handsome living. His sons will be the third generation to own it, yet they are still 10–12 years away from taking the reins. Doug lives with passion and enjoys challenging himself and his business team to become greater and greater. Yet there is a motivational disconnect. As Doug explained: "We're consistently profitable and have plenty of money in the bank. We've got a core of talented people who are more toward the great side, with the good ones and not so good ones carried by the great ones. Relative to our competitors, we are winning the race. Yet we could be so much better. It's like having an elastic waistband that stretches: I don't have to accelerate payables, we've got plenty of orders and in general there is a comfort with regards to being better than the competitors. The general feeling inside the company is that as long as we are ahead of them we are ok! We don't have to be perfect; we just have to be better than everyone else."

Doug is worried; in fact this keeps his mind active at night. He knows that this false bravado of "good is good enough" leads to a gaping vulnerability—especially if a competitor were to change or a new competitor were to enter the market with more rigor and determination.

The challenge for Doug, both in his fitness and at work, is no different than the challenges we all face. How do we motivate ourselves when life is working well in the moment? How do we stick to the discipline and persistence when a little wiggle doesn't appear to cost us that much reversal of fortune?

In Chapter 5, we briefly discussed the motivational aspects of pain and pleasure, which, when we experience them, can give us the proverbial kick in the tush. Yet, as their intensity diminishes, we tend to curtail our grand Action plan and miss the opportunity for true change. The question is: how do you become firmly committed to Action when you are not inspired (or terrified)? Remember, that is where the discussion of discipline starts. During the course of this book we have explored the consistent, diligent and methodical mechanisms of Right Action, regardless of the fear or joy factor. Self-discipline is something that we can teach ourselves at any stage of life. Just because you may have endured a zany home life that interfered with your ability to be self-disciplined, it has no bearing on your ability to implement the Right Action structures now. A company is no different; at any stage it has the ability to change and become disciplined, systematic, focused and accountable. Excuses be gone!

When there are not enough powerful emotional motivators such as fear, joy, pain or pleasure kicking you into sustained action, start with the basics. Discipline and Right Action will take you a long way. You can and must practice them by taking little steps. Just start with one area and follow through. These create more magic than anything you can stir into a pot and sprinkle with hocus-pocus! Here is a quick Habitually Great thought pattern exercise that Doug and I worked on together.

Disciplined "In Order To":

Here's what Doug wrote:

Goal/Aspiration:
To weigh 175 pounds by June 1 (lose 35 pounds in 18 weeks).

I will be disciplined and create Right Action to achieve the above goal/aspiration in order to:
Feel better, to achieve the success, so that my old clothes won't fit anymore and I'll buy a nice new wardrobe, to have a sense of accomplishment, to succeed in anything! It will flow over to everything. I will gain a confidence that I can do anything. I'll be able to get up on 1 slalom water ski much easier (the straight one, not the big easier one)! I'll wear

my bike clothes without being laughed at or feeling self-conscious. I will feel great and light on my feet!

NOW IT'S YOUR TURN:

Goal/Aspiration:

_____

_____

I will be disciplined and create Right Action to achieve the above goal/aspiration in order to:

_____

_____

_____

_____

_____

_____

_____

Using another metaphor let me introduce you to stock car racing (NASCAR style). This is high speed racing around an oval track. For a stock car racer, momentum is everything, as it takes laps and laps to get up to peak raceway speed. If you ease up on the momentum because you've got a nice lead, watch out. The other cars are also building momentum like a slingshot. In one instant they are far behind, so far that you don't even see them in your rearview mirror. Then a moment later, seemingly out of nowhere, a car zooms past and you've been left in the dust. At this point, it is often too late to recapture your lead. The car that passed is orbiting at a much higher sustained velocity. You realize you inadvertently slowed down with the cushion of your big lead, and now there is a lag between you and the fellow who blew past you. This is what happens to companies who ignore the realities of the "Gathering Momentum Habit" of their competitors. They get complacent and – whoosh – they are passed by a competitor they didn't think was viable and run the risk of slipping so far behind they can't get back in the race.

Another great example is Lance Armstrong. When this famous bicycle racer beat cancer and healed his body, he overpowered the odds. Put your Habit Wisdom thinking cap on you'll understand just how he did it. There was no wiggle room, the motivation was unambiguous: life or death He doesn't live in a world of wiggle. He lives in a world of success, really of greatness. And that is where he gets his satisfaction – out of his discipline and the results that arise from his discipline. That is where I want you to get your satisfaction from. I want you to get the satisfaction of the accomplishment of anything you set your mind to achieve. That is far more satisfying and much longer lasting than having a moment of temporary wiggle satisfaction at the cost of the big game.

As you practice Shifting your "Wiggle Room Habit" to the "Squash The Wiggle Habit," you will find that each time it is easier and easier for you to keep your mind's eye directly aligned with your discipline and your aspiration.

Breaking Through Your Success Ceilings

When we start to climb the peaks in many areas of our lives, we may find that on one or two of these journeys our Habits seem more stuck than in others. We may throw up our hands and say, "Help! Why won't these Habits budge?" That's ok! On your journey toward your ultimate life, you can expect to run into a Success Ceiling or two as you step out of your comfort zone of "good." A Success Ceiling is a stationary comfort level, a cap on how successful we are willing to be in a certain part of life. We may fear the accountability of reaching a heightened level of success, so we remain at a lower point instead of breaking through the ceiling to a higher level. We can recognize our arrival at a Success Ceiling when we see ourselves becoming distracted or complacent rather than continually growing better and happier.

Success Ceilings show up in all areas of our lives. For example, you might be great at making money yet at the same time be on your third marriage or in a perpetually rocky relationship. In that case, clearly you have hit your Success Ceiling in relationships. Have you noticed a few areas of your life that are in a plateau (career, relationships, fitness, etc.) or perpetually less than satisfactory? In every real life example we've looked at so far in this book, the individual was pressed up against their Success Ceiling, proverbially bumping their heads at a demarcating line.

Within the shadow of a Success Ceiling are Limiting Habits such as the "Waiting For The Shoe To Drop Habit," "Why Bother Habit," "Procrastination Habit," "I'm Right Habit" and others that determinedly hold you in place. Instead of continuously improving, we get stuck and complacent. As we saw in the previous section, companies have Success Ceilings, too, where they get "good enough" and become complacent. Over time they are eclipsed by their competitors, the ones who are not satisfied with "good."

A Success Ceiling really means that you have hit either a blockage or a comfort level about how successful you are willing to be. Sometimes there is a Master Habit holding you back, such as the "I'm Not Good Enough Habit," "I Don't Trust Anybody Habit" or "Insecurity Habit." Often there is a Belief wedged underneath those Habits about relationships, money, health, etc.

Consider the "Loyal To The Family Habit" from Chapter 3. That Limiting Habit can lead straight to a Success Ceiling. In some instances, as great or as not so great as our parents and early life role models were/are in their successes and achievements, we seem to follow the tracks of their patterns. Maybe we get a little bit ahead, though not too far. Interestingly, sometimes the relationships with our mates seem to have the same dynamics that we didn't like watching with our parents. Have you ever woken up to realize (and perhaps scream silently or aloud), "Oh my gosh, I'm just like __!" That can be a very unsettling wake-up call. Have you noticed that your lack of awesome success in your career, relationships, parenting, fitness, etc., has some hooks embedded in the patterns of your family? We may equate higher degrees of success as likely to cause a disconnect between ourselves and the patterns of family members and others we feel strongly bonded to. Paradoxically, we put the brakes on our potential for greatness.

Remember Lisa, who was the first one in her family to go to college and the first to have made $100,000? She said, "It was really unnerving, you know?" Exactly. Exceeding her parents' success was not part of her pattern. You must deploy your "Courage Habit" and head into uncharted waters and learn how friendly those waters are. You must be the model. Today Lisa is a multi-millionaire who sponsors college scholarships for kids at her former high school.

As you uncover the origins of any Success Ceilings, ask yourself questions such as: Where did I get these Habit-Stamps? What are the originations of my Beliefs? Who owned those Beliefs and then innocently (or not) stamped them into me? What conversations did I hear as a child? What did I observe about success and failure? What did my role models do that I am now repeating? What do I remember my mother or father saying to me? Did they call me a winner or a loser? What messages am I left with in my belief system? What language did they use? What did failure feel like in my family? What were the Success Ceilings that I observed and now have repeated? With my newfound Habit Wisdom, what are the Actions I will take now?

Some Success Ceilings have nothing at all to do with our families of origin; they are all about us. The key is to break through the Success Ceilings that you know are limiting your happiness and potential, no matter where they have come from. When you find yourself bumping against a Success Ceiling, begin by asking, "Why is it that I'm only here and not moving forward in my career and my life?" Then, once you've found your answers, apply Right Action success structures and catapult yourself to the next level of success.

The many real life people you have read about in this book have a common thread: they are just like you and me, and they have blasted through their Success Ceilings! Are you ready to break through to greater heights? Play with this and take yourself to the next level. We always want to be looking for ways to power ourselves through a Success Ceiling and reach the next peak.

Breaking Through
My Success Ceilings

1. A Success Ceiling I am currently experiencing in my life is:

   _____

2. What Master Habits and Habit-Clusters are influencing this Success Ceiling?

   Master Habits: _____

   Habit Clusters:

   Where did these Habits come from? _____

   What Beliefs do they support? _____

3. The Breakthrough Of Success That I Want In This Area Is:

   _____

   _____

4. What Peak Life Habits (pick 3) am I going to deploy to Power me to that new height of greatness and success?

   Peak Life Habit:_____

   Peak Life Habit:_____

   Peak Life Habit:_____

5. Here's My Plan of Action:

   _____

   _____

   _____

   _____

6. I Am Scheduling These Actions To Occur On:

   _____

   _____

Appreciate Your Failures

One of the utmost impediments to success is the "Fear Of Humiliation Habit." Are you afraid of making mistakes? Have you stopped taking risks? Have you ever become depressed over a failure? Failures are often hard to take and difficult to understand. We have all cried pretty hard in moments when failure felt devastating. Paradoxically, when practicing Habitual Greatness, it is easy to see the logical connections between the successes and failures in our lives. One of the very best ways to reach success is by failing. Often it is the only way. To succeed we must grow, expand and learn. The best thing to learn from is our failures. In fact, sometimes the best thing that can happen *is* a failure.

Habitual Greatness includes the extraordinary humility of failure; embrace this and transform your fears, now! Did you ever meet a lucky child who did not fall off their bike while learning how to ride? Seeds of success are within every experience that doesn't work out as planned. Professor Randy Pausch expressed this idea elegantly:

"Experience is what you get when you don't get what you want. The brick walls that are in our way are there for a reason. They are not there to keep us out; they are there to give us a way to show how much we want it."[6]

Right Action embodies the most important learning of all – from failure. Don't allow rejection to derail your dreams.

> ### EXPERIENCE IS WHAT YOU GET
> ### WHEN YOU DON'T GET WHAT YOU WANT

Embrace each adversity as a success being born. Revise your Belief-Links so that you use failures as a springboard for learning and change. What if failures empowered you because of great learning? What if they were something you came to welcome rather than avoid? That is the miracle of practicing the "Learning From My Failures Habit," a Habit that admittedly takes a lot of Habit Wisdom and fortitude to embrace.

---

[6] Dr. Randy Pausch. Oprah Winfrey Show. October 22, 2007.

Robert is an entrepreneur in the process of raising a $15 million seed round of financing to help launch a biotech enterprise. He estimated he would have to approach 300 accredited investors to get 30 to commit the necessary money, and he decided to chart the rejections on a "failure board" along the way. His staff thought he had lost his mind when they learned that they were going to celebrate their rejections and put the letters on the wall. He later conceded that there was a lot of "fake it till you make it" going on at first—even he had to fake feeling good about his initial failures (Pattern Interrupt #1c). He understood that the "Learning From My Failures Habit" acknowledges the statistical predictability of life, which he believed in his case indicated that 300 prospects were more than enough for his financial goals. With that in mind, his team members were not attached to each yes or no, and they could go on to learn from the rejection they encountered on the way to the goal they visualized as inevitable.

In the end, it took fewer than 200 contacts to raise the money. Robert is so convinced of the merits of the "Learning From My Failures Habit" that he is now using it in his search for a perfect mate. He figures it will take 100 dates to find her; he's up to number 35 and shows no signs of slowing down!

Thomas Edison tried thousands of different ways to get the light bulb to work before it did. How many times will you falter on the path to your summits? Learn every day from your failures. Welcome them, even begrudgingly. Remember that you are invoking success, so build a positive, powerful relationship with failure. Don't just beat yourself up. Make it fun! Create some new Habit Chains around failure that reinforce Belief-Links about how virtually every achievement you've ever had occurred after you failed. Anticipate success by letting failures be the signs that success is around the corner!

PEAK LIFE HABIT SPOTLIGHT:
The "Learning From My Failures Habit"

The key to all growth is failure. Failure is how we get to success. We can capture valuable lessons by asking often, "What can I learn from this experience?" This is a particularly important question to ask ourselves if we think a similar situation could arise again in the future.

As you analyze any of your past experiences and or relationships, identify the Limiting Habits that you exhibited during those times. The knowledge will clarify what your mistakes were and how to Shift to more positive Peak Life Habits and Right Action if you find yourself in a similar situation. Be careful to sidestep any regrets, guilt, or shame you may feel as you are remembering. Failures and "almost" moments are the best teachers of all! Accept the life you have lived until now and embrace your humanity, your flaws, your failures and your successes.

The "Learning From My Failures Habit" Interrupts:

I'm A Failure Habit, Blame Habit, Fear Of Failure Habit,
Self-Sabotage Habit, Playing It Safe Habit, Perfectionist Habit

SL 10.3

The key to your inquiry on the next page is to apply your "Ground Truth Reality Habit" and examine an experience you prefer not to repeat. Take a peek at one of your *big* failures and sharpen your Habitually Great practice of growing from the valuable lessons embedded within that experience. One popular definition of insanity is "doing the same thing over and over and expecting a different result." Let's break that logjam. Smile, bite your tongue and get on with it, brutal facts and all. Learn from your failures, appreciate their lessons, and enjoy real progress in your life!

WHAT LESSONS CAN I LEARN?

1. One of my recent and biggest failures was:

_____

_____

2. Identify any Limiting Habits that you exhibited during this experience and what effect they had on the Outcome.

    Limiting Habits: _____

    Impact: _____

3. What lessons did you learn from this experience (or what could you learn)?

_____

_____

4. What Peak Life Habits could have been helpful and will be helpful next time?

_____

_____

5. What could you do differently if this situation arises again? Ask yourself, "How could I be wiser next time? What could I improve? How could I have even greater results?"

_____

_____

6. What preemptive cues did you get that you didn't notice or chose to ignore?

_____

_____

7. What specific and measurable Actions are you going to take? When are you going to take these Actions?

    Action: _____

    I've scheduled and will take this Action on: _____

Action: _____

I've scheduled and will take this Action on: _____

Action: _____

I've scheduled and will take this Action on: _____

The challenge with failures is to learn from them and avoid creating Limiting Habits because of them. That is the difference between running our Habits and being run by them. In Chapter 1, we learned that the very first aspect in the creation of a Habit is a Belief born of an event. Failures are events. Gain Habit Wisdom by learning from and appreciating all of the failures in your life (as well as the successes). Those instances may have a lot more to do with shaping the powerful person you are becoming. Failure *is* one of the most important ways that we get to success. There is even better news: the preemptive aspect of the Habitually Great program is designed so that you can fail less and succeed faster, with great pinpoint accuracy, often circumventing most—if not all—unnecessary failures on the roadway to your successes.

Any Fear of Failure In There?

Another key to Habit Wisdom is transcending any and all manifestations of your "Fear Of Failure Habit." Perhaps the kid in you is afraid of failing and not wanting to disappoint or fall short in any way. Certainly the adult in you gets no pleasure in missing the mark. It is time to Shift. This is the work of greatness. What does failure mean to you and why does it mean so much to you? Where does that conversation come from? Which of your Limiting Habits reinforces your fears of failing? Maybe there is some deep familial grieving because failing meant something unacceptable with your father or mother. Pause right now and locate any stigma of losing and failure and the associated stories in your head. Identify the Habit-Stamp of this conundrum.

There is an inconsistency that you must eradicate in order to fulfill your dreams: if you are afraid of failure, you are not likely to reach your full potential because there are lessons to learn that your Habits will prevent you from experiencing. Your fear blocks the lessons and closes the pathways to brilliance. Untwist all of this! Remember, fears often manifest into reality because of your automated focus on what you don't want. Transform your internal and external conversations about failure, fully embrace and examine the lessons gained, and use that knowledge to propel you to excellence. Play big and if you happen to come up short or lose (it is actually never really about losing because of what you gain in the experience), you will learn things that you never knew you didn't know about the path to that success. Learn to be a great loser and you will win. It is guaranteed, because once you transcend your fear of losing you won't have any issues with all the learning that losing offers. Once you are no longer blocking your passion with a wall of wasteful fear, there will be no stopping you! We have all looked back at the failures in our past and said, "Oh my God." You'll now want to say, "Oh, thank God!" Learn and power forward – you are on the Right Action path.

* * *

Ok. The rubber meets the road right here. Now, what if you look deeper into yourself? Can you open up even more? What are your fears that are still unspoken? What are your ground truths, if you lift the façade? What are you afraid of about your future? What are the vice grips around your heart? What are your pains and distresses that you are still carefully glossing over? Talk about it, think about it, clarify it and put it on the table. Be clear and open about what is really there.

There are plenty of misguided "gurus" in the transformation and self-improvement business who don't want you to even look at that stuff. Their concern is that you will get stuck by focusing your attention on the downside. That *is* the paradox: they misunderstand the leverage of our Beliefs, Habit-Stamps and Limiting Habits. We've got to unplug and flush those out rather than ignore the elephants in the room! If you don't look at all of it, you will limit your possibility and sustainability of change. Those hypnotizing pulls are extremely strong. This is why so many ecstatic "ah ha"s are followed by the same old same old. Confront your fears, confront your unspoken thoughts, confront and reveal the twisters and conundrums that haunt you. Pack them up and move them out.

Take a moment here, go back two paragraphs and answer the questions. Reveal the fears, concerns, deliberations and hyper-extended indecisions. Clear your head by acknowledging the elephants in your room. Those are the conversations beneath the conversation. No more playing it safe by staying on the superficial truth level. What gummed up thoughts are stopping you? What Limiting Habits are running them? Interrupt them cognitively with your conscious mind! Disempower them and let change happen.

* * *

In November of 2007, I was walking on the beach in Maui with Dr. Wayne Dyer after an invigorating swim together. Wayne stopped walking, turned to me and looked me straight in the eye. He said, "Mark, you have to finish your book, you have to finish it now, no matter what hardship that causes, no matter what difficulties that creates financially or with your clients. You have to finish writing your book now!" I knew part of the "hardship" was to combat all my Limiting Habits that had made themselves known for the past few years during the course of this book project: Procrastination, Distractions, Incompletion, Confrontation With Success, and Perfection, to name a few.

I had to apply every Right Action Habit and success structure that I am sharing with you, from Stop Doing to Being Proactive, from Discipline to Teamwork, from Pattern Interrupts to Power Scheduling. Vocally invoking Positive Results Language was a huge challenge. I knew that if I told my clients that I would have Chapter 6 written by the end of December I had no wiggle room, so I went ahead and told them. That was difficult. I like wiggle room. _Habitually Great_ had already been over six years in the making, and I wasn't close to finishing. Sabotage, failure and well crafted excuses were definite options. The rigor, discipline and determined Right Actions also involved some sacrifice, as Wayne had forewarned me, including a lot of solitary time, writing whether or not I felt like it, cutting my income and missing holiday gatherings with friends and family. Some family members didn't understand; some clients clamored loudly. Those hardships are investments. Embrace your aspirations and your world will come around and champion your efforts. You hold in your hands the Outcome. When you point your compass to your "true north," hold onto the location, make your investments and follow your bliss!

Manifest and instill yourself with Right Action and Success Habits to take you beyond where you are, and go to where you want to be in this lifetime. It is the right time to step onto your path of joyful power in creating the life you love. If you are not sure of what the end goal or result is that you want to focus on – it doesn't matter. What is important is for you to be in Right Action throughout your life. Let me invite you to turn the page and open the door to Chapter 11, Master Habit Wisdom. Come on in!

CHAPTER 11

MASTER HABIT WISDOM

"When you are inspired ... dormant forces, faculties, and talents become alive, and you discover yourself to be a greater person by far than you ever dreamed yourself to be."

—Patanjali

Congratulations! You have reached the summit of *Habit Wisdom*, the ongoing mastery of your Habit mechanism. This is the launching pad to your goals and aspirations. From this vantage point you have the power in each moment to circumvent any Limiting Habit that attempts to take over your thought processes and control your Actions. You have the skills and wherewithal to immediately insert and Shift to the control and authority of a Peak Life Habit. You are ready to apply Right Action. You are the master of your Habits instead of an unwitting slave to them.

My intention has also been for you to fully grasp that *all* human beings are run by Habits, and not just the "brush our teeth and floss" kind. One Outcome of Habit Wisdom is expansively opening up to your "Compassion Habit" and "Lighten Up Habit." With your Habit Wisdom you are now an expert on the why and how of the Habit mechanism of both your and those around you. In this chapter we will discuss managing this playful wisdom. Even if someone you know has done many kinds of counseling workshops, and read countless self-improvement books, they still may not be able to Shift. Their Habits are running them, which you can appreciate from you own inquiry in this book!

Now that you have mastered Habitual Greatness, you are well-versed in Right Action. You have the information, the Right Action tools, and the Habit Wisdom necessary to Shift and create whatever you choose for your life. You have the ability to masterfully generate changes and create a life that exceeds your dreams. From all of the previous chapters, you have an overflowing toolbox of training and development. Now the practical application requires just one final spice: the discipline of Right Action. U-Turn your fingers and get started, patiently, step by step. Figure 11.1 summarizes the "Seven Practices Of Habitual Greatness," all of which fall under the Right Action umbrella:

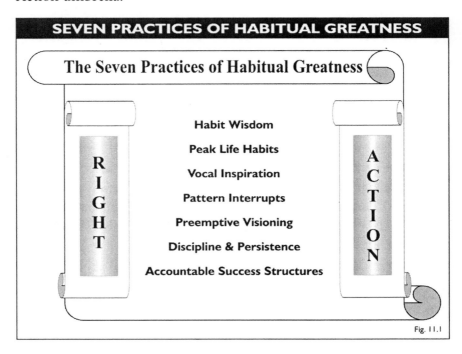

SEVEN PRACTICES OF HABITUAL GREATNESS

The Seven Practices of Habitual Greatness

R I G H T

Habit Wisdom

Peak Life Habits

Vocal Inspiration

Pattern Interrupts

Preemptive Visioning

Discipline & Persistence

Accountable Success Structures

A C T I O N

Fig. 11.1

A Habitually Great Life Is Meaningful

The journey along the path of Right Action is a fulfilling quest of aspiration, not a contrived goal expedition. Have you noticed that we humans don't generally sit around and blindly ignore our immediate surroundings or the world? Even in oppressed societies, people ultimately rise against their oppressors. Kids eventually tire of video games and television and go outside, and while some of us may be pretty good couch potatoes, even the most sedentary among us can Shift to make things happen! This appears quite innate, and it has been going on for centuries. Without JFK's bold declaration that we would put a man on the moon, it is unlikely that such a convergence of Right Action to achieve that goal would have happened. What are your bold declarations?

The goals you focus on are selected by you to fit your shoes. At times, your goals may be sourced in practicality: losing weight, finding true romance (yes, that's practical!), making more money, increasing your education and credentials, creating time for what you love, and relaxing. Those goals are real, important, achievable, and meaningful in the context of your ultimate life.

There are likely to also be aspirational goals, the ones that take your breath away as you think about your place and purpose within their possibilities: the dream of your beautiful wedding, receiving your diploma, being elected President, having a Ferrari in the garage, the birth of your child, traveling the world first class or with a backpack, or winning *your* proverbial Super Bowl. You can imagine the ones that are perfect for you. Some practical goals may inspire you in the same way! The key with all of your goals is to be both aspirational and practical. Think of your fulfilled life in terms of what you want. Pause and imagine the pursuits, pleasures and achievements that are still to come, particularly as you become masterful at their fulfillment.

Sometimes your goals will be laden with passion and the desire for greatness; other times they will be sourced in that oh-so practical side of you. When you blend the two, you will find a deeply sourced motivational combination. In all cases, you must take Right Action to fulfill on your goals. Remember, inspiration comes from the discipline of persistent Right Action along with patience and a good dollop of faith in the form of the "Believe In Myself Habit."

Recently a coach of mine said, "Why limit yourself? How about setting a goal of exceeding any goal you set?" Even the smallest changes in our language can make a big difference in our goal orientation. Picture going beyond, above the top.

At the annual meeting with her sales team, Josie used the phrase, "We've had a very high closing ratio of 35% this year, great work everyone!" I later explained to Josie that while her positive gratitude and acknowledgement to her team was awesome, her phrase made it sound as though 35% is not only acceptable, rather it is also better than normal and leaves nothing more to achieve. Even though she was making a positive and complimentary observation about how high it was, she was capping the possibility. At the next meeting she asked, "Now how about a great conversation together on the pathways to exceeding 40%? Who has some good thoughts on that one?" The conversation that ensued opened doors of Action that she had never considered. By the end of the year, instead of accepting the baseline of greatness as 35%, her sales team put together a 43% closing ratio!

Always focus on and imagine yourself exceeding your goals (whether they are individual and personal for you or a team effort as in Josie's example). Your Actions will surprise you! That is a slice of Habit Wisdom.

A Habitually Great Life is Peak-to-Peak

I use the phrase of Peak Life Habits because a mindfully created life – one that attracts robust success and big happiness – is what catapults us from peak to peak. As you climb the peaks, here is where the cliché "life *is* the journey" completes the picture. The journey is "peak to peak." You are at this peak today and your internal voice has some questions for you: "How do I enjoy this scenery while ascending to the next one?" "How do I traverse the slopes to get there?" "How do I hike that next peak in my sights that I really want to climb?" Peak Life Habits are how.

A discreet little saboteur may come in the form of the following question: "What if everything gets to working so well that there's nothing else for me to do or achieve?" You may start to worry that your work will be done; perhaps you will even become bored with having fulfilled all of your dreams. Some of us have used this very excuse as a reason for why we don't quite get to our ultimate lives. Let's stop that in its tracks! There is good news: there is always a bigger and greater goal to achieve, always another peak to climb that launches you to the next level of joy, challenge and accomplishment. Sometimes you may have a strong feeling that *this* one is the big one, and when you have attained whatever that one is you will have finally made it. This is likely not the case. Often we cannot see what is next until we get on top of the peak we are ascending. Standing on the success of that milestone you will then see all of the mountain ranges that were obscured from view. They were just hidden by the peak you were climbing. You aren't tired when you reach the top of each peak; you are inspired and more committed to climbing the next one. It is all about being limitless in your achievements. You'll say, "Okay, there's the next one. I want to climb that one now."

When you bask in the moments of a great success such as a promotion, financial achievement, communication breakthrough, baby's birth, wedding, degree, fitness goal, etc., savor the wonder of the moment, and then, when you're ready, look at the beautiful peaks from high upon your summit and select what is next. Sometimes it might even be just a great period of R & R. There are so many things in life to take on and experience. Look at what is right in front of your nose and power forward!

You may encounter some familiar Limiting Habits along your path, such as the "Paralysis Habit," "Fear, Doubt & Worry Habit," or the "Seeing What's Wrong Habit." A lot of us create struggle and break down because we are paradoxically more comfortable struggling to achieve success (perhaps an old Habit-Stamp from a distressed childhood) than actually reaching our goals. Perhaps experiencing that anguish feels safer than simply having and exercising Peak Life Habits like the "Success Habit" or the "Being Unstoppable Habit." Here is the good news: don't worry about getting rid of your struggle Habits because this is life on earth. There are periodically going to be disconcerting issues to address in your life. Kids break arms, fender benders happen, people live and die. Why invent things to worry about? Life will give you plenty of challenges. Since your struggle Habits will by default have some air time, perhaps now is the right moment to stop investing in your suffering and start paying attention to Peak Life Habits like your "Going Beyond Almost Habit!"

A final note on distress: great human beings use the energy of aggravation positively! Yes, they use it to focus on improving rather than sabotaging possibilities. This is a simple way to channel your negative energy into positive Right Action. Use your "Seeing What's Wrong Habit" as a starting point. Then Shift to seeing what you want and focus all of that energy on creating exactly that. Channel your negativity into Right Action directed at Shifting your life positively! In other words, don't drop into the "Woe Is Me Habit;" instead ratchet up to the "Taking It On Habit!" Take on the discipline of making the necessary changes while patiently following through, regardless of the chatter that your internal voice offers. Go for the gold medal of success in your life and enjoy the journey, peak by peak!

A Habitually Great Life Harnesses Power versus Force

There is a clear distinction between being determined and powerful versus being forceful. Do you know many forceful people that are also humble and display compelling modesty? That's not a likely combination of Habits. Through his empirical study of greatness, Jim Collins discovered that the most effective style of leadership is determined, modest and humble. With your Habit Wisdom comes the responsibility to be powerful in a new way. Habitually Great leadership is your tangible purpose for life, having what Collins calls "quiet, calm determination…never boastful…never blaming other people…[giving] credit for success to other people and good luck… demonstrating an unwavering resolve to do whatever must be done."

That's the practice of the "Power (vs. Force) Habit," and what Collins calls "Level 5 Leadership,"[7] the top wrung.

PEAK LIFE HABIT SPOTLIGHT:
The "Power (VS. Force) Habit"

When we use our power, we attract what we truly want through Right Action. When we use force, we impose. Even if we are able to force results into existence, the Outcome will be at the expense of our health, attitude, relationships and long-term success.

Realizing our own personal power our agency in every situation allows us to take on our lives. Our goal is to be powerful about focus rather than trying to force an outcome. The "Power (vs. Force) Habit" is about cognitively using our minds as the most powerful place to be, and taking Actions that champion our commitments, dreams, intended outcomes and delights.

As we play with this Shift, we will start to notice when we are making other people wrong and then be able to take our fingers and pull them back into a U-turn toward ourselves. Instead of blaming and forcing others, we will check in with our own power and vulnerability. Powerful human beings are compassionate and let other people be who they are. If a mate or employee doesn't fit in with what you want, forcing them to fit your mold won't work. Powerful people recognize that and communicate authentically and make appropriate decisions that support their life's goals. Power is about being centered, appropriate and clear. There is an identifiable feeling of balance and core focus when your "The Power (vs. Force) Habit" reigns.

This Habit is also about using positive language. Use the "The Power (vs. Force) Habit" to practice (with patience and persistence) your mastery of Positive Tentative and Positive Results Language.

The "Power (vs. Force) Habit" Interrupts:

Blame Habit, Forceful Habit, Bully Habit, It's All About Me Habit, Being Critical Habit, Domination & Control Habit, Self-Sabotage Habit

SL 11.1

A key to power is listening well with a larger openness in your heart. Be more willing to hear others and accept their truths as being just as important and real to them as yours are to you. Remember, their Habits are often the determinants of their perspectives, and you know just how strong Limiting Habits like an "I'm Right Habit" can be. You will be practicing the "Great Listener Habit." As adults, the power of vulnerability is not a sacrifice of power; it is about being open so that the world can communicate with us and we can really

---

[7] Collins, Jim. *Good To Great.* (HarperCollins, 2001, p. 36.)

hear. Information is where the power is, and one of the best ways to be powerful in the world is to be wise in the world. Powerful human beings are compassionate and let other people be who they and their Habits are. Take notice when you are making other people wrong and U-turn your finger. Instead of blaming, check in on and access with intention your own Habit Wisdom center of power and openness.

For an illustration about the "Power (vs. Force) Habit," turn to the Middle East, a tinder box for eons. Force does not work in the Middle East, yet it is ever-present. Making somebody else wrong is often an escape from dealing with ourselves and the mistakes we are making. It seems that history has all parties in the Middle East pointing fingers at someone else, never back at themselves. It's no wonder there has yet to be a long-term resolution and peaceful co-existence. It is the same in our own lives. Behaving in a righteous and forceful way, focusing on problems with disregard for synergistic, healthy solutions, makes situations worse and stymies the path to your ultimate life. Be a model of the Shift from perpetual internal sabotage and blame to a paradigm of camaraderie and resolution.

Powerful living is an exceptional slice of Habit Wisdom, and it requires a deft touch of focus, discipline and humility as you make the Shift from force to power in your family, career, hobbies, fitness, nutrition or any other area. Put a spotlight on your "Create Destiny (vs. Fate) Habit," "Great Listener Habit," "Teamwork Habit" and "Leading By Example Habit." Focus on Right Action combined with your "Power (vs. Force) Habit" and bring masterpieces of joy to fruition.

Modeling: Who Are You Doing This For?

Who are you doing this for? A healthy answer is "me." Just like when the stewardess instructs you that when the oxygen mask pops out of the compartment, put yours on first. The best way to help others is to focus on the truth in your heart, your life, your happiness, and create it well. That may sound counter to the Habit-Stamps in your family of origin. It may even sound selfish and narcissistic. Now let's look closer. The path to Habitual Greatness is taken with integrity and perseverance. Who do you have the most influence over? U-turn your finger. What is the best way to influence your peers, staff, family, the world?

Think back to what Nelson Mandela said:

And as we let our own light shine, we unconsciously give other people permission to do the same. As we are liberated from our own fear, our presence automatically liberates others.[8]

[8]Who do you respect the most? Who do you most want to emulate? Who has inspired you with their approach to life? Are they living their lives to influence you, or are they living their lives well because that is who they are? Ok. There's your answer. We are often influenced by people we respect, appreciate and admire, those who live well because they choose to. They focus on their place and purpose.

Whether you are aware of it or not, people watch you and even make decisions in their lives based on observing yours. Yes, you are that powerful. It is time to be responsible for that power. You are always modeling for someone: a coworker, child, friend, even strangers. The "Modeling Well Habit" is the best way we can help people find their own path. Yet there is nothing for us to do except focus on being exceptional with who we are, how we behave and what we achieve. When you do things because of your commitment to your own joyful excellence, others will notice. We look for examples that support who we want to be in life. We search for mentors. Accept the role, accept the light, and enjoy the "Modeling Well Habit" with humility and grace. Michael Jordan won't walk out of a hotel room unless he is in a crisp suit and tie. He carries himself with dignity and grace in his manners, language and generosity. He knows he is always modeling on an international stage. As it turns out, so are you, even if the stage is smaller.

---

[8] Williamson, 190.

All organizations have energy – and it can be either positive or negative – that reverberates from the top down. This is what I call the *Pyramid Effect*. Even if you don't happen to be the head of a company or your family, as the CEO of your life you are at the top of your personal organizational chart. In this position, you cannot expect people around you to be any better than you are willing to be. Your behavior—what it is and is not—will be emulated. Take the example of accountable communication: keeping your commitments to people is the key because the Actions are more important than words. So if you say to Drew or Matt or Carol—anybody—that you are going to get them something by Tuesday, then make sure that you get it to them by Tuesday. If at the end of Tuesday you don't have it to them, put it in your schedule to update them. Send them a note or call saying, "I know I promised it by today. I did not complete it and I apologize. I'll have it to you tomorrow at 5:00 pm." It's that simple. *You* create the culture that exists around you. Because of the Pyramid Effect, your style of leadership, level of accountability and Habits are likely to permeate many others in your life.

Most importantly, you are modeling for children. In Chapter 3, we discussed how what you say matters a lot to the children who watch and listen, often creating Habit-Stamps and Beliefs in their own minds about happiness, success, worthiness and failure. The good news is that in addition to what you have been saying, your Actions are a model for them. Ultimately it is what you do in your life, with your Actions, integrity, successes and failures that they will come to emulate. If you disappoint them, if you consistently fall short, if you are sloppy, if they see you blame others and avoid accountability, then that pattern is likely to be Habit-Stamped into your kids, too. Now here is the beautiful thing about modeling for kids: if you keep growing, Shifting and improving, it is likely to have an indelible imprint in the children who witness you even when they are in their 20s, 30s, and beyond. Be unstoppable and those you love just may catapult their lives too.

PEAK LIFE HABIT SPOTLIGHT:
The "Teamwork Habit"

The "Teamwork Habit" is an important Right Action Habit. Every day you participate in teams within all of your roles. You create a "team" in your personal relationships, with co-workers and staff, children, relatives, in your everyday interaction with vendors, doctors, coaches, trainers, friends, etc. Teamwork catapults your aspirations and accelerates the achievements and joyful circumstances you desire. Importantly, it also places you into the larger context of the help you can offer to others, opening your heart with both the "Humility Habit" and the "Modeling Well Habit."

The foundation of the "Teamwork Habit" is trust, starting with trusting the people at home, working, carpooling, or telemark skiing. Not blind trust, but rather the trust of knowing that they are capable, smart, effective human beings with their unique bundle of Habits, just like you. Trust that everyone around you has Limiting Habits and Peak Life Habits. Discern what Habits they have and recognize how those Habits will impact your teamwork with them. That is your responsibility and it disengages your "Seeing What's Wrong Habit." Is there a team you're on where trust is broken or seriously impeded? Here's an interesting nuance: if you don't trust a situation, group or individual, trust them not to be trustworthy. Because trusting people to be who they are and who they are not gives you a lot of freedom.

Some teams we are on are not by choice; for example those with our siblings, kids and parents, even some with our co-workers and classmates. Our accountability with those teams is to be responsible for our Habits and wise, compassionate, and preemptive about theirs. There are many teams you build and select, even your marriage(s). In those cases, participate on your team with compassion and wisdom, using the balance of your "Being Appropriate Habit" and "Authentic Habit." Hold yourself accountable for your impact and manage your "Cut & Run Habit" while at the same time improving or changing your teams when there is a mismatch, calling on your "Ground Truth Reality Habit" (remember that Peak Life Habit is also a "U-Turn My Finger Habit") and taking Right Action in order to fulfill on your goals and happiness.

Teamwork synergistically blends with the "Healthy Vulnerability Habit." Recognize the strengths of others; acknowledge and ask for assistance in areas that you are uncertain or weak, as well as the areas where you can just use some help. Build great teams and you will climb the highest peaks, individually and together!

The "Teamwork Habit" Interrupts:

Difficult To Deal With Habit, Seeing What's Wrong Habit,
I Don't Trust Anybody Habit, Doing It My Way Habit, I'm Right Habit

SL 11.2

Integrating The Shift From Your Limiting Habits

Take a moment to go back and review Figure 2.4 (page 31) in Chapter 2, looking at those Limiting Habits that are the big ones, the Master Habits. They have always been in the background. You know what they are there; a handful became your allies in those "almost" experiences. The idea of being Habitually Great is not that they go away, rather they Shift—you Shift with them. They are muscles that are so well defined, so familiar that they are part of your emotional constitution and how you live life.

Your Limiting Habits have served you. For example, if you are obese because you don't want intimacy, your Limiting Habits have worked. If you are impoverished because you are afraid of success, your Limiting Habits have worked. If you are distressed and aggravated because of what's wrong, your Limiting Habits have worked. Limiting Habits have been your allies and they have served their purposes.

The time for change is now. Those Habits are no longer useful. You are ready to address your ground truth and Shift your path from "almost" to all the way.

INTEGRATING THE SHIFT TO YOUR PEAK LIFE HABITS

How are you going to deconstruct your Limiting Habits and build the muscle of your new Peak Life Habits?

Step 1: There are a few Limiting Habits that are your core foundational "Master Habits" and have a tendency to show up more than others. List two or three of your Master Limiting Habits that you've been most run by in your life:

1. Master Limiting Habit:_____

2. Master Limiting Habit:_____

3. Master Limiting Habit:_____

Step 2: Now, since you know the Limiting Habits that stop you from reaching your goals, what is *your* personal formula for Right

Action going to be? The core formula is about identifying the Limiting Habit that is rearing its head, naming it and then choosing one of your Peak Life Habits to step in and create the change. Apply the Pattern Interrupt that performs best for you. These steps are yours to identify and integrate. The best formula is the one you create for yourself, as it is personal and unique. This is where you access your own personal power. You create the specifics of how the change is going to occur.

Reference the Shift Chart on pages 261-271 or Figure 4.6, the Top 15 Peak Life Habits (page 80) and see which Peak Life Habit intercepts the Limiting Habit and changes the whole paradigm, causing you to look through a whole different lens within yourself:

1. Peak Life Habit:_____

2. Peak Life Habit:_____

3. Peak Life Habit:_____

Step 3A: Here's the fun and powerful part. What are you going to do to take steps to integrate this Shift? How specifically are you going to be deliberate, intentional and aware as you develop that Peak Life Habit muscle? This is your internal tracker. The list you make below is the one that tells you how you will know that the new muscle is well defined and working. "Here's what I'll be doing instead of being stuck."

- _____

- _____

- _____

Step 3B: Now finish your formula by defining specifically and measurably how the world around you will know that this is different, that change has occurred and been implemented in the way you now live your life. List the tangible Shifts by which your family, co-workers, and friends will know that a significant change has taken place. They will know and notice because:

- _____

- _____

- _____

You have set up a powerful accountability within yourself to step past any barriers. Good. Now walk straight to your ultimate life!

* * *

When Roger Bannister became the first human being to run the mile in less than four minutes, he broke more than a Success Ceiling; he broke a Belief barrier. He stepped out of the box that said humans could not run a mile any faster than four minutes. Who makes our boxes? We do. What box are you challenging yourself to step outside of?

Take some time and focus on what it is that you want to do and who you want to be in this lifetime. What do you want to create and become? What are your dreams and passions? What roles are you playing in those? What are your challenges? What can those challenges teach you? Have fun! If you get the lesson, they will go away. Are you committed to transforming your life? Are you ready to step into your ultimate life?

How does change happen? Call off your search. The answer is within you. (It's not a sound bite coming from me.) You have all the answers inside that you have been searching for. Your reading of this book simply reinforces those truths while providing you with more tools to listen to your inside voice.

No Finger Pointing!

Don't "try" this at home! If you have already begun doing this, immediately retract all those fingers pointing at your friends and family, the ones making comments such as, "You've got the 'Seeing What's Wrong Habit,'" or "There's your 'Insecurity Habit' again" or "You're stuck in your 'Avoid Accountability Habit!'" They are not likely to appreciate your uninvited newfound perspective and instead will look at you like you are off your rocker. They don't have the Habit Wisdom that you have gained from reading this book. It is better to be kind, playful and gentle with those around you. Buy them their own copy of this book and take them to a Habitually Great program!

In the meantime, lighten up and see the ground truth reality: we've all got people and circumstances in our lives that push our buttons, those sore toes that trigger our emotionally charged Limiting Habits. That doesn't simply change when you do; after all, their Habits are running them. What has changed is your interior landscape and management of *your* Habit mechanism and understanding of where they are coming from. Those insights are invaluable in human interaction. Since we can't change people (even though we all know we "try") imagine now the folly of attempting to change someone when they are not even in charge. As you take on your Habit Wisdom, develop a "Lighten-Up Habit" and keep a sense of humor and playful detachment. Have a nice laugh about how futile it is to be upset – after all, no matter how much they may want to change too, they haven't yet chosen to do so. You could even share this program with them and they still may not change, because human beings change when they want to, not when you want them to. Lighten up, go play with life and go for your own joyful greatness!

When you find yourself reacting to someone or something, look to see which of your Limiting Habits they are inadvertently triggering. Be accountable in your self-reflection and assessment of what is truly going on. Is it your "Insecurity Habit," "Avoid Vulnerability Habit," "Disappointment Habit" or "Anger Habit?" Remember, when your emotions rise, your intelligence declines. In that moment use your Habit Wisdom, be compassionate and generous and work with *their* Habits. In other words, if you know your co-worker or mate has an "Avoid Vulnerability Habit," with your Habit Wisdom you know not to challenge their vulnerability or insist on it because, after all, they are determined to avoid it. Make sure their vulnerability is protected and cared for so that their Limiting Habit doesn't get triggered.

When you are interacting with a loved one, family member, friend or co-worker, do not expect them to be different from whom they are – no more blaming them for what they cannot change. Remember, they are run by their Habits and not the other way around. What Habits do the people around you have, and how can you adjust to accommodate those? It is powerful to be able to take responsibility for whatever crosses your path in full preparedness and awareness using your "Walk My Talk Habit" and "Responding (vs. Reacting) Habit."

When you choose your mate, your job and your friends, you take on their Habits, too. You can predict how they will and won't be, and that is data you can work with. Apply your Habit Wisdom with evocative compassion and power. Here's an example:

Jean made an agreement with her husband that they would stop drinking. Jean had already quit, and she felt strongly that they would stop arguing if alcohol was taken out of the equation entirely. David recognized the problem, too. One of Jean's Master Habits is her "Insecurity Habit," while David has a dominant "Avoid Vulnerability Habit." What do you think was the predictable Outcome of this agreement? His "Avoid Vulnerability Habit" took over immediately, and he created all kinds of "special occasions" to continue his social drinking, which triggered Jean's "Insecurity Habit." This became a Habit-Duel.

For most couples, Habit-Duels are oil & vinegar Habits that lead to consistent unhappiness and often, divorce. Jean (who had taken a Habitually Great workshop), interrupted the pattern and invited her Habit Wisdom to take over. She made a conscious decision to choose David and his Habits. Jean recognized that David's "Avoid Vulnerability Habit" had to be carefully soothed. With Habit Wisdom, knowing that this Habit runs him, she substituted her "Compassion Habit." Together they modified their agreement and made a "special occasion" list while including a reasonable cap on the number of drinks David would have on those occasions, giving his "Avoid Vulnerability Habit" room to breathe and her "Insecurity Habit" a timeout. Great solutions make all the difference in creating a Habit Shift.

Theirs is a happier marriage because of Habit Wisdom. Jean, instead of being triggered into the "Seeing What's Wrong Habit," "Being Critical Habit" or the "Domination & Control Habit," made a much more powerful choice. That was a choice of Habit Wisdom, with compassion and the possibility of happiness. Soon thereafter David quit drinking on his own.

Habit Wisdom is the ability to begin seeing what is predictable based on life experiences and the Habits we create during and in the aftermath of those events. Let's take a look at what would be predictable for a person if they had a devastating abandonment experience as a young child, such as a parent dying or leaving them behind. With the Habit-Stamps from that experience, a person would likely create Habits where they could (to the best of their ability) avoid risks of vulnerability, particularly as it relates to commitment, in order to preclude that terrible feeling of abandonment from ever reoccurring. Tragically, this would limit their lives as the "Fear of Abandonment Habit" and "Avoid Commitment Habit" would likely be running them. The following Habit-Pattern would likely be established: they become "leavers" who leave people, jobs and situations before those situations can leave them. This way they protect themselves from the risk, pain, vulnerability, etc., of being left or not being in control of how something ends. This is a misuse of the "Being Preemptive Habit!"

That example is what really happens. You likely know someone who has demonstrated this and other Habit-Patterns. You can really Shift to that wise place of compassion and generosity of letting people be who they are as well as (here's the key) *who they're not*. Smile wisely with the knowledge that it is essential to respect differences...look in the mirror as no two people are alike! This is life on earth. People are perfectly imperfect, and you are in training to discover your Habit Wisdom and also practice your "Detachment Habit" so that you can allow other people to have their Habits and to understand with compassion that Habits run most of us. If you want them enlightened, share this book or get them their own _Habitually Great_ book or a ticket to a Habitually Great Workshop. In the meantime, no finger pointing at their Habits; they won't understand.

PEAK LIFE HABIT SPOTLIGHT:
The "Detachment Habit"

Emotions up; intelligence down. That inverse relationship is overlooked by most of us when in the throes of a Limiting Habit. Executive and personal decisions made in the midst of triggered emotions are not often brilliant. Choosing the "Detachment Habit" allows us to pause and Shift to Right Action
.

The "Detachment Habit" is an important cog of Habit Wisdom because it allows us to make choices that are appropriate; and from it we gain clarity and level-headedness. It is an important antidote to many Limiting Habits, including the judgment, distress, drama and finger-pointing ones. When we are detached we don't need to struggle, we don't need to be right, we don't need to win and we don't need to lose. This Peak Life Habit is a great stepping stone in a Pattern Interrupt moment and is the source of centered, powerful decision-making.

For example, Rachel became an expert at shifting to the "Detachment Habit." She had been highly emotional, on and off stabilizing medications, and was a true drama queen. Then, after several months of Peak Life Habits coaching, discipline and Pattern Interrupts, she found herself consistently in a new frame of mind that she described this way: "Detachment is being revitalized and fully present, energized, reengaged and recommitted. It's like you wake up one morning and the Shift has happened." Shift Happens.

Often you will simply notice that a Shift has occurred, like Rachel did, after a healthy period of time of working to be detached. There are many practices that help with detachment, from spiritual to meditation to great workouts.

Detachment has nothing to do with indifference. This is about being detached from the hook of Limiting Habits and putting yourself in the "zone." You know it when you feel it: the freedom to be fully present and accountable, being wise in your thoughts and actions, fully availing yourself to people, moments and situations. What we will be detaching from is the Limiting Habit attachment of doing things our way, suffering, making a situation all about us, assigning distress, aggravation and meaning to the events in our lives. Detachment allows us to make choices that are appropriate and level-headed. Detachment is akin to being clear-headed, powerful and compassionate.

Practicing the "Detachment Habit" brings you to a high level of discipline while relaxing your stranglehold on struggle and force Habits. It's like instantly saying to yourself: "Hold on. Let me detach; what Habits would be better in this circumstance?" Then consciously choose those Peak Life Habits.

The "Detachment Habit" Interrupts:

Obsess Habit, Righteousness Habit, Can't Let It Go Habit, Defensive Habit, Fear, Doubt & Worry Habit, Life's Not Fair Habit

SL 11.3

Compassion, Happiness & Balance

Compassion

Recently I asked a client, Kyle, a psychologist who was good at taking care of everyone else except himself, the following question: "If you were compassionate with yourself in a generous way, what would that look like?" Our discussion follows:

> Kyle: "I think it would be with me taking more time off for myself and doing the things that I want to do, interests that I have for myself."
>
> Coach: "Good, like what?"
>
> Kyle: "Well, I've wanted to get back into flying. You know, to get my pilot's license. I started probably seven years ago."
>
> Coach: "What else? What else if you were compassionate with yourself and really gave yourself some loving?"
>
> Kyle: "I want to be with the right partner...someone who is smart and sexy and compassionate and clear-headed and loves me for who I am. And does pretty well financially also by herself – how about that? Yeah!"
>
> Coach: "What else if you were being compassionate with yourself?"
>
> Kyle: "I want to move into a nice, bigger house that is clean and organized."
>
> Coach: "You want to be with a really terrific partner. And have a bigger home and a nice clean space that's organized. And fulfill your dream of getting your pilot's license."
>
> Kyle: "Yeah, and I want to be financially secure."

Coach: "So what do you want? Picture your liquid net worth. Being compassionate for yourself and specific… What do want to you have?"

Kyle: "Well, I'd like to have seven-figures, with a lot of it earning a high rate of return."

The discussion drilled down to several more particulars with clarity and detail. It is important to be specific in creating the change that you want. Remember, being specific and measurable is where all aspirational goals start! Make sure your mind has the clear picture. If you just say, "I want to make more money," be prepared for the possibility of a few dollars more, even a penny more. If you say, "I want to make $150,000 more," now you have a data point around which you can create a Right Action success structure.

Kyle had created a structure for success and accountability (he has a coach), and he had already tackled some other elephants (Limiting Habits) along with having ended a toxic relationship that was in the way, so the likelihood of his achieving his goals became pretty high. Will he be happy? That is a good question. Let's extend our discussion about compassion into happiness.

Happiness

Bob Lutz, perhaps one of history's greatest, most admired and respected automotive executives, was asked at the age of 75, "What's your idea of perfect happiness?" His answer was: "Having enough material wealth where you feel no financial stress and being surrounded by humans and animals that you love and they love you."[9] That is one of my favorite definitions. The key word in that last sentence is "my." What is *your* idea of perfect happiness? That is the one that matters.

Perhaps a better question is the Habit Wisdom question: "What's in the way of my happiness?" That is the question this book and all Habitually Great programs tackle. What stops you from feeling and being joyful, successful, healthy, happy, relaxed, balanced and

---

[9] Lutz, Bob. *Automotive News* (March 19, 2007. 4.)

content? What gets in the way of your heart's desires? Answering a question about happiness by definition requires that you start by looking at what is in the way of happiness. *Beliefs, Habit Chains and Limiting Habits are in the way of happiness.* Mastering your Habitual Greatness and the law of Right Action will get you all the way to your ultimate life, *your happiness.*

> ## HABITUAL GREATNESS AND THE LAW OF RIGHT ACTION
> ### WILL GET YOU ALL THE WAY TO YOUR ULTIMATE LIFE:
> #### Your Happiness

Chasing after wealth and prestige is not a guaranteed formula for happiness. Data suggests that once our basic needs are met, money does not buy additional happiness (though the material dreams we realize are often the source of an aspiring smile). Money comes with its own set of issues; the more you have does not diminish the issues, rather simply changes them.

In his book, The Happiness Hypothesis, Jonathan Haidt summarizes the following:

"Happiness is not something that you can find, acquire, or achieve directly. You have to get the conditions right and then wait. Some of these conditions are within you, such as the coherence among the parts and levels of your personality. Other conditions require relationships to things beyond you: Just as plants need sun, water, and good soil to thrive, people need love, work, and a connection to something larger. It is worth striving to get the right relationships between yourself and others, between yourself and your work, and between yourself and something larger than yourself. If you get these relationships right, a sense of purpose and meaning will emerge."[10]

Throughout this book, we have been working on the "conditions" as Haidt aptly summarizes. Getting the conditions right requires a lot of bulldozing of our Limiting Habits and reforestation with Habit Wisdom. Creating the conditions of happiness in conjunction with

---

[10] Haidt, Jonathan. *The Happiness Hypothesis* (Basic Books, 2006. 238-239.)

disciplined adherence to the principles of Habitual Greatness is our work (or play) for all ages and times in our lives. Whatever you decide happiness means to *you*, it is yours to define. The sky is the limit!

The Balancing Act

Here is the final elephant in the room of change and happiness: how can you achieve real happiness if you are spending the majority of your days distractedly managing the busyness of your life? What can you do to Shift your roles and Habits effectively in order to allocate time and establish the conditions of happiness and the accomplishments you desire? You are accountable for putting Peak Life Habits into practice, as well as the important Right Action structures that will liberate you. Remember, a key Peak Life Habit is "The Right Time Is Right Now Habit." Create a Right Action success structure. Become a leader in the "Saying No Authentically Habit" with compassion and authenticity so that you can practice the "Saying Yes Powerfully Habit" with confidence and truth. Begin immediately to take Right Actions that invigorate your place and purpose in the here and now and for the future. Start to live in ground truth reality about how much time there really is in a day, a week and a lifetime. Focus your time well.

Here is an important Habit Wisdom recommendation: hire a coach! Having a coach will help you see what to delegate, what to hand-off, what to Stop Doing, and it will assist you in the accountability of creating a life you truly love. If you think you don't have time for a coach, think again. Purposefully select a coach who will help you learn to prioritize your roles, get into ground truth reality about your life and hold you accountable to making real Habit changes. If you feel you don't have a budget for a coach, then hire one that fits within your budget. Throw out your "Excuses Habit." With a coach as your ally, you will limit your wiggle room—always a good thing.

That said, not having a coach means nothing – in other words, no excuses allowed here! This book provides you with all the means required for you to become Habitually Great and master the Law of Right Action. You can do all of this yourself, every part of it! That's what this book is for. Create the results and joys you desire; everything is within these pages. Dig in, get to work, stay with it and go all the way to your ultimate life. Just do it!

The View from Up Here

Your Habit Wisdom provides insights into the Habits of your colleagues and loved ones, and you may even see that their Habits and your Habits are sometimes in direct confrontation with each other. For instance (look out!), sparks can fly when an "I'm Right Habit" meets another "I'm Right Habit." With Habit Wisdom you are accountable. You can choose to immediately side-step whatever gets in the way of your balance, detachment, compassion and greatness, and you can bring yourself right back into your power center.

Habit Wisdom is what allows us to live in harmony with those around us. By gaining a breakthrough understanding of our own humanity, we can accept our foibles and become compassionate with ourselves and others. In short, we acquire the strength to release our Limiting Habits and instead learn to be more forgiving, show acceptance, patience, understanding and love. On the next page you will find a Peak Life Habit spotlight illuminating the power of your "Compassion Habit," leading you to more smiles and a hearty dose of the "Lightening Up Habit."

PEAK LIFE HABIT SPOTLIGHT:
The "Compassion Habit"

The entire Habitually Great program is steeped in the *"Compassion Habit."* Compassion works on many levels. Compassion walks hand in hand with appropriate and authentic communication and ground truth reality. The distinction of the *"Compassion Habit"* is to be satisfied with who you are and compassionate with others. In the card deck of Habit Wisdom, compassion is the ace of hearts.

a. Even if someone you know has experienced many sessions of counseling, coaching or workshops, and read every self-improvement book, they still may not change and may not be able to change. Habits can be pretty tenacious! Your *"Compassion Habit"* helps you stop judging and better understand this predicament in yourself and others.

b. In the important arena of the *"Teamwork Habit,"* use your *"Seek First To Understand Habit,"* and *"Great Listener Habit"* to become more powerful, compassionate and effective in groups and with others. You will build a lot of trust with your *"Compassion Habit"* leading the way.

c. Stop thinking that when someone steps on one of your "sore toe" Limiting Habits that they are doing it intentionally. Habit Wisdom mandates that your "It's All About Me Habit" detaches in those moments and that your *"Compassion Habit"* takes over. Most of the time those other innocent souls are not aware of and have no power over what they are doing; their Habits are in charge.

d. Most of the circumstances in your life you have helped create and you retain the power to change. So lighten up, have compassion, relax. Take Right Actions with the *"Gathering Momentum Habit."* Be compassionate along the way.

Interrupt virtually all Limiting Habits with your "Compassion Habit!"

SL 11.4

You have all the information, all the tools, and all the Habit Wisdom that is necessary to Shift your life in whatever direction you choose. Allow yourself to bask in the sense of completion and success that comes from reaching a peak that you selected. Completion opens a door to greater success.

This is life on earth and there is always something to learn, grow, Shift and achieve. As you have more fun, enjoy more success and cultivate more passion in your life, you will discover more and more rewarding peaks ahead. Your Peak Life Habits will assist you as you climb the faces of new and higher peaks.

We started this book together in a discussion on how large and powerful Habits really are. In fact we called them the *elephants in the room*. What you are left with is the power of your own Peak Life Habits and a new mastery for your entire lifetime – Habit Wisdom. Right Action is your partner. You can deploy Peak Life Habits as your agent provocateurs, facilitating your magic carpet ride to greatness. You are in charge as soon as *you* start running your Habits and disallow them from running you. Your old Limiting Habits may hover around, waiting for a break in the rhythm, a change in the beat or an almost indiscernible pause in which to cut in. In those moments when you feel a pull back to a familiar argument or an old dissatisfying (yet familiar) pattern or situation, STOP. Be preemptive and SHIFT. Know your elephants.

Gracefully block your Limiting Habits. With your Habit Wisdom you are astute about how the world is and how the world isn't, about who the people in your life are and who they are not. Practice your Habit Wisdom well and always in tandem with *Positive Tentative* and *Positive Results* Language Habits. Remember that in the world of language, "needs," "shoulds," and "tries" generally don't get met or accomplished. Your desires, goals, passions and aspirations are predictably fulfilled by keeping your internal and external voices calling forth Right Action.

Alison was over 300 pounds and with her "Put Myself Last Habit" she was always helping everyone except herself. She lived alone and hadn't expressed a romantic interest for two decades. At work she seemed to create drama and breakdowns anytime things were going nicely and was well versed with her "Self-Sabotage Habit." Yet these issues did not arrive in a vacuum. Their genesis was a very real belief that Alison had held ever since she was a girl growing up in her grandmother's house. Nothing she ever did was good enough for her grandmother, and anytime she indulged in her own childhood she was berated with "You selfish, selfish girl!" The pain ran even deeper; it was an abusive environment with personality disorders present in the adults around her. In that unhappy home, she was powerless in the face of those unfriendly outside forces. With the Beliefs that life is hard and unfair and any focus on oneself was bad, Alison's Habits were born and entrenched. Addressing those experiences is what great therapists are for, and as an adult Alison had peeled her onion with experienced and helpful counseling as well as self-improvement programs. The cognitive step was now up to her.

When Alison enrolled in the Habitually Great coaching program, she was mired in a cluster of sabotage Habits. Like many of us, her head was a dangerous place to be. She had never before labeled or distinguished her patterns of breakdown and distress in this manner. The Habitually Great methodology often strikes an immediate chord in people, and it did with Alison. She noticed Shifts immediately. To start, Alison chose to be coached by phone for 30 minutes every week for several months. That was a rigorous commitment that she created and followed through on with spirited determination.

Through weeks of Pattern Interrupts and plenty of ground truth realty checks, she interrupted her "Put Myself Last Habit, "Victim Habit" and "Self-Sabotage Habit." There were plenty of challenges along the way; Limiting Habits always look for loopholes until you close them all, tight. Early on there were moments where her Limiting Habit saboteurs created disappointing setbacks. In those moments Alison often doubted her ability to Shift. I didn't dissuade her from those thoughts; instead we acknowledged them to be real. Since she didn't fight those Habits, Alison was able to see her Habit mechanism more and more clearly, and with perseverance she became adept at Pattern Interrupts. Alison became vigilant in preempting old and familiar lapses into her old Habits. Over time, with her "Patience Habit" and her "Determined To Succeed Habit," Alison persevered!

Today Alison is an extraordinary woman who is respected and liked by all who meet her. She has had a series of promotions, growing in her position from Marketing Manager to Chief Executive Officer. Alison travels the world for work and pleasure, enjoys her rediscovered romantic interest in the opposite sex, works out regularly, takes pleasure in healthy eating and has lost over 140 pounds. Her "Self-Respect Habit" has bloomed! Most heartening is the contentment that she feels in her heart, having deep gratitude and satisfaction for having cleared the path to become who she really is. Alison appreciates her wonderful life and maintains a vigilant watch for her old Limiting Habits, which, as they do in all of us, show up every now and then.

Alison's story is an extraordinary example of rising above deep Habit-Stamps. Yet even if you had the perfect childhood, fulfilling your dreams is still likely to include overcoming an obstructive cluster or spiral of Limiting Habits.

Every day focus your mind on your successes, as happiness comes from focusing on what goes well. Positive thoughts create positive experiences. Consider a "Seeing What's Right Habit" of writing and reflecting upon five things that go well every day. Every Habitually Great program and Habitually Great coaching session starts with recent successes! Remember, happiness is a set point in your head; you are the color coordinator of your life on earth. Use that cognitive brainpower, manage it, control it, know your elephants and take the specific, measurable steps toward your own joyful existence every day, no matter what. Measure and pay attention to the soft metrics, too—the ones about family time, nurturing your relationships, relaxation, giving back and fun activities.

The Right Time Is Right Now

"I have learned a hard lesson trying to help *real* people, change *real* behavior in the *real* world. There is no "couple of weeks" (when things won't be crazy anymore, when the unique and special challenges of right now will be over and I can take a "couple of weeks" to get organized and focus on this program). Look at the trend line! Sanity does not prevail. There is a good chance that tomorrow is going to be just about as crazy as today. If you want to change anything about yourself, the best time to start is *now*."[11]

- Marshal Goldsmith

---

[11] Goldsmith, Marshall. *What Got You Here Won't Get You There* (Hyperion, 2007. 197-8.)

Right now in this moment, I am your coach and there is a Limiting Habit hovering called the "Waiting For The Right Time Habit." Let's Shift that immediately to "The Right Time Is Right Now Habit!" In most of life the *right time is right now*, yet many of our Limiting Habits convince us to wait for a right time that never arrives. Is there really a perfect time to ask your boss for a brief sit-down? No. How about for when you'll find that girl or guy in just the right frame of mind to say "yes" to whatever your question is? No. Am I coaching you to be inappropriate? No. Be respectful of situations that are defined by timed structures and metrics. I am coaching you to step out of your box, be bold and unreasonable with yourself. Stop your procrastination in the midst of waiting for the "right time" and get on with it!

As Wayne Dyer says, "When you change the way you look at things, the things you look at change." Are there situations and circumstances where you have been inventing a safe haven story that you use to justify staying *out* of action? You bet. Now and for all time be powerfully unreasonable and have some breakthroughs! Information is power; if there is a rejection to be had, get to it soon, because failures lead *to* success. Since they are often inevitable, speed them up; get to them and over them. There is no Hall of Fame baseball player who ever got more than four hits out of ten at bats on average during any one season of his career; in other words, the majority of the time they failed! It is time to fulfill the aspirations you have been dreaming of and ascend the ones you have already achieved. Your accountability is to get started, right now, as an expert in the Seven Practices of Habitual Greatness.

Welcome To The Summit!

Life is a blessing. You have enjoyed many successes, large and small (getting out of bed today counts), just to get to where you are in your life today. You were born with a perpetual drive to learn and grow, achieve and ascend. That drive resurrects itself often. We experience that resurrection as "wake-up calls" at different points in our lives. We rub our eyes, scratch our heads, look around and wonder, "How did my life get to be like this? How did I get the Habits, Beliefs and life results that look like the ones of my parents? What happened to the direct path to my dreams? Where did I derail and get off course? I'm ready to make a change. How in the world do I get from here to there?"

Your Habit Wisdom can answer all of those questions. We are, after all, creatures of Habit. We are all Habit-Stamped unknowingly based on life events and experiences. The good news is that a whole bunch of Peak Life Habits are also imprinted in your Habit mechanism and have helped you move your life toward new heights and positive directions. The not-so-good news is that Limiting Habits were also formed way back when and have been running you when you thought you were in charge. A few tyrannical Master Habits became the pit bosses. Now you have lifted the cloud and illuminated your Peak Life Habits and Habit Wisdom. You have the cognitive ability to choose your Habits in any given moment. Remember to be friendly, caring and compassionate with your own internal critic, ease up on that old "Hard On Myself Habit" and keep going. Know what you want; achieve what you want; enjoy what you've achieved! Would you like to leave a legacy that makes a difference in the world even after you have moved on? If so, challenge yourself to orchestrate that!

You have all the tools of Right Action to create and exceed your expectations in the fulfillment of your inspired life. You are in the driver's seat; you have all the controls. Use them well! That is Habitual Greatness!

Welcome home,

Mark F. Weinstein

HABITUALLY GREAT APPENDICES

Appendix A: Peak Life Habits

    Peak Life Habits are positive, Actionable Habits that we deploy to preemptively circumvent our Limiting Habits. By consciously choosing these Habits we can catapult with ongoing disciplined action to the joys and successes we truly desire to achieve. For an in-depth description of each Habit, please visit **www.peaklifehabits.com**.

- ☐ Accountability Habit
- ☐ Acknowledgement Habit
- ☐ Acting As If Habit
- ☐ Always Learning Habit
- ☐ Apology Habit
- ☐ Authentic Habit
- ☐ Being Appropriate Habit
- ☐ Being In Action Habit
- ☐ Being Unstoppable Habit
- ☐ Believe In Myself Habit
- ☐ Compassionate Habit
- ☐ Completion Habit
- ☐ Create My Destiny (vs. Fate) Habit
- ☐ Creating A Powerful Future Habit
- ☐ Courage Habit
- ☐ Courage & Humility Habit
- ☐ Detachment Habit
- ☐ Determined To Succeed Habit
- ☐ Discipline Habit
- ☐ Emotional Fortitude Habit
- ☐ Empowered Language Habit
- ☐ Excellence Habit
- ☐ Feeling Good Habit
- ☐ Focus & Clarity Habit
- ☐ Gathering Momentum Habit
- ☐ Going Beyond Almost Habit
- ☐ Gratitude Habit
- ☐ Great Communicator Habit
- ☐ Great Listener Habit
- ☐ Greatness Habit

- ☐ Ground Truth Reality Habit
- ☐ Healthy Exercise Habit
- ☐ Healthy Trust Habit
- ☐ Healthy Vulnerability Habit
- ☐ Humility Habit
- ☐ I Can Do It Habit
- ☐ I Remember Habit
- ☐ I'm Organized Habit
- ☐ I'm Worthy Habit
- ☐ Integrity Habit
- ☐ Keep The Faith Habit
- ☐ Keeping My Word Habit
- ☐ Kindness Habit
- ☐ Leading By Example Habit
- ☐ Learning From My Failures Habit
- ☐ Lightening Up Habit
- ☐ Living In Reality Habit
- ☐ Living Powerfully Habit
- ☐ Making Powerful Choices Habit
- ☐ Modeling Well Habit
- ☐ No More Excuses Habit
- ☐ On Time Habit
- ☐ Open Heart Habit
- ☐ Patience Habit
- ☐ Pattern Interrupt Habit
- ☐ Persistence Habit
- ☐ Playing Big Habit
- ☐ Positive Results Language Habit
- ☐ Power Scheduling Habit
- ☐ Power (vs. Force) Habit
- ☐ Proactive Habit
- ☐ Preemptive Habit
- ☐ Putting Myself First Habit
- ☐ Resolving Past Issues Habit
- ☐ Responding (vs. Reacting) Habit
- ☐ Right Action Habit
- ☐ Right Action Momentum Habit
- ☐ Saying No Authentically Habit
- ☐ Saying Yes Powerfully Habit
- ☐ Seeing What's Right Habit
- ☐ Seek First To Understand Habit
- ☐ Self-Love Habit
- ☐ Self-Respect Habit
- ☐ Specific & Measurable Habit
- ☐ Squash The Wiggle Habit
- ☐ Solution-Focused Habit
- ☐ Stop Doing Habit

- ☐ Success Habit
- ☐ Success Structures Habit
- ☐ Taking It On Habit
- ☐ Teamwork Habit
- ☐ The Right Time Is Right Now Habit
- ☐ Time Is Just Time Habit
- ☐ U-Turning My Finger Habit
- ☐ Walk My Talk Habit
- ☐ Fill In:_____
- ☐ Fill In:_____

Appendix B: Limiting Habits

Limiting Habits hinder your greatness and interfere with the goals and successes you desire in your life. Limiting Habits cause your "Habit-Gaps." For an in-depth description of each Habit, please visit **www.peaklifehabits.com**.

☐ Acting Small Habit

☐ Afraid To Be Wrong Habit

☐ Almost Habit

☐ Anger Habit

☐ Appeaser Habit

☐ Artificial Harmony Habit

☐ Acting Small Habit

☐ Afraid To Be Wrong Habit

☐ Almost Habit

☐ Anger Habit

☐ Appeaser Habit

☐ Artificial Harmony Habit
   Avoid Accountability Habit

☐ Avoid Authority Habit

☐ Avoid Commitment Habit

☐ Avoid Conflict Habit

☐ Avoid Disappointment Habit

☐ Avoid Vulnerability Habit

☐ Backsliding Habit

☐ Being Critical Habit

☐ Blame Habit

☐ Bully Habit

☐ Can't Let It Go Habit

☐ Can't Say No Habit

☐ Chaos Habit

☐ Confrontation With Success Habit

☐ Covert Unconscious Habit

☐ Cut & Run Habit

☐ Defensive Habit

☐ Difficult To Deal With Habit

☐ Disappointment Habit

☐ Distraction/Interruption Habit

☐ Distress Habit

☐ Distress & Aggravate Habit

☐ Do It Myself Habit

☐ Doing It My Way Habit

☐ Domination & Control Habit

☐ Don't Rock The Boat Habit

☐ Doom Loop Habit

☐ Drama Habit

☐ Entitlement Habit

☐ Every Other Monther Habit

☐ Excuses Habit

☐ Expect You To Know Habit

☐ Fantasy Habit

☐ Fear, Doubt & Worry Habit

☐ Fear of Abandonment Habit

☐ Fear of Commitment Habit

☐ Fear of Failure Habit

☐ Fear of Humiliation Habit

☐ Fear of Success Habit

☐ Feeling Incapable Habit

☐ Forceful Habit

☐ Frustration Habit

☐ Good Is The Enemy of Great Habit

☐ Good Person Habit

☐ Guilt Habit

☐ Hard On Myself Habit

☐ Hold Myself Back Habit

☐ I Always Have An Enemy Habit

☐ I Can't Habit

☐ I Don't Deserve Habit

☐ I Don't Trust Anybody Habit

☐ I Don't Wanna Habit

☐ I Have The Title Habit

☐ I Have To Worry About Money Habit

☐ I'm A Failure Habit

☐ I'm Alone Habit

☐ I'm Disorganized Habit

☐ I'm Not Good Enough Habit

☐ I'm Not Great Habit

☐ I'm Not Worthy Habit

☐ I'm Right Habit

☐ I'm Too Busy Habit

☐ Impatient Habit

☐ Incomplete Habit

☐ Insecurity Habit

☐ It's All About Me Habit

☐ It's All My Fault Habit

☐ It's Never Enough Habit

☐ Knight In Rusty Armor Habit

☐ Life's Not Fair Habit

☐ Limiting Language Habits

☐ Logic & Justify Habit

☐ Looking Good Habit

☐ Loyal To The Family Habit

☐ Need to Be Needed Habit

☐ Official Truth Habit

☐ Obsess Habit

☐ Open Door Habit

☐ Optimist Habit

☐ Over-Committed Habit

- ☐ Over-Think Habit
- ☐ Overwhelm Habit
- ☐ Paralysis Habit
- ☐ Perfectionist Habit
- ☐ Playing It Safe Habit
- ☐ Playing Small Habit
- ☐ Pleaser Habit
- ☐ Procrastination Habit
- ☐ Put Myself Last Habit
- ☐ Reactive Habit
- ☐ Regret Habit
- ☐ Resentment Habit
- ☐ Resignation Habit
- ☐ Reward Habit
- ☐ Righteousness Habit
- ☐ Rubber-Band Habit
- ☐ Safe In My Misery Habit
- ☐ Scatter Habit
- ☐ Seeing What's Wrong Habit
- ☐ Self-Deprecating Habit
- ☐ Self-Sabotage Habit
- ☐ Skepticism Habit
- ☐ Set Myself Up For Failure Habit
- ☐ Sob Sister Habit
- ☐ Someday/One Day Habit
- ☐ Spacey Habit
- ☐ Stress & Obsess Habit

- ☐ Struggle Habit
- ☐ Unable To Be Specific Habit
- ☐ Unsafe World Habit
- ☐ Victim Habit
- ☐ Wait And See Habit
- ☐ Waiting For The Right Time Habit
- ☐ Waiting For The Shoe To Drop Habit
- ☐ Why Bother Habit
- ☐ Wiggle Room Habit
- ☐ Woe Is Me Habit
- ☐ Fill In:_____
- ☐ Fill In:_____

Appendix C: Shifting Limiting Habits to Peak Life Habits

LIMITING HABITS	Shift to	PEAK LIFE HABITS
Acting Small Habit	→	Playing Big Habit Making Powerful Choices Habit
Afraid To Be Wrong Habit	→	Humility Habit Courage Habit
Almost Habit	→	Living Powerfully Habit Right Action Habit
Anger Habit	→	Being Appropriate Habit Compassion Habit
Appeaser Habit	→	Ground Truth Reality Habit Saying No Authentically Habit
Artificial Harmony Habit	→	Authentic Habit Ground Truth Reality Habit
Avoid Accountability Habit	→	Accountability Habit The Right Time Is Right Now Habit
Avoid Authority Habit	→	Healthy Vulnerability Habit Accountability Habit

LIMITING HABITS	Shift to	PEAK LIFE HABITS
Avoid Commitment Habit	→	Playing Big Habit Discipline Habit
Avoid Conflict Habit	→	Courage Habit Authentic Habit
Avoid Disappointment Habit	→	Playing Big Habit Courage Habit, Humility Habit
Avoid Vulnerability Habit	→	Healthy Vulnerability Habit Emotional Fortitude Habit
Backsliding Habit	→	Proactive Habit Discipline Habit
Being Critical Habit	→	Compassionate Habit U-Turn My Finger Habit
Blame Habit	→	Seeing What's Right Habit U-Turn My Finger Habit
Bully Habit	→	Power (vs. Force) Habit Kindness Habit
Can't Let It Go Habit	→	Detachment Habit Seeing What's Right Habit
Can't Say No Habit	→	Saying No Authentically Habit Putting Myself First Habit
Chaos Habit	→	I'm Organized Habit Success Structures Habit
Confrontation With Success Habit	→	Success Habit Believe In Myself Habit

LIMITING HABITS	Shift to	PEAK LIFE HABITS
Covert Unconscious Habit	→	Pattern Interrupt Habit Emotional Fortitude Habit
Cut & Run Habit	→	Right Action Momentum Habit Persistence Habit
Defensive Habit	→	Humility Habit U-Turn My Finger Habit
Difficult To Deal With Habit	→	Teamwork Habit Being Appropriate Habit
Disappointment Habit	→	Success Habit Learning From My Failures Habit
Distraction/Interruption Habit	→	Focus & Clarity Habit Completion Habit
Distress Habit	→	Lightening Up Habit Seeing What's Right Habit
Distress & Aggravate Habit	→	Solution-Focused Habit Detachment Habit
Do It Myself Habit	→	Open Heart Habit Teamwork Habit
Doing It My Way Habit	→	Seek First to Understand Habit Teamwork Habit
Domination & Control Habit	→	Great Listener Habit Power (vs. Force) Habit

LIMITING HABITS	Shift to	PEAK LIFE HABITS
Don't Rock The Boat Habit	→	Playing Big Habit I'm Worthy Habit
Doom Loop Habit	→	Right Action Momentum Habit Success Habit
Drama Habit	→	Lightening Up Habit Being Appropriate Habit
Entitlement Habit	→	Teamwork Habit Gratitude Habit
Every Other Monther	→	Accountability Habit Determined To Succeed Habit
Excuses Habit	→	Completion Habit Apology Habit
Expect You To Know Habit	→	Seek First To Understand Habit Great Communicator Habit
Fantasy Habit	→	Living In Reality Habit Ground Truth Reality Habit
Fear, Doubt & Worry Habit	→	Courage Habit Emotional Fortitude Habit
Fear of Abandonment Habit	→	Keep The Faith Habit Believe In Myself Habit
Fear Of Commitment Habit	→	Courage Habit Create My Destiny (vs. Fate) Habit

LIMITING HABITS	Shift to	PEAK LIFE HABITS
Fear Of Failure Habit	→	Learning From My Failures Habit Squash The Wiggle Habit
Fear of Humiliation Habit	→	Playing Big Habit Humility Habit
Fear Of Success Habit	→	I Can Do It Habit Going Beyond Almost Habit
Feeling Incapable Habit	→	Determined to Succeed Habit I'm Worthy Habit
Forceful Habit	→	Power (vs. Force) Habit Responding (vs. Reacting) Habit
Frustration Habit	→	Patience Habit Detachment Habit
Good Is The Enemy of Great Habit	→	Living Powerfully Habit Going Beyond Almost Habit
Good Person Habit	→	Saying No Authentically Habit Ground Truth Reality Habit
Guilt Habit	→	Integrity Habit Resolve Past Issues Habit
Hard On Myself Habit	→	Lightening Up Habit Seeing What's Right Habit
Hold Myself Back Habit	→	Courage Habit Right Action Momentum Habit

LIMITING HABITS	Shift to	PEAK LIFE HABITS
I Always Have An Enemy Habit	→	Seek First To Understand Habit No More Excuses Habit
I Can't Habit	→	I Can Do It Habit Acting As If Habit
I Don't Deserve Habit	→	Believe In Myself Habit Create My Destiny (vs. Fate) Habit
I Don't Trust Anybody Habit	→	Open Heart Habit Teamwork Habit
I Don't Wanna Habit	→	Keeping My Word Habit Right Action Momentum Habit
I Have The Title Habit	→	Humility Habit Apology Habit
I Have To Worry About Money Habit	→	Lightening Up Habit Ground Truth Reality Habit
I'm A Failure Habit	→	Learning From My Failures Habit Solution-Focused Habit
I'm Alone Habit	→	Teamwork Habit Success Structures Habit
I'm Disorganized Habit	→	I'm Organized Habit Success Structures Habit
I'm Not Good Enough Habit	→	I'm Worthy Habit Being Unstoppable Habit

LIMITING HABITS	Shift to	PEAK LIFE HABITS
m Not Great Habit	→	Believe In Myself Habit Greatness Habit
m Not Worthy Habit	→	Putting Myself First Habit I'm Worthy Habit
m Right Habit	→	Leading By Example Habit U-Turn My Finger Habit
m Too Busy Habit	→	Power Scheduling Habit Stop Doing Habit
npatient Habit	→	Patience Habit Detachment Habit
ncomplete Habit	→	Completion Habit Accountability Habit
nsecurity Habit	→	Playing Big Habit Healthy Trust Habit
's All About Me Habit	→	Great Listener Habit Open Heart Habit
's All My Fault Habit	→	Lightening Up Habit Learning From My Failures Habit
's Never Enough Habit	→	Gratitude Habit Seeing What's Right Habit
night In Rusty Armor Habit	→	U-Turning My Finger Habit Modeling Well Habit
ife's Not Fair Habit	→	Right Action Momentum Habit Keep The Faith Habit

LIMITING HABITS	Shift to	PEAK LIFE HABITS
Limiting Language Habit	→	Positive Results Language Habit Empowered Language Habit
Logic & Justify Habit	→	Authentic Habit Ground Truth Reality Habit
Looking Good Habit	→	Humility Habit Healthy Vulnerability Habit
Loyal To The Family Habit	→	Resolving Past Issues Habit Detachment Habit
Needing To Be Needed	→	I Am Good Enough Habit Stop Doing Habit
Obsess Habit	→	Detachment Habit Patience Habit
Official Truth Habit	→	Ground Truth Reality Habit Authentic Habit
Open Door Habit	→	Saying No Authentically Habit Power Scheduling Habit
Over-Committed Habit	→	Stop Doing Habit Power Scheduling Habit
Over-Think Habit	→	Lightening Up Habit Acting As If Habit
Overwhelm Habit	→	Saying No Authentically Habit Discipline Habit

LIMITING HABITS	Shift to	PEAK LIFE HABITS
Paralysis Habit	→	Right Action Momentum Habit Persistence Habit
Perfectionist Habit	→	Playing Big Habit Right Time Is Right Now Habit
Playing It Safe Habit	→	Taking It On Habit Going Beyond Almost Habit
Playing Small Habit	→	Greatness Habit Modeling Well Habit
Pleaser Habit	→	Stop Doing Habit Saying No Authentically Habit
Procrastination Habit	→	Accountability Habit Right Time Is Right Now Habit
Put Myself Last Habit	→	Healthy Exercise Habit Put Myself First Habit
Reactive Habit	→	Detachment Habit Responding (vs. Reacting) Habit
Regret Habit	→	Learning From My Failures Habit Courage Habit
Resentment Habit	→	Compassion Habit U-Turning My Finger Habit

LIMITING HABITS	Shift to	PEAK LIFE HABITS
Reward Habit	→	Discipline Habit Squash The Wiggle Habit
Righteousness Habit	→	Humility Habit Great Listener Habit
Rubber-Band Habit	→	Right Action Momentum Habit Preemptive Habit
Safe In My Misery Habit	→	Playing Big Habit Determined To Succeed Habit
Scatter Habit	→	Focus & Clarity Habit I'm Organized Habit
Seeing What's Wrong Habit	→	Seeing What's Right Habit Lightening Up Habit
Self-Deprecating Habit	→	Empowered Language Habit Walk My Talk Habit
Self-Sabotage Habit	→	Pattern Interrupt Habit Squash The Wiggle Habit
Set Myself Up For Failure Habit	→	Preemptive Habit Create My Destiny (vs. Fate) Habit
Sob Sister Habit	→	Seeing What's Right Habit Determined To Succeed Habit
Someday/One Day Habit	→	Right Time Is Right Now Habit Power Scheduling Habit

LIMITING HABITS	Shift to	PEAK LIFE HABITS
Spacey Habit	→	Focus & Clarity Habit I Remember Habit
Stress & Obsess Habit	→	Feeling Good Habit Patience Habit
Struggle Habit	→	Lightening Up Habit Success Habit
Unable To Be Specific Habit	→	Accountability Habit Specific & Measurable Habit
Unsafe World Habit	→	Emotional Fortitude Habit Keep The Faith Habit
Victim Habit	→	Living Powerfully Habit Accountability Habit
Wait & See Habit	→	Preemptive Habit Leading By Example Habit
Wait For The Right Time Habit	→	The Right Time Is Right Now Proactive Habit
Waiting For The Shoe To Drop Habit	→	Right Action Momentum Habit Living In Reality Habit
Why Bother Habit	→	Determined to Succeed Habit Ground Truth Reality Habit
Wiggle Room Habit	→	Squash The Wiggle Habit Gathering Momentum Habit
Woe Is Me Habit	→	Lightening Up Habit Seeing What's Right Habit

Appendix D: Glossary

Accountability: To be accountable means to be responsible for our Actions. There are three important aspects to accountability. The first is communicating and accepting accountability with the people in our lives. The second is our own self-accountability. The third aspect is the accountability structures that we create for ourselves.

Action: Being in Action is the key to Peak Life Habits. Actions are part of our Habit Chains, which are comprised of a Belief, which leads to an Action, which then leads to an Outcome and ultimately to the Habit that they generate. By our Actions, we create the Outcomes that we want and the positive Habits that will change our lives.

"Almost" Habits/"Almost" Moments: "Almost" Moments and "Almost" Habits prevent us from achieving what we want in life because our Limiting Beliefs and Habits stopped us short of our goals and dreams.

Belief: Beliefs are what we have been telling ourselves – about ourselves or about our Actions, Outcomes or goals – whenever we choose to take a certain Action. We all have our own thoughts and Beliefs that cause us to choose the Actions we take in life.

Belief-Link: A Belief can be stated in terms that begin, "I believe that…," and the Belief-Link completes that sentence: "…and so with that Belief as my guide I choose to…." The Belief and our decision to act upon it in a certain way are in fact separate, and we have created the link by our choice. Our Actions are guided by Beliefs, with Belief-Links becoming Outcome predictors.

Conversation Under The Conversation: The conversation under the conversation is what is not being said. In other words, it's the real reasons, thoughts, feelings, excuses, etc., that we experience in a given moment and are covered up by the top layer of the actual conversation or interaction. In many cases our Habits are the conversation under the conversation, which are controlled by our unconscious and forceful Beliefs. Our Habits are ultimately formed when we have a layer of conversation (Beliefs) on top, under which is often a deeper layer of conversation that we often do not articulate.

Default Beliefs/Habits: These are the whole bundle of Beliefs and Habits (the good, bad and ugly) that make up who we are. Our Default Beliefs and Habits are the ones that run us everyday.

Entrenched Habits: All Entrenched Habits are Master Habits (though not all Master Habits are Entrenched Habits). If a Master Habit is really deep and ingrained, then it's an Entrenched Habit.

External Dialogue: There are two ways we communicate with language: internally and externally. The external dialogue is the dialogue of our spoken words, out loud, in conversation and communication with others. It speaks our thoughts to people and to the world out loud. Our internal dialogue will often mirror the Habits of our external dialogue.

Habit Chains: The Habit Chain is comprised of the Belief linked to the Action, which is then linked to the Outcome, which in turn is linked to our Habits.

Habit-Clusters: Habit-Clusters are Habits that are grouped together, often with a Master Habit at the top driving them (though there are Habit-Clusters without Master Habits as well). In either case, Habit-Clusters are groups of Habits of a similar nature that operate together.

Habit-Duels: Dueling Habits are Habits within us or in our relationships that are contradictory. They are often Habits that keep us paralyzed. When we have Peak Life Habits that contradict our Master Habits, we then have a challenge, a clash, a struggle, or what is known a Habit-Duel. In a relationship, a Habit-Duel can lead to conflict and – in the worst cases – is a deal breaker, ultimately destroying the relationship.

Habit-Gap: This gap is the difference between what we have/are in life today and what we want to have/be either today or in the future.

In the middle are the Limiting Habits that stand in the way of our fullest potential.

Habit Mechanism: Our Habit mechanism is a system wherein our conscious and subconscious Habits are composed of our Habit Chains of Beliefs, Actions and Outcomes. However, we all have a unique package of Habits and also a very individual mechanism for how we enact our Habits in our lives.

Habit-Patterns: When we have a tendency to practice the same Habits repeatedly, we have a Habit-Pattern. Our Habit-Patterns often consist of Habit-Clusters or Habit-Spirals of closely related Habits that are interwoven together into a pattern of Habits that pop up in our lives over and over again. We also can "inherit" a Habit-Pattern from our family of origin or an early life experience in which we saw specific Habits played out again and again.

Habit-Spirals: Master Habits and Entrenched Habits are at the top of a Habit-Spiral and have Subordinate Habits that reinforce them. One Master Habit triggers a domino effect among other Habits. The Spiral metaphor is used because it captures a sense of hierarchy: the Master Habit kicks in, followed by the next Habit, the next Habit, and so on.

Habit-Stamp: During our formative childhood years, and as we get older too, we are strongly influenced by events and experiences with our families, friends, significant others, strangers, television programs, music, movies, the Internet, the news and advertising media, at school and early work. From those experiences we develop Beliefs about virtually everything. Often we don't participate in the conscious choice of those Beliefs, as they are imprinted upon us by those experiences, people and events. Those early Beliefs become Habit-Stamps, stamped into our subconscious, and we develop Habits based on our Habit-Stamps.

Habit-Triggers: Habit-Triggers can be a person, place, thing, action or thought that sets into motion one or more of our Habits. Triggers are an important facet in recognizing how to Shift our Habits with Pattern Interrupts. When we are interrupting and Shifting our

Habits, we first want to notice the Habit-Triggers that are setting our Habit mechanisms into place.

Habit-Trance: This is when we immediately and unconsciously default to a Habit. The change is so automatic that we go into a Limiting Habit-driven trance, and we don't ask the questions that will help us understand why.

Habit Wisdom: Habit Wisdom involves gaining knowledge and understanding of our own Habits as well as the Habits of the people around us. We want to learn all we can about our Habits, Habit-Mechanisms, Habit Chains and how all of us are absolutely run by our Habits. With Habit-Wisdom comes the possibility of taking over control of our Habit-Mechanisms and consciously creating a life designed around great Habits while having much more compassion for others. Like us, they are controlled by their Habits.

Habitually Great Power Scheduling: Power Scheduling lends structure to our days, enabling us to be at our best and most productive. Scheduling the Peak Life Habits way means identifying our time-wasters and distractions so that we can restructure our schedules in a positive, powerful and productive way.

Habits: A Habit is a pattern of Action that is acquired and has become so automatic that it is difficult to break. It is a tendency to believe, perform or behave in a certain way. Habits can be either negative or positive – i.e., Limiting or Peak.

Internal Dialogue: Internal dialogue chats incessantly, buzzing our head with thoughts and ideas about the world around us. It is the first place to listen when we want to begin Shifting our Habits.

Inquiry: An Inquiry is when we ask questions. Inquiries are important in Peak Life Habits because they allow us to dig deep and inquire as to what our Habits are, when and where were our Habits formed, how we play out our Habits and how do we want to Shift our Habits to Peak Life Habits.

Law of Right Action: The Law of Right Action says we attract our success by aligning our efforts with our intentions, i.e., by transforming our thoughts and feelings as well as our actions. This transformation requires a Shift that ultimately attracts a greater life.

Language Habits: Language Habits perpetuate the style and types of phrases we use while supporting and reinforcing our Beliefs and Habits. Language Habits are both external and internal, both negative and positive. The phrases we use may have come from our parents, teachers, friends, books or movies. Without realizing it, we adopted a Cluster of Language Habits that has nothing to do with success, happiness or fulfillment. Often what we think and speak is likely to become our reality. (See Vocal Invocation.)

Limiting Beliefs/Habits: This is the core element of the Habitually Great Program. Our Limiting Beliefs and Limiting Habits are the patterns and behaviors that have bedeviled us for a lifetime. These Limiting Beliefs and Limiting Habits have stopped us from achieving our goals and dreams. They have held us back and kept us at "almost" in key areas of our lives.

Limiting Language: Language contributes either to our wellness or our illness. Our Limiting Language is negative and brings us pressure, struggle, fatigue, stress, suffering, overwhelm, guilt and burden. Some examples of Limiting Language are the use of words and phrases such as: "I should," "I'll try to," "I need to," "I have to," "I can't," "Why did this happen to me?" and "I'm not good enough."

Master Habits: Master Habits are the big ones! These are the Habits that are pulling the strings of our human mechanism just like a marionette. Master Habits are so controlling that they run us, and we are in many ways addicted to their control and to the life context that results from them.

Outcome: The Outcome is part of the Habit Chain. The Habit Chain is comprised of a Belief, Action, Outcome and the Habit that they generate. Our Beliefs lead to Actions; our Actions produce or generate an Outcome. The Outcome is the result or consequence of the Action.

Pattern Interrupt: The Pattern Interrupt is a key step in the Peak Life Habits process of attaining breakthroughs. One of the best ways to change a Habit or a Habit-Pattern is to interrupt it. To put a Pattern Interrupt into Action, the first step is to recognize the Habit, then consciously interrupt the Habit or Habit-Pattern, and then Shift into a Peak Life Habit instead.

Peak Life Habits: We are creatures of Habit; our behavior is Habit-Driven. Habits are synonymous with our routines, customs, practices, strategies and processes that we use in our life. Peak Life Habits are positive, Actionable Habits that allow us to take forward steps to gain control and mastery of our Limiting Habits and catapult us past "almost" to the lives and successes of our dreams.

Positive Results Language: Intentionally selecting a way of speaking that is specific, measurable and holds us accountable to Right Action. Positive Results Language includes phrases such as, "I will…" and "I am going to" and "Here's my plan of action."

Positive Tentative Language: The first step toward Shifting to your ultimate goal of Positive Results Language. It allows you to modify your language toward the positive rather and provides a first glimmer of the accountability and specificity. Positive Tentative Language includes phrases such as, "I want to…" and "I am working on it."

Right Action: Right Action is positive, disciplined, persistent Action undertaken with clarity, focus, specificity and measurability. It reinforces and strengthens our commitment to generate the changes that lead to our desired Outcomes. Importantly, a key element to Right Action is being respectful and appreciative of others and of ourselves. Right Action is the antidote to the undertow of Limiting Habits.

Right Action Success Structure: This is the Peak Life Habit of creating Action structures that lead us step by step to the Outcomes we desire. It is the means to organize and support your Right Action Momentum Habit to break through your Success Ceilings. These are structure and Action plans by which you can tackle your goals and fulfill on them. A Right Action Success Structure is specific, measurable and focused while delivering a sense of accomplishment.

Right Action Success Structures include the mastery of scheduling, the discipline of completion and the steady deployment of Pattern Interrupts.

Rubber-Band Effect: When we Shift into new Habits and Patterns, we often experience something akin to a gravitational pull, yanking us backwards. Those feelings may manifest themselves through a powerful discomfort with our successes, because the new Habits and successes are very different from the struggle and the suffering that we are used to. In such moments we may actually "snap back" to our old Limiting Habits and failures, because we feel more comfortable with familiar suffering.

Self-Sabotage Habits: "Sabotage" is a strong word and an apt one. There are times when we sabotage our successes, relationships, fitness, careers, etc. in a covert way that we may not even be conscious of. Rather than reaching our goals, we put up our defenses and resist. An example of a Sabotage Habit is the Confrontation With Success Habit. With this particular Sabotage Habit we are confronted with becoming successful because we may feel we don't deserve it, thus creating a disempowering effect. We are usually Habit-Stamped with our Self-Sabotage Habits early in our lives.

Shift: Another key to Peak Life Habits is Shift. When we recognize our Habits and learn to do Pattern Interrupts, our Habits will start to change or Shift, and then we can be even more intentional. Our conscious minds will begin to see what our subconscious minds are up to and therefore allow a Shift to occur. Shift Happens!

Subordinate Habits: Our Subordinate Habits are the ones underneath our Master Habits. These Habits reinforce a larger, more Entrenched Habit that heads a Habit-Cluster or Habit-Spiral.

Success Ceiling: A Success Ceiling is our comfort level, a measure of how successful we are willing to be. We may fear the accountability of reaching a certain level of success, so we remain at a certain point instead of breaking through the ceiling to a higher level. We can recognize arrival at a Success Ceiling when we see ourselves becoming distracted or complacent rather than constantly growing better and better.

Vocal Invocation: Vocal Invocation is when we actually call forth into existence something that we speak either internally or externally. Examples: saying something like, "It drives me crazy," which then invokes aggravation and distress. If we say, "It's dreadful," we may unwittingly summon a bit of dread in our life. The opposite is also true: if we say, "I am going to win this promotion!" it becomes a more likely Outcome.

<u>RECOMMENDED RESOURCES</u>

Habitually Great Programs

Habitually Great Intensive Seminar

As a thank you for purchasing <u>Habitually Great</u>, I invite you to attend the Habitually Great Intensive Seminar, free! At this course we can change your Habit mechanism right on the spot. This seminar will take you to a whole new level of success, and I want you to share those smiles. Included in this offer is a complimentary tuition scholarship for you *and* a friend or family member. That is a value of $2,599.

This offer is for a limited time. To guarantee your seat and for dates and schedules, please register at www.habituallygreatbook.com. For planning purposes there will be a $150 no-show deposit at the time of registration that will only be charged if you do not attend. This offer is made on a space-available basis and all seating is first come, first serve.

Habitually Great Coaching

Every great athlete around the globe shares an important competitive advantage: great coaching. The *Habitually Great* coaching system is designed to make certain you achieve your ultimate life. The knowledge that you have amazing potential is within you. Take it to the next level and achieve the happiness and success you desire. Your Habitually Great coach is your ally as your one-on-one coach, with the goal of doubling your velocity to your ultimate life.

For details on how to get started with your Habitually Great coach, call 1-877-271-PEAK (7325), visit www.habituallygreat.com or send an email to coaching@habituallygreat.com.

Habitually Great Corporate Workshops

There are many reasons why organizations across the country choose Habitually Great corporate workshops. Call now to discuss your situation and desired outcomes. In these workshops we get to the heart of the obstacles blocking success or, as we prefer to say, achieving greatness. Through group interaction and workbook exercises we tackle issues contributing to many Habits, including the "I Don't Trust Habit," and the "Avoid Accountability Habit." During corporate workshops we examine Habit-forming patterns across all levels of staff, management, and the executive team. We introduce simple and useful cognitive tactics that are lasting and create real culture, real communication and real accountability breakthroughs.

For details and to schedule a customized Habitually Great corporate workshop, visit www.habituallygreat.com, send an email to corporateprograms@habituallygreat.com, or call 1-877-271-7325.

Habitually Great Speaking Engagements

How would you like to experience a keynote speaker who your participants will love and who will provide takeaways that will last a lifetime? Mark Weinstein is not a magician or a mentalist. He is not going to pull out a guitar and make up songs about relationships or talk about his career in the big leagues. Mark is a professional keynote speaker who will give your audience something great that they can use right away and for the rest of their lives in both their work life and their home life. Mark Weinstein's Habitually Great keynotes and breakout sessions will have your audience engaged, inspired and enlightened. As a keynote speaker his impact upon audiences is immediate, long lasting and life changing.

To have Mark Weinstein or one of our Habitually Great Master Trainers appear live at your next event, call 1-877-271-Peak (7325), or send an email to: speaker@habituallygreat.com.

ABOUT THE AUTHOR

Mark F. Weinstein is the founder and president of Peak Life Habits, Inc., a firm specializing in personal development and organizational greatness. Mark is the author of _Greatness In Communication: Creating A Culture Of Accountability & Trust_, as well as _Peak Life Habits: Workbook 1_, and _Peak Life Habits: Workbook 2_. In addition to providing life and executive coaching programs for individuals, Peak Life Habits has delivered leadership workshops and seminars to many top organizations including Wells Fargo Bank, FedEx Kinko's, Coldwell Banker Legacy, American Red Cross, Hyatt Regency, and others.

Prior to founding Peak Life Habits, Mark was the CEO of SuperGroups.com, an early pioneer in private group and social networking on the web. The company was recognized as a PC Magazine "Top 100 Site" and won many awards. Believing that mastery of the habit mechanism is the missing link to greatness, he changed his career in 2002 and fully developed the methodology that is the cornerstone of _Habitually Great: Master Your Habits, Own Your Destiny_. Mark is a frequent speaker at conferences and leadership events.

Mark splits his time between East Hampton, NY and Albuquerque, NM. You can contact Mark at: author@habituallygreat.com.

2480951